KINNING

ALSO BY NISI SHAWL

Everfair

KINNING

NISI SHAWL

TOR

TOR PUBLISHING GROUP

NEW YORK

This is a work of fiction. All of the characters, organizations, and events portrayed in this novel are either products of the author's imagination or are used fictitiously.

KINNING

A Tor Book
Published by Tom Doherty Associates / Tor Publishing Group
120 Broadway
New York, NY 10271

www.tor-forge.com

Tor® is a registered trademark of Macmillan Publishing Group, LLC.

The Library of Congress Cataloging-in-Publication Data is available upon request.

ISBN 978-1-250-21269-6 (hardcover)
ISBN 978-1-250-21267-2 (ebook)

Our books may be purchased in bulk for promotional, educational, or business use. Please contact your local bookseller or the Macmillan Corporate and Premium Sales Department at 1-800-221-7945, extension 5442, or by email at MacmillanSpecialMarkets@macmillan.com.

First Edition: 2024

Printed in the United States of America

0 9 8 7 6 5 4 3 2 1

For Chip, my fairy godfather

Anarchists of the May Fourth Movement refused to distinguish between means and ends, holding that the process of revolution lay in the creation of the future society in the present.

—"Anarchism in China," Wikipedia

SOME NOTABLE CHARACTERS

Crew of *Xu Mu*

Ho Bee-Lung, pharmacist, botanist, Tink's older sister

Ho Lin-Huang/Tink, inventor, engineer, Bee-Lung's younger brother

Kwangmi, steering, Tink's love

Ma Chau, steering, Kafia's love

Kafia, Ma Chau's love

Chen Jie-Jun, twin sister of Min-Jun

Chen Min-Jun, twin sister of Jie-Jun

Gopal Singh/Umar Sharif/Vinay, Dalit laborer, film star, intelligencer, Bee-Lung's love

Brinda, cook, originally servant and intelligencer to Italian ambassadors

Raghu, navigator

Everfairers

Prince Ilunga/King Ilunga, son of Josina and Mwenda

Princess Mwadi/Queen Mwadi, daughter of Josina and Mwenda, aka "Bo-La"

Queen Josina, Mwenda's favorite wife

King Mwenda, abdicating ruler of Everfair

General Thomas Jefferson Wilson, converted U.S. missionary, devotee of Loango

Serenissima Bailey/Rima Bailey, intelligencer and Mwadi's love

Raffles, colobus monkey

Carmelita, cat

Lady Fwendi, educator

Hafiza/Luliwat, servant to Queen Mwadi
Lisette Toutournier, retired intelligencer, married to Daisy
Daisy Albin, retired poet, married to Lisette
Sifa, favored serving woman to Queen Josina
Lembe, favored serving woman to Queen Josina
Yoka, diviner and advisor
Bahir Haji, Hafiza's father

Europeans

Alan Kleinwald, physicist, prisoner
Hubert Chawleigh, intelligencer and assassin, married to Clara
Clara Chawleigh, intelligencer, married to Hubert
Deveril Scranforth/Devil/Scranners, intelligencer, explorer
Herr Paul Schreiber, printer, intelligencer, married to Hanna
Frau Hanna Schreiber, printer, intelligencer, married to Paul
Signore Ercolano, intelligencer and Italian ambassador
Signore Gentileschi, intelligencer and Italian ambassador
Signore Gravina, intelligencer and Italian ambassador
Signore Quattrocchi, intelligencer and Italian ambassador

Sundry Allegiances

Sevaria binti Musa, Ceylon and Malaysia, film star, director, producer
Trana, Ceylon, servant to Sevaria
Jadida, Ceylon, servant to Sevaria
Rosalie Albin, Zanzibar and Everfair, merchant, daughter of Daisy, sister of Tink's dead love Lily, Amrita's love
Amrita, Zanzibar and India, merchant
Dr. U Shin, China, creator of Spirit Medicine (played in film by Umar Sharif)
Qadi Ahmed ibn Amir, Zanzibar, government official

KINNING

AXIOMS

1. That in 1893 an alliance of British socialists and U.S. missionaries bought a vast tract of land in Africa's Congo River region from its ostensible owner, Leopold II of Belgium.
2. That with the inclusion of the region's displaced indigenes, the citizens of this new nation, Everfair, vanquished Leopold's traitorous attempt to re-conquer them.
3. That the integration of Everfair's disparate populations proved so difficult that the country reverted from a loose democracy to monarchy.
4. That combined with respect for traditional wisdom, Everfair's technological proficiency in the use of steam, gasoline, and nuclear energy, and in automatic weaponry, lighter-than-air flight, and medicine, helped it to flourish into the twentieth century.
5. That despite choosing to fight on WWI's defeated side, Everfair inspired a global anticolonialist movement that worked for change in tandem with rising revolutionary sentiments.

IMAGINARY CHAPTERS

Stories want to tell themselves. But real stories go on and on, without ends, without beginnings, all middle all the time.

Did you read *Everfair*? If so, that may be how you have come to these words. That may do to lead you into what these words mean. Or you may prefer an alternative.

You can start telling a story with what you hear first, and where, and when. Your beginning can be there and then.

For Example

The story could begin with one man. Dr. U Shin is the name for that man and what he signifies, though the name's bare translation carries no such import. A wanderer of many kinds of lands in his early days, eventually he settled at the confluence of plain, rivers, and mountains known as the Northern Capital. Beijing. He studied, then taught, at Beijing's Normal College, formalizing his already extensive understanding of plants and animals. He also became convinced by his students and colleagues that the brutalities he'd observed in his travels—soldiers gutting sons before their fathers' eyes, starving villagers buried alive by heaps of their neighbors' corpses—were the exact opposite of inevitable. Revolution could cure the deadly disease lying at their roots. The anarchists gathering under the banner of the May Fourth Movement were busy formulating and fomenting it.

In the low, airy laboratories he shared with his movement comrades, Dr. Shin sought a natural means to develop the relationships necessary for the triumph of social anarchism. Like the graceful aspens whose groves filled the high valleys he'd visited on his journeys, like the crows wheeling in black flocks through the stormy skies, people must be connected. So he believed. Otherwise, the world would destroy itself with war. That it had not already done this was owing to the very tenuous threads tying humans together into groups larger than the nations they officially belonged to, nations bent on mutual slaughter. To prevent another such planetwide disaster, these threads must be spun tighter and stronger, and there must be many more created. So he thought. And so he directed his research.

He found some answers.

Led by the brilliance of Hoshi, a Japanese woman who had stubbornly stayed in China when her emperor's troops withdrew, Dr. Shin discovered the organic precursor to the Spirit Medicine that was afterward used by the May Fourth Movement. And in concert with Hoshi and others—the names these others were assigned at birth don't matter as much as what they did—he created the Spirit Medicine out of this precursor fungus, nourishing it and making of it a substance capable of binding humans to one another in new ways. He also developed protocols for its administration. The most effective of these protocols were those performed in person, but mass administration could predispose large populations to easy influence and incorporation into the whole later, as long as individual sympathizers to the revolution followed it up.

Still, there were drawbacks. For one thing, the sensual nature of *kinning*, as Hoshi and Shin came to call the process of forming Spirit Medicine–bonded groups, could frighten off potential recruits. Some already in sexual or romantic relationships brought their partners along with them. These attested to its healthiness. But some—mother-daughter pairs and others anxious to avoid the slightest hint of incest in their doings, and those who wished to live their lives completely chaste—hung back. They promised they would fight in May Fourth's revolution without benefit of the special abilities bestowed by treatment with the Spirit Medicine—the heightened empathy shared with fellow inoculants, and the enhanced sensitivity to the smell of lies.

For another thing, each act of kinning led to the formation of only a small affinity group, groups that Hoshi dubbed "cores." Anywhere from three to six people could join together so. In the presence of seven or more, no further kinning took place. Trying to add a seventh to an existing core only resulted in the sort of incomprehension with which decadent white men viewed their brown servants.

Seeking to combat the limitations imposed by their size, Dr. Shin adjusted the Spirit Medicine's application procedures and its subsequent growth patterns so that, in each core, one member was able to connect with other, similar members and so to influence their cores—powerfully, though indirectly. He called such members "nodes."

The erotic charge that permeated kinning proved stubborn. Neither Shin nor Hoshi nor any of their revolutionary colleagues were able to eliminate it before the May Fourth Movement requested a large store of spores to be carried abroad by their newly commissioned aircanoe, *Xu Mu*. Fortunately, Ho Bee-Lung, sister of *Xu Mu*'s designer, Ho Lin-Huang, had come up with a promising new Spirit Medicine strain that seemed to work as well as the original, but without its troublesome, potentially sexual side effects.

Which is the point at which Chapter One starts. Perhaps, however, you'd like a broader view?

In That Case

The antagonist's perspective offers a completely different angle on any story.

To the minds of many Europeans, much of the world appeared useless during much of its history. Widespread warfare heightened this perception. There were winners and there were losers, and the winners of the Great War—France, England, Russia, and the United States of America, chiefly—had no patience with its losers—Germany, Hungary, Turkey, and their allies. These minds classified the losers as beggars pleading for scraps of the winners' wealth and culture, with that traitorous side-switcher Italy bottom of the rank.

Even lower in estimated value than Italy, though, stood the Europeans' colonies, whether friendly or hostile to the winners' cause. Lands that were home to non-Caucasians were deserts, swamps, jungles, wildernesses rank with the odors of untamed savages . . . they were worth only whatever could be ravished away from them.

Until the colonies provided answers to two questions. The first of these was: Why were the vast majority of the victims of the Maltese Influenza white? Review of their living circumstances brought a touch of clarity to the issue, because when whites lived abroad and in close proximity to coloreds—in cities such as Alexandria and Bombay and Mombasa—the disease caused them far fewer casualties. Rumors of a secret vaccine coincided with the discovery of early trials of May Fourth's Spirit Medicine and led to the conclusion that that was the source of the lower orders' protection and its extension to the higher orders.

This conclusion was erroneous. The protection was due to an earlier epidemic caused by a more benign version of the same disease.

In any event, acting upon the Europeans' incorrect conclusion would have been hard. What were they supposed to do? Steal and reproduce a formula developed by their inferiors? Should it work as they hoped, the chance of unwanted consequences was still fairly certain; not only were the originators of the substance that they believed to be a vaccine Orientals, they were anarchists. Perhaps the vaccine would give those who partook of it subversive tendencies.

The idea of an alternative to May Fourth's Spirit Medicine was an enticing one for Eastern Europe—especially for Russia, which shared long stretches of its border with China. Russia's ruling dynasty had barely survived a homegrown revolt, a revolt destroyed almost as much by the epidemic as by the efforts of the Romanovs. The ranks of the insurrectionist party's majority faction, the so-called Bolsheviks, were decimated by deadly waves of disease. Because of their foreign appearance, May Fourth's anarchists were easily spotted when they attempted to fill the void that caused. Frightened agriculturalists quickly responded to the allure of the anarchists' Spirit Medicine with a vaccine of their own, and shared it with the rest of Europe almost at once in order to prove their purity to skeptics of Russia's whiteness.

Some consequences of the so-called Russian Cure they came up with could be just as unpleasant as those of the Spirit Medicine, though: a statistically significant number of the Russian Cure's recipients underwent a strange transformation, seeking out open fields and sinking knee-deep into the soil. Gradually, over the course of several summer weeks, they became sedentary and voiceless, though responding to the presence of friends through their facial expressions and gestures. Estimates varied, but this syndrome seemed to directly affect only about 5 to 8 percent of those treated.

Its indirect effects were more widespread. Religious cults developed around the afflicted, who were believed by the most popular new sect to be God's chosen, and by a large rival group to be possessed by evil demons. Theological arguments on the topic sundered churches, cities, nations, became heated, devolved into fear-fueled riots, and Europe's functional population, already ravaged by the 'flu, shrank further.

But the continent's hunger for land grew beyond all previous bounds.

Often the loved ones and relations of the victims of the Russian Cure's unfortunate side effects camped beside those victims, joined by devotees waiting for their "quickenings"—returns to their former vitality heralding their ascendance to heaven. No one knew exactly when and how these quickenings would happen, but many faithful adherents of this theory stayed nearby, singing hymns and ministering to the planteds' needs, fending off those who attacked them as devil-ridden. Still-weary veterans of the Great War fought to keep the various factions separate, leaving wide strips of land between the planteds' enclaves abandoned.

Thus the need for a second question and a second answer. This question, in fact, had been asked earlier and ignored: What would it take to turn the salt-drowned acres under the Mediterranean into inhabitable land? The Italian intellectuals who proposed to demonstrate the idea's feasibility were at first laughed off. Their "Atlantropa" was too obviously a ploy to increase their own country's territory. Also, given the extent of the Maltese 'flu's casualties, the need for expansion wasn't all that pressing. Not at first.

But then.

Quickly, the unforeseen reaction to the Russian Cure spread on the heels of its wide administration. Responses varied; relatively progressive governments, and the governments of the countries hit hardest by the 'flu, refused to stop giving it out, despite certain religious groups' demands. More conservative regimes cut back—until it was discovered that 'flu patients on the verge of death could be semi-revived, roused at least to the side-effect victims' vegetative state. All clamored for this service to be granted to those in their care.

Gazing out from their tall towers, their high halls and gilded palaces and polished marble courts, viewing a landscape filling with mysteriously sessile citizens who took over an increasing number of farm plots and sparked a deepening feud promising to spill massive quantities of blood, those in power found that building a dam across the Straits of Gibraltar suddenly became not just conceivable but quite a practical project.

Within Possibility
The birth of Atlantropa could be considered the best of all this story's potential beginnings, because of the project's status as a

rising threat, and its plain path from hope to execution. As an idea, it came seemingly from the depths of night: a Romanian man named Horatiu, citizen of one of the nations worst devastated by the strange, crippling reactions some had to the Russian Cure, mentioned it as a dream in his daily journals—though all but immediately afterward the Italians adopted it as a concept, becoming Atlantropa's most vocal champions.

And the Italians were also among the very first to station operatives and engineers on the sites of Atlantropa's future dams. They disguised their agents as diplomats, but only thinly; most knew why Signores Gravina and Gentileschi served their government on the shores of Gibraltar's straits. And everyone expected Signore Ercolano's simultaneous mission to Cairo to succeed, for the plan to enlarge and improve the canal connecting the Mediterranean and Red Seas was immensely popular, regardless of its importance to the Atlantropa scheme.

What no one anticipated was the opposition arising in India. Thousands of miles, mountains, glaciers, and language and cultural barriers lay between the subcontinent and the lands to be drowned and dried out by Atlantropa's completion. Why was it of any concern to the Indians? Why did it move pan-Indian separatists to found the rebel nation named Bharat—a name stolen from anti-Muslim bigots?

Britain's pro-Atlantropans attributed the Bharatese secession to the heavy-handedness of their rival faction, the Restorers. Britain's Restorers sought to take advantage of their country's lower death toll to reestablish their fast-loosening hold over an empire where, just a short while ago, the sun never set.

But Atlantropa would guarantee a larger playground for Britain's ambitions: new territories could be claimed along Africa's and Arabia's extended coasts. Betting that continued 'flu casualties would weaken Europe and so hinder the majority of white nations from cashing in on the coming land rush, British proponents of the Atlantropa project fielded their own secret operatives. They cooperated with Italy but maintained a separate organization. They were so successful that they even managed briefly to cross into the outer fringes of Bharat. Only the unaccountable (to the spies) tendency of their guides and contacts to misunderstand directions kept them from truly penetrating into Bharatese territory and learning the source of the mysterious opposition to their cause.

It was in the celebration of a local ritual, Raksha Bandhan, that the roots of this resistance could have been found—had the British known where and how to look for them. A student of Dr. Shin's brought one of the earliest iterations of May Fourth's Spirit Medicine with him to Patna; a teacher there whose notions of the importance of national identity exceeded those of the leading secessionists invited him to participate in the ritual with her. The student filled the role of brother, receiving from the teacher a bracelet binding them to protect one another (for the teacher's views on gender roles were unconventional). The bracelet's freshwater pearls, and drilled seeds, and cut and felted fur, spoke of life's intertwining strengths. Inspired, the traveling student not only kinned with the teacher and her aunt and uncle but trained her to administer the Spirit Medicine's spores herself, and then settled in to help her inoculate the rest of the region.

In this way the vast majority of northwest India's populations came to declare themselves an independent nation. And because their nodes recognized the threat Atlantropa posed to cores kinning along the Mediterranean's shores, they pledged themselves to fight it.

The Bharatese sent a delegation westward to Arabia and Egypt, where they tried, with very little success, to infiltrate European operations. The growing use of the Russian Cure stymied them. There was as yet no thought of blending that organism with the Spirit Medicine, which anyway still consisted of just the original variety.

Closer to home, the Bharatese had better luck, inoculating high Ceylonese officials who worked directly under Governor Manning.

But their greatest achievement involved sending a delegation east to Bangkok, May Fourth's nearest official outpost at the time, to urge speedier sowing of the Spirit Medicine's spores. They also incubated and delivered the quickly accepted plan to inoculate telegraph cables and weave the resulting growths into a revolutionary alternative: a worldwide communications web.

This was a difficult accomplishment to aim for, of course. And time-consuming: though Ho Lin-Huang was going to fly the movement's aircanoe over two continents and lay spores along lines connecting two more, that itinerary would leave an entire hemisphere yet untouched.

Beyond Possibility

So far you've been treated to visions of story beginnings situated in the Spirit Medicine's creation, in its opposition, and in some of the scenarios of its distribution. All within the realm of the senses. All verifiable.

But true visions can also be born behind closed eyes. True visions rely on more than facts. Think of fairy tales.

Think of what you've just read. Do you see pictures in your mind? Do you see those waving fields of human wheat? Those earnest, revolutionary cables swimming over golden sand and sinking under black, mud-filled bays? Those salt-soaked bottomlands rising pale and stinking behind swift-built dams?

Now bend your thoughts toward the blankness to these lands' west. Neither dark nor light, this emptiness is the perfect ground for the dreams that answer questions before they're asked. Like the idea for Atlantropa that initially came to Horatiu, images emerging from our unconscious possess their own gravity. Dreams shape worlds. They shape worlds and they seed them, and therefore, dreams may be the best way to begin telling a world's story.

So. What does the first dream of this world's story feel like?

China's anarcho-socialist May Fourth Movement undulated into being out of a breathless fear of drowning in others' greed.

There were similar crusades elsewhere: in Ireland, in France and Russia (among those who managed to escape the tyranny of both the Maltese Influenza and these two countries' rampant imperialism), in Argentina, and in Bolivia. And colony after colony attempted to emulate Everfair's independence, while descendants of enslaved and conquered people living under imperialist regimes took secret heart from their example. Only May Fourth, though, yearning above and below the waters separating them all, dared to imagine universal success. And only May Fourth's Spirit Medicine promised to guarantee it.

Given the slowness of the spread of the Spirit Medicine's organism via inoculated telegraph cables—speedy as vegetable love— May Fourth sought another way to transport the revolution's empathy inducers to the Americas. But the United States shut its shores to keep away the 'flu. So did the dictatorships to its south. However, in dreams . . .

In velvet silence the archetypes assembled, strained out of memories filled with the struggle to overturn our oppressors. Evil in the guise of an assassin; good in the guise of royalty, a child, the rightful ruler of a wakened land; random chance in a monkey suit. Evil slew good, strangling it. And yet good did not die.

Over and over such dramas played through sleepers' heads, in parts and wholes, submerged in the streams of other narratives, broken into bits and laced together to form new versions of the same events.

Here's a fairly coherent example:

The blond beast stalks up the rippling staircase on two legs, long hands held out from its sides in readiness. Night's darkness flows away from its path like music, pooling and spilling downward, filling the steps the beast leaves behind as it turns, mounts, turns again, and strides past guards steeped in drugs or strong drink or spells of blindness. Curtains fall open. The victim stands up from their couch and stretches imploringly toward the beast, which is suddenly our viewpoint. Then the victim shrinks back and edges toward the wall

*behind it—behind him? Her? Gravity tilts and the victim contin-
ues backward, climbing to the ceiling to dangle overhead. Our arms
raise our hands to grab and drag it to the floorwall and choke its
slender throat and hold and hold and hold until there is no air to
breathe for anyone. And we are about to suffocate, but then . . . then
there is something else. Something more. A window in the wallfloor
and it cracks and between its shattering edges peeps a face with eight
eyes staring so hard they draw everything into their black shine.*

Such dream sequences were common in North, Central, and
South America. Sometimes the strangling hands were replaced
with lynching ropes; sometimes the staring eyes became those of a
crowd of slumping, work-worn women, or men hunched and staggering with weariness, or smiling children who reached eagerly to
embrace and revive the beast's dying prey.

Influencing the interpretation of these scenes as symbolic
of the revolution took careful judgment. May Fourth partisans
sent letters to painters, speakers, actors, singers, journalists, and
the like, explaining how to understand the dreams in an artistic
light. The theory they offered those tending toward a scientific
outlook—the hemisphere's scholars, inventors, and researchers—
was that the living mass of the planet willed a change.

If so, it willed that change on several fronts, in several ways.

But was such a change the story's beginning or its middle? Or
maybe its conclusion? Could all these divisions overlap with each
other, perhaps?

Or could it even be that *Kinning* begins before *Everfair* ends?

CHAPTER ZERO

June 1916
Kisangani, Everfair

Princess Mwadi knelt in the jasmine's warm shade. Both Sifa and Lembe slept. That had never before happened, but the eyelids of both her mother's women stayed shut when Mwadi whispered their names. And Lembe snored, though lightly. And Sifa smacked her lips, which she would never have done in Mwadi's presence while awake.

Daring discovery, the princess stood, still lapped in the vines' deep green shadows. Her brother Ilunga lay within the palace walls, recuperating from the new illness under the care of Yoka, one of their father's most trusted and discreet counselors, and visited frequently by King Mwenda himself; her mother, Queen Josina, had established rooftop gardens to house the hives of her holy bees upon her return from her diplomatic mission to Angola, and there she was to be found most days. Though ostensibly the queen dwelt here in the palace courtyard with the other royal wives and daughters, Mwadi had quickly learnt how to amuse herself without expectation of her mother's praise or censure. And also how to seek out and enjoy her mother's company without being shooed away from the secrets Queen Josina liked to gather.

How, as Miss Rima Bailey would have put it, to sneak around.

The trick was to become something else. No longer content as a velvet-faced, sturdy-armed thirteen-year-old girl, Princess Mwadi concentrated on her resemblance to the sighing rain, then slipped free of the pavilion's overhanging roof to join the rain's fall.

Languorous in the midday's moist heat, ranks thinned by the ravaging new illness, the palace guard proved no impediment to

Mwadi's departure. And Kisangani's thoroughfares led her where she wanted to go so easily—the dwindling waters between built-up roads coming no higher than her knees, so that she might wade unmolested the whole way.

The city had grown since her father first established his court here, back before she or Prince Ilunga had been born. And it had grown even more in the two years since she acted the role of Bo-La alongside Miss Rima in Sir Matty's play. The atolo tree planted near the shelter of the king's ancestors stood surrounded now by many similar shelters sharing the tree's protection. So broad its branches, by itself the tree darkened almost all the sacred precinct's ground. So high its crown, the misting rain wreathed around its leaves like dagga smoke. So snaking its roots, she had to stoop to the soil and feel her way among them with her hands. So fat and slick the trunk, she didn't even try to climb it, merely clasped it to her, breathing in its clean, wild scent.

She had reached her goal! She threw back her head in joy and saw it—the king's original ceremonial shongo, yes! The green of its copper was duller and bluer, the curves of its blades were fuller and longer, than the intervening foliage.

So high above her head . . . impossible to touch it. It had stayed lodged in the gleaming brown bark higher than the ceiling of the palace pavilion for more than forty seasons—ever since her father hurled it there and decreed that whoever drew it free would rule after him. Warning stories told of the injuries borne by pretenders to Everfair's throne in their pursuit of this prize: multiple bones broken in sudden, inexplicable falls; crippling wounds gouged in their flesh by the beaks of invisible crows. But from the overheard conversations of her mother's rivals, the princess knew for certain that once she released the shongo from its resting place she could call herself her father's heir, as these women's sons had attempted to do. As her stupid brother Ilunga had tried to do as well. She had to retrieve it for herself, successfully—but how?

Arching her back, she continued gazing upward. A limb emerged from the tree's main body to the shongo's right, and just a little lower. Thinning gradually, gracefully, the long limb drooped near its end—Mwadi whirled to check—low enough! Or nearly so; she picked her way to where it waved almost, almost within her grasp. A glance around: no one was present. As she had planned. Offerings would be made later, at the time of the evening meal. Nobody had been here when she arrived, and nobody had arrived since.

With practiced swiftness she unwound her headwrap—a wider strap than babies wore, as Mwadi was soon to be a woman. A couple of tosses and it went over the limb. First she dragged the limb down. When the wood no longer bowed to her weight she paused to make sure again she was alone, then jumped! Still hanging by the loop of her headwrap she swung her legs high and locked ankles around the lowered limb. Of course it held her. Creeping along its under-side like a caterpillar—bunch, stretch, bunch, stretch—she moved toward the tree's center. Once there it was a struggle, but she got herself upright and facing in. No dizziness or loss of grip or bal-ance. No plunge from this hard-won height. No flock of ghosts.

Now. Bracing herself by tightening her thighs she leaned left, took the wooden haft of the king's shongo in both hands, and tugged. It came free slowly, like a well-watered cassava plant.

Triumph! Everfair was hers! Entranced by her happy prospects she sighed and stroked the glowing, newly naked blade, largest of the shongo's three. Burial in the atolo tree's flesh had kept it shin-ing bright. As bright as the future reign of Queen Mwadi.

Now to tell King Mwenda, so he could make the succession of-ficial. And to share the news of her good fortune with her mother, his favorite. And to gloat openly, in his face, upon her victory over Ilunga.

No, she would be kinder to him than that. Appoint him minis-ter of something. He was her brother, after all, by both father and mother.

Surely that mattered.

According to Queen Josina, every relationship entered into

mattered. Each was of the utmost importance. Slowly, thought-fully, Mwadi came down off of the atolo limb and untied her head-wrap. She wound it around and around the shongo's shaft, pulling it tight, then laid it loosely over the sharp-forged cutting edges.

Her mother shared wisdom like it was chocolate, always pos-sessed of a personal supply from which she doled out small bits, seemingly on a whim. Mwadi had learned as a child to savor her mother's pronouncements, to chew them over and extract their constantly changing, ever-refreshing truths.

As the princess left the grove surrounding the atolo for the ramp leading down to the partially flooded thoroughfare, she frowned at the ground on which she walked. She was going to reign over this land—over this earth, over the very soil clinging to her bared feet. Was that a relationship? Even now, at this point, before she actually ascended to Everfair's throne? Or perhaps not even then. Perhaps only relationships with living entities should be counted? The trees, then? A low branch brushed the top of her head as she stepped onto the ramp's gravel, as if in a tender farewell.

The peak of the day had passed, and Mwadi met a few others on her way home to the palace. Other subjects: young people run-ning errands for their elders, whites ignoring the inconvenience of doing business during the heat's height. Were the Europeans whom King Mwenda had demanded fealty from also in import-ant relationships with her? Or only those she knew personally, such as Sir Matty?

No one stirring about recognized her without her attendants, and Mwadi reached the palace steps quickly and easily. Sifa still slumbered in the courtyard; Lembe woke, but fell in immediately with the princess's pretense of being on her way to the bottom of the staircase that climbed from courtyard to rooftop.

For Lembe to do otherwise would have been to alert Queen Jo-sina to her inadequacy. It would have been to admit that she'd ne-glected to do her job. Instead, when the queen came out onto the roof through the door of the interior stairway, her serving woman was diligently oiling the carved wooden stand of one of her holy hives.

Mwadi watched the queen walk slowly between the tubs containing her budding flowers and fragrant blooms. Reaching the sheltered platform where the princess reclined, Queen Josina paused to observe her woman at work.

"How is my brother?" Mwadi asked dutifully. She sat up and reached beneath her couch to retrieve the cloth-swaddled shongo and began to unwrap it.

Her mother stepped onto the platform and sank to the cushions beside her. "Well enough. The disease is coming to accept his superiority." She swung her head one way, then the other, checking for any who overheard them. None of the other wives were visible; though supposedly it belonged to all, this garden was known as Queen Josina's private retreat.

"All signs indicate Mwenda will take my advice on the succession. So eventually, Ilunga will rule over all the rest of our land just as he'll rule very soon over the organism causing this illness."

No he would not.

"Naturally, a position of such distinction brings with it a high measure of risk. We must guard him carefully. . . ."

Josina's long, proud eyes rested lightly on the bundle occupying Mwadi's lap. "What are you about to show me?" Not waiting for Mwadi's answer, the queen twitched aside the last of the veiling headwrap. "Ah. Is this—this is the knife your father threw!"

"Yes. I pulled it from the atolo tree. That means I—not Ilunga—am my father's heir."

Her mother smiled with closed lips. "You are his heir when he says so."

"He will! He has to! Mother, you can help me to persuade him of my rights!" Mwadi took the shongo by its handle and tried to lift it from her lap.

Josina's hands barred hers from rising. "Are you sure you should do this?"

She drew back, staring. "Of course I am!"

"Are you sure this is how to get what you want?"

All certainty drained from Mwadi's head. Why would her mother object to her becoming queen? Why would she favor buffalo-headed Ilunga?

"Do you even know what that is? What it is that you want?"

"Everything! I want everything!"

A wider smile now. "Yes. You are truly my child." And now her mother's long, strong fingers curled over Mwadi's own, reinforcing her grip on the shongo. "We will have it. Everything you want. Trust me."

Mwadi had always trusted her mother. The question had always been whether her mother trusted her in return. Some secrets, the queen kept saying, it was impossible to share.

"Can you tell me how we will win?"

"You know that I am an initiate in the mysteries of the Yoruba, a priest of the orisha Oshun, yes? She who is the owner of wealth and learning?"

"I do."

"She who invented the form of divination I practice. She who holds high her golden light to show me which path of the many I can see that I should take. Which leads most surely to my desires."

Queen Josina's exploration of foreign cultures was well-known— but had adoption of foreigners' beliefs undermined her faith in her daughter's abilities? Or did it somehow, by some devious means, support it?

"*Your* desires?"

"We are in harmony. I have learned the best melodies to play, the best places in which to move our feet." The queen stroked the back of Mwadi's clenched hand. "You must relax. As I said, trust me." She beckoned, and Lembe abandoned her task to approach the platform.

"Accompany Princess Mwadi to Prince Ilunga's chambers,"

the queen instructed her serving woman. She leaned forward, speaking softly into her daughter's ear, again stroking her hand. "You'll give this to him for safekeeping."

"To Ilunga? No! Never!" She lowered her voice, too, but fierceness filled it, hardened it the way blows and heat harden iron. "*I! I* will be this country's rightful ruler!" She jerked her hand, trying to free herself—and the shongo—from Josina's grip. She couldn't.

"What if I agree with you on that point?" The queen was whispering, was close, her cheek touching Mwadi's. The sweet scent of her hair oil threatened to wipe out all other smells, all sights and sounds and—

Mwadi stood. She swayed only a little, only a moment. She kept her hold on the shongo. So did her mother, which Mwadi found steadying. "Then you do? You agree and acknowledge—"

"Listen to me! Can't you tell? Stop your insolence and obey me!" The queen stood too. "I know what I'm doing! I know this reality! I am ready to enter it—though if Oshun had not prepared me for your stubbornness I would have you poisoned!"

Quickly Josina wrested the shongo away from Mwadi's surprised grasp. But only to hold it before her, between them. "You will present this to your brother. You will explain to him that you found it at the atolo's foot, in a bowl filled with black sand such as we use for metal casting. You'll make sure others hear your story, and that they repeat it.

"Do these things and anything else I instruct you to do. The throne and the land will be yours."

June 1916 to June 1920
Kisangani, Everfair, to Cairo, Egypt

Should he lie? Prince Ilunga shifted his weight from one aching elbow to the other and gazed away from his sister's gift. Then back. Resplendent on a fur-covered cushion it lay, his father's first ceremonial shongo, a three-lobed promise of sovereignty. He who pulled it from the trunk of the atolo tree was to be named King Mwenda's successor.

Should Ilunga claim the feat of retrieving it as his own? With the shongo in his possession, his claim would have real weight. It would ease the pricking soreness lingering from that earlier attempt, that ugly failure seen by all.

But what of those who'd seen Mwadi bring the shongo to him here? The guards outside his door? Or the flat-chested woman seated by his bed, the one his mother had assigned to attend to Ilunga as his illness receded? Not to mention anyone his sister might have met on her way to his rooms. Not to mention his sister herself, gone now. Gone to report to someone? To his mother?

There was no hope of untangling the threads of Queen Josina's intricate plots. He must just believe she always put his interests first, as she swore she did.

"Why does my sister want it, anyway?" he grumbled.

The flat-chested woman spoke, startled. "She doesn't! She gave it to you!"

He ignored her words. But her presence was not unwelcome; though you couldn't call her attractive, at least she was a woman. He was young and needed practice. "Here. Use some of that salve on me. My limbs—" Clacking beads interrupted him as his mother swept through his bedchamber's door.

"Queen!" The woman—he ought to learn her name—dropped to the floor. "Your son's health improves by the hour. I was going to you with my news as soon as those bringing the evening meal arrived."

"No need for that." Josina touched the woman's shoulder and she got up. "I see his progress." An arched brow and the delicate flare of the queen's nostrils indicated her approval. "He'll be able to join his father tomorrow when he holds court."

"Is that when we'll receive the Portuguese envoys? Are they on—" A sharp glance from his mother stopped the prince's questions mid-spate.

"The *secret* envoys spent last night in Mbuji-Mayi, and they rest there again today to observe a feast of their religion." She paused and he had time to absorb the full strength of her emphasis on "secret." "Rosine, go fetch the prince's evening meal yourself."

The poorly endowed woman left. No great loss. The coaching in diplomacy Queen Josina gave him once she was gone more than compensated for missing a chance to flex his love muscles. During the formal reception held for the Portuguese the next day, and in all his dealings with subjects and foreigners afterward, he did his best to remember her teachings.

Regularly she received visits from foreigners—often from those who had initiated her in her religious mysteries. When these visitors departed she would spend long night hours treading intricate dance patterns to music audible only to her ears. Some whispered that his mother was mad. If so, it was a cunning madness.

"Do not reveal the extent of your intelligence to those who assume you lack it," she counseled him, again and again. "Play the fool in public and in private act the sage, and you'll both surprise your enemies and please your friends."

He watched as she accepted without protest the Portuguese ambassadors' reluctant refusal to speak to the other European governments on Everfair's behalf. Later, in the markets following his country's surrender to the English, Ilunga learned how invisible activity—spying, magic spells, nested schemes—bore visible fruit. Despite the attacks on their sovereignty instigated by Thornhill and other British agents, his mother cultivated Everfair's ties to certain of England's factions. Because, she said, "Our enemies are made of more than one kind of cloth."

As the seasons passed, Queen Josina encouraged Ilunga to dig his own information channels and direct their flow. She expected him to use these to help her keep up with schisms developing between those who planned a return to Europe's fast-vanishing superiority.

The so-called War to End War resulted in a litter of smaller conflicts, most fought with words and smiles, in hidden rooms, on metaphoric battlefields. Judged a harmless playboy, Prince Ilunga was easily able to observe the Europeans and their surrogates as they jockeyed for knowledge and position. He journeyed from city to city, avowedly in pursuit of pleasure: west to Lagos, south to Maputo, east to Mogadishu, north to Cairo.

Where, at the age of thirty-five seasons—eighteen-and-one-half years—he found his first real friend.

Deveril Scranforth grinned when Ilunga introduced himself as the future ruler of Everfair, and leaned back to balance his wooden chair on two spindly legs. "Ha! One day you'll outrank me, then. But for now—" Without looking he stretched wide both arms and hooked each around the waist of a deep-chested beauty. "—for now, I'll be teaching you a thing or two, what? And you'll be grateful for that—and show it!"

Smoke from their host's hookah drifted between them on its way to the night-curtained windows. Attending this soiree was part of the standard plan Ilunga's mother had devised for gathering intelligence: woo the offspring of embassy personnel and allow himself to be drawn into their social groups.

Attendance was part of the standard plan, making this a completely unremarkable evening, but ever afterward Ilunga remembered it as the beginning of a new phase in his dedication to savoring the world's glories. Heightened awareness of his surroundings, helped on by the judicious consumption of cocktails, filled him with the sense of his surroundings' divinity: the satin sheen of the throw pillows scattered about him on his divan, the jewels winking in a passing guest's cuff links, the sweet residue of honeyed melon coating his lips, the tinkling chime of the golden chains adorning the wrists and ankles of the laughing woman who leapt up from Scranforth's lap and snuggled cozily onto his own—despite his weak protests.

"Not a virgin, are you?"

As if Ilunga were still a boy! "No!"

"Good. Nothin wrong with it if you were, but I'd want to start you out a bit slower." The white crooked his finger and two more beauties congealed out of the crowd to stand beside him. "Which of em d'you want? All three of em? Like to keep one for m'self."

To go from the glittering heat of the party to the dark fragrance of the house's fountain-fed garden took only a few steps. Only a moment. And then the prince was enveloped in flesh. Above, below, on either side, perfumed skin slid and slipped against his clothing. Then against his nakedness.

Touch receded, returned, receded, returned, new waves rippling over old ones like the music of the fountain waters rising and falling somewhere nearby . . . like the fickle breezes laden with the party's distant murmurings, or the thickening breaths of the women wrapping him in pleasure.

Then Scranforth's voice came crashing through their panting sighs: "What d'ye say? Good play? Best hoors in Maadi—in all Cairo! Agreed?"

The soft lips kissing Ilunga's eyelids went away. He opened his eyes and his mouth, about to bellow furiously at the European's interruption—but the soft lips came back, to graze his jaw and cling moistly to the ridges and valleys of his throat—and his delight at this found its reflection in the pale, half-shaven face hanging over him.

The prince realized he wasn't actually angry.

Delight mirrored was delight doubled. Bliss upon bliss proved this new truth. To receive a caress and cry out at its shivery progress—from spine to buttocks to tight and tingling testicles— was to share and deepen its effects.

Was this increase in his arousal a sign that Ilunga wanted sexual congress with the white man? He tried asking his mother. Sometimes he believed she knew him better than he knew himself. But the coded messages he sent her went unanswered. All the queen responded with were instructions: stay in Cairo, enroll in Victoria College, rent a home there that his sister Mwadi could run for him.

His father wouldn't blame him for a trait only Europeans

and missionaries abhorred. Would he? Probably not. Although Ilunga's usefulness as King Mwenda's heir would perhaps be compromised. . . . No. That sort of thinking belonged in the head of Queen Josina. Who, if she said nothing of her son's predilection, must not consider it to be a problem.

And for him it wasn't. Adventures with Devil—so Ilunga came to call his new friend, adopting the pet name employed by his fellow students—filled most of the prince's nights, and quite a few of his days as well. The white man knew the town's best brothels. Even more conveniently, he introduced "Loongee" to several women willing to entertain them for no money—though not exactly for free, as Ilunga quickly learned.

His first such encounter was with a buxom, cheerful matron whose nephew controlled the stock certificates of the Great Sun River Collector Company. She was easily satisfied. In addition to plowing the slick delta between her thighs—Devil stationed titillatingly nearby, ostensibly to watch out for the woman's husband—he only had to purchase fifty shares of the company, at a surprisingly moderate price.

But soon the prince learned how to fend off these requests. This meant that sometimes, to his regret, he also had to fend off the proposals of erotic exercise they accompanied. Enough of those remained to keep him happily occupied, though. And despite a couple of petty disagreements, and one serious quarrel involving a firearm, he made sure to include Devil in any activities of that sort.

Ilunga dedicated an entire suite of his Maadi villa to sexual pursuits. He arranged a door communicating with the room where Devil often stayed. Once or twice he invited others to visit, hoping to experience the same intensified gratification in their presence.

As far as Prince Ilunga could tell, his experiments failed. He felt no comparable increase in sensation when he shouted his satisfaction in the hearing of his sister's European protégés, the Schreibers; no wider or even equivalent overflowing of deliciousness when he hosted other college friends for similar nights of sexual indulgence.

Nonetheless, his efforts made a difference.

How? Chiefly through his memory. Ilunga knew he was reaching for connection to others. He was aware that he cherished the touch of the women who attracted him, and that he yearned to share it. He realized how he longed to drench the strangers of the world in these women's musk, to be soused in their sweat, to drown in it while drowning his white companions with him.

Memories of these desires dug their grooves deep into his mind. Incompletion kept them fresh and sharply edged.

Memories, like all stories, want to tell themselves. Asleep, Prince Ilunga dreamed that his fantasies came true. Awake, he forgot the specifics of how that occurred. But the happiness his dreams left behind haunted him.

Awake, the prince pretended stupidity, as Queen Josina had advised him to do. He acted as though ignorant of Devil's plan to use him to access Everfair's mineral wealth—and of some points in that plan he really *was* ignorant, because ignorance was easier than action. Ilunga always preferred to avoid unnecessary effort.

In fact, it was Devil's drives rather than the prince's own unsteady ambitions that moved most things forward—especially things concerning the succession. Much of what the European wanted to do depended on Ilunga inheriting the throne. So in between their college's lectures on the histories of dead empires and their evening assignations with willing women, Devil did his royal friend's tedious yet necessary political work.

Who, then, do you suppose gathered and treasured together Prince Ilunga's unrequited attempts at blurring the boundaries dividing him from the rest of creation?

Who do you think?

CHAPTER ONE

December 1920
Tourane, Vietnam, Aboard Xu Mu

Dragons. Best to follow them. Bee-Lung looked up at her brother. His long, appropriately handsome face became clear as the winch cranked her higher, toward the aircanoe's open hold. His expression was calm. Those born in Dragon years expected to lead others even more than they enjoyed doing so. He really was the perfect node. The decision to share her specially bred new strain of May Fourth's Spirit Medicine with him was proving wise.

Nodding acknowledgment to the Bharatese man on the crank, Bee-Lung hitched her robe tight against her hips and thighs and hopped over the cargo basket's low rim. Normally she wore trousers, but her appearance at the French administrative palace had merited the wearing of this concoction of peach-colored silk trimmed in crimson cord. It seemed to have done the trick; she would have to store it properly till the next stop on their trip.

But first to tell Tink. He was already walking toward the hold's narrow door out, sure she'd be behind him. She smiled at his back and ran forward. He paused at the threshold and turned, one foot still raised to step through. "Success?" he asked. The beginning of a furrow indented his brow.

"Of a sort." Without moving her head, Bee-Lung indicated the Bharatese man with her eyes. He had joined them too recently to be trusted, his inoculation only taking place today.

"Come." Out the door, along the corridor, to their shared cabin in *Xu Mu*'s gilded prow. "Now." He closed the thick cotton curtains and pushed a sack of dried mushrooms out of his path to the glassed window. Porthole.

"They've stopped short of giving consent for the cable's inoculation, but they won't stand in our way. As long as no one can implicate them."

"The French wish to seem ignorant of what we're doing in their colony?" Tink's voice had the sheen of sarcasm.

"So I interpret our interaction." A crate of clay Spirit Medicine containers on the floor—deck—rattled as the aircanoe rocked in a momentary gust. "Naturally we must prepare to leave as soon as the spores are distributed. But my recruits will tend the threads they produce to expansion and fruiting, and will make sure the resulting conduits connect with the ones we started for our May Fourth friends." Ducking under a small hammock filled with empty paper envelopes—she would use them to organize future botanical samples—Bee-Lung made her way to the cabin's second and larger porthole. It was shaded. She pushed the white pleats to the round frame's bottom and looked out over the city the French called Tourane. *Xu Mu* faced away from the mouth of the Han River and away from the telegraph cable's landing station on the shores of the East Sea. The red roofs under which Bee-Lung had lately intrigued lay almost directly below. The French invaders' mooring facilities were barely adequate—a rope was all that held the aircanoe to their mast.

Low clouds gathered and parted and gathered again, veiling the inland mountains in pale obscurity. "At least it's warm," her brother remarked. "If the rain keeps off we'll have no trouble tonight."

"No need for you to go yourself, then."

"But I want to." Of course he did.

"No need," Bee-Lung repeated. Uselessly. Not just Dragon, Metal Dragon.

"Would you rather I sent you?" This was a jest on Tink's part; it had been determined earlier the differing roles she and her brother would assume on this voyage.

"No." She pulled the shade back up and frowned. "They've already seen me."

"Ha! They'll never see me! I'm not getting caught!" He went to crouch over the jars of Spirit Medicine. "They accepted the tea we brought them without noticing?"

"Even so." The threads of Spirit Medicine that they had secreted in bundles of fragrant tea leaves were so thin as to escape detection. Stored in the palace pantries, these would be available to May Fourth's new kitchen agents for later inoculations. Of which there would assuredly be many. "Enthusiasm for our venture will greet—"

A scratching at the bulkhead interrupted her. The Bharatese man shoved the door's curtains aside and came in holding a tray. "Raghu!" Yes, that was his name. Of course Tink knew it. "Are you ready?"

"And eager!" Light from the glowing sponges in his tray of bowls winked off of Raghu's sudden grin. Like that, it was evening; the day had been dark enough that the change had slipped past her without fanfare.

Bee-Lung took a sponge lamp and hung it from its hook on the cabin's ceiling. One of her favorite discoveries; the radiance of the powder impregnating it was fired by water. So gentle its shine. So sad, like a setting moon.

There was no reason for sadness. Tink would be fine. Her trepidation over the deployment of a gang numbering unlucky four was mere superstition. The May Fourth Movement's very name repudiated such backward notions.

She took a second lamp to hang.

"You should sleep," Tink told her.

She tugged fretfully at the tight cuffs of the silk robe's sleeves, which had crept up to pinch the fat of her upper arms. "I should get out of this abominably restricting dress."

"And then sleep."

While changing to her accustomed clothes, she imparted the

intelligence obtained by the kitchen agent regarding approaches to the cable's terminal station. Then, because it was her policy to obey her brother, even when he didn't realize he'd given an order, Bee-Lung did manage to sleep—for several hours. She woke well before sunrise to dimness and silence. The water fueling the sponges would have partially evaporated by now, so the cabin's dimness was to be anticipated. But not its silence. The lamps' low glimmering showed that the hammock beside her own hung limp. Empty.

Tourane, Vietnam, Aboard Xu Mu to the Governor's Palace

Seated with three of his chosen kin in the cargo basket, headed down to his first ground sortie in service of May Fourth, Tink felt a happiness he hadn't known in years. If there was no conventional beauty left in the world for him since Lily's death, he could at least be of some practical usefulness. The Chen twins seemed filled with the same high hopes for the mission he himself held, giggling as they hunched protectively over the braided coils of spore-laden root sheaths. Before the basket's descent plunged them into the starless night's darkness, Tink could see that Raghu's expression looked less sanguine. Then there was only his scent to go by: the Bharatese man's sweat, bitter with nervousness; his noxious inner winds released to be dispelled by gradually rising offshore breezes, which carried the sweeter smell of dying kelp. At last came the muddy odor of the freshly trodden road to their target, as promised by Bee-Lung's intelligence.

Climbing from the staging platform down to the ground along the bamboo stairway at the palace's back, they encountered only one guard. Before he could raise others, Chen Min-Jun grabbed him by the throat. His scream softened to a grunt. "Come with us," the girl suggested, her strong hands twisting left and right, then loosening.

"Or decide to stay," said her sister. "In which case we'll be forced to kill you."

No surprise that the guard became at least a temporary recruit.

Between the homes of colonialist collaborators clustering near the palace's walls they walked—quickly, quietly, avoiding the treacherous, gravel-strewn entranceways of the more elegant establishments. Then these were left behind.

Removing their lone lightsponge from his shirt, Tink lowered it to soak in a puddle and activate. He squeezed out the excess water and returned it to its former home, his body and clothes serving as its shade. They should not rely on their eyes alone. It would be best to frame their perceptions in the fashions nourished by the Spirit Medicine while on this mission.

Soon the tingling air of the woods encroached more closely, and soon after that it enveloped them. Tink wanted to rest here, to lie among the enchantingly damp fallen leaves as if he, too, had come to the exact right place. But the road. The mission. The spores.

The target. At last they'd reached it. Fragrant, new-turned earth, steaming with life, sat wetly mounded over the trench in which the cable traveled from its landing station in the bay to the terminal house on the forest's far side. Here they would insert the latest of their spore batches, whose emerging threads would reach along that cable's length to find the previous, the next, the next. . . .

He waited for Raghu, who lagged behind the twins and their captive. "Tools?" From a sling over his left shoulder the man removed a pair of collapsed shovels. Unfolding the one handed to him, Tink sank it into the soil. He directed the Bharatese to start digging a few paces farther from the road.

The actions he performed were pleasurable: sinking in the shovel's blade, lifting out the muck of knowledge, heaping it up next to one serenely expectant hole after another. He couldn't delve too deeply; the holes' round sides wanted to melt and sag. But once in place and active, the spores would sense their goal and reach down for it with quick-growing tendrils.

When he and the Bharatese had excavated a dozen of these miniature gullets, they switched duties with the twins, tending the prisoner and watching for intruders while Min-Jun and Jie-Jun unspooled the precious root sheaths into the waiting orifices. This far from shore there would be no steel wire wrappings—only rubber and gutta percha layers to protect the buried cable's copper core, materials that would help as much as hinder the growth of the spores' tendrils. The Chens poured mud back into the holes. It overflowed them.

Was this spot too wet for the fungus to flourish?

Tink felt how long it would be till dawn. "Onward," he decided.

The covered trench went straighter than the road, but in the same general direction.

As they came nearer to the telegraph's terminal station, the waters soaking the black earth drained somewhat away. Though still flat to his useless eyes, the land slowly rose, so that in good time an orchard of mangos surrounded them on both sides. Excellent. This was a sort of terrain Tink was very familiar with.

The digging this time was not much more work, though they made the pits deeper. Another twelve. That ought to be enough. Again he and Raghu traded with the sisters. But the prisoner had been flirting with the girls, and he sulked, unhappy at the change.

"What's your name?" Tink asked. If he could, he would learn from the guard himself how best to persuade him to their side permanently.

"Zhou Yong-Lei." Honest pile of rocks. Well, one could gain purchase there, if one were stubborn.

"And of what do you dream, Master Zhou?"

"I—"

"Terrorists! Seize them!" Shouted orders and blinding white beams shattered the orchard's dark calm. Off of the road poured a clotted flood of frightened-smelling men. BANG! BANG-BANG-BANG! Rifle fire from two different points flew mere handsbreadths from Tink's face. He fell to embrace the earth, catching at Zhou's clothes to drag him down too and save him. Another explosion and the sudden salt of spilling blood told Tink that he had failed.

Sadness. The guard died, life leaking soundlessly out of his wounds and into the orchard's accepting roots. Tink surrendered to the men—they were all men—who had shot him. No chance now to win Zhou over to the right side. Hustled toward the road and back the way they'd come, Tink wasted precious time in regret. Only as they left the countryside behind did he begin to return to full function.

Coals smoldering in iron baskets flanked the wide stairway leading to the palace's grand entrance. By their smoky light he saw that the Chen twins still accompanied him, though Min-Jun had a dark swelling on her right cheek. Twisting as far as his captor's grip allowed, he made out Raghu's slumping form at the group's rear, supported between two soldiers.

They didn't climb the stairs. A pair of soldiers at the bottom challenged them in French. Tink had learned a little French from Lisette and the Poet. Only a little, and long ago, and this version was differently accented. His sister had made a study of the language for diplomatic purposes. Not he. The tones of the challenger's and the respondent's voices told him more than the shapes of their words. The challenging man seemed satisfied with the other's answer, but rather than lead them up to the governor's receiving rooms he took them to a shadowed servants' entrance near the building's southwest corner. With a last deep breath of the night air in which *Xu Mu* flew, so near, so unreachable, he followed his captor's insistence within.

It wasn't all bad. The lights were far apart, but steady and shielded with glass. His vision was restored to utility. They walked to the end of a corridor and turned left. A door on their right would have delivered them to the bamboo scaffolding and stairs up to the roof platform and the aircanoe's mooring post. But that door was shut, and they turned away from it, into the palace's heart.

Or if not into its heart, if hearts must lodge higher in metaphorical bodies, then into its rectum. A small chamber, poured concrete for walls, no windows, square flagstones paving the sloping

floor save for a wide, shallow hole at its center. Old odors of stale
sweat and cold embers and roast—pork? monkey?—fought with
the odors they carried with them: the knowing mud and the new
blood and the trace scents of gunpowder, steel, the fat greasing the
soldiers' boots and the laundry soap lingering in their uniforms.

The soldier who had hauled Tink into the room flung him
across it. He fell on his side. The flagstones soothed him, cool
against his exposed skin where his short trousers were torn. The
Chens landed beside him, then Raghu beside Jie-Jun, grunting and
trying to stand again at once.

"Attawndayzeesee." Wait here. No doubt a joke; the soldiers
were all laughing as they left, laughing even louder as they locked
the door's rattling lock.

No electricity. No light. Tink turned the sponge around inside
his shirt so that it shed the brightness fed by his perspiration out
onto their surroundings.

"They didn't chain us!" observed Jie-Jun.

"Why should they need to?" Raghu asked glumly. "We'll never
escape."

True, perhaps. By the smell of things the door out was guarded.
The room's walls stood as stout as such walls could stand; given
time they would crumble, but for now—the floor? Tink half-
rolled, half-crawled to the bared earth at the room's focus. It actually stank—even before he had taken the Spirit Medicine, Tink
would have noticed its reek of charred wood. His heightened sensitivity to chemicals revealed nastier details: a spatter of urine,
and small but insistent clots of vomit. And the sweat was reminiscent of grief and fear. These things combined with the faint
hints of old roasted meat to tell him why they'd been brought
here, what they'd been left here for. Torture.

He buried his fingers in the sullied soil. As always, it lived.
But sourly, blindly, in solitude. To make contact with even a rudimentary core such as they had started growing on the palace

grounds would take too long—weeks, during which time he'd be unmoving and apparently unconscious. And preferably unobserved. Unlikely.

The ceiling? Tink got to his feet and pulled the sponge from his shirt. He raised it high so its soft brightness showed him that yes, as he'd sensed, there was wood above his head. But wood long dead, infused with some decay-retardant poison, so that there was no communing with it, no way to use it to tell his sister of his whereabouts.

The Chens came to kneel beside him, eyeing him expectantly. They knew him for a node. "We must simply wait for Bee-Lung to find us," he informed them. Eventually she would catch his scent. "She's bound to come soon."

Tourane, Vietnam, Aboard Xu Mu to the Palais du Gouverneur

Of course both of the cargo baskets were in use right when Bee-Lung needed them. *Xu Mu*'s loaders had filled them the prior evening, doing the heaviest of their labor before the warmth of the day. She hurried to put on the stupid peach silk robe again, but by the time she arrived in the hold the industrious workers had already lowered one basket to the platform; the other dangled in midair. Obviously it had gone too far down to be recalled.

Breathing as calmly as she could manage, Bee-Lung composed herself to stand out of the way, a distance from the open hatch. The winch operators unwound the cable with what seemed to her unnecessary deliberateness. Surely the second basket's journey wouldn't take too long—the landing platform was no farther away from the gondola's hold than the bottom of the aircanoe's envelope was from its top. Yes, the gifts of porcelain it contained were delicate, but very carefully wrapped. She had delayed sending them down till now to make certain of that. This was her fault.

The full basket reached the roof's level without incident, was hooked and hauled into place, and at long last the winch line was attached to the emptied basket. Up it came and in she got.

"You won't go alone?"

That had in fact been Bee-Lung's intention. But the question came from Kwangmi—the only woman Tink had voluntarily sought out since his love's death, and the core member who—though she was deemed unnecessary to the sowing mission—would have made them five rather than unlucky four. Bee-Lung ought to overcome her disdain. "Not if you'll join me." She climbed into the basket first, then held out her hand to help the Korean, who despite her name was dark-complexioned. "Shining Beauty" indeed. Trust her brother to find the unorthodox attractive.

"Hurry! Quickly!" Ignoring the lurch and sway of the cargo basket's initial drop, Bee-Lung pleaded up through the hatch for the workers to lower them fast, faster! Not till they reached the platform did she realize she still held Kwangmi's hand.

Bee-Lung loosened her clenched fingers. A rag-clad loader offered his dirt-smeared arm. She pretended she needed it, clung to it, and with a false show of age tottered stubbornly away from the bamboo stairway running down the palace's back, dragging the loader and his arm alongside. Kwangmi, smart if not conventionally good-looking, followed her example. Yesterday's intelligence—how long it seemed since she'd received the skinny little kitchen maid's report—said there was a door to the attics on the inner slope of the east wing's roof.

Yes. A short hop onto the regrettably slick tiles—an inadvertent slide halted by Kwangmi's swift snatch at the peach dress's collar—a gap in the door's shutters—she was in.

A round window covered in brown paper provided some light, but it was in the western wall and not exactly bright. Bee-Lung let the air currents tell her where she was, what surrounded her. Mostly empty space. A pile of trunks filled the corner to her immediate left. A velvety cluster of bats hung from the peaked roof's rafters, the white of their feces a stark circle on the attic's dark floor. Which way down? The bats would not know.

Kwangmi entered behind her. "Bar the shutters," said Bee-Lung.

The sounds of Kwangmi's searching ended in satisfied mutterings and the knocking of wood on hollow wood. "It's done," she pronounced, padding forward on rubber soles. "No one will follow us in. Can you smell where he is?"

"Vaguely." Bee-Lung shook her head. "He's below us. Quite a distance—" Maybe she should have presented herself formally instead of entering this way. Who knew how many floors lay between her and Tink? Was it too late? Perhaps not. After all, only the no-doubt lowly loaders had seen them arrive. Perhaps Kwangmi could be directed to render occult aid if Bee-Lung could find her way to a regular receiving room. There she'd do her best to distract the colonial officials with a petition for their help in solving the mystery of Tink's disappearance—a mystery Bee-Lung suspected the French themselves of causing.

Wherever the exit to the rest of the palace was, it would not reveal itself to her if she simply stood in one spot. "Come, Kwangmi," she commanded, walking past. Together they moved through the door in the wall dividing them from the attics' main area.

The new room was wider, and higher ceilinged. And emptier. And still so much dust! She saw no nearby windows, but there ought to be vents—

"CHUHH!"

No! Bee-Lung whirled, but before she could silence her, Kwangmi let out two more loud sneezes: "CHUH! SHH-CHUH!" Then she had her hand over the woman's disgustingly wet nose and mouth.

The sneezing fit stopped. They stood in a ringing quiet. Faint murmurs from the bats in the previous room ruffled its surface. Bee-Lung plunged deep underneath the noiselessness, sinking into the slumbering lumber of the building, swimming with the pollens floating—floating down? Down! The wood confirmed it, and also what she now remembered of the sneezes' echoes.

Removing her hand momentarily from Kwangmi's face to wipe it on the silk robe, which was good at least for this much, Bee-Lung brought it back up to pinch the woman's nostrils shut, then drew nose and head low enough that her lips touched Kwangmi's naked ears.

"Follow me to the storey below. But stay hidden. From there go where you detect his scent."

Softly as she could, Bee-Lung crept ahead and to the left. These stairs must connect with the set running from kitchen to servants' quarters. She began her descent, then paused. Now she recalled seeing a narrow door in the cramped back passage's plastering, too high to reach without a stepladder. Would she hurt herself? Kwangmi would be fine. And so would Bee-Lung; she'd have to be. Pulling free a few pins, she disarranged her hair. She rubbed her eyes red and lamented that the steps on which she stood seemed to have been swept clean. But doubtless the robe's hem had gotten dirty enough during her trek across the dusty main room. She checked to make sure there was no visible sign of the Korean woman. No. If Bee-Lung hadn't sensed her, she would never have known Kwangmi was there.

Smiling, Bee-Lung began to scream. Like a unicorn she thundered down the rest of the stairs to pound on the locked door at their bottom. "Demons! Demons!" she screeched. "Save me! Save me! Demons!" For greater effect she added a string of wordless yelps.

Soon the door opened and two wiry men with muscle-knotted arms pulled her out. Servants—not her target audience. She clasped them to her and wept, acting too frightened to answer their questions. They supported her ostensibly uncontrolled steps and steered her helpfully toward the front of the palace, where the Frenchmen worked and lived. But she balked at the broad stairs leading down to the ballroom and library levels—her task was to divert attention away from those lower floors and give Kwangmi a chance to free Tink.

Her ears caught the click of a metal latch retracting. It was followed by a phrase: "Portayzellah." A woman's rich scent flooded Bee-Lung's nose; she looked up to see a proud, high-browed face peering from a doorway to the stairs' right. She had not met this one yesterday; judging from intelligence she'd gathered this should be the gouverneur's wife's primary attendant, Madame du Strigile.

The room into which the servants ushered Bee-Lung was not as spacious as those in which she'd been welcomed the day before. A narrow bed on one side, chairs with embroidered cushions on the other, arranged next to a small and totally unnecessary fireplace. Bee-Lung fell onto the bed as if in a faint. It stood beside a pair of open windows and so was blessed by a cooling breeze.

"Keteelareeve?" said the Frenchwoman. Bee-Lung's recall of the language was returning. Qu'est-il arrive. What was wrong. Moaning, she modified her babble, murmuring now in French her distress-fractured claims of fiendish assault: "Came upon me where—snakelike wings—horrible laughing teeth—"

A cup touched her lower lip and she gulped water from it gratefully. "Fetch Doctor Blanchet," the madame ordered. A servant left, but four others took his place. The room and the corridor beyond were nicely crowded now. "Clear the—"

Desperately Bee-Lung sat and grabbed for the madame's shooing hands. Won them. "NO! Don't leave me! Don't let anyone go anywhere alone!" Bad enough that the important ones, the soldiers, were still missing.

The madame's high forehead ridged in annoyance. "Really!" Fortunately at that moment the smell of a European man asserted itself. The gouverneur! His bushy brown beard covered his face like a prickly shoe-cleaning mat. Gold spectacles shivered on his unremarkable nose, reflecting away her sight. "What's all this nonsense? Haven't I enough to deal with already, holding prisoners for that Christ-beloved cable company? House servants are your responsibility!"

He was leaving! Bee-Lung jumped to her feet and pushed through the throng. "Master! The demons want you! *You!*" The gouverneur paused in his ponderous pivoting.

"This is no servant of ours!" the madame sneered. "Don't you know who works for you?"

"If it's not ours, what's the little monkey doing in here? A beggar? Turn it out!"

"She's the ambassador, fool!"

Close enough now, Bee-Lung seized the gouverneur's wrist and clung fiercely despite his frowning attempts to wrest free. "They wish to eat you up!" she insisted. "You must—"

"Here! Let me go!"

On the contrary, Bee-Lung buried her face in the man's satin-covered chest, wrapping his fat waist in her other arm. Temporarily, the hands of servants pulled her away from him. But sagging back as if in a faint, Bee-Lung fell against her captors. They staggered and dropped her. She crawled back to the gouverneur and grabbed at his ankles. He kicked. She howled and pleaded. The madame strove vainly to insert reason into the scene. "Let Blanchet come treat her— If only you will stand firm, Antoine, she cannot possibly move you!"

The gouverneur ignored this sage advice and kept kicking. The sharp toes of his stinking leather shoes hurt. Bee-Lung slipped them off his feet one after the other, which perplexed him. "To me! Guards! Guards!" he yelled. At last, at last, soldiers began arriving. Dark blue uniforms swarmed up the stairs and filled the passageway. By this time she'd been dragged to the room's threshold and had, between kicks, an excellent view of proceedings. And an even better perspective via her other senses.

Not all the palace's soldiers had run to the gouverneur's defense. A few, faintly distinguishable, remained in the service area four stories below her.

However, Tink did not. His scent now found her mainly by way of the madame's open window, with Kwangmi's and that of some familiar others joining it. They had gotten out. Success!

With a show of reluctance Bee-Lung finally allowed herself to be detached from the white man's ankles.

Tourane, Vietnam

Thorny hedges laced with drooping, brown-spotted leaves sheltered the path between the kitchen and formal gardens. Fat berries colored a fiery orange hung at intervals. Tink saw Kwangmi snatch a few, then ran to follow her into the shadow of the south court's tall fountain.

"We're hidden here?" Raghu asked.

Tink and the Chens were too busy slaking their thirsts to answer such a stupid question. "Not hidden," Kwangmi told him. "Only unseen. For the moment." She drank from the fountain too, then put a few of the berries in her mouth and began chewing them.

"For how long?" The Bharatese man rose nervously.

"Sit." Tink tugged at Raghu's sheer tunic. "Till we must board *Xu Mu* again."

Raghu sat, but looked back at the palace, up at the aircanoe looming overhead, back, up, back, up—

Kwangmi spat the chewed berries into her palm. "Tear off the bottom of your shirt." She spoke to Raghu.

"Me? My kameez?"

She nodded impatiently, then gestured to Min-Jun. "Come beside me. Please. Just the front, Brother."

Tink placed a comradely arm atop Raghu's shoulders. "Best to humor her."

Grinning in embarrassment, the Bharatese tore his white cotton garment from side-slit to side-slit and gave the resulting rag to Kwangmi. She dipped it in the fountain and twisted it into a bandage, packing the berry mash into its pleats. With not a single glance at the trouser top Raghu had been so reluctant to reveal, she tied the makeshift poultice into place on Min-Jun's black and swollen cheek. "Sister Bee-Lung says the healing properties of rose hips are fast acting. You'll feel better soon."

"Are we waiting for her?" asked Jie-Jun.

Tink peered around the fountain's lowest aerial basin. "We were, but we should go." Though no one was visible yet past the masking roses, the chase was on. Several palace doors had suddenly opened, and in the near distance he heard waves of sandaled feet crash out of them, their noise spilling loudly over the steady trickle of the fountain.

"We'll weaken them—divide them! Let's separate!" Even as he proposed doing this he dreaded a course that could leave Bee-Lung behind. He didn't want to part with the twins, either, or poor Raghu, and certainly not Kwangmi, who had proved so useful so often. And yet how else—

"Yes," Kwangmi agreed. "That was Sister's plan. I will lead them to their closest temple of Christ, where the French, being superstitious, will avoid killing us. And you will climb directly to *Xu Mu* and rendezvous to pluck us off the temple's high tower."

"But surely—"

"It is in accord with our core's wishes." Tink knew she was right, felt it in his blood and glands. "No more arguing. No more time." Urging Raghu and the Chens before her, she ran toward the street-side wall of the palace's compound.

And he ran where he was meant to run, to the palace itself, to the ramp the stairs the landing deck the mooring mast, shoving aside five soldiers in his way. The Spirit Medicine lent him speed. One soldier, regrettably, went over the deck's too-low rail. He bounced nastily as he fell; before he landed Tink had topped the mast and begun his swarming ascent up *Xu Mu*'s mooring line.

Some waft of information had reached high enough. The cargo basket was being lowered; Tink would easily be able to reach it with a few more pulls upward. He did.

Secure in the basket, Tink looked earthward again. The palace disgorged a hurrying stream of soldiers, his sister in her improbable peach dress in their lead. They cascaded down the steps to the carriage path and onward to the gate, in apparent pursuit of Kwangmi and the others. Faint shouts rose from a portly man in European costume walking briskly among the stragglers. Lastly, a woman also in European attire appeared. She stood in the middle of the steps and clasped her hands.

A light breeze scattered any scents emanating from the ground. Tink raised his eyes. The basket was nearly to the hatch. Already he could distinguish different cores by their individual members' arms as they reached down to touch him, to learn what he could pass along of the mission's success and the others' safety.

"Cast off!" he cried as they hauled him into their embrace. "Immediately!" Two newer recruits scurried away to the prow to reel in the mooring line. Surrounded by the rest, Tink traversed the cramped corridor running aft between hold and bridge; as they went, some fell away to share his news with others in the crew. At the corridor's end, on his own, he came to the companionway and ladder down to *Xu Mu*'s many-windowed steering and observation pod. It was narrower than the main body, feeling full when during flight four were stationed there. But even as he rushed to the lever bank on the pod's far side he indulged himself in a burst of pride. The bridge pod had been his innovation, his favorite modification to the very basic aircanoe design May Fourth had initially adopted.

Xu Mu's control levers jutted inward from the hull at waist height, just below the pod's two rear-facing windows. Tink seated himself on the bench before them and pushed up the small switch lifting the barrier between the Bah-Sangah earths of the engine. Now they would mix and produce enough heat to create steam. In a quarter hour the steam's pressure would suffice to turn the aircanoe's propellers. But *Xu Mu* would need to fly to Kwangmi's rescue sooner than that.

Outside the pod's windows, the lowest clouds had torn apart to show those higher and thinner; now these began to melt like silver. No rain for a while, then, it appeared—but if the wind strengthened, trouble could develop.

A subtle shudder ran along the bridge's woven ceiling. Well, if the wind caused problems they would have to solve them. *Xu Mu* was unmoored. His vista shifted as Tink maneuvered the aircanoe's flaps and rudders, trying to swing its nose 180 degrees. Pitching, yawing, creaking, straining, *Xu Mu* struggled in and out of the wind's fickle grasp till at last he saw the palace retreating slowly behind them. They rode the bay's breath landward.

Normally he shared his bridge shifts with Kwangmi, he and one trainee keeping watch to the fore while she plied the control levers aft with another. But not now—he strode to the pod's forward windows alone and there! There rose the Christian temple's square towers, shedding the morning's mist like smoke in the sunlight. The temple seemed somewhat to his south—Tink returned to the control bench to engage corrective fans—and was the aircanoe rising? Too high? He ran back and forth a few more times, and once, when Kang Woo-Hyun peered down the ladder to ask for instructions, he clambered halfway to the hatch to ask him how swiftly the crew might distribute themselves toward the bow.

"Will that not cause us to descend, Brother?" Woo-Hyun asked.

"Yes! But wait upon my signal!"

"What signal? How shall we—"

"Do I care?" he shouted. Clenching the ladder's rails, Tink forced himself back under control.

"Those who have received the Spirit Medicine will sense my signal and relay it to any still waiting for inoculation." That should work, provided he allowed sufficient time for transmission. He descended the ladder to check again on their progress. They had better not arrive too soon, or their passengers would not yet be in place.

"Leave the hatch propped open," he shouted upward. "Bring Ma Chau to stand by it."

A sudden calm struck. *Xu Mu* hung motionless in a thickening murk. A storm was brewing—out of what? Out of nothing! While preoccupied with coaxing the motiveless craft toward the temple to the west, Tink had discounted telltale signs of a squall coming in from the sea in the east. He knelt on the bench and scanned the sky anxiously. The pause in the wind might indicate that it was about to worsen—or that it would altogether cease for hours—which was likely if the associated precipitation was heavy enough—

A spatter of rain dashed against the glass. Another, louder, and then others, more, blending together, a constant flow, a bankless river and *Xu Mu* drenched and sinking, sinking, far too soon, with their goal now lost from sight.

How long had it been since he threw that first switch? The inexactness of the sense of time's passage that the Spirit Medicine engendered in him was so annoying. Yes, all life was interdependent, and matching the aircanoe's arrival at the temple with his kin's was a most useful ability. Also valuable was the Spirit Medicine's improvement in his piloting skills. But was the engine hot enough yet? The steam high enough? Could he call on its power now to drive them on through the blinding rain?

"Ma Chau!" he shouted.

"Mr. Tink?" So she called him, according to her people's custom. "I do not smell the signal to send us lower."

"No! No longer necessary!" If this were a junk they could row. If he were a giant he could set *Xu Mu* on his palm and blow. As things stood . . .

"Direct four good winch-workers to the hold. Make sure they're ready to lower the cargo basket at your word."

He would delay no further. At the distance the Bah-Sangah priests had insisted on incorporating into every aircanoe's design, the brass pipe wrapping the earth-fueled engine must surely be glowing with readiness. Beads of water would be evaporating off of it like sweat in a desert.

The lever releasing the engine's steam into its turbine chamber fitted smoothly between his hands. He pressed it flat against the hull wall. A slow surge forward began; Tink let it rock him to his feet. But he stayed at the controls, his back to their destination. The heavy rain wiped away the distances normally revealed to him by his keen sight, and did the same to a lesser degree to his sense of smell. His hearing, however, had increased. He untied the ribbons holding shut the louvres set between the aft windows. He let the sound enter him. Below, above, around the engine's vibrant thrum the rain's echoing bounces told him of the changing shape of the landscape.

The glad dampness of leaves outsang the stoic stones and placid clay tiles of buildings. This was a neighborhood of several inns, as he recalled, each with its stables and gardens. Patient wooden sheds used as storehouses lined a strip of dull, packed earth—a road. It ran a long way behind them but not far ahead, so *Xu Mu* had reached its end.

In his last clear look before the rain Tink had seen that this road led to the temple's cemetery. He guided the aircanoe past the graveyard's iron gates and found the headstones' slight, isolated pretensions to endurance gently funny.

Longer intervals in the raindrops' echoes indicated a slope downward to starboard, which in turn gave way to the pattering surface of a pond. Next came the temple's rear courtyard: cobbles packed tightly together around a high prominence, most likely a large devotional image. Just beyond loomed the temple itself—the "church" they called it—facing west, toward Europe, toward the architecture it mimicked with its "gothic" arches and colored windows and tall towers filled with bells of iron.

CLANG! CLANG! CLANG! Who dared to ring the temple bells? The chiming came from the closest of the twin towers. Its clamor ceased and he heard the soldiers in the relative quiet, swearing and panting and smacking their sandals on the tower's winding stairs, higher and higher. Then Bee-Lung's gleeful cackle and her scent! All their scents—the clouds did no more than drizzle now, and first smell then sight returned. The low, pierced wall surrounding the nearest tower's roof appeared; it was at his level. Would they hit it?

No. Dark blurs streaked past the pod windows and struck the ground. *Xu Mu* leapt in the air. The crew had dropped sandbags. Tink stood and ran to the control levers. He fell twice: the change in altitude. Even so little. He shunted the steam off the turbine. Of course this didn't stop them moving, only slowed them down. Soon they'd be past— But there went the cargo basket, whirling away as fast as the workers could unwind it.

And there were his sister and kin, emerging from a hatch in the green copper roofing. Too late, though: the basket dangled now over the church's broad front steps.

They must go back. Turning was easier this time. He used *Xu Mu*'s forward momentum to execute a tight circle, and made the second attempt as the last of their kinetic energy bled away. The alignment was perfect. They hovered in position.

Soon he heard Raghu's joyous shouts of relief, the Chens' ribald jokes at the expense of the men working the winch, Bee-Lung's loud laughter, Kwangmi's silence. Kwangmi came down the pod's ladder and without comment took her usual spot. Tink got up from the bench to give it to her.

Then he shook his head and sat back beside her. "No."

"No?"

He shook his head again. "No. You are as sure as I am of where we're going. Take the observation post. Direct me."

CHAPTER TWO

January 1921
Cairo, Egypt

Did Ilunga even care? Mwadi doubted it. This was his fifth suspension since starting at Victoria College, only a year ago, only two seasons. She frowned down at the letter her royal brother had left crumpled on her writing table, along with the remains of his "English breakfast": half a crumpet, a congealed pool of egg yolk, dregs of chocolate in a thick-walled white mug. This was his way of handing off anything requiring complex thinking while at the same time making light of his little sister.

Princess Mwadi had inquired into the college's disciplinary policies when Prince Ilunga enrolled—for just such cases as this, and also (though she admitted this aloud to no one) in the unlikely event that she too would eventually get accepted. The maximum number of suspensions allowed before expulsion was four. Here was number five. No surprise that special allowances were made for the favorite son and projected successor of a king, but best not to expect such leniency to last.

Mwadi indicated the scraps to Aloli, who piled cutlery, napery, and mug on the dirtied platter and carried them out of the library's open door. With the room restored to order, Mwadi relaxed into a cushioned wicker chair rescued from the balcony outside her brother's bedroom.

How would Mam'selle Toutournier have handled this situation, Mwadi wondered. Pled with the college chancellors for further exceptions? No. Most likely she would have fled Cairo long ago, well before Ilunga had worn out all Mwadi's patience with his wastrel habits. Or maybe Mam'selle would never have emigrated from Everfair in the first place. Yes.

If only Mwadi were more like Rima Bailey's old lover. More than envy went into that wish—she had a great deal of respect for her former rival. Who was also her former teacher. Mam'selle Toutournier would have claimed successorship to Everfair's throne seven seasons ago, even in the face of Queen Josina's seeming opposition. As Mwadi should have done.

Would have, should have. Neither phrase told her what to do now.

She got up and went over to the windows giving onto the garden. She should have rung for Aloli or Hafiza—that phrase again. Instead, she herself pushed aside the windows' drapes, still closed against the night's rain. Impatiently she wrestled up the bar of the casement's stay and shoved it outward. Immediately a black-and-white monkey leapt through and landed on her shoulder.

Mwadi screamed! The monkey screamed back and launched itself into the air. A brown gob of monkey shit plopped to the polished floor. She screamed again, now in anger. How dare it? The monkey climbed the library's half-empty shelves. Did it think to escape her so easily? She ran and yanked the bell pull. Aloli appeared in the doorway almost instantly.

"Princess?"

"Scranforth's disgusting 'pet'!" She pointed at the rigidly silent animal. "It's gotten loose, and look!" She pointed now at the small but pungent lump of dung. "Soiling the room! It's another of his insults to me!"

Aloli—smiled? "May I speak, Princess?"

"Of course. Though you'd better clean that up before it—sets." Or stains, or did whatever unpleasant thing shit did left to its own devices.

Turning for a moment to face the passageway, Aloli clapped her hands and gave instructions to the boy who came. "It's attended to. As for poor Raffles—" The servant woman came to stand with

Mwadi in front of the wall of shelves. "He's a pet, and spoiled, true—but he's not, if you'll allow me to say so, a well-kept pet. Doesn't he appear neglected to you? And scared? Where is his owner?"

Mwadi scowled up suspiciously at the monkey. "What has such a creature to fear? What does it want in my apartments?"

"Perhaps he is looking for something to eat? No telling when Raffles was last fed."

"They eat bird eggs, right? And spiders, insects—"

"Not this sort. As do many holy men, they partake only of plants."

The monkey made a noise like a sneeze crossed with a roar. It leapt down a shelf and ran back and forth along the edge of its new base of operations.

"Capture it!" Mwadi ordered. The boy mopping up the monkey droppings ducked his head obediently and scrambled up from his crouched position, rag snapping. "No! You'll only frighten it away! Bring me a plate of fruit." She would tempt the thing down from its inconvenient perch.

The plate came; Aloli took it and presented it to her. Mwadi selected a slice of orange dripping with juice and raised it toward a pair of black, shocked-looking eyes peering out of the bookcase's dark corner. The monkey gave off a series of tsks like a worried old woman. Patchy white fur encircled its leathery face. The orange's juice dribbled onto her palm and trickled in a tiny stream along her wrist, her arm, headed toward the belled sleeve of her cotton blouse. It would be sticky—

The monkey jumped! Almost she screamed again—but that would not become a king's daughter. Mwadi received the monkey with open arms, as if catching a child. It stunk. No doubt there would be lice, fleas. . . . She tried to give it to Aloli but the monkey clung fiercely to her shoulders. It embraced her, brushing her cheeks with its soft beard, patting her back, briefly nuzzling her throat and collarbone. That tickled! She tried again to put it away from her, smiling but firm. It grabbed at her hair, loosing long braids from their underlying basketry. Its busy fingers fiddled with one braid now hanging close to her face and she saw its hands. Had Scranforth *mutilated* it? The poor thing had no thumbs!

Apparently becoming more at ease, the monkey stopped tampering with her hairdo and turned its black-and-white gaze toward Aloli and the boy with the rag. And the plate of fruit. Mwadi felt its body lean away, though its feet gripped her tightly and its prehensile toes had been insinuated beneath her skirt's waistband.

"Another piece of orange," Mwadi ordered. "Or better yet, a strawberry." It was the end of their season.

The monkey took the berry and stuffed it into its straight slit of a mouth. It reached toward the plate with one hand but kept its hold on Mwadi's coiffure with its other. It ate an orange slice, skin and all, then chose a guava wedge like an old ivory moon and presented it to the princess.

Mwadi gazed at the monkey's sad, maimed hand for an instant, then opened her lips. Fleas and dung be damned.

Three servings of fruit later, her brother's guest, Deveril Scranforth, stumbled in from the passageway. "I say," he said. "Good old Raffles! Glad to see he's turned up! I'll just take the wee scamp back—"

Moving with his accustomed awkwardness, the European approached. Mwadi retreated in the direction of the still-open window. "Hi, now, don't let him get out again!" Scranforth lunged forward. She evaded him easily.

"And why not? Won't he come back?"

"Be so kind as to remove your hat." Prince Ilunga grinned as he entered the room. Mwadi had observed that though her brother commanded this Scranforth more readily since their falling-out, his authority over him continued polite. "There's a good fellow!" Ilunga added placatingly, as Scranforth doffed the slouch hat he wore day and night, within and without the house.

"Aha! Is this your missing monkey?" asked the prince.

Mwadi shook her head in denial. "The monkey is mine now."

"No such thing!" Scranforth looked aggrieved.

The princess rolled her eyes at the white man's rudeness. "You withdraw your gift?"

"I— What? I never gave— Never said I would make a present of—"

"But you want my sister to look favorably on our upcoming contracts? Of course you do!"

Upcoming contracts? Mwadi flattened her brows, leveled her eyes on Ilunga. The monkey fretted in her arms, wriggling and whimpering like a sick baby. This Scranforth had previously persuaded the prince to dump his shares in the Great Sun River Collector Company, a promising solar energy venture that had come near to failing as a result of the white man's interference. Only by exercising her skill at riding in the bodies of birds had she saved her brother from death at the hand of his "friend"—and by spying on him in partnership with the beautiful Rima, whose career had since taken her thousands of miles away.

Was it time now to send an urgent message pleading for Rima Bailey's return? Or perhaps should she ask for someone else's help—Mam'selle Toutournier would know what to do. If only Mwadi understood exactly what sort of mischief the British were planning. Did it involve the Atlantropa project, as her German protégés were convinced?

If she knew for certain what was in the works, she could bring her parents proof of it. She'd show them. She'd root out the traitors, rain down retribution on the heads of their enemies. They'd see then that *Mwadi* was the one truly worthy of becoming Everfair's next ruler.

Cairo, Egypt

"Curse it!" Prince Ilunga popped his injured finger in his mouth and sucked the blood. His favorite servant girl, Sabra, appeared in the open French window and he beckoned her onto his balcony.

She carried a bowl of scented water, which she set at his feet with a graceful obeisance.

"Blessed one," she murmured, head still bowed. "If you permit, I will bathe your wound."

"What's this jibber-jabber?" Scranforth asked. He spoke surprisingly little Arabic for one who had lived in these parts more than five seasons.

"She is attending me." He gestured for Sabra to rise. Her body uncoiled, and with sinuous arms she set the bowl on the wicker table to his right. There would be honey in it to fight off infections—what else? Red and orange petals danced just below the water's surface. Cautiously, the prince held out his bitten hand. Sabra received it gently and finished unwrapping the linen bandage he had already partially removed.

"Have the bugger destroyed, that's my vote." Devil hunched forward on his cushioned stool. "Vicious little beast. I'll take it to the butcher's, have them chop its miserable head—"

"No."

"—right off. What? You can't be serious, Loongee! Bugger bit you!"

"It was provoked. I say again, no." The scene they'd played out below ran before his mind: Devil prying the monkey from the princess's arms despite her protests, the ridiculous chase around the room that followed. "We should have shown more dignity." Though he'd all but decided to have the monkey shot, the way that Devil assumed he would irked Ilunga. The white man's offenses were forgiven, but not—despite the startling nature of their shared experiences—forgotten.

"Besides, my sister likes the filthy thing. We'll delay execution till she tires of it."

"Loongee! You're a positive genius! Raffles will distract her from our real business—yes! You'll want to see the latest—"

The glare Ilunga turned on Devil stopped the European midsentence. How could they be at such odds now, so synchronized when aroused? The prince paused to make sure the silence would last, then assumed a pleasant expression and stroked Sabra's bare upper arm. "Is it deep?" he asked. "Is it serious?"

"No, blessed one. You are the son of fortune. Monkeys will usually bite quite deeply, and their bites are inclined to fester. But praise God, my ministrations and your strength will avert that outcome." As she talked she dabbed at his hurt hand with a dry cloth. "See, where I lay these lion's tail blossoms your bleeding ceases. I'll leave them in place beneath the dressing, if you don't object."

"How should I object? You're good at this." He stroked her arm again and smiled benignly.

Sabra finished and, somewhat to his regret, withdrew. The prince shifted his focus to Scranforth. "We must deal with these matters *discreetly*. I beg you to remember that my servants, while loyal, are but human, and as susceptible as anyone to threat or bribery.

"And now that the coast is as we say clear, you may go and fetch me your draft agreements."

"Got them here." From the wallet on his belt Devil extracted a sheaf of tightly folded papers. "Safer to always have them with me." He unfolded the sheaf and spread it out on his lap. "This one on top pertains to your country's interests in the potential lakebed sites on the borders with Uganda and Tanganyika. It says—"

"I am quite able to read." Prince Ilunga took the bulk of the pile in his unbandaged hand.

"Yes, but it's dashed confusing, all party-of-the-first-part and legal lingo like that. . . ."

Ilunga set the pile of papers on the table and leafed through them, nodding—till he came to one in particular. This he held up at arm's length. He wrinkled his nose. "My gifts are contingent? Contingent on what?"

"On gaining the throne, but that's a done deal, ain't it? Specially with British backing."

"It is." His father had all but publicly named him heir on being shown the shongo.

"So nothing to worry about. I'll make fair copies, have them ready for you to sign tonight."

"I doubt my wound will be healed so quickly." Ilunga was a prince, soon to be a king. He deserved a show of respect, especially from a man with such flimsy excuses for shooting him last year. A man who seemed unaffected by the proximity Ilunga found so puzzlingly piquant. "I'll sign your copies tomorrow." Devil could wait. Elsewhere. "Go."

The winter day had turned unseasonably warm. Ilunga remained on the balcony. For a little while he sprawled unattended in his accustomed chair, but soon the houseboy appeared with a pitcher of gin and sweetened lemon water. He sipped, approved, and sent the boy after Sabra; he was enjoying her soothing touch and considering how to summon Devil back when his sister entered the suite, unannounced and unwelcome. Swift as remorse the servant rolled off the bed to her feet.

In Mwadi's cradling arms rode her new acquisition, the cause of his latest injury. "The weather is so fine. Shall we take our tea in the garden this afternoon?" she asked.

Ilunga sat up. "You really needed to come in here to ask me that?" He searched the room's corners. The girl had vanished. "Right now?"

Mwadi shrugged. "Your Scranforth said you would be alone. How was I to know not to believe him?"

Regarding Devil, the prince had gotten in the habit of pretending more aloofness than he felt. "He's not my social secretary."

The princess sniffed. "If he were, he would have reminded you that we promised to entertain the Schreibers today at four."

"Those krauts again?"

"The Germans were Everfair's allies, unlike your Scranforth's government."

"The Germans lost."

Cairo, Egypt

Alone in her boudoir but for Hafiza and the monkey, Princess Mwadi admitted to herself that even the garden's sunny upper terrace would be too cool for an alfresco tea service, given the declining of the sun at that hour. Much as she longed for the caress of the open air she should deny it to herself.

A princess ought to be able to have anything she wanted. And yet . . .

She swept the scattered papers from her desk with one spiteful arm. They meant nothing. No letter from Rima, who by now must be well established in Mumbai. Travel through the wild Himalayan mountains could no longer serve as an excuse. Perhaps the concerns of her new show kept her too busy to write? Mwadi plunged face-first onto her pile of cherry satin pillows. She would not weep. She turned right side up.

The monkey had fled her histrionics. It sheltered under Mwadi's vanity, hunched in shadow and silence. "It." Must she call this new companion "Raffles"? Did the monkey know itself by that name by now? "Come here!" she commanded. No response. "Raffles!"

Hafiza cleared her throat, which meant she wished to speak.

"Well?"

"Perhaps you could use a softer voice, Your Prominence? More of your customary sweetness of tone?"

So was she now to become a seducer of monkeys? Surely she had better business to undertake.

"Make certain my white tea gown is fit to wear. And the collar with the pearl embroidery needs fresh ribbons—the gloves with the matching buttons should be about somewhere. And tell Aloli we'll take our tea in the conservatory." A compromise between her desires and the weather.

Hafiza left on her errands and the monkey emerged from its hiding place. Its slanting eyes glittered wistfully. "There's no way for you to tell me your real name, is there?" she asked. It approached her. She didn't want its vermin near her bed, so she got up. Hafiza had restored the papers fallen from her desk to their proper positions. "Names are merely matters of convenience." Rima's full name was Serenissima: in Italian, "most serene." Which was nothing like her. Nothing at all.

With a glance at the door, Mwadi opened the unsealed envelope she'd shoved onto the floor with everything else. An unfinished letter to her love still lay safely folded within, still evenly coated in the powder Lady Fwendi had taught her to use to detect tamperers. No one had read it—and if Rima didn't answer Mwadi's last letter, no one ever would. Not even she to whom it was addressed.

With a snap she tossed the letter back onto the desk. Startled, the monkey scampered away, this time toward the boudoir's grenadine-colored curtains, which it climbed halfway to the high ceiling. Then it halted and turned warily back her way.

So expressive its dirty face. When Hafiza returned, Mwadi would have her give it a bath. "Do you get on well with birds, Raffles?" she asked. She was starting to see the monkey's potential usefulness in her gathering of intelligence. Too bad about its thumbs.

Suitably dressed, Mwadi took her seat in the conservatory in good time despite Hafiza's complaints of having too much to attend to—a short interval before the scheduled arrival of the Schreibers. Sending the houseboy to make sure Ilunga would show soon, she pinched a couple of dead blossoms from the apricot tree growing so prettily through the trellis behind their table—just the petals, not the tiny green fruits. Then there was nothing to do but sit and wait.

Not for long. "Frau Schreiber, Herr Schreiber, welcome." She curtsied in the whites' fashion. Hanna Schreiber's curtsy was of course much deeper than Mwadi's, since she and her husband were refugees under the princess's sponsorship. As previously, Paul Schreiber's bow brought his nose nearly to his knee, a display of suppleness which Mwadi remembered Rima remarking on salaciously.

"Please, take a place." Aloli entered with a large silver tray. "My brother will be with us directly." She hoped. He must care about something. If her protégés could report a connection between Devil Scranforth and Atlantropa, as Mwadi expected, she wanted Ilunga to hear about it. She wanted those ties severed.

It was Mam'selle Toutournier who'd begun the princess's education on the feeding rituals of whites, back in Lady Fwendi's school for spies. "Shrimp paste on your side of the lower tier, cress on mine, and Herr Schreiber's favorite honey cakes on top."

The study of cookery books and novels had continued and expanded her learning. Princess Mwadi was now an expert in polite methods of procrastination. "Isn't the pattern on the plates clever? See how the feathers change to leaves, the leaves give way to flowers, how the petals of the flowers become spearheads and the spearheads become feathers?"

"Yes. And so delicately painted! I'm reminded of our Meissen service. The pot warmer's sides were made of lithophanes. . . ." Suppressed tears threatened to overcome Frau Schreiber's composure. "I wonder where it's—where it's gotten—"

Anything could trigger this nostalgic longing for a long-vanished version of mainland Europe. Not all the Russian cures in the world would restore Germany as it once was, sans mass graves and human orchards.

Fortunately, at that moment, the conservatory door opened on Ilunga, distracting Frau Schreiber from her sorrow. "Madam," Princess Mwadi asked, "as our guest, will you pour?" The refugee woman blushed at the honor. She picked up the teapot and the danger of her succumbing to a fit of weeping was safely past.

"Are you drinking your tea slop again?" Ilunga asked, seating himself in the remaining wrought iron chair. He swiveled and shouted over his shoulder. "Hi! Boy! Bring me another pitcher of that gin mixture from this morning. And tell Devil where to join us."

Mwadi forced a smile and leaned over her brother, ostensibly to straighten the collar of his jacket. "There are no more seats," she murmured.

"You're right." He turned to face the boy's retreating back. "And find a seat for him. There's a bench that will do, just outside the door, I think."

She kept smiling. "Before your friend arrives, you should know something."

"I *do* know something!"

"Something about him. He is a spy and a conspirator. He means to flood Everfair and drown half the continent."

"Who says so?"

Mwadi turned her eyes toward the Schreibers. "Give your report."

Herr Schreiber blinked several times rapidly. "We're unable to ascertain exactly who it is, but the Atlantropa project's investors have hired an agent to protect their interests. A Briton, we think, although certain signs point to the involvement of Italy's ambassador to Egypt, one Signore Quattrocchi. However the matter has been arranged, it seems likely Mr. Scranforth is at least cognizant—"

The door opened again. The princess thought this servant's name was Gassra or Gassar or something like that. He bore the slightly damp and much cleaner monkey on his back, and balanced on one hand a smaller version of the tea tray, and on that two cream-colored envelopes. The servant knelt before her. The monkey leapt away to disappear into the greenery.

Her heart leapt also, even as she recognized the flowing script adorning the first envelope as Mam'selle's and the spikier hand on the second as her mother's. Neither could be the letter she waited for, but she picked up the queen's missive with fingers not strictly steady. Then sighed in impatience. Her mother still refused to communicate with her directly. "Brother, this is addressed to you alone."

"Really? Well, open it and read it to me." There were good

consequences sometimes to Ilunga's refusal to treat her past attempt to claim the throne seriously.

"Perhaps—" Herr Schreiber stood. "—a private matter—this is no time for us—"

Mwadi protested that they must stay—that they had not finished giving their report.

"No need," her brother declared. "I have the gist. You think Devil's plotting to use my succession to advance Europe's expansion."

"At a terrible cost to Africa!"

"Our father should be the judge of that!"

"Before or after he abdicates?"

In the silence answering Mwadi's question, Frau Hanna Schreiber's timid throat-clearing sounded irritatingly loud. "What is it?" Mwadi asked. The woman had risen to stand beside her husband without the princess noticing. "You insist on leaving?"

Herr Schreiber nodded. "But before we go—we have copies of a pamphlet written by Herr Doctor Kleinwald on his theory of entangledness, in which he touches on Atlantropa, too. We got the job of printing them just before he disappeared, and now they are ours to distribute. May we offer one to you?"

Mwadi accepted the pamphlet, escorting the Germans to the house's front entrance, where Gassra or Gassar held open the door for them. When she returned to the conservatory, Ilunga had Queen Josina's letter in his hands, frowning at it.

"Can you tell me what it says?" she asked.

"Of course. Our father is abdicating sooner than expected."

"When?"

"Soon. On our arrival in Kisangani. Here." Ilunga thrust a thin sheet of paper at her.

Mwadi scanned the words covering it quickly. "'The Royal Heir will be formally recognized at the same ceremony, which is to take place on your arrival in Kisangani. So make haste. Wait for no one. I must stress this, for the king's spirit father has spoken most emphatically on how your promptness affects the matter of who is named in the announcement.'

"What of the removal of atolo's shongo? Was that not the determining factor? Is it instead to be a race? Are we meant to compete to see who gets home first?"

"I suppose." Ilunga refilled his glass from the pitcher. "If that's your interpretation." A sip, a smack of his lips, and a small, satisfied belch followed. "Will you make the arrangements for our return, Sister? Include Devil, too; he's eager to scout out drilling locations."

"Yes." Her tone must have burned his skin with its chill.

He attempted a careless laugh that quickly choked to death on its own unconvincingness. "You dislike him, don't you, Didi?"

"I detest it when you call me that. And if you're to bring your friends, mine can accompany us also."

"The Schreibers? How long will it take them to close their business? To sell off their stock and presses and other equipment? No. They'll slow us down. No."

She turned her eyes heavenward, seeking patience. Raffles dropped from the top branch of the apricot tree onto her shoulder. The monkey's deformed paws patted gently at her braids, exploring their intricacies without deconstructing them.

She decided she was less envious of her brother's privilege than annoyed by his buffalo-headed stubbornness—or whatever had blinded him to the greed and treachery of his supposed friend. Who only a few months ago had shot him! "Certainly." She picked up a crustless cress sandwich, nibbled at it to show her nonchalance. "Must we really bring Mr. Scranforth along with us?"

"We can afford to, can't we?"

"Yes. What I mean is—"

"I'm well aware of your meaning." Draining his glass, the prince got to his feet, swaying almost undetectably. "But you see, Didi, there are—are—*things* that men share with one another that women can't—can't really comprehend. Experiences. Thoughts and ideas.

Dreams. *Feelings.* I don't expect you to understand what ties us together, but despite that trouble last year over the Great Sun River Collector Company, Devil and I are deeply, deeply, *deeply*—what's the word I want?" The sway grew momentarily more pronounced. "We're bonded. That's it, bonded together. Like we're family, like we're one. Bonded. I trust him completely, utterly, and in every conceivable way!"

Carefully the prince turned and walked away from the table. "We'll be packed and ready to leave in the morning," he called back over his shoulder. "See that the arrangements are made. Not too early."

Servants came to remove the tea things. She nodded permission but kept her seat in rebellious silence. That Ilunga was to some extent right—the Schreibers weren't yet ready to emigrate to Everfair—only made her angrier at him.

Thank goodness she had found a new partisan. Raffles clung to her as if surrounded by evildoers while the servants worked. When they had gone she offered him the remains of her sandwich and he let go of her blouse to accept it. "You'll come too," she told him. "And be most welcome." The monkey made a series of soft kissing sounds and scrambled across the tablecloth to take her brother's seat.

Red Sea, Aboard Madiz

A week later the royal party crossed the border between Egypt and Sudan. On the deck of the yacht the cool wind of their progress picked up gradually. In their wake, the customs cutter sailed back to shore. "Good to be moving again," Scranforth proclaimed. Ilunga nodded agreement with him, but privately he preferred the sheltered warmth of the cabin beneath them. The nearer to the Equator they sailed, the hotter the weather—he waited impatiently to resume sweating away the night. Tepid Cairo had only been made tolerable by the knowledge that his time there would end in another year at most, depending on how speedily Victoria's chancellors tired of his shenanigans.

A blur of black and white dashed down the raked flagpole at the edge of Ilunga's vision. "Raffles!" Scranforth opened his arms to welcome his former pet into them. It ran past him along the polished brass railing. Another passenger screamed: not a bad-looking woman for a white. Her bizarre coloring—yellowish "blond" hair and blue eyes—could not detract from her shapeliness. And according to Devil, the yacht's other passengers were all British, and therefore most probably safe. Britain had never been as hard hit by the 'flu as the rest of Europe. Ilunga hurried to comfort the sufficiently pretty passenger.

"It's completely tame. I assure you—" He attempted to possess himself of one of her pink-fleshed hands. "—the thing's harmless."

Scranforth had followed him. "Even if the prince and I weren't here to protect you, Mrs. Chawleigh—"

"Prince!" The white woman stopped resisting Ilunga's grasp. "You're the heir to the crown of Everfair who's listed on the manifest?" Ilunga bowed graciously, retaining the hand.

"How is it we haven't encountered each other before? With only a dozen people of any consequence on board, I would expect otherwise! We should have made one another's acquaintance at a meal, or on taking a trip to one of the attractions ashore, don't you think?" Perhaps they would have met earlier if Ilunga hadn't spent the first four days of the voyage recovering from his overindulgences.

"And your brave companion? Who is he?"

"Deveril Scranforth at your service, ma'am. The little, er, beast that brought us together so fortuitously is mine. Apologies for its lack of manners."

"No need!" But she frowned and cast a nervous glance along the deck in the direction the monkey had disappeared.

"Most likely the little rascal headed back to Princess Mwadi's cabin. That's where it's been holed up the majority of the time—till we hit customs. Didn't want—"

"Princess Mwadi—your sister, am I right?" Ilunga had both the woman's soft hands now. "With her I managed a more conventional introduction. Miss Glen is related to her mentor Lady Fwendi's husband, so she was happy to—"

With Ilunga steering Mrs. Chawleigh adroitly, they walked the width of *Madiz*'s stern and took the starboard companionway down to the reception area. The barman had closed up operations while they passed through customs, but he was open again. "Gin and lemon for me," Ilunga ordered. "And what for you?" He meant the woman, but Devil answered.

"I'll have the same. Mrs. Chawleigh, think I recall hearing that the yacht's supplied with your favorite cherry cordial?"

"How flattering that you took notice of such an insignificant detail!"

Devil winked a roguish eye at him over the table and maneuvered their prey into a seat between them. "Insignificant? Never say so! If Sir Geoffrey bothers to cater to your desires, they're important! Ain't that so, Loongee?"

He nodded but said nothing till the barman finished serving their drinks. Fresh peel corkscrewed down through the pale liquid in the tall glass. No ice; he'd only had to specify that once. "Our friend is famous for his hospitality and good taste. We're truly grateful he offered us his spot." Sir Geoffrey owned *Madiz,* and the captain's cabin was reserved for his infrequent use. After Ilunga had dealt with his succession to the throne he intended to exploit his host's hospitality further.

The door opened and a well-endowed older woman walked in, followed by a more slender one. "Miss Glen!" exclaimed Mrs. Chawleigh. "I was just telling the prince how you were able to introduce me to his sister—"

A third passenger entered. A man. "Hubert? I thought— I believed you slept?"

"And then I woke."

The old women sat by Devil, on the table's far side. One seat remained vacant for the man Hubert. "Good afternoon, Scran-forth. I take it you're Prince Ilunga? My name's Chawleigh. I see you've met my wife." He turned to the barman. "Scotch."

Ilunga found he disliked Chawleigh. Why? Was it the wife? Though she stared at her husband as if she expected him to scold or slap her or send her to their cabin, there was nothing in the man's attitude to indicate that he planned to interfere with her flirting. The man sat, and it was an act of controlled violence: smooth, un-conscious, arrogant, practiced—but how was that violent? What made him distrust Chawleigh instantly and read into his actions intentions impossible to justify?

The prince was not a naturally reflective man. Miss Glen—the sleeker of the two older women—remarked favorably on his man-ners as he called out to make certain the barman poured her and her companion's cognacs. She was sure he must have learnt "how to be a gentleman" from Sir Matty. He smiled and turned the con-versation aside as he'd gotten used to doing attending Victoria: If her knowledge of Matty Jamison's politesse was born of firsthand experience, where had they met?

"At school." Miss Glen looked away. With whites this often meant they lied. "Actually, it was my brother with whom he was best acquainted; they attended Glasgow Academy together—but Quentin often brought him home to visit."

"Quentin was your no doubt much older brother, then? Sir Matty is soon turning sixty, while you can't be over forty-five." Ilunga had learned that whites took no pleasure in aging. Miss Glen proved this by giggling and returning his regard again, now from beneath fluttering lashes. "No wonder you require the escort of—" What was the other woman's name? The one with the larger breasts?

"Mrs. Wulfe?" Devil raised the companion's dried-petal hand to his gin-moistened lips. "And who escorts you? Mr. Wulfe?"

"Yes. He is always with me."

A startled glance over his shoulder showed Ilunga that this

woman, too, lied. Or else she spoke of spirits, because he saw no one else alive in the room but those seated at his table—and the barman. Who since he was a servant would probably not be this woman's husband.

Devil didn't even flinch. "And where will the three of you head from Djibouti? Are you bound for Everfair, like us? Going to brighten up our weary way, what?"

"Not quite. We're traveling to the court at Zanzibar."

"But that's splendid! We'll take the same route for a while longer, till we depart Mombasa. Splendid!

"And you, Mr. Chawleigh?"

"I have some business in the Dahlak Archipelago, so we'll be forsaking you shortly. Why do you ask?"

"Just passing the time, y'know. And in case you have a little leeway?" Devil tipped his chair back on two legs, as was his custom. Ilunga imitated him. It was more difficult than it looked, but he had mastered the technique. "Thought you might want to take in some African sights with us. Cross the Equator, squire your lady here on a bit of a tour."

Mrs. Chawleigh swung to face Devil. "Oh, that sounds exciting! What adventures you and the prince must have had on this dark continent!" She switched her gaze to Ilunga. "How very brave you must be! How fearless, to face down the evil shadows lurking in your country's black jungles!"

His country's jungles? He had never set foot in one.

"Danger all around us—but you would protect me, Prince Ilunga, would you not?"

He understood then what she wanted. "With all my savage strength—"

Gasser broke through the door. "Your Prominence! Your sister's monkey—it's gone mad! Come capture it—please!"

Devil's front chair legs thumped on the floor. "Right. My monkey." He pulled out a revolver, apparently from the thin air. "Lead me to it."

"You don't mean to shoot the poor creature!" Miss Glen protested.

"And why not? A few moments ago that 'poor creature' was on the point of assaulting me!" Mrs. Chawleigh shuddered dramatically.

"Should have killed it when it bit Loongee. Or given it to a zoo." Devil strode out of the lounge door before Ilunga could beat him to it. Even the servant supposedly leading the white man was left behind.

"Gasser!" The serving man halted at his voice. "Where's the princess? Why isn't *she* dealing with this problem?"

"Prominence, Hafiza tried to wake her out of her nap. She sleeps sound as the mountains."

From overhead came the noise of fast-thudding feet running along the upper deck. Shouts drifted in the open door and portholes. Well, if Mwadi wasn't roused up by all that hubbub, he'd have no luck himself. He followed in Devil's wake.

In the open, the noise's source could be pinpointed: forward. Loudly chattering crew and servants crowded the yacht's bow. Devil was trying to squeeze past a sailor. "Get away, man!" he cried, adding to the general racket.

Out of reach, beyond the heads of the sailor, Hafiza, and Ilunga's houseboy, the monkey danced slowly up and down the flagpole— apparently its favorite perch. This time it used only feet and tail, its hands filled with a sheaf of writing paper.

"Move them aside, Gasser," Ilunga instructed. Speaking Arabic, the servant cleared his path. Then he and Devil shared the arrowhead-shaped area off which the pole jutted. A gull circled above its golden finial.

"Clean shot now." Devil grinned. He took aim.

"No! Wait!" Ilunga struck his friend's arm. The shot whizzed wide.

"Loongee! What are you at?"

"You might have hit that bird!"

"So?"

"Superstition." His sister had charged him to keep her spirit work secret. "Bad luck to kill that species. We don't want these idiot sailors quitting on us if you break one of their rules." How great was the danger? What were the chances that if Devil's bullet took down the gull, it would injure Mwadi too—if she rode it?

"All right. I'll be careful." Planting his feet well apart, Devil gripped the pistol in both hands. But the monkey made a bad target. It kept dancing—away from Devil, toward the gull. Sliding, ducking its head, shifting the papers it held for better balance—something familiar about those papers? Something about the shapes of the letters, the lay of the lines—

"What has it got?" asked Mr. Chawleigh. He and the other passengers had joined the larger group.

The monkey and bird were so close now—mere inches apart! So strange their fearlessness! Then the monkey thrust the papers up, high above its head, and the gull swooped down to carry them off like a stolen fish.

"Bloody hell!"

"Devil, there are ladies present!"

"Apologies. But I think the rotter may have made off with some of my correspondence!"

Ah. Hence the familiarity of the handwriting.

"Nothing incriminating, I hope?" Chawleigh said.

"How's that? Couldn't be—not married." Nonetheless, Devil followed the gull's flight with longing eyes. It disappeared quickly into a bank of clouds sweeping up from the south.

CHAPTER THREE

No. They're not graven images," the movie star insisted. Bee-Lung nodded, accepting this Malaysian woman's explanation of why she, a practicing Muslim, was so enthusiastic in her support of Ceylon's film industry.

"They are made entirely of light." Sevaria binti Musa rose from her divan to extinguish her projector's lamp. Her two servants unbarred the viewing room's shuttered windows. "Lives are shadows. Light is grace. We perform bathed in God's grace, and the flickering our watchers see when looking on us guides them to that greater brightness."

They conversed in English. Previously familiar with the tongue only as a means of trade, Bee-Lung had begun to study it seriously en route between Tourane and Kuala Lumpur, and had completed her studies before they moored here in Trincomalee.

In polite English her hostess ordered iced juices brought as refreshment; Bee-Lung had long ago attained the necessary basic fluency to translate what she said. After the servant's departure, though, Sevaria resumed her interesting monologue on how the British links tying Malaysia to Ceylon had given birth to her career. A complex subject now comprehensible in all its nuance. Alas, it required splitting most of Bee-Lung's attention away from the garden aromas flooding in the open windows. How she yearned to touch the iridescent black petals of the bat orchids whose delicate scent permeated the air so teasingly. But there was work here before her: a recruit to be won and tested.

"When the Great War began, Alexander Butler was shooting

David and Jonathan in the Malaysian archipelago. He was stranded, yet a mistake in ordering supplies meant he was blessed with ten times the blank film needed. He adapted the remainder of his script to our local conditions, and his leading lady took me under her wing. Rather remarkably, she went beyond employing me as her dresser and understudy—she saw to it that parts for me were written into the play the crew put together after that first film finished."

A story. Bee-Lung respected the power of stories to change minds. She noted that Sevaria had not cast herself as this one's hero. "So when they recorded the new production, your first role was immortalized," Bee-Lung mused.

The actress laughed. "And I so clumsy! But yes, there was stock enough and to spare, owing to that clerical error I mentioned. Mr. Butler chanced to see me hamming my way through *Cannibal Queens of Cook Island* and decided I was his company's future!"

Listening carefully, Bee-Lung heard the irony in the play's title.

"My father . . . my father grew used to the idea before he died." The servant who had been sent for their drinks returned, carrying sweating silver cups on a round platter. She offered it first to Bee-Lung. Honey, melon, cassia, mint: a delicious mingling of plant life. Bee-Lung swallowed a sip, swallowed pleasure.

"You enjoy it?" asked Sevaria, taking up her own cup. "My mother's recipe."

"I should like to pay my respects to the lady. She is alive?"

"Yes, she's still alive—but she sleeps so much, and at any hour these days, so that I hesitate to arrange a visit."

"Has your mother also come to approve of the course your life's taken?"

Again the actress laughed. She fanned one hand like a preening bird's wing, indicating the room's silk hangings, painted scrolls, bead-strung lampshades, fluted crystal vases, and its dozens of other treasures. "Why wouldn't she? I provide our home with all the little luxuries."

The words were those of a high courtesan scornful of her status. Did Sevaria inwardly regard herself as such?

"May I also provide her with something—a small gift?" From her jacket's wide front pockets Bee-Lung pulled a bundle of incense sticks and a simple porcelain holder, a pierced disk. "The scent of the trees of my homeland invigorates me, and will likely invigorate your mother too. And to watch the curling thread of smoke as it rises toward the sky can lift one's heart."

A brief, sincere smile lit the star's dark lips. "Yes. That's thoughtful of you. Jadida, take the good doctor's presents to Madame Amirah." The younger of the servants took the incense and left.

"And now the rest of your tale?" Bee-Lung prompted.

"The rest?"

"You have explained how you came to act in the moving pictures but not how you and the pictures come to be situated here." Over a thousand miles lay between Trincomalee and Kuala Lumpur, even leaving off side trips such as the one *Xu Mu* had made to Dacca.

"It was my brother. He's the reason I came here."

Bee-Lung shifted on her cushioned chair, suddenly uncomfortable. Had her queries as to who would make a suitable subject for application of her special Spirit Medicine been too general? Too hit-and-miss? "I didn't know you had a brother."

"He, like my father, lives now in Paradise. But as children we played many games, our favorite being the one in which we sailed to Trincomalee to liberate our oppressed fellow Muslims. We found imaginary treasure buried among the temple ruins; we rescued princesses about to have their hearts removed in primitive Hindu ceremonies—all nonsense, of course—ignorant and chauvinist and totally unworthy of followers of the Prophet.

"Still, when Rayyan asked me to bring him here, I knew I must do as he wished. He was suffering from wounds he had sustained the year before as a volunteer at Gallipoli. We knew these would be his final days. He died peacefully on the voyage."

A brother alive could have been an impediment. A brother dead and buried, however— "You interred him here?"

"About a hundred miles south, near Batticaloa."

Perhaps a plant grew on the brother's grave. Bee-Lung would find out and get a sample. Any trace of a precursor for the bond she wanted to replicate would help. "It's good that you honored his last instructions."

"Well, yes. I'm glad of that. And once we arrived here my mother and I hadn't the heart to go back to Malaysia and leave his final resting place behind. So with the store of money he'd set aside for us we sent to purchase much of Butler's equipment. A cameraman came with it, seeking employment, while Butler returned to Britain— Why do I tell you all this?"

Sometimes sympathy was all it took, Bee-Lung thought. Aloud she answered, "We are humans. We need to share our feelings."

Trincomalee, Ceylon

Tink eyed the tunnel stairs doubtfully. Not that he disbelieved what he'd been told: that they led down to a secret room filled with sacred Hindu idols. When his guide had described the spot he'd smelled completely truthful. Even on the tunnel's threshold, Tink caught no whiff of treachery in the man's effusions. But in the darkness, as he himself had discovered in Tourane and since, he . . . changed. His senses came more powerfully under the sway of the Spirit Medicine. Which process his rational bent of mind equated with loss of control. Not that he felt any hesitation at all in giving himself—and others—over to the Spirit Medicine's revolutionary influence.

"There are torches?" he asked.

"But surely you've brought sponges?" replied the guide. "Your sister is our best supplier for the dust by which they shine!"

"Yes." Over long periods, though, sponges weren't bright enough to keep the Medicine's tendencies dormant. He stood nearer the edge of the stairs' landing, peering forward, but didn't start down.

"Smoke from torches would give away our activities," the guide explained.

"True. Until throwing off the colonizer's yoke we must take every precaution we can." He grimaced at the blackness below, then pulled a pair of dry sponges from his sleeves. The guide dipped water from the stone jar beside his feet and poured it over both. As the sponges began to glow, Tink countered his fear firmly and explicitly within his mind, where that fear was born. He was not about to die. He would remain himself, and whatever aspect of that self the Spirit Medicine made manifest was its truest essence.

A last glance at the sliver of day just visible behind them: the tunnel's entrance, guarded by the Chens. Raghu would be stationed farther away, among the green ruins, seemingly a pilgrim engaged in innocent prayers. And Kwangmi . . . reliable Kwangmi stayed at *Xu Mu*'s helm, ready to dispatch help on the relaying of his signal. Which he must trust he would know when to give.

Down. The walls' lichens thinned, vanished. The drip of moisture echoed quietly between the scrapes of his soles on stone after stone. Rootlets sometimes grew this deep. Not often. But the network of tubules via which the ruins' trees connected continued till Tink and his guide reached the stair's bottom.

A shallow gutter drained off gathered moisture. Across the short floor, one steep step led up to an arch of darkness filled with invisibly decaying grass. Tink walked bravely forward, casting ahead his sponge's flameless light. A curtain of woven bamboo fell from the arch's curving heights—taller than one man standing on another's shoulders.

He touched the curtain. The rotting vegetation hummed with change. "Go in!" the guide urged. "See why we brought you here."

Mounting the single step, Tink parted the curtain. His eyes adjusted rapidly—no, this was too quick a brightening for that. The room's radiance—*blossomed*. All around him, golden statues shone like fire—like the sun—a thousand suns! A thousand *living* suns—fluttering with shadows, dancing with leaves—vines climbed around a score of figures in the likeness of men stern and laughing, standing and sitting, blessing the space before, below, above, and beyond them with powerful and countless arms.

"Lord Siva welcomes you," explained the guide. "He has caused the clouds to part unseasonably early." The light lessened somewhat, became more bearable. Looking upward, Tink discerned its source: an opening in the underground chamber's roof, showing the sky. Blue sky and swiftly scudding clouds like grey rags filled the center of the wide ceiling, an irregular patch of day in this sunken night.

Lowering his eyes, Tink saw the gleaming statues more clearly. Not all were golden; not all were men. Some, shaded by the plants' winding tendrils, matched the color of the naked heavens; some were shells, tridents, and other shapes too obscure for him to name.

"What is it?" he asked, though not exactly sure which of the mysteries confronting him he questioned.

"Butterfly pea, it is called: a sacred flower, and these individual examples of it more sacred than most. Typically they grow only in full sun, yet here belowground, sheltered as we are on the surface by the temple's crumbling walls, they thrive! And thus they demonstrate how luminous is Lord Siva's glory. By the month of the sawan they'll be in full bloom, ready to be used."

"Butterfly pea . . ." Bee-Lung would know the species. "And with these holy flowers you will—you'll do what?"

"We make offerings of them, chiefly in the form of garlands for our lord to wear. And we use them to cleanse ourselves, within, without—we bathe in them, drink them as tea, dress our hair with them, consume them at the ends of fasts—"

Consume them. Eat them, drink them, soak in their infusions.

He had found the perfect medium for creating the basis of multiple cores. The rewards of courage were sweet. The cores now being established would advance more easily because of him. Still, though,

he must discover some way for festival attendees to volunteer for
inoculation against hierarchy—even if they did this without their
full understanding of what it involved.

That understanding would come later. It would.

Also there were practical issues. He'd have to devise a feasible
plan for following those up.

Trincomalee, Ceylon

From the balcony opening off of the guest chamber assigned to
her, Bee-Lung did her best to distinguish *Xu Mu*'s silhouette. High
though Sevaria's house stood on Fort Frederick Hill, the docking spires and the six aircanoes moored there refused to look like
more than a set of chopsticks surrounded by an ungainly clump of
rice grains. Even up here, on the first storey, the two long miles lying between the film star's bungalow and Trincomalee's shipping
yards defeated Bee-Lung's eyes.

But eyesight was not the Spirit Medicine's strong suit.

The last of the monsoon's prevailing breeze blew against her,
east to west, north to south. Yet there would be countercurrents.
She waited several minutes for the fragrant news they were sure to
bring. Finally, interweaving with the scents of the back garden's
acacia flowers, she smelled Tink's contentment, mingled with the
odors typical of *Xu Mu*. He was back aboard—and from other in-
dications, in the company of his adored Kwangmi.

That determined, Bee-Lung relaxed onto the bench provided.
Tink and his coremates would return tomorrow morning with a
consignment of Spirit Medicine spores to bestow on the latest recruits, and would carry with them her special strain, the one she
had used to deepen empathy between her brother and herself. And
using that empathy, she would develop the perfect strategy to take
best advantage of the opportunity he had found in the sawan festival. All was in good motion.

Bee-Lung shut her eyes and let touch overwhelm her other

senses. Silken bat orchid blossoms slipped softly between her fingers. Wiry root filaments tickled her palms, and then her sample's ruffled leaves skimmed over them, soft dimples dragging her contact with its outer cells in and out, up and down. . . .

The dressing gong roused her from her reverie. Evening dew was gathering on foliage already damp with the day's light rains. On her bed lay the ensemble Sevaria had given her, hinting strongly that it ought to be worn to dinner tonight. At least it was comfortable, and more practical than that regrettable peach silk. In Dacca she'd spilled a large quantity of a green soup down the gown's front. It had been restored to not quite its former glory.

This salwar kameez business suited her much better: a tunic to go over a matching pair of pantaloons. As Bee-Lung was adjusting the trousers' waistband Trana, Sevaria's most senior maid, knocked and entered.

"You have no difficulties, Aunty?"

Bee-Lung smiled at the honorific. She and Trana were of an age. "So far I'm fine. Look!" She gestured at the garment's securing sash, which she'd tied in the clever and decorative bowknot Ma Chau taught her.

"Yes, that's nice. Let me assist you with the kameez? It will be easier—" Trana made the tunic's satiny sleeves glide down over Bee-Lung's upraised arms, made no fuss when she refused the loan of a matching choker of pearls and opals, and conducted her through the upper and lower house, across the swiftly darkening courtyard, then into the candlelit dining room just as Jadida rang the gong by the room's entrance a second time.

Both servants left. Bee-Lung stood alone, studying the problem: they were to be confined to a Western-style formal table arrangement, and a most unharmonious one. As well as a vase holding dying branches lopped off of budding trees, the table's white cloth was topped with four identical sets of gleaming porcelain plates, silver, and cut glasses. Should she seat herself in one of the table's high-backed chairs in defiance of the trouble thereby invoked—as her rationalist brother would have urged her to do? Or should she wait, as she was inclined, in hope that the unlucky number of diners would be lessened or increased at the last minute?

Murmurings of English entered through the courtyard door. She detected a strange accent—American? "—callin us 'darky' and—"

Blown in by the night's breath, a tall black woman draped in grey scarves and amethysts interrupted herself to pause and laugh on the room's threshold. "Hey, this your Chinese lady-doctor, Sevaria? Doc, you know my old friend Tink? Ho Lin-Huang, I *should* say."

Behind the woman came Bee-Lung's hostess, clad in a more opulent version of her earlier attire. Heavier embroidery surrounded this tunic's neckline, and its front was spattered with gems. Still no veil, something Bee-Lung had often seen worn in Dacca and Kuala Lumpur. Perhaps it was unnecessary without the presence of men. Or perhaps a film star was always going to be more daring than functionaries' wives—a positive trait to discover in one destined for the forefront of world change.

"Come." Jadida and Trana had reappeared. They slid two chairs out from opposite sides of the table. Sevaria nodded at Bee-Lung to take one and indicated the other with a hand. "Miss Bailey?"

This was the woman who had for a time stolen away the Poet's lover? This was Rima Bailey?

Sevaria took the seat to Bee-Lung's right. The place to her left, at the table's head, remained empty. At least they were only three—for now. The servants poured them iced water and garnished it with sprigs of mint. Trana stepped back, the deep brown of her uniform blending with the walls' wooden paneling. Jadida vanished again—most likely to the kitchen.

"I am Ho Bee-Lung. Ho Lin-Huang is my younger brother."

"Rima Bailey. You got a funny name, Bee-Lung. Sound like a bug's body parts."

She was used to the giggles and remarks of less mature English speakers.

"You're already acquainted, then? Bee-Lung—" Sevaria carefully emphasized the last syllable's "oo" pronunciation. "—where did you meet my next film's costar?"

"Everfair's where we shoulda met, am I right?" said Miss Bailey. "If Tink hadda stayed just a season more till I come back. You been there lately?"

"We go there now." As everyone on this island must surely know.

"Ain't the same, what I hear."

What did Miss Bailey hear? And how had she heard it? "No?"

"No ma'am, it ain't. King Mwenda's son Prince Ilunga is pretty much flunkin outta school up in Egypt. Princess Mwadi stay with him. They two got a house together in Cairo. Yeah, Queen Josina cain't be caught havin nothin to do with her daughter since the princess try an lay claim to the throne, so last time I seen Mwadi she was a exile from her own mama's court."

Bee-Lung looked away, confused. If the princess wanted to steal his throne, why would the prince give her shelter?

"Late last year, that was when we got together. Ain't had not one letter from her since I went travelin after that."

The louvered door on Bee-Lung's left opened and Jadida entered, carrying a covered brass serving bowl. Steam trailed behind it, billowing out as Trana removed its lid. Coconut, lemongrass, fiery peppers, garlic, onions, the eggs and flesh of chickens . . . these sweet and sour and hot and salty flavors would suit the slippery blandness of noodles well, yes. This soup she would not spill.

"I heard that the King of Everfair threw out all the country's whites, much like our friends in Bharat," Sevaria said as she was served.

"Not exactly." Miss Bailey stirred her soup rapidly, her spoon ringing against the porcelain. "King Mwenda ain't too much concerned about anybody so-called race. He more worried whether they acknowledge how he their ruler, how Everfair their home. You do that you all right, no matter to him if you spozed to be white."

She pursed her lips and blew, still stirring. "So the Poet an her son, her daughter, them an a buncha other white folks hangin on."

"Then what is the difference you say I'll find?" Bee-Lung asked.

"Motes hasn't been meetin." A swallow, a pause, a second swallow. "Nobody gettin they hands cut off no more, that's good. But it seem like people hardly interested in the way they king—"

CRASH!! The sound of running feet and a panting stream of Arabic swear words came from the kitchen door's direction, swelling louder as it opened. Jadida stumbled forth, appeared to struggle for her balance, gasped, and said, "The shrimp, my lady. Madame Amirah is unsatisfied—"

"I am." Her hostess's mother stepped out of the kitchen corridor to stand straight as a nun before them, hands clasped as if in prayer: composed, alert. "They're not fit for guests. Too old—I am so very sorry." No sign of ingrained melancholy despite this statement of regret. And the posture was not that of a woman exhausted. Bee-Lung's treatments were working after only a day's application. The aroma of past-their-prime shellfish confirmed that the Spirit Medicine element of Mother Amirah's cure was effective too, sharpening her senses.

"Will you take your chair? Jadida, please help Madame to be seated."

Bee-Lung pushed her own chair away from the table, but before she could formulate an excuse to leave, Miss Bailey, much closer to the courtyard door, had it by the handle. "Y'all ain't gotta feed me. I ate before. I just come here on account a Miss Sevaria's movie. You can send your script by the hotel."

"The rest of the meal is not worth eating." Mother Amirah remained by the kitchen entrance. Now only two sat at the dining table—a much more favorable number. But if her hostess persuaded her mother to sit, the constellation the diners formed would become both neutral and chaotic. Bee-Lung leaned forward, preparing to stand on her slippered feet.

"Sweets!" Sevaria's voice was edged with desperation. "Partake

with us on the verandah—we've prepared honey rings and sher-
bets and bibikkan cake and aggala balls of course, and it will be
cool—"

Bee-Lung nodded. If they weren't confined to a table, the servants' presence would prevent any unfortunate configuration.

"Awright, yeah." Miss Bailey tugged the door open. Her scarves
fluttered gently in the draft she created. "Where we headin?"

Trana conducted them to the main building's rearmost porch.
She set a branch of burning candles on a metal-topped table and
arranged a padded footstool near the only other furniture, a long
settee. Miss Bailey claimed the stool, bare legs emerging from
the froth of her skirts like tree limbs from river foam. She leaned
against the balustrade, stretching her arms to rest along its top.
"So kin we discuss particulars?"

"I don't want to bore anyone." Sevaria gave Bee-Lung a significant glance. "I'll have the script fetched. Read it over tonight, and
when we meet tomorrow you'll know better what to ask."

Trana returned, accompanied by Jadida and the fragrances of
honey and dates, of cinnamon, cloves, ginger, and myriad other
spices. Slices of sugared lemons, brightly quenching, floated in a
pitcher of orange sorbet, bobbing on the syrup's tiny waves. To
smell was not quite as good as to taste. Bee-Lung accepted a small,
moist cake and was glad of the springiness filling her mouth as
she chewed, rendering her unable to answer Sevaria's suddenly
pointed questions about the continuation of her mother's therapy.

"The infusion you prescribe may be brewed by anyone, I trust?"

Bee-Lung shook her head no. Though of course it could. But best
this recruit believe that Bee-Lung's presence was indispensable.

"No? Why not? For what reason?"

Bee-Lung continued her chewing.

"If you leave us instructions and the proper materials I'm sure
we'll manage." A momentary hesitation. "There's nothing—
superstitious involved, I hope? No scrying or casting of horoscopes
or . . ."

The unfinished sentence trailed off suggestively. A reply could no longer be avoided. But an answer could.

"You should be healed as well." Bee-Lung knew most people enjoyed centering a conversation on themselves. "Have you been fatigued, yet had trouble sleeping? Does your stomach ache with loneliness in the early morning?" She forestalled Sevaria's negative: "Or perhaps the late afternoon? Your pulses are too slow. Especially for one so young. To my knowledge you are unique! It will be my honor to consult on such an interesting case—I'll happily attend you in addition to your mother for the rest of my visit."

Sevaria fell for Bee-Lung's stratagem. "Am I in danger?"

"Not yet. And see how sprightly Mother Amirah is now, after just a single day in my care? I can fix your pulses like that!" She snapped her fingers.

"How much more will you charge?"

"Practically nothing." Bee-Lung felt greedy; she ought not to accept any money at all from Sevaria for conducting an experiment on her. But her fee would go to fund a good cause: the purchase of homes with spacious gardens where other recruits could live and grow fresh crops of Spirit Medicine under their grounds. So progressed the spreading of the May Fourth revolution.

A high whistle from Miss Bailey interrupted Bee-Lung's reflections. "You ain't playin!" She flourished a sheaf of papers in one short-nailed hand. "Trincomalee Harbormaster seen this? You run your plans for this picture by the governor, by anyone?"

"He has seen the ending—and approved it! You can't judge till you read the whole." Sevaria sounded as if she were trying to disguise a deep worry. "That's a copy for you to take home."

"You sure I ain't about to get put in jail for sedition just by havin this—thang?" Miss Bailey shook the script.

"No one takes such fairy tales seriously. Be easy."

But Miss Bailey appeared far from easy. She surged up from her stool to pace before the settee. "Okay, you win. Kinda. Ima go to my hotel room and read it all and tell you what I think after that.

Drum me a jitney. I be back here teatime tomorrow." She whirled and left, the candle flames wavering in her wake.

Sevaria sighed. "Jadida, go with her." The younger servant scurried off obediently. The older servant stayed and accompanied the rest of them to their chambers amid Sevaria's apologies and Mother Amirah's breathy singing. From a snatch, Bee-Lung recognized the lullaby she had crooned while dosing and bathing the woman. She'd only sung it once, but her patient knew every word. This was yet more proof the medicine was working, tying them together via that song's story as if they belonged to the same core.

As she had hoped, Sevaria beckoned Bee-Lung into her room. A round bed, showily curtained in shimmering lengths of insect netting, occupied its center. Sevaria seated herself in front of a low chest of drawers topped by a mirror. "Please?" She indicated a backless chair upholstered in expertly tanned tiger fur.

"It will be easier to examine you while on my feet." Bee-Lung took Trana's lamp and began with tracing the star's hairline, then peered into her ears, her eyes, put firm fingers to her chin and turned her head this way, then that.

"Smile for me. Wider—show your gums." These were darker than she had expected. Entirely healthy, of course. But Bee-Lung tutted and sent Trana to retrieve her workbasket. Safely alone with the recruit, she set the lamp on the chest to reflect itself. "Tip your head back. Stick out your tongue. Further—I realize how unladylike you appear, but I must see its roots. You may wish to close your eyes." With a flourish, Bee-Lung extracted a silk handkerchief from the sleeve of her kameez and used it to aid her grasp of the star's wet and slippery tongue muscle. Turning it over, she found its underside as ordinary as its surface: blood vessels and glistening skin. She let the cloth's edges soak up a tiny pool of saliva, let go of the tongue. Withdrew. Sevaria closed her mouth at once; for good measure Bee-Lung used the handkerchief's corners to dab off a dewing of perspiration just starting under the delicate curl of her nostrils. She would see if using these fluids improved the efficacy of the special Spirit Medicine's application.

The door opened silently wider as Bee-Lung carefully stowed away the now-drenched silk. She sent the softly entering servant to fetch a pot of hot water with which she would brew the basic Spirit Medicine. From the top of her workbasket she took an iron beaker and emptied into it the remainder of the packet prepared for Mother Amirah. This she set beside the lamp.

Then she unpacked the rest of her workbasket. The top of the chest was now far too cluttered for her to lay out her tools properly. She used the tiger chair, despite its unhelpfully curved and padded seat. Wooden bowl, bone-handled rocking blade, clay jars—each packed with hollow, purplish-white threads harvested from a dozen different underground networks. She pulled out the smallest jar and transferred a quarter of its contents to the bowl. Then she selected a thin, flexible length of dried bamboo and balanced that on the bowl's rim.

What else? She needed to produce an immediate sensation so that Sevaria would be satisfied of the mixture's efficacy. What would convince her that her pulses were responding to Bee-Lung's treatment? Lion's tail? No—this should be a stimulant. Tobacco! She sprinkled a dash of snuff over the bowl's contents. Only a dash—too much and her subject would sneeze out the Spirit Medicine along with the tobacco powder. And cacao! She added the last of her store from Everfair. That should do it.

The knowing settled in Bee-Lung's blood. The new node she constructed would amplify May Fourth's anti-hierarchical attitudes just as hers and Tink's did. Her native empathy was colored by the dye of Sevaria's curiosity, infusing her perceptions, freshening them: the crackle and whisper of the fungal tubes pulverizing beneath her knife, the hollow *thok* of the knife's metal knocking against wood when a granule of cacao gave way, the spicy pungency of the blend climbing the chamber's subtle air currents to tickle her sensitized nostril hairs. The two of them were kinning.

Sometimes, the best times, it went like this: a connection would form between inoculant and inoculator, before the Spirit Medicine's actual application.

Bee-Lung finished her mixing. She lifted her head and met her subject's eyes, dark and beautiful. But void of understanding.

"What now? You'll brew this as a drink for me?"

The connection went in only one direction so far. Perhaps that was as well; Bee-Lung's deception would remain hidden, and the tie to the planned terminus—the artificial brother—would be stronger.

"No. That will be done with the treatment's other part, the portion identical to your mother's, once Trana has returned. This additional mixture is meant to be inhaled. Through your nose." She mimed using the bamboo to breathe in the Spirit Medicine. "Now you."

Ceylon, Aboard Xu Mu *and in Jaffna*

Tink kissed Kwangmi's rough braid. "Stop!" she commanded him. "Let me concentrate!" He obeyed. Only the temporary emptiness of the bridge pod had emboldened him to offer such intimacy. Beyond *Xu Mu*'s stern-facing windows, the sparsely jeweled night began to move steadily, in one direction. No more arcing back and forth with the wind. They were unmoored, underway.

"Are you sure you want to go this time?" he asked. "It will be Raghu's first mission as leader. Perhaps I'd better come along instead, in your place—to guide him."

"Perhaps you'd better not. He'll have more self-confidence if you stay on board." Tink wanted to reason with her, but the hatch above creaked open, warning him their time apart from the others was at an end.

It was Min-Jun, the elder of the Chen twins by twenty heartbeats. "We're packed. Raghu says we're to sleep in the hold."

"Yes. I'll join you as soon as Brother Kang relieves me." Kwangmi watched Min-Jun climb back up the ladder to the main gondola, but didn't wait for the hatch to close. She took Tink's suddenly clumsy hands in her own. "My Steel Dragon. Don't scold. Don't frown. Though unruly, I'm yours: I pledge you my love."

Tears sprang to Tink's eyes. Was he doomed to repeat all his life's mistakes? He had lost Lily Albin despite pleading for her to act safely, on such a similar night, such a similar adventure, years ago in Everfair. And on this return trip was he to lose Kwangmi too?

No. Nor would he try to argue further against Kwangmi's descent into danger.

"And I pledge that you have mine. And something more: my intention to marry you." He knelt like a white man. "I have no engagement gift. Not yet—but when we meet again—when you find your way to our rendezvous I'll be waiting there with gold, gems—"

"Why?"

Tink stared up, surprised. "It's traditional! Don't you want proof of how I feel?"

"I neither want nor need it. Such objects would only hamper me in our work and mark me as a grasping materialist to be defeated—an enemy!"

Again the hatch opened, slammed loudly back. Kang Woo-Hyun skipped the ladder and vaulted to the deck. "Captain! Big Sister! We're dropping!" He ran to the elevator levers.

Kwangmi followed him. "By how much?"

"Significantly."

Tink got to his feet. The forward windows showed more lights than stars. He felt a distinct slant upward as he walked to the stern controls. "Quickly!" He pointed at the emergency weight release cords. "Both sides!"

Kwangmi's gaze was low-lidded, assessing. "We could hit someone."

"Better a bag of sand on your head than an entire aircanoe." Pressing Brother Kang aside, he pulled the port cord and let the imbalance caused by the bags' release throw him starboard, then pulled that side's cord too.

Xu Mu straightened and rose. Trincomalee's twinkling streetlamps fell below and behind them. "Adjust trim," Tink ordered, and was surprised to see Woo-Hyun's pale hand on the stabilizer grip. He looked over his shoulder. Kwangmi's sandals were disappearing up through the hatch.

Well. She had told Sister Chen she would report to the hold on being relieved. And it would be hours yet before *Xu Mu* was in position. He could bid Kwangmi farewell for the few days they'd be apart once they came within walking distance of their target, Mount Lavinia station. Till then it was Tink's job to fly.

The night passed. The island passed, northeast to southwest. The moon's shadows spread over narrowing valleys, and the ridges between those valleys reared higher and higher, becoming mountains. Higher still, Tink reveled in the air's revealing thinness. The scents of mist and sprouting grass, of wild sheep and wandering leopards, floated up to him unmasked, infiltrating *Xu Mu*'s bridge pod with their ephemeral stories. Holy men had walked these peaks once, and would again someday.

Tink's shift ended and Ma Chau took his place. Freed, he ascended to *Xu Mu*'s main gondola and walked the narrow corridor forward to the hold. A damp sponge flickered next to the doorway.

He entered. With the cable station just over the approaching horizon, the other members of Tink's core were already up and about their preparations. Rubber-backed silk jumpsheets—an improvement on the original barkcloth—hung in whispering pleats from overhead hooks. Ma Chau had devised a particular way of folding the new versions' wider dimensions so that they opened smoothly when held by two corners, like square flowers blooming on falling stalks. They would slow his coremates' plunging descents—if properly arranged.

"Brother!" Tink seated himself next to Raghu where he perched on the central hatch's low coaming. Raghu's uncertain smile stopped Tink's questions in his throat, unasked. "Success awaits," he said instead. "Let's review your final instructions to me."

"*My* instructions to *you*?"

True, they could as easily be thought of in the reverse. "You'll jump just after we pass over Meegoda, have I got that right? You'll take cover for the rest of the day and make your way to the coast tomorrow night. And then when you've sown the spores for communication within the exposed cable housing, you'll procure a boat and head north to Jaffna, where I'm to meet you."

Raghu nodded and added, "And as you sail, you'll broadcast spores in the paddies and vegetable patches." His thick brows furled together like stylized clouds. "But will the Spirit Medicine grow and prosper, treated so? We don't want to squander our seeds."

They weren't seeds. "Bee-Lung believes enough threads will be produced and ingested so that the revolution will have a good number of easily converted sympathizers among the ranks of its Buddhist enemies." He stood and went to Kwangmi's side. Had she been ignoring him, or was she merely distracted by Jie-Jun's attentions to her head? Kwangmi's single braid had been reworked into many, and these were now being woven into a tight, sleek cap. It was not terribly becoming, though it looked practical. As practical as the silk harness she wore.

Tink squatted before the basket on which his adored one sat. He spoke without preamble, as he had learned she preferred: "So gold is not pleasing to you. Would you rather I offered you something else as a betrothal gift?"

Sister Jie-Jun's face warmed. Tink felt rather than saw it in the hold's dim light. A blush? Surely all the core knew of their attraction. Jie-Jun made as if to move off and allow them a small bit of privacy.

"Stay." Kwangmi lifted one hand. "We're saying nothing to each other you too can't hear." A grave-sounding sigh escaped her. She bent her head closer to his. "I repeat my question. Why?"

"To—to mark the occasion."

"No, not that. Why marry me?"

"What?" Tink sank back to sit on the hold's gently swaying deck.

"Why marry me? What's the need? Aren't we already bound together in a much more intimate relationship than that of man and wife?"

"What do you mean?" He smelled a sudden upwelling in the salt-bearing ground breezes. He heard the soft brushing together of detached hatch-securing lines being coiled up. Had they reached their destination so quickly? "What are you talking about? Our core?"

"Of course." She drew back to address Jie-Jun. "Are you done?"

"Almost. I'll just—"

Tink lost interest in Jie-Jun's words. He reached for and found Kwangmi's high-arched, natural foot, big and strong like a peasant's. He stroked its bony top. Kwangmi bent forward again and caught his caressing hand under hers. But she didn't remove it, only stopped it in place.

Jie-Jun left. "Think about what I've asked," said Kwangmi. "I truly want to understand your reasons for wishing to marry me. Explain them when we rendezvous." She released his hand and stood. A rush of dampness swept upon them from the open hatch. Tink lifted his head in time to see Raghu push himself off the coaming, jumpsheet correctly harnessed and held. The Chen twins followed suit.

As Kwangmi tied together the last two straps of her harness he attached its jumpsheet. She ran the few steps to the hatch. "Figure it out!" she shouted, and threw herself overboard.

Tink found himself hanging on to the top of the hatch coaming with clenched fingers. He was not doomed to a loveless life. He swore it.

He stared down into the dark sky in vain. Naturally none of the core were visible; that was very much the point of dropping them like this. For a moment longer the slender ribbon of Kwangmi's odor unfurled into his nose. Then the progress of *Xu Mu*'s insistent engines broke that connection, too.

He forced his hands to loosen, his body to relax back. Someone else from the crew entered the hold. They helped him shut and resecure the main hatch and open the smaller one. It was by this hatch he would scatter the Spirit Medicine spores Bee-Lung had deemed sufficiently hardy. When their cores were widely enough distributed that empathy was the world's standard and hierarchy a declining minority's tendency, there would be wild reserves at every hand to complete the revolution.

He spoke with the crew member helping him as they worked, but could not have said their name once they'd gone away.

Dawn came. Pink clouds swam above and below them, reflected in paddy waters broken by black soil and green leaves. Which would be the best medium for growth? Tink tied knots in a spare line to indicate spots along their route where he scattered the spores. He used a scale of twenty to one. As twilight enveloped them and Palk Bay crept into view, he wound the line into a pillow and lay with his tired head in its lumpy cradle. Jaffna lay on the bay's far side. This part of the mission was accomplished, and rest was his reward.

But he didn't dare rest here all night. Only a little while, really, till *Xu Mu* had safely moored above the fat base of the Ariyalai Peninsula, on the town's outer edges. Otherwise he'd miss his chance. When the motion of their flight stilled he woke from his nap and climbed down to the bridge pod. All was well there: shift changing smoothly, route to Trincomalee readied for their return tomorrow night. Or perhaps the next morning.

He'd assigned himself to the Jaffna landing party. He was forgiven for putting himself forward in this way. Everyone understood his eagerness to be with his core again as soon as possible.

In the cargo basket with his companions—members of his sister's core, so able to render at least rudimentary medical aid if needed—Tink could tell his distraction and silence were attributed to pin-ing for his own kin. But in fact he was focused inward, dissecting his thoughts and feelings for Kwangmi, trying to fashion them into an answer that would satisfy her last-minute questions and get her to agree with what he knew would be best.

He rode down to the loading facilities in a fog of reflection, and passively shared the freight wagon hired to take them to the town's one good hotel. He must have registered there, for when the knock came he was standing in a bedroom with a door between him and the knocking hand, between him and a high, inquiring voice:

"Sir? Apologies for disturbing you so late. You are willing to receive a lady visitor?"

For the first time in hours Tink came fully awake. A window to his left showed uncompromising night. How had his core arrived here so quickly? Had they failed to inoculate the telegraph cable? He didn't sense Kwangmi in the passageway—she must be waiting in the hotel's lobby. He strode to the door. Around its edges, along with the scent of the speaker, a familiar smell seeped in—familiar, but out of place. How did he know whoever it was? He pulled the door open.

"Much obliged to you, Mr. Ho! I knew you was better mannered than to keep me waitin. Now scuse me while I take a seat." Rima Bailey! In she walked, brash as truth, slamming the door behind her. She sat on his bed and leaned forward, propped on long, strong arms.

He'd last seen her on stage, in Everfair. "Why are you— What are you doing here?" he asked.

"Lookin for you. Findin you. Wasn't you expectin me? You acted like it a minute ago."

"No." Tink shrugged and sat down suddenly on a wooden stool, the only seat provided. He was tired of thinking. Tired of wondering if the Spirit Medicine weakened his thinking. "I expected—someone else."

"Well Sevaria was already gonna send me, so your sister didn't need to come herself." Let Miss Bailey believe it was Bee-Lung he meant. He was too tired to explain. "Said our film might not get off the ground if I don't make Governor Manning approve it. Said the governor like his berries black." She straightened and smiled with her lips shut, pressed tight together as if they held back a secret.

Fruit was usually a metaphor for sex. "So you've come to seduce this Mr. Manning—"

She interrupted. "*Governor* Manning." She stood to tower over him. "Yeah, he spozed to check in here tomorrow. Meanwhile I can set you up for your spywork the way Bee-Lung payin me ta do."

"You're going to get me ready for 'spywork'? What kind? And how?"

"You gotta plant them spore thangs ahead a time so revolutionaries able to start inoculatin people when they preparin for them festival days. And you ain't wanna be caught." Miss Bailey clasped her hands together and stretched her arms above her head, towering even taller. "So you an Raghu hafta act like you pilgrims."

"Wait—Raghu's here?" Jumping up, he flung himself at the door.

"I say that? No! Course he ain't here yet."

She wasn't lying. He could smell. He let his hand fall from the door's knob.

"He landin in Jaffna tomorrow mornin, maybe a little later, yeah? All accordin to plan, and I ain't got no business with him anyways. He do what he already done. Meanwhile—" From a small velvet bag chained to the low waist of her skirt, Miss Bailey pulled a jar of the sort Bee-Lung used. She removed its stopper and held it out to him.

"Pretend this in here be the spores. Show me how you gonna carry they container."

Tink assumed an air of confidence. "I can easily hide it in my sleeve."

Miss Bailey sniffed and shook her downy head. "Naw. Too heavy. An how you know you be wearin sleeves? What your guide had on?"

"Short trousers. No shirt," he conceded. "But he let me keep mine."

"So? You expectin to sneak back in the shrine he showed you? An wearin what you usually wear?" She bent to set the round-bottomed jar on a pillow and stepped away. "Ima let you think a minute how shady that sound."

Tink tried to concentrate, but Miss Bailey's movements distracted him. First she opened the window and leaned out, then she abandoned that for the washstand, balancing the white soap bar on its side and snapping the washcloth at an errant moth.

"You got your answer?"

"No." He had nothing for Miss Bailey. Nothing for Kwangmi, yet, either, and he'd had hours longer to come up with a response to her question. He was certain he'd solve that problem, though. Eventually. Maybe sleep would help. He wanted to lie down, but Miss Bailey was back on the bed, blocking him.

"Lemme tell you what's happenin then. You gonna be plumb stark naked. Won't nobody suspect you a smugglin in nothin."

"Naked! Naked?"

"Yeah right. Naked. See, your sister worked up a skin condition to afflict you, for which she is now workin up a cure." She tipped the jar and poured its contents onto her palm. "This here powder gonna make you itch fierce once I get done sprinklin it in your sheets. All over. Take a day or two, but by the time you get back to Trincomalee you be in bad shape! So then you show your guide and tell him you gotta go back where he took you. Say you pledged to bring Lord Siva a broom—"

"A broom?"

"That's right, a broom. That's the proper offerin. And tell him you made your vow to have the healin ceremony in that secret chamber. While you prayin your guide be sweepin you clean of whatever curse—all over—an sweepin Spirit Medicine spores into the very air! Inoculate them flowers for sure!"

And the flowers would host the Spirit Medicine in their root systems, and introduce its empathy-triggering chemicals into festival celebrants' brains. By then *Xu Mu* would be long gone—their latest recruits would be in charge of generating the final cores. After first generating, of course, those recruits' consent to the process.

How would those on the aircanoe know they had succeeded? The plan seemed complicated and farfetched. But if Bee-Lung thought the idea would work, it would work. The Spirit Medicine was going to find new homes; the revolution was going to breed new heroes.

So why this prickling in his liver? Why this sinking hollow in his belly, like a lead-walled bubble awaiting the worst moment to pop? Why this weariness and dread?

INTERLUDE W

ORIGINS OF THE MAY FOURTH MOVEMENT

When imprisonments and executions completed the destruction of Russia's 'flu-ravaged Bolshevik Front, the last of the supporting cadres of sympathizing Chinese students returned to their homes. On benches in roadside gardens, in passages between crowded lecture halls, they exchanged the fruits of their foreign-learned lessons with student comrades who'd remained behind with the intent of being taught by the Chinese proletariat—an element at that time largely nonexistent, since in 1919 most of the country's population were peasant farmers.

The confluence of the pragmatic attitudes instilled by these peasant instructors with returnees' memories of the grim realities of Russia's failures produced a new approach to fomenting revolution: a doubly determined effort to model the best possible outcomes, to commit to building and living in the most dynamically joyful anarchies imaginable. Immediately. Now.

Already there were inklings as to how such societies could work: Everfair and the fledgling nation of Bharat, various maroon settlements on the edges of increasingly abandoned empires, and so forth.

But how to wrest from capitalism's clawing grasp the resources necessary—the food and land and fuel and lumber, the knowledge and the machines that would transform today into tomorrow? And how to do this without the violence underlying the Bolsheviks' downfall?

The answer: Science. Radical applied research provided easy means to coordinate the massive strikes from which the movement took its name. On May 4, 1919, cores that had been formed with the spores of Dr. U Shin's Spirit Medicine led thousands of insurgents in hundreds of cities, towns, and villages to claim the streets as their own. The streets and everywhere the streets went.

CHAPTER FOUR

February 1921
Mombasa Island

Princess Mwadi squeezed her eyes shut in frustration. Her monkey scrambled up over the hotel balcony's low wall and patted her cheek with a warm, reassuring paw.

She patted him back. Raffles had done his part, stealing Scranforth's correspondence and passing it along to the gull Mwadi rode. Which she had then made fly east, to Queen Josina's closest agent. But the response to her information about Britain's scurrilous plan to exploit Everfair's resources? Skepticism. Questions. Inaction.

Another touch, softer than the monkey's, caressed her face: the evening breeze. February was Mombasa Island's coolest, driest time. She reveled in the air's movement, longed to take wing—but she must finish this letter first.

Her servant came out with a lighted lamp. It would draw insects. The princess sent it away, along with instructions to leave her undisturbed till morning. But now she must choose between being able to see and being able to breathe freely.

She went inside. If she finished her letter to her mother quickly enough, she could go out again soon. Raffles came in behind her. He leapt onto the dining table to examine the remains of her dinner, tucking one of the doughy puddings she disliked into his mouth. Since her acquisition of him, the monkey had gained weight and audacity. As Mwadi searched for the best way to frame her protests and pleas for the queen's serious reconsideration—her words must be carefully chosen for this missive to be sent via normal channels—Raffles clambered into her lap, blocking her view of what she was trying to write. Mwadi caressed the low division parting the fur atop his head, and he leaned to one side to follow her fingers.

The letter began well enough, subtly underscoring the evenness so far of the competition between prince and princess:

My dearest Mama,

Though my absence hasn't precisely been an exile, I'm so relieved at being called home again! Ilunga and I *really are hurrying to be with you, though we arrived in Mombasa only yesterday—you must blame the backwardness of British air service for that.*

As you know

And there it stopped.

What did her mother know? Best not to refer openly to the intelligence Mwadi had gotten to her earlier. And however much she wished to remind Queen Josina of her daughter's special abilities, however supportive these might be of Mwadi's claim to rule, they had to go unmentioned in this uncoded missive. So:

As you know, we travel accompanied by Ilunga's old friend Deveril Scranforth, who continues in British employ.

Mwadi prayed that, as with her first hint about the seeming race home, changing the script in which she wrote those last five words would emphasize her hidden meaning: in this case, the depth of her distrust. Her perfectly justified distrust.

New paragraph:

I can hardly wait till we reach the shores of Lake Kivu, where the black-headed gull rests on peaceful waters. For then it will be but hours till your loving arms embrace and welcome us. And then I shall be able to tell you all our adventures!

Again the switch in script styles. Combined with Mwadi's mention of a rare bird and of explosive Lake Kivu's "peaceful" waters, this must be sufficient to warn the queen to expect more news—news of an explosive nature. Which news she hoped to harvest tonight.

She signed and sealed the letter, setting it aside to be sent first thing next morning. What was the charge for postage? It would be added to her bill.

Now. Removing the lamp's shade—the same sort of pierced brass globe as was used on the glamps of her childhood—and extinguishing its flame, the princess stepped out again onto the balcony. Bats swept moths and mosquitos from the air for their supper, their fluttering wings a whisper, their high squeals of satisfaction practically inaudible. She'd tried to ride them the night before, but they were too different from her family's traditional mounts. Perhaps if she made a few more attempts her will would prevail.

For tonight's excursion, though, she planned on keeping things simple and using another bird. Its cage hung from the balcony's arched opening. It had slept all day there, cooled by shadows. Now that twilight was emerging, expanding those shadows, the nightjar's brown feathers stirred. Its eyes blinked open, gleaming in the last of the sky's luster.

The princess unhooked the cage and lifted it free, then settled on the cushioned divan with it balanced on her lap. She held it to her face and unlatched but did not open its door, imitating the little swamp bird's chup-chup-chup to ease its nervousness. Her call became a song, a petition for admittance. When the answer came her body closed its eyes. She saw them shutting. She pushed open her cage's unresisting door and hopped through it onto a shoulder rising and falling slowly with calm, even breaths. No worries. All would be well. She flew into the deepening darkness.

Mombasa Island

Prince Ilunga sighed happily and untied the white napkin from beneath his chin. The meal had been good, and had merited most of his attention for the past two hours. Giving his business to public dining houses such as Violetta's Grotto was a Cairo custom he expected to indulge less frequently once secure in his succession. But not immediately.

Cutlery clinked against china; murmuring voices washed against walls of a subdued, greyish blue—meant, he supposed, to represent granite or some other stone. Devil had backed the recommendation of Violetta's by offering to come along. The Englishman's thin lips, reddened by tomato sauce, curled upward like a moustache at their ends. "Cigar, Loongee? Got the right sort—Honduran, none of that Sicilian rubbish."

The prince glanced around the room. It was full of well-off travelers, gentlemen like himself. And ladies. "Here?"

"Of course not. There's a garden. Got a fountain, walkway— very pretty. Guests welcome. Nice and cool, and besides, if we can get away from these damn prying eyes there's something I've been meaning to show you."

Their waiter led them by way of an abandoned private room to a curtained door and three stairs down to a platform near to ground level. As Ilunga's eyes adjusted to the dimness—night had fallen while he dined, but a little light spilled onto the garden from within—his ears took in the splash of water falling on water. The fountain. His skin shivered with the knowledge of its nearby coolness.

"Here we are. Already cut it for you." Devil handed him a long, fragrant cylinder. A gun-like silhouette appeared in Devil's hand and Ilunga twitched despite himself. "Light it?"

He made himself lean toward the white man. "Yes." It was a Ronson Pisto-lighter. Harmless. Devil had shown it to him many times before. It sparked and flamed and he reached to hold it steady at the end of his cigar, with no betraying tremble in his hand. Inhaling carefully, he savored the smoke's spicy perfume. He exhaled without coughing. "What is it you want me to see?"

From a shadowy shrub came the chup-chup-chup of a night bird. Not, he hoped, a species his sister had mastered.

"Something I've got back. Queries and promises, mostly. Responses to my letters—you know, ones I had to write out again thanks to that damned Raffles." The Englishman paused to clip and light his own cigar. "They're behind you, Loongee, a hundred percent. Just want me to make sure you're a sure thing." A chuckle. Another draw on the cigar. The prince matched it. He and Devil were manly, important.

"But you wanted to show—"

"Can't let you keep anything, of course, but look if you don't recognize that seal!" From the wallet ever present at his waist, Devil produced an envelope. Wax that looked black in the feeble illumination clung to its flap. That crest—Ilunga took the envelope and ran his fingers over the seal's broken surface to make certain. "King George!" he exclaimed. "King George supports me!"

"Shh!" Devil lurched forward and snatched the letter back. "Secret! Can't let you keep it," he repeated. "Too dark to read here anyway. Dangerous. Only wanted to show you. Since I have—" Clenching his hand, Devil crumpled envelope and letter into a ball and set them aflame. Dangerous indeed!

"Careful!" The blazing paper plummeted like a star to the wood at their feet. Cursing and stamping, they extinguished it.

Curious staff poked their heads out of the restaurant's small rear window. Caught! But the prince pretended to be showing his friend steps in a new dance, and after a few moments the questioning looks changed to encouraging grins and laughter at the clumsy white man's expense.

Luckily Devil was immune to blacks' low opinions. He laughed too, and was in his normal good humor as they reentered Violetta's and retrieved their walking sticks. A good humor soon to improve.

"Loongee! Eyes right!"

They stood by this point at the restaurant's main entrance, a sunken area set off from the tables by a low papier-mâché balustrade. Evidently Devil's greater height showed him something—*someone*—of interest sitting at one of the tables. The prince refused to stand on tiptoe. "What? Who is it?"

"I call dibs on the first time the husband leaves."

"Husband? Is it—"

Devil was off to the hunt, bounding up the entrance area's two steps, snaking through crowded tables. Ilunga hurried to catch up with him before he disappeared, chasing him to a booth in a corner spectacularly got up to resemble a crystal-bearing cave wall. The plaster was embedded with actual low-grade gems that flashed and sparkled in the candlelight.

"Splendid!" Devil exclaimed. But he was referring to the booth's occupants, not their surroundings. "Mr. and Mrs. Chawleigh—hadn't expected to see you here so soon!"

"The business on Nocra took less time than expected, and I found myself able to renew my acquaintance with an old friend also in transit: Signore Quattrocchi. Won't you join us? Let me introduce you." The invitation sounded somehow false. No welcoming smile or gesture accompanied it.

Devil eyed Quattrocchi's thin form and sharp-chinned visage with apparent unease. Did he fear additional competition for Mrs. Chawleigh's favors? "Just leaving, actually, but perhaps breakfast tomorr—"

"Perhaps a nightcap," the prince interjected. He made as if to sit on the blushing white woman's ample lap and an attentive waiter brought up an empty chair for him. "Now."

Mombasa Island and Aboard Omukama

What was her range? Flitting from perch to perch across the dark and lively city, Princess Mwadi doubted she could fly the nightjar as far as she truly needed to go. According to the letter they'd received in Cairo, Queen Josina would be waiting for her children in Kisangani, Everfair's capital, thousands of miles away. An enormous distance, one it would take several days for the poor bird to cover—weeks, even. And much of the route was over territory inimical to a swamp creature: high grasslands, mountains, a wide lake offering no shelter from eagles and other predators.

If the princess followed her heart she'd be led in an entirely different direction: Rima-ward. But wherever she rode, she would need to leave her body behind. Best to focus on her current path.

A tree. A wall of bricks still radiating the day's warmth. A rooftop clothesline. An arm of iron from which swung a merrily creaking sign. She picked her path back to the hotel cautiously, one bright eye cocked for watchers. Though it was unlikely anyone hereabouts but her brother knew of Mwadi's skill at riding.

Arriving safely on her balcony, she flew up another storey to listen for activity in Ilunga's suite. Silence. She paused, waiting. The prince ought to have come in right behind her, or even ahead of her, given her circuitous course. She had observed his departure from the restaurant's garden, post-cigar, had figured the timing. But the suite's quiet continued minute after minute.

Surrendering, she swooped back to the balcony below and forced her reluctant mount to reenter its cage. The body she was born into roused easily and hooked the cage's latch.

Everfair's old enemies, the English, backed Ilunga to replace Mwenda as king. The messages Mwadi and her monkey had stolen from Scranforth on *Madiz* had revealed his intent in that regard. Tonight she'd learned that these intentions were shared and advanced by the highest of high powers—the sovereign of the only European country not devastated by the Maltese Influenza.

She needed to consult Lady Fwendi about what she'd learned. Maybe Mam'selle Toutournier too. But she and Ilunga were booked to leave in the late morning on *Lukeni*, which would fly to Everfair via Mwanza, bypassing Kalemie and Lady Fwendi's school. Her brother must somehow be persuaded to postpone their passage by a day so that they could both take the alternate route. If necessary, the princess would feign illness—though the thought of resorting to that ploy rankled. She hated admitting any weakness—especially to Ilunga. And she'd be hard-pressed to catch up with him if he left her behind.

She called back her servant to remove her jewelry, her rings and hair ornaments, and prepare her for bed. She missed Aloli's sure touch greasing her scalp, but endured Hafiza's more perfunctory massage without complaint. Raffles jumped on the bed's canopy— and back off with frightened speed when it sagged under his weight. Mwadi laughed at the monkey's antics—a little bitterly, but she laughed. She was without question lighthearted. She was not distracted from her surroundings, not in despair. She was thinking only of her country, and how quickly she could arrive there. Not of Rima.

She slept and was almost sure she didn't dream of Rima, either.

At dawn the princess woke. She should supervise the packing, but she lay stubbornly still. Raffles poked his head up from her bed's foot. He had become accustomed to spending the nights nearby since their voyage began.

After a bit, the need for the chamber pot drove her to get up. Then Hafiza roused from her pallet and took the pot down the hall to empty. On her return, Mwadi sent her to the kitchen for tea or coffee, or chocolate if it could be had. "And fruit," she added as the servant left. "Or something else to feed my pet."

On the balcony, the nightjar sat dejected on the floor of its cage. Mwadi chided herself for not setting it free before. She had been selfish. She cradled her hands to pick it up and discovered as she lifted it that its eyes were glazed, its feathers fluffed as if to ward off a chill. Its heart beat sluggishly against her palms—please, let the poor creature not die! Let its death not be her fault!

What could she do? As if Mam'selle herself spoke, Mwadi heard her answer in her matter-of-fact voice: if the bird was cold, she should warm it. She tucked it inside the lace top of her negligee, soothing its speckled head with her fingertips. What else? Perhaps Hafiza would have some clue—she'd been helpful with the monkey back in Al Maadi.

The suite was empty. No breakfast yet. No servant. Hearing footsteps on the landing outside her door, Mwadi went to open it, monkey in attendance. But the steps were not Hafiza's. A blond-haired white woman stood hunched with embarrassment at the top of the stairway, headed down. Her pale face flushed a bright pink and she turned away—just as Mwadi recognized her former fellow sailor. "Mrs. Chawleigh!"

As if helpless to stop herself, Mrs. Chawleigh looked back up. A soft, hiccupping scream escaped her mouth and she jerked herself around to run away downward. Scrambling noises echoed up the stairwell in her wake; gradually they diminished and ended. From the landing above came the sound of a closing door. Prince Ilunga's door.

Raffles emitted a trilling hoot. Steps sounded on the stairs again—getting louder, coming nearer. Hafiza's scarfed head appeared; she was climbing up from the kitchen at last, and carrying a promisingly heavy-looking tray.

Set on the suite's low table, the tray's contents fulfilled that promise: hot chocolate, sweet rolls studded with fragrant cloves, a basket of dried dates, a bowl of raisins, and another bowl filled with juicy wedges cut from a crimson-fleshed blood orange. Mwadi arranged herself on the nearby sofa—and as she sank into its cushions remembered the bird nestled in her bosom.

She brought it out. "Hafiza—" she began. A knock at the door interrupted her. It opened on the prince.

"May I come in?" he asked, entering without waiting for an answer. "Chocolate? Fetch us another cup," he ordered Mwadi's servant. Who glanced at the princess to check whether she should obey. Mwadi nodded. She wanted her brother in the best of moods. She tucked the shivering nightjar back between her breasts.

Ilunga eyed her with an expression of mild annoyance. "Starting up a royal menagerie to replace London's, Sister? Can't it wait till we get home?" As if to underscore the prince's point, the monkey scampered over to snatch a pawful of dates from the breakfast tray and stuff them in his mouth. With the same paw he grabbed a pastry.

"Ugh! Nasty thing! Shoo!" Ilunga's disgusted shouts scared Raffles out onto the balcony.

"I must get him better trained." She wished she didn't sound so defensive.

"Do you have someone around here in mind to do that?" The prince took the cup Hafiza had reappeared with. "I fear our stay in Mombasa must be prolonged."

The princess leaned back in surprise. "Prolonged? How? Why?"

The prince ignored her questions. "I'm sending Gasser to switch our booking to *Lukeni*'s next flight." He took a sip and smacked his lips appreciatively.

"But *Lukeni* won't head west from here again till next Friday! Two markets! Our mother's waiting! Are we supposed—"

"How is it you're so familiar with aircanoe schedules?"

She brushed aside her brother's sudden suspicion. "I made all the provisions for our travel, do you forget? That is, I did so until you decided they were no good. So now are we to be stuck here in this primitive hotel—"

"'Primitive'! Is that what you call it? Well, who selected this 'primitive' hotel?"

At her breast the nightjar fought to fly free, its wings half-beating like a weak but furious heart. She tried to calm herself so as to soothe her bird. Hadn't she actually *wanted* a change in plans?

"*Omukama* leaves in just four days. Monday. One market. If we must delay our departure, isn't that a better option?"

Grudgingly, Ilunga agreed. "Four? That could work."

What did he mean, "That could work?" Work how? What was Ilunga up to?

Womanizing was what. She got verification of this that same evening. Overseeing an insect-hunting expedition on the hotel's rooftop garden, Princess Mwadi leaned out over its parapet and spotted Mrs. Chawleigh five floors down. Twilight, distance, and perspective made of the white woman a small, round shadow, but her telltale yellow hair framed the purple dot of her bonnet. That and her odd, sneaking behavior—approaching the hotel along a trash-strewn alley, darting forward and hanging back at irregular intervals—identified Mrs. Chawleigh and her mission.

"Prominence?"

Mwadi turned her head. "Yes?"

Her servant carried the bird's cage one-handed. "I think she likes these best." Among the wood shavings and plant clippings covering the cage's bottom, a much-recovered swamp nightjar tore the wings off a struggling moth. Mwadi scolded herself again, as she had since realizing the cause of the bird's suffering: she ought to have let it feed last night.

"Catch more of them, then." A movement below captured her attention and she faced forward again. Now who was this? A man was following Mrs. Chawleigh. When the white woman looked over her shoulder and saw him she extended one gloved hand in a wave. Judging by his costume, and by the pallor of what little skin it revealed, he too was a European. And though Mwadi could not be sure of his identity from this vantage, the man's calm, deliberate pace was exactly that of Mr. Chawleigh.

Mrs. Chawleigh disappeared. The spot where she vanished matched Mwadi's memory of the hotel's rear entrance, a memory gleaned from previous reconnaissance rides. Hurrying to the stairway and descending half a flight toward the top floor's landing, she heard a door below open on quiet hinges. Crouching, she witnessed Mrs. Chawleigh slip inside Ilunga's suite. So. It was for such an affair her brother postponed their travel. She didn't need to hear or see anything more.

She returned to the roof, which by this time was much darker: a boy lit glass-shielded candles. She took one from a wooden table and peered over the roof's parapet for a final look. The man she had assumed to be Mr. Chawleigh was gone.

"Come," she told Hafiza. She walked down to her suite slowly, staring into her candle's flame as if mesmerized, trying to understand the implications of what she'd seen. Mr. Chawleigh knew of his wife's assignations? Mrs. Chawleigh knew that he knew of them?

By the day of *Omukama*'s departure, Princess Mwadi had still not puzzled out what was going on.

This aircanoe was larger than *Lukeni,* though of the same vintage. But most of its gondola was filled with freight: tubs of creamy white fat rendered from the flesh of locally grown coconuts, which provided a soft undernote for the sharp odor of cloves and the near-hallucinatory cloud of perfume drifting up from baskets of precious vanilla. Only twenty passengers could be accommodated. Yet among those seated in the aft viewing cabin she found the Chawleighs.

Ilunga entered beside her, feigning surprise at their presence. "What? I thought you were all settled on the coast for the rest of the season—how is it you venture to explore the interior?"

Mrs. Chawleigh gazed up at the prince in what was surely meant to be a seductive manner. "Since you'll be at hand for most of the journey, we'll be in not the slightest danger!"

"You're visiting Everfair?" the princess asked. "You must come to see us at the palace in Kisangani." She kept her voice flat and empty of enthusiasm.

"Ah, no." Mr. Chawleigh shook his head and grinned as if ruing his answer. Though his expressionless eyes remained leveled on hers. "It's business again, unfortunately. King George is sending me to establish a consulate at Usumbura. We're only flying in as far as Kalemie; we'll sail the rest of the way."

So much information, and given so voluntarily. Could she trust in its truth?

"Sit down. Please." The white man had risen from his seat when she and Ilunga first approached, as was his kind's custom with those they designated "ladies." Now he placed two chairs from another of the cabin's tables at his own and gestured welcomingly. "Is this enough? Should I get us one more? For your friend?"

Her friend? "Raffles?" the princess asked.

Mr. Chawleigh laughed. "No! The monkey? No. I mean Mr. Scranforth. Isn't he to join us? Where is he?"

"Resting in our cabin," said the prince. "Aircanoes put his stomach out of sorts."

"Really? Motion sickness? He seemed fine aboard *Madiz.*" From a vest pocket, Mr. Chawleigh took a silver flask. He unscrewed the top and poured colorless alcohol into a cup on the table before him. "Too bad. You'll have to drink his share." He moved the flask's mouth over the other cup.

The prince giggled nervously. "I couldn't. And isn't that Mrs. Chawleigh's cup you're about to pour—"

"You don't mind, do you, Clara? Or you, Princess?"

Mwadi did mind. The bored irritation Ilunga's vices normally caused her frothed over into anger. She stood up, knowing this would force Mr. Chawleigh to follow suit. "Brother! Hadn't you better continue your inspection?"

"My inspection of what?" Ilunga asked as she dragged him from his seat and back out into the corridor. She shut the door and they were alone.

"Have you lost your senses, Sister? I am *not* going to allow you to make me look like a fool!" The prince straightened the kilt he wore in imitation of the Sapeurs.

"A fool indeed! Bad enough that you play the sot in your own home—here in public, you're ready to consume strong spirits at practically the break of day!"

Ilunga made a great show of bringing forth a watch tucked in the kilt's smallest pocket. "It is ten sixteen precisely. Hardly the 'break of day.'"

Mwadi pinched her lips together. She was not going to argue in this unseemly manner, in this unseemly spot. She nodded in what could be taken as acquiescence and left him to head for her cabin. Most likely the bird would be slumbering there, but Raffles had been fretting to escape its confines and explore *Omukama* ever since they boarded. She could divert him and herself at the same time.

She reached her door and opened it, but before she could step through she heard a whispered command: "Stop." She paused on her cabin's threshold out of curiosity. Not obedience; never that. "I know you hate me," the hushed voice continued. "Know you stole my monkey and set it against me too."

Scranforth. Now she could see that the door to Ilunga's neighboring cabin hung somewhat ajar. Mystery solved. "What do you want?"

From beyond the door to her own cabin, Hafiza called out to Mwadi softly, "Prominence? Is that you? Are you coming in?"

She replied yes, with equal softness, so as not to wake the nightjar. But Scranforth kept speaking, so she stayed where she was to hear him.

"Wanted to warn you. Watch out for Chawleigh. Quattrocchi's pawn, and if he enjoys anything it's dirty work. Chap's a real bounder."

Kalemie, Everfair

Prince Ilunga smiled approvingly at the many subjects lining Kalemie's busy streets. "The people rise early to greet us. It's good!" He leaned forward to wave out of the carriage's window.

On the seat opposite him his sister stuck out her lower lip and blew an impatient-sounding sigh. "'Early'!" The princess's tone implied that the hour was on the contrary late. Really, though, his rising had been quite timely considering the length and extent of Clara's amorous attentions. He turned to grin at Devil. It had been Ilunga's idea to purchase berths aboard the ship on which the Chawleighs booked their passage to Usumbura, and look how well that had turned out! Over his sister's protests—which he had expected—and the reluctance of his friend—which he had not.

"We'll be at Lady Fwendi's establishment for elevenses—isn't that right, Didi? Very soon. Plenty of beautiful young ladies to be found on the school's premises," Ilunga reassured Devil. Probably his eagerness to be quit of the Chawleighs stemmed from the solitariness of the night he had spent.

The carriage swung right, following the steam bicycle towing it along this new, narrower thoroughfare. Less of a crowd had gathered in this smaller space. The bicycle's engine noise seemed louder now, with fewer cheers to mask it. Then they reached the school's grounds and rounded the curve of the graveled drive leading to its front door. A garden planted with palms distanced the cheers of the populace further.

Several staff members—or were they students?—lined the wide steps up to the school's main building: most female, including the drummer, who began to play as soon as the carriage door opened.

Lady Fwendi descended from the building's entrance. The simplicity of her gown revealed that her figure had not changed much since Ilunga and Mwadi appeared in her husband's play, twelve seasons back. Prince Ilunga, of course, was now in his prime. He bowed and kissed her brass hand. She withdrew it a little too quickly. "Sir Jamison will be so sorry to have missed your return."

"Where has he gone?" asked Mwadi, climbing out behind Ilunga and embracing Lady Fwendi as if they were old chums. Instead of, as Ilunga knew, teacher and former student.

"To Kenya, actually, via Mwanza. He'll be landing in Mombasa tonight. So you might have crossed paths with him if you'd waited and flown on *Lukeni*. He'll be back next market; he just wants to have a look at a yacht he thinks of buying."

The door on the carriage's far side scraped open and shut, and Devil appeared around its back. Ilunga introduced him. Lady Fwendi looked him up and down. And up and down again. She smiled. "So this is our famous English lion fighter?"

Incredibly, Devil blushed. "Didn't think you would have heard of that, but no, not exactly—that was m'cousin Granny. Grandison. Not me." He dropped the slouch hat he'd grabbed from his head and fumbled it up off the ground. "Awfully proud of him of course. Can't say I'm brave as—"

"And who have we here?" Lady Fwendi was peering up at the carriage's roof, where much of their luggage was stowed.

Mwadi lifted her arms and the monkey leapt down into them, its long black-and-white fur flying like a cape. She smoothed the fur back into place and cradled it like a doll. "This is Raffles. A silly name, I know, but it was already given him."

"May I?" Lady Fwendi tried to take Raffles in her own arms. The tangled line with which Ilunga had secured the animal to the luggage rack got in the way, so she untied it.

"You will be staying in Mademoiselle Toutournier's old apartments. I hope they'll be suitable accommodation for King Mwenda's offspring—" She smiled at Ilunga for the first time since his arrival. "—and big enough for all three of you?"

"If not, Devil can look for lodgings elsewhere." Ilunga expected a hostess's typical objections to his joking offer, but Lady Fwendi only nodded as if in agreement, then nodded again to the drummer, who finished their welcome with a flourish. At this signal, several pretty students or servants or whatever swarmed forward to unload their belongings. The boy Gasser and Mwadi's maid got out and helped.

Lady Fwendi led all of them up the stairs and into the building's coolly echoing entrance hall. Another, steeper flight of stairs filled the dimness opposite. Again Lady Fwendi took the lead, mounting it. "I wish you could stay longer, but I understand that tomorrow you must catch *Okondo* and hurry home," she said over her shoulder. "Only one night! We had hoped for two—we expected you when *Omukama* arrived yesterday, but I understand you made other arrangements?" The scuffling of the girls' many sandals on the staircase behind them muffled Mwadi's reply. He was happy, actually, not to have to hear his sister rehash their argument and eventual compromise. It would have been just as sensible to stay aboard the ferry and sail to Usumbura, then fly home to Kisangani from the other side of Lake Tanganyika. Just as sensible and far more enjoyable—for him. But Mwadi would not be "cheated" of this visit, and it was true, as she insisted, that his favored route would have involved leaving Everfair as soon as they got here. Though only temporarily.

At the top of the stairs the procession paused; the prince was at a loss to understand why until he arrived there himself and saw his sister and Lady Fwendi stooped over a sleek grey cat. Mwadi stroked its head and Lady Fwendi its tail.

"Whose pet is this?" he asked.

Both women straightened up. "No one's," said Lady Fwendi. "She moved into the washhouse only last week." The cat approached him fearlessly, a look of pleased expectancy in its round green eyes.

"A stray?" The prince stooped likewise and paid his respects. One never knew who lay behind an animal's presence; this was part of why he'd been reluctant to have Raffles shot. His sister had admitted there were others with her skills. He suspected Lady Fwendi. Who else might there be?

Mademoiselle Toutournier's suite of rooms occupied half of the second storey, but was reached separately from the rest of the floor. They walked deeper into the school building, then ascended a twisting staircase. It emerged in the center of an airy, white-walled parlor, sparsely but comfortably furnished. Dark gold curtains covered glass-filled doors in one wall; where the curtains were incompletely pulled together, Ilunga saw the railing of a balcony. In two of the room's three other walls stood two wooden doors. The third wall, to his left as he came away from the staircase, was covered in empty bookcases.

He moved toward the balcony, skirting a sofa and an extremely broad desk. The gold curtains parted to show a crystal doorknob. He turned it and—

"Loongee! A room each!" Devil had opened all the apartment's other doors in the time it took Ilunga to approach one. "But what about your sister, eh? Can't have her sleepin with us bachelors, can we now." This was stated, not asked, with an over-obvious wink.

Lady Fwendi made a mock-tragic face. "I didn't realize how many were in your party! I thought Mr. Scranforth was a sort of secretary who could bunk with our groundskeeper. Clearly not.

"Mwadi shall share my rooms—it's no inconvenience to me for such a brief visit, and especially as my husband's away. And none at all, I hope, to you?" She directed the servants and pretty girls to distribute his and Devil's luggage as necessary, then left with Mwadi.

The slam of the door at the bottom of their private staircase recalled Ilunga to his deferred explorations. The door to the balcony opened easily. A leafy trellis with scraps of fabric woven between its slats provided a shallow pool of shade for the hammock tied to its supporting posts. Yet the air was warm. And still. And heavily scented with tobacco.

Going to the balcony's edge and leaning forward, Ilunga saw no obvious source for the smoke he smelled. His idle curiosity sprouted questions like a fledgling bird sprouts wing feathers.

Scranforth joined him. "Sure you don't mind me taking the biggest room, Loongee?"

The prince shook his head. "No." He craned his neck in a vain attempt to spot anything above. The vines growing out from the trellis defeated him.

"Yours has the best view—courtyard and the flower gardens. Nothin out my window but a bean plot and some sort of shack or shed or—"

"The washhouse?" Home of the nameless cat—and who knew what else? "Have you seen anyone enter it?"

Devil's clean-shaven jaw dropped an inch. "Righto! It'll be a parade of comely laundresses in and out—don't ask! Wouldn't trade places for the world! Come, let's set up an observation post."

Ilunga found no trace of tobacco smoke in the bedchamber Devil had claimed. Nor, when he retired to his own room, could he find any there.

He refreshed himself with a splash of perfumed water—not too cool—from a basin standing by a chest of drawers. He chose another shirt and put it on himself rather than call his boy back from Devil. Who was not as stupid as he pretended to be.

Neither was Ilunga.

His dress kilt of plaid linen would do for supper, he decided. Lady Fwendi would recognize her husband's sett and be softened by the compliment.

He passed Devil's half-open door and crept down the unfamiliar stairs. By the prince's reckoning he had an hour or more to explore. If come upon by anyone—his sister or hostess, say—he'd use the excuse of being lost. A patent lie, to be sure, but the actual truth, the thirst for knowledge instilled by his mother, would be obscured by his reputation for womanizing.

In fact, it was Prince Ilunga who came upon Mwadi and Lady Fwendi, and not the reverse. The two women were seated in the courtyard on which the back garden bordered, perfectly in the open. As he left the shelter of the school's back porch, his hostess was finishing what sounded like a speech of protest: "But he denounced Chawleigh to you! And you say he admits only that he works for an oil firm."

"Business. Government. How are they different? I trust neither of them," Princess Mwadi replied.

Lady Fwendi sat facing his direction. She looked up and saw him approach. "Prince?"

Ilunga tried for her hand again. It eluded him. "I couldn't help but overhear. You're talking about Devil? He's harmless enough."

"Harmless!" Mwadi spat on a brick for emphasis. "He shot you! He mutilated my monkey!"

"What! He hurt an innocent animal?" asked Lady Fwendi.

"Nothing of the sort—" Ilunga objected.

"He cut off Raffles's *thumbs*! Yes! An innocent and helpless— Ma'am! How can you laugh at such—such cruelty?"

Lady Fwendi shook her head. "No, I'm not laughing, merely— Child, your monkey Raffles, he is a colobus, yes? They are born this way naturally. All of them. Sans thumbs."

"They—"

"I told you Scranners was incapable of such a thing! Didn't I? He said the same!"

"Yes, but—"

"So you're ready to free me from my confinement?"

That was a new voice. It came, Ilunga saw, from a slender white man in loose brown trousers. Apparently he had emerged from behind the glossy hedge on the garden's far end. In his left hand he carried a curve-stemmed tobacco pipe. The right hand was hidden.

Ilunga tipped his bowler. "Pleased to meet you. I'm Prince Ilunga, House of Mwenda, Everfair's heir apparent. And your name?"

"Ah. Kleinwald. Alan Kleinwald."

Ilunga thought he must have come across that name before. But where? He lost track of the thought as Mr. Kleinwald came forward and held out his right hand. It was made, like Lady Fwendi's, like his father's, of brass.

The prince shook the man's prosthetic hand warmly. "How do you do?"

"All the better for being allowed out of hiding."

Ilunga felt no return of the pressure of his grip. A quick glance showed him that Kleinwald's prosthetic wasn't as sophisticated as the models he was used to. It was merely decorative: a metal cast of a man's open hand. "Why were you hiding? What from?"

Mwadi answered in Kleinwald's stead. "He hid from you and your mercenary so-called friend!" She stuck out her chin.

Lady Fwendi laid a restraining arm on his sister. "Herr Doctor Kleinwald was until recently imprisoned by the Italian authorities on the island of Nocra, in Ethiopia's Dahlak Archipelago."

The prince frowned. "So he escaped? Why is that a problem? I'm not Italian, and neither is Devil."

"Devil's an English agent—perhaps working also for these same Italians!" Mwadi shook off Lady Fwendi's touch and rose to interpose herself between the prince and Dr. Kleinwald. "Don't worry—you're under my protection!"

"Didi—"

"I've told you not to call me that!"

"Children! Calmly!"

From the washhouse came a long, flute-like whistle. Lady Fwendi stood too. "Supper's about to be served," she said. "I am decided. Prince, Mwadi, after you. Doctor Kleinwald, do you care to join us?"

Ilunga worried for a moment that Devil might not know where to go, but he came down the stairs in Gasser's train as the prince and princess entered the building. "Loongee!" he exclaimed. "Thought you'd given me the slip and rendez-voolayvoo'ed with one of the local lovelies!"

Under Mwadi's glare, Devil was seated at the high table's far end, with Lady Fwendi sitting at its head. Dr. Kleinwald took the chair to her right, opposite Ilunga on her left. Two instructresses occupied the places to *his* left; the plump one closest to him introduced herself as Miss Janota, which he knew from his years at court to be a Portuguese surname. She must be Angolan, then, like his mother. Whom she did slightly resemble.

Devil had an empty seat on one side and, unfortunately for him, the ugliest of the instructresses on the other. The ugliest and the unfriendliest as well, it seemed, for Devil's attempts to ingratiate himself to Miss Turtleface (Ilunga didn't bother learning her real name) by sopping up her spilled soup and disposing of her fish bones only resulted in frosty silence. From a seat off, Ilunga sensed its chill.

Across the table, Dr. Kleinwald picked negligently at his food. "Tell me," asked the prince, "if it's not rude of me to ask: Why had the Italians thrown you in jail?"

Pushing his dish away, the white man smoothed his black moustache thoughtfully. "My guess? Signore Quattrocchi found the presence of a German opposed to Atlantropa inconvenient. Publicly, though, they said it had to do with my work teaching at Lalibela Seminary."

"The Italians are Christians too, though. So why would—"

"They're a different denomination—a different branch."

Ilunga nodded his understanding. Europeans, he had learned, loved to split religious hairs.

"Besides, I myself was raised a Jew. Despite the chief priests' interest in my theories, some government officials backed the embassy's claim that this disqualified—"

A pleasant warmth against his left thigh distracted the prince. It could only be Miss Janota! Her own leg—no, her arm and hand—the pressure ebbed, then became a light and provocative friction, barely sensible even through his kilt's thin linen. Barely but wonderfully. Back and forth, back and forth . . . He opened his eyes. When had he closed them? No one seemed to have noticed. His sister was busy fending off the attentions of Devil, who had moved from the table's foot to the vacant place beside her. Lady Fwendi was intent on Dr. Kleinwald's plate, disjointing his newly served game bird, while the doctor himself gazed vaguely out over the tables crowding the rest of the dining room.

Ilunga gave Miss Janota a brief, sidewise look. Nothing in her face's expression indicated how busy her hands were. Why the subterfuge? Why not approach him later, less publicly?

Because she wanted something other than the simple joy of coupling: a favor from the man who would soon be king. His own experience had warned Ilunga that this was going to be the way of things.

With a dissatisfied sigh, Prince Ilunga captured the woman's groping fingers in his own, clasped them tightly, transferred them to her lap, and released them. Best not to engage in any promises—especially not those made without words. Best to seek fulfillment with others, later, elsewhere.

CHAPTER FIVE

March 1921
Ceylon

Bee-Lung knew she must stink. Surely her anger must flavor the droplets of her breath. There was nothing she could do to stop their broadcast, and Tink's stoic absorption of them along with Big Sister's spoken scolding only irritated her further. His feelings fed into her own, threatening to choke her.

"Come," she said. "Let's walk." Though he was a Dragon, her brother let her lead him out of the now familiar bungalow, along the graveled drive to the street running past Fort Frederick. A small girl carrying a pot of glue cooked from horse bones scurried to get out of their way as they continued onto the promontory. The stiff breeze there helped to disperse Bee-Lung's wrath.

She picked her favorite tactic: mirroring. Rational arguments such as he used on himself would win over Tink's mind, and the rest of him would follow.

"There's nothing you can do now to reverse your agreement with May Fourth on this tactic. Distribution is a fact," Bee-Lung said, facing her little brother calmly.

"Not entirely true," he replied. "We acted in accordance with their precepts in Tourane, in Kuala Lumpur, in Dacca, yes. And yes, I did make the offering here, and as the broom swept me with your cure it also dispersed the Spirit Medicine's spores. But even if the plants incorporate them as you hope—"

"As I calculate," Bee-Lung corrected him. A much more Tink-ish word.

"All right. If the plants accept fungal companionship as readily as you calculate, there are still two more steps. They must next be persuaded to spread a newly fruited generation of spores with their blooms' pollen. And then the inoculating blossoms must be harvested and used by worshippers. At which point you'd have us interfere."

Among the stones and shattered columns scattered around them, anyone could have hidden, their scent blown away before it could be tracked or recognized. Bee-Lung shepherded their course toward the trails winding down the cliffs' sides.

"So you doubt my teaching ability?" she asked, switching tactics.

"What?" Taken off guard, Tink had failed to follow Bee-Lung's mental leap.

She returned to logic, approaching her conclusion step by step. "Our Hindu recruits will be responsible for ensuring the butter-fly pea flowers manifest the Spirit Medicine in a properly trans-missible form. They will also see that all supplicants ask for and receive spore-infused garlands." She paused to pluck a sprig from a wind-stunted, silver-leafed tree, and tucked it in a pocket for later appreciation. "Why assume they haven't been trained for these tasks? Is it my skill in this area you doubt, or my commitment to our cause?"

"Bee-Lung! Neither!" The sound of Tink's shoes on the path's sparse soil ceased. Bee-Lung backed up and saw that her brother had halted behind the last bend. His eyes were tightly closed, his hands clasped together before his chest as if pulling each other off of his arms. "It's just that I wonder if what we're doing is—worth it? If it's right?"

"'Right'? The revolution to overcome the last remnants of cap-italist colonialism is beyond 'right'! It's essential to preventing a worldwide conflagration! It's—"

"We won't win the revolution with numbers alone. We need—more. Something more. We need our stories to erase theirs, to overcome."

Coming closer, Bee-Lung practically tasted her brother's internal struggle. "We won't win with numbers, perhaps. But they're a start."

Tink's eyes blinked open. "No they're not. Not a start in the proper direction. How much further are we going this way?"

She chose to take him literally. "We won't reach the beach; in a few more turns we'll come to a flattish area where this trail ends. Trana recommended it as a picnic site. From there the cliff drops sheer to the sea."

Taller, greener trees covered the tiny plateau. Threading her way through them, Bee-Lung avoided a group of white schoolboys gathered around a ministerial-looking man. He held something in his hands that seemed to fascinate them; in wayward bits of breeze she scented rust and rock powder.

Emerging from the woods' shadows she gloried in the freshness of the wind: air blown for miles over the ocean's unsullied waves. But quickly Tink caught her up, and the miasma of his questions floated out to envelop her.

She turned her face from the sky. "I can't read your thoughts," she reminded him. "Only your feelings. Ask me what you need to know."

"Have you ever successfully administered Spirit Medicine to someone who was unaware of what you did? Will you try doing that this time?"

"You already have that information."

"No! I'm unsure of everything! How even will our friends whom we've left behind provide proof that the method we've picked works?" Anger spiced Tink's anguish. "Will we poison them? Will the Spirit Medicine transform them into helpless slaves?"

"No, no, Little Brother." She grasped his strong wrists, pulled slowly downward to stroke the backs of his broad hands. Again and again and again. Grandmother had soothed him this way when they were young. "No, not poison—"

"Stealing their minds! Putting them in thrall—"

"Not so! They'll be free, truly free! Immune to the dangers inherent in hierarchy; invulnerable to the disease of capitalism. And once inoculated they can form cores with whomever they want." Cores that would be based on whatever stories they adopted as their truths. Bee-Lung had a good idea about how to give the best story the best chance.

Ceylon

Tink hung his head in shame. His sister had convinced him they would be doing no harm. How? Eyes lowered, he followed Bee-Lung back up the cliff, wishing he could have been half as persuasive as she was in his latest quarrel with Kwangmi.

He was a node. And he was Metal Dragon. His sister was Fire Rat. Her horoscope made her the perfect companion, but it hardly qualified her to be his leader. Even the advantage of her age should not have inclined him so irresistibly to go along with her plans. Could his submission be the Spirit Medicine's work? Perhaps it had to do with the special Spirit Medicine they'd absorbed together?

He didn't have the stomach to ask. He left her mounting the steps to Sevaria's verandah and continued walking, alone, to the tea shop where his love had agreed to meet him.

As he walked the afternoon rain set in, washing the air clean. Flags on ropes crossed the road, drooping as the falling water weighed them down. Each drop kissed the spot it landed on: stone, timber, mud, straw, flesh . . . The glass window of the tea shop reflected his somber face and framed it in diamond rivulets. Entering the darkness, he stumbled on a seam in the floorboards, but quickly regained his balance and homed in on Kwangmi's table. She sat alone.

Farther back, barely visible in the walls' and rainclouds' shadows, a bearded man stood behind a short counter. This would be the "wallah," the tea factory and shop's proprietor. Tink bowed in greeting. There were three more customers; all sat at the shop's other table. They were older, so he bowed to them as well before lowering himself to his wooden stool. A warm and fragrant pot already occupied the table's center. Reaching past it, Tink took Kwangmi's stub-nailed left hand in his right. "I see you got me a cup," he said.

"Of course." No smile. She poured for him—which could have been nothing more than an excuse to make him release her hand. When he attempted to repossess it she picked up the milk jug. "You must try your tea with this. Be sure to add a spoon of jaggery too." She gestured to a dish of sticky-looking brown crystals.

"All right." He managed to brush her sleeve with his as he took it.

Kwangmi heaved a heavy sigh. "Brother."

He waited. Behind the shop's now empty counter space came the noise of rain drumming faster and faster on the warehouse's tin roof. The old women at the table were waiting for Kwangmi to say more too, their conversation suspended.

The rain died suddenly. He couldn't stand the silence any longer. "Sister," he began. "I owe you an apology. My explanation to you in Jaffna was obviously no good. I'm sorry."

"Are you sorry? Indeed? For what?"

"For—" For failing to satisfy his beloved. Which he seemed to be doing again. "For getting it wrong."

"We can't lie! We can *not*—not to each other! Brother Tink!" Kwangmi slapped the tabletop with both palms. "I know you don't believe any of that irrational rubbish you spouted!"

His tea had slopped over his cup's brim. He'd overfilled it. "You don't accept that I wish to marry you for eternity? How can you say so?"

"Because it's not true!" Kwangmi leaned forward, oblivious to the puddle running to stain her jacket's front. "Stop telling me stories you think I want to hear!" she hissed. The customers at the other table nodded sternly in agreement.

"But I want to spend my whole life with you—"

"Yes! That smells right—and with the Chens and Raghu too! But you will! You do!"

"—and ever after."

"'After'? After you live, you die!"

"After that."

"After you die, you're dead." Now the women at the neighboring table shook their heads. Going by looks, Tink judged them to be Hindu, but whatever their religion, it promised more than that.

He'd had enough sleep since Jaffna. He chose his words with better care. "We belong with each other beyond time's limits. Beyond our bodies' bounds. The Spirit Medicine was the first thing to connect us; from that connection we have grown closer and closer. Our marriage will celebrate the profound depth of our togetherness."

"Bee-Lung approves?"

"What?" Shock at Kwangmi's question made him draw back.

"Big Sister Bee-Lung. She has a unique association with you, doesn't she? You two share ties the rest of us can't."

"A mother and father, yes, but our simple family relationship alone—"

"Not that. Your second dose of Spirit Medicine. The one she took with you; it was a very particular strain she used. Very exclusive. Wasn't it?"

He had to answer her if he wanted to maintain the faintest whiff of integrity.

"Yes."

Ceylon and Aboard Xu Mu

Even with a month's accumulations, Bee-Lung estimated her baggage would take up only one trunk. Sevaria had sent Trana to help her pack. Bee-Lung sent her right back. Then she realized she needed fresh paper to wrap around her clay pots. She'd removed her tools and supplies from her workbasket to make room for dried plants and other delicate samples she'd gathered during her stay. If left unprotected, the pots might knock together and break. Paper—or if paper was less plentiful here than at home, sawdust, lengths of cheap cloth—or better yet, some way to protect the samples separately so she could empty and reassemble her workbasket. No telling how soon she'd need it again.

In Sevaria's chamber all was bright chaos: scarves and kameezes crowded the bed's surface; Jadida knelt before the empty slippers encircling it, shuffling them so their colors matched the gowns and trousers laid out above. Trana and her mistress bent over the mirrored chest, scooping fistfuls of jewelry from the top drawer into a metal box. Bee-Lung made her request.

"Specimens?" Sevaria asked. "Film cans should be big enough. How many will you need? We can spare ten or so. Jadida, leave those and take Madam Ho to the cellar."

Film cans were like lidded metal plates. Bee-Lung found she was able to enclose multiple plant samples in each, and could even layer some of them between peach-colored silk torn from the ruined dress. The cans didn't all fit in her trunk, though, so she left her room once more to search out a rope or belt to strap them together.

Swearing male voices came from the direction of the back garden. Earlier, when Bee-Lung had returned from her walk with Tink, the yard surrounding Sevaria's house had been empty. Now a cart filled the rearmost portion of the house's drive, and a gang of serving men struggled to pack it neatly with a pile of ungainly appearing film equipment. "Hey, Cousin," she shouted to one she remembered from a trip into the neighboring hills. "Do you have a length of cord I can use?" She held out her hands to show the desired measure.

"Ha! What does it look like?" The man hopped down from the

cart's high bed. Darker-skinned than Raghu, he wore his hair in a neat knot at the back of his head. "No. If you want to secure your luggage, better give it to me."

"It is such precious cargo." Bee-Lung frowned to show her worry.

The man's name was Gopal. He frowned back in a way that quickly became a flirtatious grin. "How could it be otherwise? A woman of your stature wouldn't be concerned with anything petty. Let me take care of it for you. I'll—"

"Madam Ho! I hope you aren't being annoyed?" Jadida had appeared. She stood now between Bee-Lung and Gopal.

"Of course not. This man is going to bring down my trunk and the bundles I've made. Follow me." She turned to go in the way she'd come out.

"Through that door? No! He's dirty!"

Perplexed, Bee-Lung peered around the servant woman's shoulder. Gopal was sweating, yes, but no more covered in grime than Jadida herself. "What do you mean?" She thought further. "And how are we to get all your lady's belongings loaded in time for our flight if he can't come in to carry them?"

"He and the rest of the loaders must use the *back* door. Trana and I will supervise. We're just now ready for them—I was sent to make sure you had no further needs."

"There's nothing."

The path the men were made to take between first floor and cart seemed unnecessarily circuitous to Bee-Lung, but they moved quickly, and by the time the afternoon's rain began the household was on its way to the airfield. She was glad for the manner in which the water washed the busy air of the city's distractions. And of most others. Bee-Lung and Sevaria and the two servants rode in a separate carriage, a cab, but Gopal's very interested aroma floated forward to her from the cart he rode in behind them.

The rain intensified as soon as they arrived. There was time enough to wait for it to lessen, so they did—the laborers and drivers huddling in the mud beneath the cart, as Bee-Lung was able to see while shuttering the window on her side of the cab.

"We're in no danger of being stopped," said Sevaria. "Now that Rima's gone ahead, Governor Manning is eager to see us leave, too."

Bee-Lung hadn't needed reassurance on that score, but it seemed the film star thought she did. She nodded in calm agreement, then realized the shutters made the cab so gloomy inside that Sevaria wouldn't have seen this. "Yes."

"Your brother is waiting on board?"

No. "He'll be here in time. He knows *Xu Mu*'s schedule; he's the one who drew it up."

Soon the rain had all but ceased, and the field's drummer signaled *Xu Mu* to lower its baskets. The drivers and loaders crawled out from their shelter. The loaders began working with the direction and assistance of a woman employed by the airfield; the cart's driver helped them too, but the cabbie busied himself with his bicycle's furnace and gears.

Bee-Lung rode up on the first basket's first trip, alongside her samples. She was able to commandeer Gopal's presence and bring him with her. Then she got him to carry the trunk and film cans forward to her cabin, though his well-muscled arms and back ought to have relegated him to working the winch.

She thrust the door curtains aside and went into the cabin ahead of him. While both Hos had been away, their shared space here on *Xu Mu* had become the temporary home of others—Ma Chau, it smelled like, and her Dacca recruit Kafia. Those two had been happy here. Bee-Lung smiled.

Gopal came in and she had him set the trunk against the corridor-end bulkhead. "What now, Cousin?" he asked. "Shall I return to the ground and prepare another load?"

"I'm not Sevaria. I'm not in charge of you. What do you want to do? You can go back down and check with her."

"I would rather stay up here." He laced his fingers together, bowed, and raised his head. "And I'd be honored if you let me kin with your crew."

As she had suspected: Gopal wished to join *Xu Mu*'s mission. But how did he know to use the word "kin"? "You're aware we may never return here? Friends, family—you must abandon them. You can't expect them to wait for you to come back."

"The revolution is my family."

Well. This *was* serious. "The revolution?"

"The way we're going to change the world and rid ourselves of the parasite owners. I have heard lessons taught by May Fourth's pilgrims. I traveled here from Jaffna to help." His genuine concern for the future wound around his sexual curiosity like a tendriling vine.

So young. Men of his age barely knew their bodies, much less their minds. But let him find that out for himself. "And you can help—absolutely! The sawan is coming. We need Hindu infiltrators on the ground—there's so much work to do!"

"I am Hindu, but also Dalit. I won't be welcome inside the temple until the festival, only allowed to dispose of its garbage."

"You don't know what that means, 'Dalit'?"

"A Dalit is a peasant." So Bee-Lung recalled from Tink's summarizing.

"Yes, but worse. Poorer. More deeply despised." He shook his head, clenched his long-palmed hands, made a visible effort to relax them. "My journey here—I walked. No money to buy passage on a boat or anything else. So I walked."

The deck dipped. Another load had come up through *Xu Mu*'s main hatch while they talked. Also there was a faint trace of Sevaria in the air, growing more definite by the moment—a live scent, not mere exudations from her belongings. The secondary hatch must be open and its winch deployed. The film star would board soon.

Gopal was ready to be recruited; with every breath Bee-Lung inhaled his thick truth and willingness—and also the low but steady thrum of his arousal. "Shall I buy your work contract?" she asked. Official power over him would put an end to any question of romantic involvement.

"I don't have one yet."

The cabin was crowded with stacked crates and hung with hammocks and dry lamps; to get closer to him she stepped over things and ducked under them. "I'll ask for the loan of your services till we reach our next port, since that's where Sevaria's headed."

Their next port: Zanzibar, where they would make the movie Governor Manning had prohibited.

"As for a permanent position, I'll consult my brother. Meanwhile, yes, you'd better help with the rest of the luggage."

"Then you'll take me on?"

"That's not what I said. But let's go." She saw him realize he blocked her path to the door and move. Good. Though it would be difficult for a while to harmonize his actions with those of the Spirit Medicine's previous imbibers, the quickness of Gopal's understanding boded well for smooth integration. Tink would have no objections to Gopal, she was sure. And Kafia could be inoculated at the same time as him, which would please Ma Chau.

However, there was one slight obstacle: before long the two new recruits would need additional kin. The complexity of the operations planned for sawan meant that all their freshly made cores had been left behind to run things. All but one.

Arriving in the hold she finally caught Tink's odor, disappointed and faint. It was faint partly due to distance and partly because it was masked by Sevaria's scent; the star had climbed from her basket, which she shared with Jadida, to fuss over a tall, thin, canvas-covered piece of equipment. Immediately after the rest of the hold's occupants turned to greet Bee-Lung, Sevaria did too. When fully accepted she would act with them in unison.

"Hello! Our tripod at least is doing well."

"If you won't need that thing while we're in the air, why not store it here?"

Sevaria pursed her lips. "Yes, you're right; it won't be needed. Not until we approach the island—perhaps not even then, if I arrange a stable-enough camera placement for the aerial shots." She tilted her head consideringly. "Or perhaps . . . perhaps I should dangle it from a rope as we descend? It will spin and wobble and swing back and forth, which is normally a bad idea. But that could signify how dizzy The Sleeper feels on waking after a century. It could . . . it could . . ." The star's words stopped, though her thoughts seemed to continue on.

Bee-Lung left her to them and went to the passenger hatch. Tink and Kwangmi were riding up together, but something was wrong. She peered out. They stood in opposite corners of the cargo basket, and faced in opposite directions. Why?

Tink told her in their cabin as he removed his few personal belongings. "She turned me down. It's the second time."

"Turned you down for what?"

"Marriage."

"Oh, yes. I knew you wanted to marry Kwangmi. But why?"

"That's exactly what she asked. She didn't like any of my answers." He pulled a long wooden knife sheath off of a line of pegs above the door.

"That wasn't going to be in Sevaria's way there," Bee-Lung told him. She and Sevaria would share this cabin for the three days of *Xu Mu*'s flight over the Indian Ocean. Tink was shifting to general quarters.

"It's the first thing Yoka and I made." He smelled hurt; would this knife heal him? Maybe; maybe he'd be healed by the memories it carried.

He dragged a heavy shirt, a woolen coat, and a pair of leather-soled, toed socks from a bamboo box. "Let her put her belongings on top. I won't need anything else out of here." Arms full, he left without saying farewell. But after all, neither was going anywhere without the other.

The door curtains stayed open. Gopal's eagerness for Bee-Lung's company came through it almost as clearly as Sevaria's Spirit Medicine–amplified artistic excitement. Then they were there.

Gopal bore two bulging wicker suitcases under his arms and a lacquered metal pitcher-and-bowl set in his hands. Sevaria smiled at Bee-Lung. "Where shall he put them?" she asked.

Bee-Lung pointed to Tink's box. Gopal juggled his burdens, balanced them on the box's top, then went back to stand by still-smiling Sevaria. He smiled too. The air became clotted with anticipation.

A subtle increase in the tiny draft entering around the cabin's half-shut porthole let Bee-Lung know that *Xu Mu* was moving. There: the snap home of the retractable mooring line strummed along the envelope's netting. Almost immediately the aircanoe's prow swung around to starboard to put them on course. Even the most inexperienced passengers must feel that. The time had passed for anyone not traveling to Zanzibar to depart. Yet Sevaria seemed unfazed by her loader's continued presence.

Bee-Lung supposed she had better make her request now. But Sevaria spoke first.

"We're underway? Good." She bestowed a sweeter smile on Gopal. "Fetch me my chair—and the flower-printed cushion." He bowed and left.

His steps and odor faded. "You can't mind him staying aboard! He's *perfect*!" The filmmaker laid a perfumed hand on Bee-Lung's arm. "Exactly the looks and manner I had in mind when I wrote the role of Doctor Shin." In the film's version of the Spirit Medicine, Dr. Shin was the grandson of its creator.

Bee-Lung assumed a severe expression. "He must work while he's with us."

"Ye-e-e-ess, but he must also learn to act. There's only a little time before we land. Message Rima to meet us again sooner than you said—so she can help teach him. Meanwhile, treat him as you treat the rest of my staff."

They talked further. Gopal returned with the chair and multiple flowered cushions. Sevaria dispatched him again to aid Trana in double-checking the well-being of her cameras and lights and so on. Gradually, Bee-Lung allowed herself to be persuaded not to start training what was probably going to be a fairly unnecessary and quite temporary crewmember.

But he did remain a desirable recruit.

Leaving the star to settle comfortably into the hammock she'd selected, Bee-Lung exited the cabin. General quarters filled the gondola's middle section. The corridor divided it evenly; both Tink and Gopal were in the half on her right, *Xu Mu*'s port side. She opened the door curtain and went in.

The cabin's portholes were shaded so that those who needed to could sleep. It was quiet: from aft came a sneeze, a whisper, the low slide and suction of sexual congress. But Tink was much nearer, showing Gopal to an untenanted hammock. She called her brother to her. He responded and brought the new man. She held the curtains apart. "Come," she added for Gopal's benefit.

Their infirmary occupied the tiny space just beyond the companionway leading down to the bridge pod. Bee-Lung had taken advantage of its jut beyond the pod to install a waist-high counter holding a permanent basin and drain. Her square workbasket, reconstituted, rested awkwardly within the basin's curves, where she had instructed the loaders to leave it.

"Sit." She gestured to the stool over the pisshole. "Little Brother, will you step back out to give me more room? But remain within reach. I may need help."

Gopal gazed up with suddenly wide eyes. "Will it hurt?"

Foolish child. "No." She opened the workbasket's lid. "Unless that's what you want." Which jar? At this point in the journey she'd tried them all—though the strain of Spirit Medicine administered to Sevaria still needed a second recipient.

What did she know about this man, or about the woman Kafia who she proposed to kin him with? Hardly anything. Not enough.

Unstoppering all nine jars, she dropped their corks in her jacket's front pocket. "Here," she said. She picked up the basket, waved it under the recruit's nose. "Choose one."

Indian Ocean, Aboard Xu Mu, to Morne, Seychelle Islands

Tink wished he could walk away and leave Bee-Lung to do her work without him. Though he didn't know where he'd go if she wasn't insisting pretty powerfully that he stay in the infirmary's entrance. Kwangmi's scent drifted up from the companionway—partly an irritation, partly a delight. Entirely too much a temptation.

His love was not averse to coupling with him—or with any of the others in their core. He didn't blame her; sex, though not compulsory, almost always made the ties between core kin stronger. He'd seen that. Sex between cores, even. None of that was a problem; it wasn't exclusivity he wanted.

So what was it?

If he followed Kwangmi's trail down into the bridge, he'd only be in her way. He'd be a nuisance. He'd appear weak. He needed to reflect, to stew in his own meditative juices, away from the influence of others' odors and feelings. What did this latest rejection mean? He needed to find a way to be alone. Perhaps he could climb up the netting around Xu Mu's gasbags.

Tink laughed softly to himself at the image that brought to mind.

"What's funny? Pay attention, Little Brother!"

"All right." He craned his neck forward to show Bee-Lung how intently he was watching her. She prepared the Spirit Medicine tea for drinking the same way he'd seen her prepare it several times, pulling threads from the pot Gopal had picked and chopping them up in a small wooden bowl with other ingredients: ginseng roots; ginkgo leaves, blossoms, and nuts; yellow horse stems; and a crumbling brown paste his sister had always refused to identify as anything but what it looked like, which was dried mud.

Squeezed down onto the stool where he sat, Gopal's big body no longer radiated strength. His face was like a child's on its first trip to the sea: awed, scared, giddy with expectation. "You choose this?" Tink asked. "You invite the revolution to take you over? To live inside your skin? There's no way to reverse the inoculation process. Be very sure."

Anger tightened Gopal's face and edged his smell. "Of course I'm sure! The revolution's going to save the world—don't assume I'm ignorant just because I'm Dalit!"

Bee-Lung stretched out one hand to cover the recruit's head. "Hush! Peace, boy!" She stroked back his black hair.

She turned to Tink again. "Why agitate him—especially now? Look how far he has come. Every step was a decision."

"I've seen enough," he replied. "I'll send you someone else."

"Perhaps Kafia? We'll be ready for her soon."

"Fine. In a moment, then." Tink withdrew as gravely and deliberately as possible, though he knew it was pointless to try to disguise his frustration from his Spirit Medicine–linked sister.

Equally pointless to avoid Kwangmi. He stopped outside the door to his new quarters but didn't go through. Instead he walked back along the passage to the companionway and descended.

There she stood: dark against the forward windows, blithe, serene, focused on what lay ahead. He made up his mind to grasp the nettle and made his way to her side.

Silently though he approached, she knew he was there. Naturally. Without looking, she reached out one hand for him to take. Her hand was cool and her grip firm, like his own. "You don't mind?" she asked.

"Mind what?" Below, the edge of the shadow trailing *Xu Mu*'s silk envelope teemed with white seabirds. They flew in purposeful circles, a hunter's stratagem. Dragons hunted too. "Do I mind that you won't risk deepening our commitment to one another? Yes. Of course I mind. But I'll wait. Eventually you'll decide I'm right."

"No!" Now she did look at him. "That's not what I meant! And if you persist in misunderstanding me I'll ask Bee-Lung to sever me from our core!"

"You won't!"

"I will!"

"She can't." Perhaps his sister could do such a thing, though no one had yet tried it.

"At *Xu Mu*'s next stop, I'll leave."

Tink still held his love's hand. He tightened his hold on it. "All right then. As you wish. I give up. What did you mean?"

No use. Kwangmi pulled to free her hand, and Tink knew he had to let it go. "You don't care."

"Yes I do." He cared too much. "Tell me."

Raghu's feet appeared at the top of the ladder down from the main gondola. "Tell me," Tink repeated.

"We're heading straight for the Seychelles. That's what I wondered about. We're not mooring first at the Maldives, as you wanted us to do. As you voted to do, and urged everyone else to vote."

A good node gave way to his group's wishes. "One British protectorate is much like another. No, you're not talking about a real concern of mine. There's no cable station to infiltrate in either place." May Fourth's plan was for *Xu Mu* to fly back to China by way of Arabia, and continue their mission along that route. It would take time, months—maybe years—for the spores they sowed now to knit together into a complete messaging network. Meanwhile, additional missions would use its newborn fragments, test their scope and capabilities. The simultaneous inoculations of human beings could go in any order.

And hopefully the Russians' rival organism would never become so widespread as to compete. No one on *Xu Mu* had yet encountered any Russian inoculants. The unfortunate consequences visited on some Europeans who'd received it had scared away people from more civilized countries.

Raghu came to stand with them, eyes and perspiration full of confusion. Tink understood his puzzlement: Kwangmi radiated hurt and pride at the same time, while Tink himself must reek of spoiled desire. "What's wrong?" the Bharatese man asked. He slung an arm over each of their shoulders.

"Nothing, Little Brother," Tink lied.

"Obviously that's not true," scolded Kwangmi. "Tink wishes to form a separate alliance with me within the core."

"What? How?"

"Marriage. A contract."

"Between just you two?"

"Didn't she just say so?" Tink ducked out of Raghu's loose embrace. "But since Kwangmi's not in favor of the idea we're not carrying it out. Nothing's happening. As I said. Nothing."

He changed the topic. "Where's Kafia?"

"With Ma Chau, in the hold," Raghu replied.

"Then excuse me." Rushing to the ladder, Tink climbed up it two rungs at a time. Once clear of the hatch he slowed. He had promised to bring to Bee-Lung her patient's potential coremate, but he could smell that he still had plenty of time.

The curtains were open on both crew quarters' entrances. Snoring and sleep odors wafted out of those on his left, where for the next few days he would hang his hammock. More activity was happening in the compartment on his right: whispers and farts and worry filled its exhalations.

He passed into *Xu Mu*'s hold, grateful for its spaciousness. Ma Chau and her new protégée sat on the far forward catwalk, legs dangling. He ascended to their level, made his way around to them, and made his announcement. Ma Chau accompanied Kafia to the infirmary and agreed to shepherd the newly made partial core to one of the oversize hammocks reserved for first nights.

Then he was alone. The hold was somewhere he hadn't considered. He would have claimed it as his retreat and strung up a hammock—if only they hadn't packed it so full. Though that was probably the reason for its abandonment.

Nearest to Tink stood crates of minerals destined for factories in Everfair's industrial heart, Manono: sheet mica and calcite, mostly, and a tin locker of low-grade gemstones. Filling the more accessible area by the door to the corridor were water barrels and fruit baskets, consumables needed during their flight; between these and the Manono-bound shipment lay bolts and bundles of superior-quality textiles: diaphanous fabrics dyed purple, pink, green, blue, and black, sewn with beads of quartz and fringed with coins—luxury goods meant for sale to Zanzibar's sheikhas, and perhaps to a few Seychelle merchants as well. The hatch his core had leapt out of on their last mission was barely visible in the shining welter of goods surrounding it. His love's injunction to him that night to "figure it out" replayed in his memory.

He had attempted what Kwangmi asked, but to no avail.

Two skylights overhead and a high line of slits in the outer bulkheads let in the day's gradually dimming light. *Xu Mu* chased the setting sun, but would never catch up with it. Soon night would settle over them. And there was yet another night after this to pass before arriving at Victoria, which was only the next stop on their voyage. He and Kwangmi must somehow adjust to the intermingling of each other's dreams.

As was standard practice, their whole core had been assigned to the same quarters. Tink switched hammocks with one of the Chen sisters, who was happy to give him her spot by the door. He willed himself to go to sleep quickly, so that when Kwangmi came in from her shift on the bridge he'd be unconscious. To his surprise that worked. He woke early, of course, but was able to leave without disturbing anyone. A swift sniff between the curtains on the doorway across the corridor assured Tink that Gopal and Kafia had begun a satisfactory bond.

He spent most of that day at the bridge pod's forward windows, enjoying the view. His shift took him to the aft end of the pod around noon; from there things looked about the same. *Xu Mu*'s rough-edged silhouette trailed behind them over a wave-wrinkled sea. The aircanoe's height flattened what must be fifteen-foot crests into silver tiger stripes against a background of dark water.

When his love came down the ladder to relieve him at the helm, Tink left without lingering, without voicing his resentment over her rejection. Though that was certain to be apparent. The best he could do was refrain from putting his thoughts into words.

Another night. This time slumber was denied him. Kwangmi's entrance was his cue to get up and go out. He drifted quietly between hold, infirmary, and bridge. Sponges wan with hours of exposure flickered and subsided. At last dawn blazed up at him as he climbed down to the bridge. Soon there were flocks of birds keeping pace with *Xu Mu*, their glide seeming stationary. And then a grey smudge rose over the horizon, resolving into Mahé Island, and then they were mooring at the Morne Seychellois mast.

Tink was included in one of the two landing parties. He felt glad to be leaving Kwangmi behind, but sad also. The cargo basket descended to a crudely built platform on a brush-strewn hillside and its other passengers—not his core—dispersed with parcels of fabric, bags of treated sponges, and bundles of metal tools. The earlier party, Bee-Lung's, had gone out of range. The landing area was practically deserted; the Seychelles didn't receive many aircanoes. One loader went up to *Xu Mu*'s hold to help with the final cargo basket, leaving just two loaders on the ground to receive and store its goods.

And here was where those goods would go: an open-sided wooden shed huddled against the platform's posts, with a few logs piled in one of its five bays. Crew and loaders stowed *Xu Mu*'s imports on simple plank shelves in a second bay. The other three were completely empty.

Beyond the shed, a stony trail led down to the town in one direction and up to the mountains in the other. His sister's scent came wafting solo to his nose. "Little Brother?" Leaping off of a boulder, Bee-Lung ran toward him with cupped hands. "Look! I found it blown free of its branch—no need to pluck it! So strange! So rare and beautiful!"

In her hands rested a small, fragile-looking brown parasol, about the right size for a moth to carry. "Yes, lovely. What is it?"

"The fruit of a jellyfish tree—this island is the only place they grow!"

"And what is it used for?"

She emitted annoyance. "Must everything be useful?"

Wasn't that what beauty meant?

His sister's odor calmed and sweetened. "I forget your bias some-times. To me, a thing's function is determined by its attractiveness—not the other way round."

He thought of an example. "Miss Bailey."

"Yes, exactly. Her looks make her an excellent actress."

Bee-Lung turned her head right, then left, to scan their surround-ings. "Where shall I leave this while we check on Miss Bailey's headway and see about passing on Sevaria's newest instructions? The rest of my core has already left to meet with our favored merchants—we can coordinate our return with theirs."

A table stood in the shade of a palm; Bee-Lung built a little en-closure of stones there and deposited her prize inside. She laid a dried frond from the sheltering tree over its top and they followed the wide, gently sloping path down to Victoria. The path became a road. The road led all the way through the town, ending at the foot of a long, sun-warmed pier.

Here, not up in the Morne, was where the Seychellois conducted their business. Low buildings flanked the road and crept out onto the pier, some stinking of dead fish, some broadcasting the sensual aroma of freshly cured vanilla pods, some a tantalizing mélange of scents impossible to separate and identify.

Unmistakable, though, the tangy sweat of drinkers and the sour ferment of the alcohol they consumed. Between cracks in the tavern's windowless walls came the low, threatening grumbles of eternally unsatisfied men. Tink didn't want to go in. "How do we know she left word for us here?" he asked.

"It's not certain that she did, only very, very likely; Sevaria's paying her a bonus for each message we retrieve. What would you do in her circumstances?"

He would take advantage of any chance of that bonus that presented itself. He pulled open the tavern's door. The reek intensified and the noise level dropped.

"Greetings." Tink shifted to French from the Cantonese he and Bee-Lung used when alone. Sudden silence followed. He stepped into it. The daylight at his back mixed with dimmer illumination filtering in through fishnets hung over a wide door in the room's far side.

A moment the silence held. Then it broke like a spider's web. "Greetings back at you." A woman smelling of seaweed and soapsuds came forward. "I'm your hostess, Miss Miora. What is your desire? Food? Beverages?"

"A message," Bee-Lung said, stepping from behind him as he bowed. She bowed too. "We believe a boat or aircanoe's drummer may have entrusted you with news of one of our former companions."

Miss Miora gave more of a nod than a bow. "Yes. It will be yours when you prove you're who it's meant for."

"Surely we've done that just by asking."

Tink didn't want to stand there arguing. He didn't like the odor of self-interest rising off of the customers—eight men, by his count—and he especially didn't like the tavern's relative darkness. It would bring him more deeply under the Spirit Medicine's sway.

He pulled a small jade rod from his shirt's cuff. "This ought to establish our credentials." He bowed again and offered it with a flourish.

"It does!" The rod vanished into the hostess's many-pocketed vest. "Come with me and I'll deliver what was put in writing for you and try to answer any questions about it you may have." Miss Miora led them not to a more confined space but to the far doorway. She swept the nets covering it aside.

His sister's faint disapproval pervaded the air between them as she passed. "You paid too much," she said beneath her breath. Before Tink could defend himself they were outside, on the pier, in the blessed sun, the warm breeze cleansing his skin.

The message was painted in green ink on melon-colored silk, the words English. English was the Seychelles Islands' official language since Britain's recent acquisition of them from the ailing French Empire. But reading it was still a secondary skill.

At any rate, what Miss Bailey had to say was vague and needed no obscuring:

Leaving Mogadishu now on my fourth leg. And I ain't no table! If you took off out of Trinco five markets after I left Jaffna like you was saying, you could still be a long ways behind me. Maybe when I get to Zanzibar you want me to wait for you to catch up? Let me know. But don't worry what I'll do if you're slow as I expect. I got a plan to go off on a little adventure of my own.

CHAPTER SIX

April 1921
Kalima, Everfair

Mwadi kicked the base of the naked mooring mast. Tricked! She kicked it again. So what if it hurt her? Buffalo-headed Ilunga had managed to leave her behind. She deserved to be in pain.

She tipped back her head and yelled uselessly at the cloud-covered sky. Already *Okondo*'s purple-and-red gas bag had vanished into the grey distance.

How would she get home?

At least she wasn't alone. Raffles scampered along the landing platform's rail, chittering in excitement. He adored new places, new sights and sounds. "Come," the princess ordered him. She left the platform's center for its edge and held out one arm. Her monkey ran to receive the treat she was training him to expect. Gathering him up, she gave him a somewhat limp-skinned grape from her front pocket. "Let us return to Mam'selle Toutournier's establishment," she said. It was the only sensible thing to do.

Evening was falling, and the night that followed its fall would be overcast and starless. The two warehouse workers who had escorted her up the bluff to the mast were gone home, probably to eat their suppers, but it was still light enough to find her way down the stairway without stumbling on its muddy steps.

A soft drizzle began. Nothing heavy; she didn't do much to respond to it, just pulled her silk shawl over her hair. Forge and workshop fires lighted her way through town. Throughout recent growth, Kalima had stayed true to its semi-industrial roots.

As she approached its outskirts, though, the gardens favored by the Poet and Mam'selle her wife burgeoned. By the time Mwadi reached their home, the white-graveled way before her was bordered solely by fence-covering vines and damp, green-scented darkness.

Insects fluttered around the pierced brass globe suspended from the ceiling of the house's portico, a style of lamp originating here, in the land of her birth.

The door was European, though—solid wood, with only a tiny window. She knocked for attention on the window's glass. "Hello?" Her voice sounded too timid. "Hello! I'm back!" She raised a fist to knock louder and the door opened.

It was Mam'selle Lisette. "What's the difficulty? I thought you were to continue on to Kisangani tonight. Is there a change of plans? You need a bed?"

"I've been abandoned!"

"No! Come in, child, come." Mam'selle swung the door wider and stepped aside. "Daisy!" she called over her shoulder. "Our guest is returned!"

A fire burned on the entrance room's raised hearth. Its warmth should be unnecessary so near the Equator. Mwadi lowered her shawl. Earlier there'd been no embers here, no ashes, just a vase of flowering branches—apricot, she had been told.

"Abandoned?" Mam'selle asked. "Here, have a seat. This is Daisy's chair, the closest to the fire—or would you rather mine? You and Raffles may share."

A creaking stair announced the Poet's advent. "Princess? Did your brother bring his friend with him again?"

"My brother and his so-called friend have gone off without me!"

"Gone off? Flown away on *Okondo*? They've left you behind?"

"Yes. *Yes. Yes!*"

"That's not very nice of them." The Poet went to stand by the fire. Its rosy flickering softened the roughness of her weathered face and left the time-loosened folds of her throat in shadow.

"'Not very nice' indeed!" Mam'selle took the sting from her

mockery by clasping her wife's left hand. "He vies for the crown! Of course he isn't 'very nice'!" She sat with practiced grace. "Come, let us strategize! Let us talk more freely than we could before, now we're blessed with the absence of interfering enemies!"

Kisangani, Everfair

Ilunga giggled to himself as Gasser carried the last of Didi's belongings out of the cabin they'd been forced to share. She would be so angry! He loved to see his sister struggling to subdue her temper—when young he used to tease her for just that reason.

A knock sounded on the cabin's doorway and Devil's head thrust between its curtains. "Swear we're going faster now!" he declared. "Sure you didn't shove your sister's luggage from the hatch?"

"Safe in the hold, I promise." Though its retrofit had moved *Okondo*'s "hold" up onto its former deck, open to all the elements. "We actually *are* going faster—my orders." Captain Nenzima had fussed at the request but obeyed. As any subject should—especially a woman. "We'll arrive after dark, but I guarantee some fun before we retire."

It was late, but not too late, when they glided at last over Kisangani's famous falls. The churning waters shimmered under lights made golden by the night's mist. With pride the prince ushered his companion along the gangplank to the mooring tower's lift. At his nod Gasser engaged the steam engine, and they descended toward its noisy chugging and the competing beat of the loaders' drums. "Got to modernize this," Devil proclaimed as they touched the ground. The drums finished, making his next words far too loud: "Quieter with oil!"

Ilunga laughed off the moment's awkwardness. "Spare me your European jests! You know as well as any that the truly silent motor is a mere dream!" He got in the open door of the carriage the queen had sent and made sure only Devil followed him inside.

The white man spoke first. "'Pologies, Loongee. Didn't mean to spoil any—"

"I asked you not to mention it!"

"Didn't think there'd be any harm in—"

"You didn't think at all! Why can't you wait? Why can't you just for once do as *I say*! The king hasn't abdicated yet, I'm not on the throne yet, and I haven't yet approved your plans for exploring Lake Edward."

"You sayin you won't?"

Ilunga threw back his head in exasperation. "No!" he shouted.

The sweating face of Gasser appeared in the carriage's window. "Prominence?" the boy gasped. Home. Even the night air was hot for running. The carriage pulled ahead for a moment and the boy sped his pace to draw level again. "Is all well?" he asked.

"Yes," said the prince, lowering and smoothing down his tone. "Yes. All is well." And would be.

Kalima, Everfair

After a lengthy planning session over maps and chocolate, Mwadi believed herself too excited to sleep. But Mam'selle insisted on her retiring. "You've had a fatiguing journey today, and who knows how far you'll have to go tomorrow? And by what means? Rest while you can. There are multiple factions with which you'll need to negotiate on your arrival."

At first Mwadi's fears of sleeplessness seemed justified. And worth quarreling about: neither of her hostesses were following their own advice. With the window of her room cracked open, she overheard their murmuring conversation, inescapable as perfume. But enough distance lay between their bed and hers to reduce their words to nonsense. Eventually it made of them a soothing lullaby.

She woke early to a knock on her door and a startled monkey. "Enter," she commanded, sitting up and holding her arms open for Raffles's embrace.

It was the Poet at the door, wrapped in a full robe of white cotton. "Will you breakfast with me? Lisette won't be getting up for a while yet."

"You've of course sent a servant to find out about the next air-canoe flying to Kisangani?" If she hadn't left Hafiza aboard *Okondo* she wouldn't need to ask about someone else's maid. She could have sent her own.

"A servant? There's a girl who comes twice a market to help with the baking and laundry and so on. But it's faster to drum an in-quiry. I'll do that next.

"Our washroom is on the ground floor. Come to the back garden when you're finished?"

There was a sink, a shower stall, a tall mirror, a foot bath—for too many weeks the makeshift hygiene available between Cairo and home had had to suffice. Though Raffles loudly demon-strated his corresponding joy over Everfair's more civilized accommodations—turning taps and opening drains while hooting with delight—Mwadi resisted the urge to dawdle there. Picking him up, she stepped out of the washroom onto a stone-paved path.

The sharp slaps and deep thumps of a transmission from the neighborhood's message center stirred the fresh dawn air. She should learn to translate what the drummers said herself, and not rely on others like a weak little child.

Following the path, she came to a metal table surrounded by fan-backed chairs. No Poet was in sight, but a lidded porcelain teapot steamed at the table's center, and next to it, like mountain peaks, folds of green cloth rose above a basket of sweet-smelling bread. Raffles jumped from her arms to investigate.

"Don't be frightened—I'm close behind you." Mwadi flinched but managed to disguise her reaction as a swift turn. She hoped.

It was Mam'selle Lisette. The princess frowned at being sur-prised by her appearance. "Your wife thought you would be still abed," she said. Did that sound too accusing? Let her not appear jealous. "I'm honored," she added.

Mam'selle laughed, a sound both soft as butter and clear as glass. "Don't be. I got up because Daisy brought me a message."

"What—"

"From Rima. She'll be here before twilight."

"Miss Bailey?" Mam'selle's former lover—and hers.

"We need to change our plans—she's piloting an aeroplane; you could be in Kisangani tomorrow morning, if you go with her."

"If I went with her—" With Rima! Rima!

Mam'selle had circled past her to the table. "For me?" she asked the monkey in delighted accents. She held out the palm of one hand and Raffles relinquished into it a crumbling slice of bread. "Thank you!" She turned to face Mwadi. "Shall we seat ourselves?"

"But where is the Poet?"

"She's coming. I left her in the pantry. In fact, I believe I hear her now."

Quick steps rushed toward them. "Sorry! I had to wash the cups and dry them—" The Poet bore a clattering silver tray stacked with plates and cups matching the chocolate pot. She set it down and poured. They sat and plotted anew.

Some background remained the same: the rivalry between Scranforth and Chawleigh, and the rift it highlighted between Britain's liberal oil interests and conservative hardliners' push to "mop up" the mess left behind by the collapse of Europe's colonizing efforts. And the deepening alliance between those hardliners and the most dedicated supporters of the Atlantropa engineering project.

But now Princess Mwadi stood a good chance of seeing her father before he announced his abdication publicly. "Now I can plead my case again," she declared. "We'll be beholden to neither side, and to none of the others at court."

"Are you sure?" asked Mam'selle. "What if you fail?"

"I won't! Queen Josina is your friend, yes? You'll make her see I'm right. You *have* to!"

"We're friends, yes. That doesn't mean she'll submit to my arguments."

"Write the letter! Tell her Ilunga's going to give Scranforth the rights to everything! It won't matter what he calls it: leasing, partnership, purchase, annexation—"

"It will matter to the queen." The Poet spoke quietly but with absolute assurance. "She's going to bargain for what brings the most money for the least trouble. And she'll consult her father and keep Angola in mind, too."

"All right. I'll leave partnership and annexation out of the argument." Mam'selle unwrapped her pink lace shawl in response to the day's heat beginning to rise from the damp ground. She leaned back in her chair and closed her eyes, then turned to Mwadi without opening them.

"What about the Americans?" she asked. "Would they back you? Would you accept their help?"

The Poet responded before Mwadi could. "They never did much when you wanted them to rid us of Leopold—and since the Great War they're even less inclined to concern themselves with our neighborhood."

"Would you go to them again?" asked the princess. "Be my ambassador?"

"I?" Mam'selle's eyelids lifted slowly. Her silver-grey eyes slanted upward in amusement. "I am old, retired. Surely another would be of higher suitability—perhaps an American citizen? Miss Bailey is one, isn't she?"

"She—yes." And if Rima went to the U.S. she'd once more be far, far away.

"There's also General Wilson," the Poet added.

"Ailing and in his seventies," Mam'selle replied. "Not the best qualifications for the job."

"And my daughter-in-law Mrs. Hunter. Mrs. Albin, I mean." So long a silence reigned after this pronouncement that a laughing dove came to the table to peck at the bread scraps Mwadi had saved aside for her monkey. Raffles himself called from the direction in which he'd wandered off, a querulous hoot Mwadi recognized as lonely.

"Here we are, Raffles!" She stood, scaring off the bird, pushing back her chair. Its legs scraped loudly on the bricks with which the clearing was laid. Neither woman looked up at her—they stared at each other, motionless, even when her monkey scampered out of the dombeya bushes and clambered onto the back of an empty seat.

She picked up a crust from her plate and coaxed him nearer. "You don't think Mrs. Albin would leave her husband for very long, do you?"

"No." At last Mam'selle broke the spell of her gaze. She stood now, and began to clear the table of their meal's debris, piling it on the Poet's tray. "And she's old too."

"Sixty isn't the end of the world, you know," the Poet objected. She stood as well, and picked up the half-empty pot of lukewarm chocolate.

"As you say." Mam'selle left for the house with her trayful of crockery, her wife trailing behind her. Out of sight, she threw back a suggestion with the strength of an instruction: "You may easily ask Miss Bailey if she'll serve as your ambassador when she arrives this afternoon."

Mwadi realized she had come to resent Mam'selle's assumption of authority over her. She knew the house would be more comfortable. She stayed outside anyway, first feeding Raffles the rest of her orts, then, monkey in arms, exploring the hot, insect-plagued pathways winding all around the garden and, eventually, back to the front of the property and the street.

Turning left would take her up into Kalima. She turned right, heading downward, toward the Ulindi River, and soon found her road accompanied by the flowing waters of the Lugulu—or more probably some lesser tributary.

After a while, the day began to decline downward, too, like the road. Mwadi wished she'd thought to bring along a slice or two of the breakfast bread, perhaps spread with a spoonful of the jam she had earlier ignored. A sip of chocolate wouldn't go amiss either. Or better yet—

Raffles leapt free of her loosening arms. "No! Stop!" Of course he only fled faster at her cries. The princess ran in pursuit, hopping over the low stone wall bordering the road and onto its mucky verge. "Raffles! Come back!" Her sore feet sank with disconcerting speed into the moss-covered mud. She jumped to teeter on the trunk of a downed tree. "Do you hear me? You must! Come back!"

"We hear you, yeah! Him and me both!"

The voice of my beloved.

"Rima!" Mwadi whirled to see that face, the lips and throat that made such beautiful sounds, such memories. She staggered, lost half her balance, nearly fell. Crouched and stood. "Rima! Rima—"

"That's my name. Don't wear it out." Sitting on the wall, her legs so long she could rest her chin on her trousered kneecaps, Rima smiled to take away her teasing's sting.

Then frowned an exaggerated frown. "Why you didn't write me?"

"I did write you!" the princess protested. "Even when you didn't answer. Were you holding back because of our ages? That was wrong!" She lowered herself cautiously to the ground and ran to Rima's side.

She wanted to impress her, to spring to the wall's top and dance like love on fire. She tried. One sandal stayed stuck in the mud, and the other flew off. She landed barefoot, waist a little bent, hands loose and forward, straightening, laughing, pretending she'd meant to do exactly that all along. Flexing her biceps she laughed again. "Look how much I've grown! I'm eighteen—and you're only twenty-six? You can't say I'm too young now!"

"Hunh. Lemme get on there too and then we see what I say." Up Rima climbed, arms surging like brown waves, cresting and subsiding to leave her erect body like a piece of driftwood, no, like a polished stone sculpted by wind and water into the perfect shape, her skin shining with the late afternoon's gathering mist. And then she stretched out one hand for Mwadi to hold. And then Mwadi took it. And then she held her breath, too, for fear of what would happen next.

Then she released the breath, but not the hand. And pulled Rima toward her. And stood on her toes so they could kiss. Better than wine. At last, at last. At last.

Their mouths parted, though the two of them remained in a radiantly warm embrace. Both spoke at once: "Since when—" "How long—"

Princess Mwadi laughed, delighted at their shared confusion, at anything they shared—even, now that it was over, their seasons-long separation. She began again. "How long ago did you land? You weren't expected till teatime."

"I bet it's near about that now! I landed a whiles ago, and I hurried to Mam'selle and them's house soon as I got directions—you can't say I didn't wanna see you—but you was gone, an they wasn't sure where. They went lookin one way, sent me this other."

Doubt soured the edges of her happiness at the mention of Mam'selle. Had Rima truly been that eager to see *Mwadi*? Or was her host the real attraction?

"Come on back. We need to eat an go to sleep an get up early to fly outta here." She stepped down from wall to road and held out her arms to the princess.

"Go to sleep or go to bed?" Mwadi leaned forward, hands on Rima's smooth shoulders.

"Do I gotta choose? Both. Awright? Let's go."

Mwadi hopped down to walk up the road by Rima's side. She stopped after only a few paces. "My monkey."

"Your monkey what?"

"I have a monkey, a pet. He ran away right before you came."

"You thinkin I mighta scared him off?"

"No. Maybe." The idea hadn't occurred to her.

"You want me to go on ahead an see if that don't bring him out?"

"I—" A squealing mat of black-and-white fur flew from the high branches of a nearby guinea plum to land on the top of the wall. "Raffles!" Galloping toward them, the monkey gargled and growled its displeasure.

Rima ran to interpose herself between princess and pet. "Bo-La! This thing gone hurt you!"

"Move!" she commanded Rima. Anticipating disobedience, Mwadi slipped under her overprotective arm and bent to scoop the monkey up. She raised him to her heart and held him there. He quieted immediately. She turned and began carrying him up the hill. "Come along! Don't pretend you aren't anxious to get back to your Lisette."

"*My* Lisette? Lissen, chile—"

"'Child'? So that's the problem?"

"What you mean?"

"I know your preference for . . . older lovers." Like Mam'selle.

"Bo-La—" A hand elegant as a bird in flight circled around to light upon the nape of her neck. "—it ain't like that! It ain't all about age—I mean yeah, you gotta be grown enough to know what you doin, but I ain't lookin for my mother to go with."

"Then what? What should I believe? You came here! Your attraction to Mam'selle—"

"It's over! Over! She married now!" As if a wife could never be renounced. "Bo-La, you an me make the best sense I ever seen. But we just gettin started—don't bring our love grindin to a halt fore we goin good. You gotta trust me. I ain't done nothin wrong. *Trust* me!"

For most of the way back, Rima walked silently beside her. But just before they entered the district of garden-encircled, wide-verandahed villas she stopped. "Fine. I admit I didn't write you, but it wasn't why you thinkin. Probably shouldn't be tellin you any a this, but what the hell.

"You know I work sometime as a agent."

"Like Mam'selle."

"Yeah, an like *you*. Like we done together. Ain't that different from bein in a play." A pause while Rima plucked a stalk of grass from a roadside tuft and whipped the innocent air with it.

"Well?"

"Well that's what I was doin. Why I didn't write you. I been spyin. For the Russians."

"What? Why?"

"What you think? For money!"

Rima was a Russian spy! Had she been operating against Ever-fair? Against Mwadi? She found she couldn't stand still. She set off at a near gallop, turned around to yell while running backward. "Traitor! Cheat!" She stumbled and had to look where she was go-ing. Only a moment, and when she glanced behind again Rima was right there! So fast! Raffles shrieked and urinated down her arm—the arm Rima hadn't grabbed.

"Bo-La! I ain't no traitor! I ain't tryna hurt you none: I ain't—"

"Release me!"

Rima's hands fell to her sides. "A course. I only wanna tell you what happened."

Slowly, Mwadi retreated. Rima stayed put and let her go.

But where was Mwadi going? She took a deep breath and con-sidered the situation carefully, as if she were her mother.

She wasn't going anywhere today. Certainly not to Kisangani—not without Rima's help.

"Did you gather intelligence on me? My family? On Everfair?"

"I wasn't nowhere near you all! They had me up inna mountains—Nepal, Tibet, Kashmir, places like that. They was way more worried about the Chinese, from what I seen.

"Anyway, I been finished with that job. Just thought you oughta know why I was so too busy an too far away to write. Ain't cause I don't love you.

"Here." Rima pulled off one of the bright scarves wound loosely around her long waist. "Here you go. Use this an wipe yourself clean. I know you don't wanna be walkin around dirtied up by no animal."

Mwadi mopped her arm dry, but then had no one to hand the soiled cloth to. She draped it over a leafy hedge and left it. "All right. I accept what you say." For the moment. For thinking about later.

Raffles deserted her shoulder to sample the hedge's tender shoots. As she and Rima continued up the hill to the home of the Poet—and of Mam'selle—he followed beside them, leaping from shrub to shrub. Mwadi pretended so well that things were fine between her and Rima that she half-fooled herself. By the time they came to the Poet's garden gate they were side-by-side, swinging their clasped hands. Hopping onto the garden's fence, Raffles began stripping the leaves from the rosebush that climbed it. Rima reached for the latch. Mwadi touched the soft skin of her wrist to detain her. "Remember," she whispered.

"Member what?"

"Remember what you said in Alexandria—that when your last assignment ended you would be free to love me."

"Bo-La, I ain't took no last assignment yet. Don't know when or if I will. Meanwhile, ain't what we got enough?"

Was it enough? Could it ever be—even if they really weren't on opposite sides?

The creeping mist turned suddenly to rain. She let Rima open the gate and walked slowly after her. As they approached the house the Poet appeared, a lighted taper in one hand, which she then inserted into the pierced glamp. "Excellent! You've found her! Now come in, or you'll be soaked."

Mwadi watched Rima's face carefully as they ate. Her expression was no slyer than usual. Nor did she exhibit any signs of frustrated love: no poorly suppressed tears, no sighs, no deficiencies of appetite, no sidelong glances in Mam'selle's direction. And later, abed (and not asleep), she was eager, playful, laughing loudly at the ridiculous titles and "dignities" they invented for one another:

"Racer of the Royal Blood. Nuzzler of the Royal Nipples."

"Swallower of the Royal Spit!"

They did sleep, finally, a little, then rose before dawn. Mwadi bade goodbye again to the nightjar, perched singing and alert now in its cage. By evening it would be free. Mam'selle had healed it—she had a way with her, a habit of establishing kinship with any creature with which she crossed paths. They seemed to trust her to have only the best intentions.

Mwadi fought to do the same. Mam'selle and her wife accompanied them to the aeroplane's improvised runway near the warehouse and mooring mast. Raffles leapt back and forth between the shoulders of the princess and her hosts. "I'm sorry!" she apologized. "He's probably excited—he must recognize this as the way we came when we got off *Okondo,* and I'm sure he's eager to get back aboard."

"Then he gone be disappointed." Rima waited at the top of the bluff; Mwadi hurried up the final flight of dirt-and-timber steps to stand beside her. In her haste she dislodged her monkey.

"Will he adjust to your current mode of travel, do you think?" Mam'selle asked. Neither she nor the Poet sounded the slightest bit breathless after their climb.

Rima scowled. "We ain't plannin on takin him with us. Is we, Bo-La?"

A thrill of fear passed up from the soles of her feet. "Why not?" she asked. At the same time she wondered what she needed a monkey for. What scared her about being parted from him?

"You jokin, right? He be crawlin all over you—and maybe he gonna jump out! While we flyin!"

Across the plateau's scrub and grass, the canvas-and-sheet-metal fuselage of Rima's Davis Cloud Star shimmered in the low morning light. It was a two-seater, Mwadi knew from last night's discussion, and open: no cabin, its passengers exposed directly to the air. She had not properly considered the problem of restraining Raffles.

Evidently, though, Mam'selle had, and she offered the solution she'd come up with. "If you don't object, your monkey will stay here awhile. Just till *Okondo*'s next trip north, when I may escort him to court and reinforce our intrigue." The Poet had been banished from Kisangani, but Mam'selle, a favorite of Queen Josina's, would still be welcome there. Without her wife.

Kisangani, Everfair

Ilunga let a soothing hand raise his throbbing head. He felt a pillow slipped beneath it. He opened his eyes. The face receding from view was that of his sister's maidservant, a fair-looking woman with flat breasts. He was quite certain he remembered that her name was Hafiza. He opened his lips to instruct her to bring him water, but before his parched tongue could stir from the floor of his mouth, a half-full glass appeared in her hands.

The prince sipped. Not cold. That was good. Cold water ruined the digestive—but at this thought, even though it was only tangential to food, his stomach roiled. He turned away from the glass and closed his eyes again.

The crash of beads hitting his room's doorframe woke him. He must have dozed—just briefly: the woman Hafiza still crouched by Ilunga's bed, his water clutched in her hands. But she wasn't looking at him anymore. The prince followed her gaze to a blurry figure in his doorway.

"Pardon—I hope I don't intrude? I have a favor to ask of you. If this is a bad time I'll come back later."

He knew that voice. . . . Ilunga blinked to clear the film of sleep from his eyes. "Doctor Kleinwald. Not at all. I'm a trifle under the weather—"

"I'm not that sort of doctor."

"Of course not. Come in, do— Hafiza, take away that tray and move the ottoman under it nearer."

"Yes, Prominence." She left, the curtains' beads slithering suggestively against one another.

"Have a seat. No—I'm fine." He raised himself carefully to a sitting position, fending off Dr. Kleinwald's attempts to assist him. Too-swift movement might possibly upset his equilibrium. The worst of the dizziness and nausea were receding—still, best to end this interview quickly.

"What is it you wish?"

The doctor held out his prosthetic. "I'd like an audience. I'm hoping for an improvement in this."

Ah. "Why didn't you ask earlier? An audience with my father? Or with my mother?"

"Both, if they'll listen. Whoever can get me what I need."

From his new vantage Ilunga could see daylight through his bedroom windows' carved screens. Queen Josina had left word on his arrival last night that she'd visit him this morning. Good. He'd see her first.

"Why wait till now?" he asked again. "Why not arrange for your audiences while we were both aboard *Okondo*?"

"I did. My arrangement was with your sister."

Warily, the prince shook his head. He was still somewhat disposed to dizziness. "Apparently, that was an error."

Kleinwald grinned ruefully. "Yes. Apparently it was. Can we correct it?"

Interestingly, the white man made no move to offer him a monetary bribe. In truth, he made no move at all. The two of them sat deadlocked for what seemed like the recitation period of an entire epic, but which couldn't have lasted longer than a single verse.

The prince wanted his visitor gone. "What will you give me?"

"What I promised Princess Mwadi. My work. My knowledge. My skills."

"Teaching?"

"No. My professional skills."

"And what are those? Exactly what sort of doctor *are* you?"

"I have advanced degrees in experimental and theoretical physics."

Ilunga recalled a tiresome-looking book of his sister's with Kleinwald's name stamped on the front. "Degrees from a European university?"

"One Greek university. One German."

"Are they—"

"The Greek school still operates." Kleinwald's flesh hand pinched the sleeve covering his opposite arm. "It's being run out of a convent by a bunch of nuns. The grounds of the German one were converted to a hospital."

"Did you lose anyone?"

"My fiancée, Chava."

"You were close?"

"We intended to marry."

As he moved the conversation toward more productive questions, Ilunga noted the curious absence of emotion in the white man's words. "It was as if he disguised his feelings too well," he explained later to his mother. "So well he suffocated them."

He and the queen sat at that point in the larger of the two rooms adjoining his sleeping chamber. Warm compresses and copious drafts of water had restored the prince's proprioception. He edged forward on his stool. "At any rate, what do you think?" he asked her. "He's German. Do we want his services too? Or will Chawleigh's connections be sufficient to invite the pro-Atlantropans' participation?"

Queen Josina tilted her carefully plaited head back, then pursed and pushed out her lips. "This is a complicated project we embark on. Attaining your kingship is but the beginning; the deceits we must practice the whole time are even now so multiply layered that keeping track is a formidable task. Your father's other wives, the counselors . . .

"Let me meet and assess this Doctor Kleinwald," the queen decided. "I'll give him his audience this evening."

"And the king?"

"He's not spending a lot of time in public. I will report this development and then, no doubt, he'll ask his spirit father what to do."

Ilunga felt sincere gratitude toward Mwenda's spirit father, who had advised the king to abdicate. The country accepted the decision on that basis. "Have you already mentioned Mr. Chawleigh?"

"Naturally! Your father and I keep very few secrets from one another!" She rose from her seat and made as if to leave, but paused at the door and came back. "And unless I'm mistaken, the same goes for Mr. Chawleigh and your Clara."

"Is my congress with her a problem? You never said I shouldn't partake of her . . . beauty."

"Why should I need to? You didn't say anything to her that her husband wasn't supposed to hear." Quickly glancing at the wooden door behind which her attendants waited, she added, "Did you?"

"No. I laughed with her, joked about drowning my subjects and the people of Cameroon, the land of Chad—"

"You—laughed? About the deaths of millions, about the famine and exile and loss that building the Atlantropa dams would mean?"

Ilunga sighed with shame. "I laughed like the fool she thought me."

"So. Good. My son—" Josina placed her small-palmed hands upon his closely shaven head. "—you'll rule wisely and well."

He couldn't resist. "Better than Mwadi?"

"Your sister would rule well also if given the chance. But she's younger. And female—the Europeans don't respect females. Alas. I had hoped she would arrive here with you, and that together you and I could make her understand the necessity of effacing herself.

"Sifa! We're leaving."

The prince returned to his bed. He tried for a while to trick himself into believing dreams would come if he shut his eyes, then gave up. The sun must be high, and hot, if the rain had stopped for a moment, as was usual around noon in this season. But if he left the palace to enjoy it he might miss his father's summons.

The courtyard garden seemed his best option. He went there

and found it almost deserted: only Hafiza, and Lembe, and a male servant whose name he didn't feel like recalling, were there. He had a couch set in the middle of the satisfyingly sunny garden and sent for a light repast. Gasser brought him a plate of kwanga sticks, soothing in their blandness, and another bearing a trio of horned melons cut open to reveal the seed-filled jelly of their interiors. He sucked down the slippery sweetness cautiously at first, then with confidence.

Next, perhaps, a nap? No. From the dark passage between the palace's courtyard and its front came the voice of Devil. "Loongee! Loongee! Coming to see me off?"

"You're leaving so soon?"

His white friend emerged into the garden. "Got a berth on a climber headed south along the Lualaba to the mouth of the Maiko—then they're sailing east. Puts me within a day's hike of Lake Edward."

"Oil-burning engine?" He indicated that Devil should share his couch.

"Only the best! Sorry, but there ain't that many of these type of boats makin runs—specially takin passengers. Have to catch this one—I'm off! You comin?"

He was not going to miss the king's summons. "I can't. I'm waiting to hear from my—" Ilunga let the rest of his words die unsaid. Gasser had returned, sweaty as a hard-ridden horse. He prostrated himself before the prince's slippers, then raised his head slightly to address them.

"Blessings of our king, Prominence, and his request for your attendance this evening at his ceremony in honor of the ancestor's choice for his successor."

So formal! "It is my pleasure to so serve our king. Where will I go?"

"The grove of the atolo."

So public! But the sacred precincts surrounding the royal atolo tree were the perfect site on which to announce the king's abdication and Ilunga's accession to Everfair's throne. He could stay behind afterward for a private audience, assuming that was required.

And he could escort Devil to the docks for his departure now. He leaned forward and touched Gasser's back. "Rise. Procure us a carriage."

"Goin along with me then? I've already hired a carriage m'self—oilburner, as folks round here so elegantly say. Join me?"

Unlike the usual bicycle-and-cart arrangement, this vehicle's engine and passenger compartments were combined into one blocky, bulky body. Inside, the amenities were the same—padded walls and benches, curtains over pierced shutters, nets in the ceiling for storage. He used one of the latter to hold his bowler.

Though Ilunga understood what his friend was about, showing off royal support for the fuel for which he explored, the noise as the carriage's engine started was atrocious. And the smoke and stink. Their driver—a young European—apologized for that, half his words drowned in the oilburner's belching rattle. Then they were headed downslope from the ridge of the walkway to the sunken road.

The weather lately had been relatively dry. The road's water was confined to a narrow, meandering channel at its center throughout most of its length. As the docks neared, the water slowed and spread, eventually turning into a series of shallow puddles at its end.

Devil insisted on Ilunga accompanying him to inspect the *Maria Fonseca,* second of Queen Josina's growing fleet of cascade-climbing boats. Helped by Gasser, the prince managed to avoid wetting his feet as he disembarked. He sent the oilburner on its way over Devil's protests, feeling he'd done his friend enough of a favor by riding it here. No need to undergo a return trip.

The climber's winch and engine were housed in a special man-height construction at its stern: a grass roof over four windowless walls of wood. Perhaps it was this containment that made it quieter than the carriage? It growled rather than bellowed with anger.

"Too bad the motor's been started. Harder to give you the full tour."

"No one will question my knowledge once I'm king. This will be the case in only a matter of days—markets at most."

"Still, best to have a few basic facts on call. What if Chawleigh and his crowd manage to . . . incapacitate me? What if Russia—or worse, *China*—gets a foothold in the country and you need to convince *them*?" Devil opened the door of the engine house. The noise increased, but not substantially enough to overpower the white man's mercifully short explanations of the climber's workings.

"Low gear now," he finished. "Raise the throttle as soon as we cast off."

"Soon, you say? I'd better be going back ashore." Ilunga looked longingly at the walkway down to the dock. "Your luggage is loaded?"

"Didn't mean to boot you off just yet, Loongee. Drink in my cabin?"

As the proposed libation was nothing more spectacular than a jug of Angolan ovingundu, the same sort of mead his mother made, the prince excused himself after accepting just one or two rounds.

And yet by the time Gasser had gotten him a carriage, the road was filled with shadows. Instead of heading home to bathe and change, as he'd originally intended, Ilunga directed the bicycle towing him to drive straight to the atolo grove.

The shadows grew larger and melted into one another, became evening. He arrived and mounted the steps up from the street, into the misty embrace of low-lying clouds. Seasonal weather, but he shivered in their dim coolness. Like wraiths, the outlines of courtiers and other well-placed subjects materialized before him as he walked forward. A wave of greetings rolled ahead of him. His progress divided the gathering, making him a path.

He came to the little hill where his father stood, brass arm gleaming in the golden light of the outsized ceremonial glamp's pierced globe. King Mwenda's age sat easily on him, though he had lived more than ninety seasons—or as whites measured such matters, forty-five years. And for more than half of that time the king had ruled Everfair. Why abdicate now? Only a few strokes of grey streaked his short braids and close-clipped beard. But his mother had written that that was the king's plan, and gossip gleaned since his arrival confirmed this.

The hill's top was flat and wide. King and glamp occupied its center. Queen Josina and the other wives sat to the king's left. To his right stood his preferred counselors. A troop of musicians crouched at their feet, horns and drums and harps poised to play. As Prince Ilunga approached they struck up a slow, winding melody. He circled the mound, intending to ascend it from the side least visible to the audience, so that his tardiness would be less noticeable. But there was his sister. There already, walking in his lead. How?

Careless of appearances now, he pushed people aside to plow up the hill's slope. Mwadi crested its summit ahead of him. Panting for breath, the prince struggled to catch up with her. Guards milling about in her wake sprang toward him, then fell back, recognizing him. Nothing and no one stood between him and his father. Too late.

Too late. She had beaten him. He moved forward like a priest in a trance. The princess lay on the ground before King Mwenda. Then, with the king's hands on her shoulders, she was rising. Triumphant. Smiling up at their father she clasped his arms—then turned to smile at Ilunga.

It was a smile queerly empty of hate. The prince had kept walking toward his sister without hope or reason. As he reached her, she held out a hand in welcome. So did his father. He prostrated himself, got up, and took both their hands.

The king didn't smile, but he nodded and spoke in a voice meant for only those close by to hear. "It is well. For now the land's rule will be divided, as they wish."

As *who* wished? Divided? Divided how?

With a nod of her own, Mwadi squeezed and released Ilunga's hand. She stepped back to stand beside the king and face the people gathered below. Queen Josina caught his eye and gestured for him to do the same.

From this vantage the assembly looked as if they stood in drifting smoke. "Followers! You who have sworn allegiance to the throne of Everfair—hear me this last time!" His words pitched to carry, King Mwenda swung his head in all directions so all his audience could hear him. "As my spirit father directs, I leave you now to explore the wide world. His bush awaits me! As for your well-being, it is crucial! This is why you'll have not one ruler, but two. In my absence—" He lifted both their arms high in the dimming air. "—my son, Prince Ilunga, and my daughter, Princess Mwadi, are to reign jointly!"

CHAPTER SEVEN

April 1921
Zanzibar City Aboard Xu Mu

Should she be worried? Bee-Lung wasn't sure. The warm air pushing up through the hatch to her past Sevaria's dangling head and shoulders bore no taint of fear. Was that a good sign? Or a bad one?

Through the part of *Xu Mu*'s small, square passenger hatch not blocked by the film star's body, Bee-Lung saw green palms and scattered brown roofs swelling nearer, nearer—and there, only now coming into sight, the walls of Zanzibar City. The Old Fort and its mooring mast must be just ahead.

She squeezed Sevaria's hips tighter and raised her voice to be heard over the noises outside—the distant thrum of the aircanoe's engines, the whistle of noon-hot air rushing over *Xu Mu*'s hull and rigging. "Hasn't the camera stopped running yet?"

The star's answer was unintelligible. Bee-Lung didn't care. She began tugging on the waistband of Sevaria's trousers, trying to pull her back to safety. At first she got no help; passive as a sack of grain, the filmmaker did nothing to move herself out of the opening, nothing to reel in her heavy camera.

But then Gopal's gentle hands grasped Bee-Lung's waist. "On three," he said. "One, two—" Together they hauled Sevaria over the hatch's low coaming and grabbed her shoulders. Her wrists were looped together in the rope tied to the net around the camera. "Come," said Gopal, sitting the star upright and half lifting, half shoving her behind a stack of banana leaf–bundled trade goods. "Stretch the line across the top of that and we'll have an easier time raising the weight."

"But the camera's ascent must be controlled! It's fragile! Expensive—an Aeroscope! I didn't think—"

"Don't worry! I'll go back to the hatchway and guide the camera in." Gopal nodded to Bee-Lung. "The two of you are strong enough to pull it up without me, aren't you?"

They were. Bee-Lung coiled the rope's slack around a pair of pegs driven into the hold's deck. Gopal knelt and scooped the camera's net up and in. The look he gave Sevaria made Bee-Lung wonder again as she had several times already: Was he the "brother" for whom she saved her star? The proper kin? But already she had added Kafia, and Trana and Jadida, to Gopal's cell. Though another coremate would make their number more propitious, carryover of the original mistress-servant dynamic could smother the filmmaker's acceptance. No. She would continue to wait for a better second subject for Sevaria, and would find Gopal's fifth elsewhere.

As Bee-Lung untied the rope's end from the net's bunched opening, Sevaria fussed impatiently, running her hands over the camera's varnished wooden sides as if petting a cat. She tried lifting it by herself once the net lay spread apart.

"Let me," Gopal insisted. "Where should I put it for you?"

"What do you think? My cabin, of course."

Bee-Lung's cabin. "We'll arrive so soon. Simpler to keep it here, handy for loading, don't you agree?"

"Very well. You. Gopal. Tell Trana and Jadida to help you bring the rest of my belongings to the hold. Make sure they set aside the Aeroscope's pump—I'll need it to repressurize the cranking mechanism so I can film as we moor."

Yes, confronted with such ingrained hierarchy, the Spirit Medicine would have a hard time effecting integration. Bee-Lung must find and inoculate someone Sevaria regarded as an equal.

She paid little attention to *Xu Mu*'s mooring and the by now familiar process of disembarking. Instead, she cast her thoughts ahead to consider the potential for recruiting candidates here.

Then, leaving the rest of her core kin to settle into the third-storey hotel suite they had taken, Bee-Lung ventured out with the idea of achieving that goal, among others.

Tink met her on the ground level and agreed to accompany her on her expedition. For this she was doubly grateful; first, because his pursuit of marriage with Kwangmi had weakened his entire cell: him especially, and through him, Bee-Lung herself. Best that he withdraw from such a draining and likely hopeless situation—at least for now.

Second, she was able now to share one of her errands with him, thus halving her work and hastening the Spirit Medicine's inevitable triumph. They agreed upon their itinerary and set off.

The approaching evening's relative cool drew forth a large segment of the populace—the many citizens who had kept themselves indoors during the sleepy noon hour of *Xu Mu*'s arrival. White robes and blue veils crowded the stone-paved walkways. On the streets camels, donkeys, horses, carts towed by steam bicycles—modes of transportation familiar from cities around the world—mixed with a few new motor cars. Some of these were noisy, impelled by controlled explosions of odorous palm oil, while others were fueled by hushed rivers of waterfire pouring out of dam-charged batteries.

Even in the quiet vicinity of the three waterfire-powered vehicles Bee-Lung encountered, the shouts and multi-tongued speech of the surrounding throngs made conversation impractical. That was all right; their plans were set. She and Tink would survey the nearby market's stalls for noteworthy plant samples together, and then they would part to scout out the best locations for the next step in expanding May Fourth's worldwide communication network.

Two approaches appeared to offer access to the cable running between Zanzibar and Aden in the British colony of Yemen—a line not yet inoculated. On her way to visit the city's dispensary, Bee-Lung would surreptitiously assess the first of these approaches, stopping by the telegraph company's offices on Mizingani Road.

Tink, meanwhile, would hire a cart—or some other means of conveyance—a donkey perhaps—to take him north toward the point at which the cable began its marine submersion. Somewhere along that route he would surely find a vulnerability easy to exploit.

Zanzibar

Who really understood? His sister? Tink barely remembered Bee-Lung's husband, a man who had died of the Maltese Influenza almost six years ago. Wei-Lun had been bland of face and habit, and nothing in his sister's manner then or since argued that theirs had been a true and loving marriage. The donkey between his legs probably meant as much to Tink as that man had meant to Bee-Lung: a method of reaching a goal. And not even the most efficient method.

He pulled on the beast's reins in the way its handler had shown him, and it ambled to a halt. The road swerved inland here, while the wires swooping over his head continued straight. This was exactly why he'd chosen such a mount rather than one of those intriguing motor cars; he could take the rough track that followed the parade of fresh, sap-sweating telegraph poles, stay with them despite the road's fickle behavior.

Or he could give up. Go back to the hotel. Heed the reddening of the black wires' undersides, a sign the sun was about to set. Return to his core kin before darkness rendered him wholly the Spirit Medicine's creature.

He chose the wiser course: retreat. Though the decision was harder than it ought to have been. What weighed so heavily against autonomy on the scales of his decision?

Steering the donkey 180 degrees, he tried to start it trotting back down Malawi Road to Stone Town. It ambled a few steps, then stopped. He kicked its sides and it started up again obligingly, then, provokingly, stopped again. Was it tired? Thirsty? In need of fuel? The man Tink had hired it from hadn't seemed worried about him feeding or watering Birks, as he called the donkey—he hadn't mentioned doing that at all.

After another attempt at riding, Tink dismounted. Birks peered at him a moment out of one thickly lashed eye, then ambled forward in the right direction and kept going. Tink caught up and paced alongside it, putting a hand on one of the straps tying the saddle to its body.

The road dipped to cross a stream and Birks picked up speed. Reaching the ford, it uttered a moan and plunged its head in the water to drink. So it *had* been thirsty. Now that Tink knew, he recalled having difficulty in this spot on the way out of town.

Thirst quenched, the donkey should have gone faster. But after it stood helpfully still on the stream's far bank as Tink remounted, its progress continued at the same leisurely rate. His kicks to its belly had no effect. Students headed from countryside madrassas to the city's cafés gained on him, arguing, passed him with barely nodded acknowledgments of his existence. A countercurrent of spice growers flush with satisfaction at the deals they'd made in the city smiled his way in the fading light as they headed homeward to their farms. Nearer and nearer they came, till they met him face-to-dusk-filled-face, and then they went on, their warm skins, damp with exertion, cooling and drying in the salt-scented breezes blowing off of the sea.

Dewy night descended over the leafy gardens rustling on the city's blurred edges. Tink smelled the first lamp to be lit before seeing its golden flame. One, two, five, many. Like oil-quickened flowers they bloomed, placed to guide him back easily into his cell's arms. Had he feared the darkness? Why? Nothing filled it to which he had not given his consent.

The donkey's handler met him beneath the commons' giant fig tree, as arranged. Smugness wafted off of him when Tink counted the coins still owing into his palm. The payment was too high, then. But this was only money. True wealth awaited Tink on the rooftop of Emerson House.

In the lights of the hotel's entrance and ground-floor salon, Tink's arationality abated a bit. He was aware he'd submerged his mind to other imperatives. For the moment the Spirit Medicine's hold on him was loosening. Just a little—he climbed the stairs anyway. Outside the door opening at their top twilight reigned. He located his core kin in the shelter of the flat roof's far pavilion and sank into their scents as he walked to join them.

All of them—while Raghu sang a wordless melody, the Chen twins danced with Kwangmi clasped between them. Dipping, turning, flowing, changing, the women moved with a grace surpassing unity. They did more than mirror one another, reciting poetry with the droop of a head, the drop of a hand.

His sister and Sevaria were their audience. Rather than introduce any new and possibly jarring notes into the performance, Tink took a seat beside Bee-Lung. Flashes of distant lightning illuminated his coremates' sweet motions—the promise of rain fattening the resulting traces upon the air of their aromatic sweat.

"I see them, a little," said Sevaria. "Yet also, and more completely, I—touch them? But how can that be? They're yards away!"

"You touch the atmosphere surrounding them," Bee-Lung explained. "The atmosphere surrounding and touching them, surrounding and touching you, everyone. The Spirit Medicine helps you feel how universally we are connected." She turned to Tink. "My brother. Tell Miss Sevaria about the powers and benefits we're given."

The filmmaker listened with growing anxiety. He detected her emotion but didn't understand what caused it. So he asked.

"I'm anxious because I'm not angry." Sevaria smiled with her mouth and frowned with her eyes. "I should be. I trusted you and you tricked me into receiving this—'Spirit Medicine,' this . . . fungus? I should be scared, horrified. I should be running away, far, far away— Why don't I hate you?"

For the same reason he didn't hate her. Because they were different parts of the same organism. "Because you don't hate yourself. Take some time. Realize this."

"Yes! I— Though I concluded just now that your Spirit Medicine was a danger to me, arguments welled up in its favor in my mind immediately! For all your promises of power and protection are true! And more!"

Bee-Lung took Sevaria's hands in her own. "Yes! What we've done was done from love. As you will learn. As you are learning even now—though slowly."

Nodding at the dancers, Bee-Lung continued. "The problem is that you have no core kin. I'll remedy this soon."

"How? Who will you match me with? You say I'm an experiment!"

Smelling calm, his sister squeezed Sevaria's hands and released them. "The Spirit Medicine will tell me who and how." She took up one of Tink's hands. "As it will tell us where best to initiate a new connection between the threads of its communication webbing, based on what we've learned today.

"The Spirit Medicine solves all difficulties."

Zanzibar City

Bee-Lung sighed and tucked her head down to contemplate her feet. The cloth-and-leather sandals she had purchased in the market this morning would surely please the official she was scheduled to meet. Their uppers' soft pink and sky blue harmonized so well with her sleeveless coat and trousers that it was as if they'd been dyed in the same vat, and she had varnished her fingernails and toenails pink as well.

A little breeze came through the waiting room's open doorway, the scent it bore announcing a servant's approach. She sat erect and fixed her eyes on the sultan's portrait hanging to the doorway's left, schooling her expression to interested admiration.

"Madam Ho." A person of middle years advanced toward Bee-Lung's end of the bench that she shared with several petitioners. "The effendi will see you now." She was conducted via frequently branching corridors to a door set in a white plastered wall. The servant opened it. The room's occupants were male: a young boy kneeling by the two steps leading down and into it, and the official she had come to see, seated behind a wide, European-style writing desk. He smelled like—what? Like herself? That must be the overflow of her own aura. Disregarding any such redundancies, the remaining essence indicated that this man was deeply bored. Perhaps this was for the best; Bee-Lung's visit would be memorable in contrast to the rest of his interviews.

"Will you take refreshment?"

"My thanks but no, Qadi. I dine soon, and I would rather keep my appetite."

The judge gestured to the boy to serve them. The boy rose and fetched a tray from a table in the room's far corner. It held empty cups and a full ewer. "Water, then," said the qadi. "It's surprisingly easy in this climate to neglect its necessity."

The ewer's contents were indeed water and nothing more. Bee-Lung drank appreciatively.

"Now." The qadi produced a small triangle of silk and blotted his beard and moustaches dry. "What is your complaint with my ruling? You think it unfair?"

"No! Oh, no, great Qadi! It is entirely just that you prohibit our crew from filming in public—especially as we have yet to obtain the necessary permits. Only—" She commanded the tiny blood vessels on the surface of her face to expand into a blush. "Only we don't know where to apply for the permits we need—or how to do so properly. You know we are mostly women, and woefully ignorant in this realm." Neither of these claims were true, but the qadi nodded gravely.

"And so—" Bee-Lung leaned forward to steep herself more fully in the man's scent. Could she produce complementary perfumes quickly enough to ensnare his interest? Glad of the water she'd ingested, she stoked her metabolism higher, hotter. "—we come to you for help."

The judge pursed his moist lips. "I am by nature generous. Officially such matters lie beyond my concern. Unofficially, however . . ." He glanced down at the letter lying open on his desk. ". . . you have written to say that this matter regards a Believer? A daughter of the Religion, gently reared, with no living male relatives, yes? As a devout practitioner it is therefore my duty to look after her business interests."

"Ah! So kind! So clever!" Emitting her best allurements, Bee-Lung laid her hands invitingly on the desk's edge, palms up. "And when and how will this be done? I hope it's no trouble if we give our thanks in advance?"

"You wish to—"

A burst of coughing. The qadi jumped to his feet, startlement and annoyance overwhelming his desire.

"Pardon! Pardon!" The boy—Bee-Lung had left him out of her calculations. This was an unforgivable mistake. He was right there, work-weary and watchful.

The Spirit Medicine was only as capable of providing solutions to problems as its cores were capable of formulating them. She had been omitting an important variable. Could she get the boy to leave? Alone with the judge, Bee-Lung would be able to concentrate on arousing him again and continue working toward the correct outcome.

Like the qadi, she was facing toward the boy—nothing suspicious in that. She went to embrace him, trying to appear maternal.

"Calm yourself! The qadi is merciful!" The boy's trembling lessened. His innate curiosity unfurled and diffused into the air. But most likely he was not the ideal candidate for the unfilled spot in Gopal's cell, or in any core formed of adults—though Bee-Lung noted to herself the potential usefulness of the Spirit Medicine in forming a separate children's cell.

The trembling had completely stopped. The boy was subdued. With a quick pat on his back, Bee-Lung stepped away to release him. He must still be got rid of. She knew how.

"Are certain documents necessary to accompany our petition?" she asked. "Must it be made with any special form of payment—or upon some particular kind of stationery?"

The qadi sighed. His annoyance had ebbed to be replaced by a resurgence of boredom—now mixed with a faint undercurrent of self-satisfaction. "It is quite a complicated process," he said, as if admitting a problem. Furthering its complication was likely how he maintained his high status.

"Is it possible for me to see how successful petitions have been made in the past? You have records of them that we can be shown, don't you?"

"There are archives. But as foreigners, you and those whose interests you represent won't have access to these."

"Naturally not! But what if you were to send your servant to the archives to fetch a few of the best examples here?" She swayed provocatively nearer, peeping at her target through lowered lashes. A scent of renewed arousal joined the undernote of smugness.

"Chimwala, go to the library and bring back to me the documents pertaining to . . ." Bee-Lung trained the bulk of her attention away from the qadi's words, toward his increasingly goat-like smell and the smells of others nearby reaching her from beneath the shut door. The person who had escorted her here from the waiting room bench stood immediately outside, while various others passed by, their urgency or confidence or dread building in intensity as they neared her, peaking, then falling away: a pregnant mother, a disgusted soldier, a pair of young girls—their excited whispers drawing Bee-Lung back to the domains of speech.

"And after you have delivered the papers," the qadi was saying, "you may return to my quarters to prepare my evening bath."

"Yes, effendi." The boy Chimwala bowed and left. And via the door as he opened it came the faintest trace of an unexpected odor—that of Gopal! Distant, but unmistakable—what could he want? Would Sevaria have sent him with a message? If so, Bee-Lung needed to get him to join her in the qadi's office somehow, in order to receive it. This would take some skill. What was his excuse for appearing without an appointment? And why send him, of all the crew? Gopal had no French, let alone any Arabic, or even the Swahili of the island's lower classes.

With the distraction of the child removed, she had expected to increase her exudations of sexiness. Instead she maintained each of her scents' flows at a steady level. "If you allow, I can contrive a private performance by one of the film's actors? He is a new discovery of Sevaria's and eager to demonstrate his talents—"

"'*His* talents'?" the qadi interrupted. "'He'?" The threading fumes of the man's arousal thickened. So. "When can you arrange this? Tonight?"

"Now!" Boldly, Bee-Lung reached for and possessed herself of the judge's hands. Direct contact with the skin made the influence of her output surer—though there was still that odd mirroring effect. Not quite mirroring: not precisely identical to her aroma, nor that of a member of another core . . . and oddly enough, bringing to mind Miss Bailey—of all her acquaintance! Another mental note made.

"Is the day's remaining business of any importance? Can't you cancel or reschedule the rest of your appointments? Within moments the actor and I will attend you in your apartments."

"He and you? Together?" The qadi's arousal surged higher.

"Yes. Gopal Singh is his name for the moment, but we'll think of something more romantic by the time the film is finished." What was the qadi's given name—Ahmed? Probably to propose that would be too blatant.

"He should be called Omar."

Bee-Lung doubted that. "But he's so very Bharatese in appearance. Perhaps Umar instead?" She rose to bow and ascend to the room's exit. "May I go? You'll see him when we come to your apartments and decide then."

"Yes. Where will Chimwala find you?"

Nearly a mistake! Bee-Lung concentrated on not gasping at her narrow escape. No one here was supposed to know of her

Spirit Medicine–enhanced olfactory abilities. Keeping her breath slow and even she said, as if this had always been her intention, "We'll wait for your summons in the kitchen garden." Which she could have smelled her way to, as she could as easily—but more conspicuously—have smelled her way to the qadi's living quarters.

"Good. You may leave."

She knocked on the door to get the attention of the attendant waiting in the corridor, who accepted her revised itinerary gracefully. By twisting their route just a little Bee-Lung was able to cross paths with Gopal. She beckoned him to follow her—but not too closely.

The attendant left. A moment later Gopal appeared, stopping in the shade of a walkway linking the palace's main building and the kitchen complex. The day's heat dwelt in the blue-painted posts supporting it.

"Why are you here?" she asked him.

"Will you sit?"

"Where?"

With his sleek-combed head Gopal indicated a chair behind her. It had been carved from faintly salted driftwood.

"And you'll do what—sit on my lap? Come." Taking her new recruit's hand she led him a little farther on, around the kitchen building's corner to its herb plot. Here there were no chairs; they crouched together upon a patch of creeping thyme plants.

Quickly she explained what was needed. "If we seduce the qadi, he'll take care of all obstacles to the filming. It seems his taste is for both men and women, which makes your appearance here helpful.

"But you didn't know that, Gopal. No one aboard *Xu Mu* did. So what's the cause of your coming?"

"Miss Sevaria sent me." A bee flew too close to Gopal's face and he swatted at her. The insect backed off to circle behind his head. "She no longer needs your intercession in getting licenses."

"No longer needs—or no longer wants?" The bee approached her and landed warily on the tip of her outheld finger.

"*Xu Mu* received word by drum that Miss Bailey is delayed. None of the scenes with her can be filmed here. Miss Sevaria proposes shifting locations to Everfair, where Miss Bailey meets us."

"I see. So you're to take me back aboard. The qadi will be so disappointed."

"Yes." Gopal grinned. "Unless we satisfy him first."

Tiny black feet walked the maze of whorls patterning Bee-Lung's skin. The lightness of their touch filled Bee-Lung's head with longing. As always, she kept herself in check. "Is there some reason we should?"

Gopal shifted suddenly forward and onto his knees. The bee fled. "Wouldn't the qadi's recruitment help our cause?"

"Only if he forms cores compatible with our own. Besides, I have no tools. Unless you brought my—" Abruptly Bee-Lung shut her mouth. The boy Chimwala walked the graveled path that led toward them, eyes turned downward, but ears open. "No matter," she muttered, stretching and standing. "We'll do as you suggested."

"You are ready, Ho effendi?" Bee-Lung nodded and went with him, motioning Gopal to follow. Her ethics twinged a little, but she managed to soothe them. She was doing this for the good of the revolution. The intercourse to come would be no mere selfish seeking after sexual gratification.

Gopal quickened his pace and caught up with her, nervously grasping her by one hand. She owed it to him as well as to herself to become calm. They had reached the mother-of-pearl-inlaid door to the qadi's apartments. The boy bowed and swung it open. She paused before entering to make a last effort at rationalizing the act about to be undertaken. Where was the harm in giving a powerful man what he wanted? What difference did it make that Sevaria no longer sought the qadi's immediate help in obtaining licenses? A favor that could be collected in the future still counted as a favor.

The sweetness of sandalwood spiraled up from the qadi's freshly bathed form, while the faint mustiness of incompletely mopped tiles spilled from beneath the curious sofa on which he sat. Again Bee-Lung set aside the puzzling persistence of the unnamable odor faintly underlying all.

The qadi turned his head to face them. "Greetings." Gesturing at the silk curtains toward which his sofa was oriented, he smiled. "Be welcome. Take your places." A part in the curtains revealed a low, circular dais surmounted by a circular, pillow-strewn bed. "Or do you wish refreshment before your performance?"

"Our performance?" Bee-Lung repeated. "But only one of us is an actor."

Gopal's hand tugged at the hem of her vest. What had she led this poor boy into? Though now he was leading her. Whispering as they climbed the one step up to the dais: "You are whatever he wants you to be. Both of us. We're in his power." His soft breath left dew-like traces on the curves of Bee-Lung's ear. He maneuvered her by her bare shoulders so they stood face-to-face, and leaned against her forehead with his own. Still whispering: "Our pleasure will be so very great—there will be more than enough to share." Now he unfastened her clothing, removed it, and stripped off his own. Now he sank to lie upon the front of the bed, pulling her down beside him. Now he caressed her back, the muscles, fat, and bones covered by skin with a scarce but eager supply of nerve endings.

"Stop thinking!"

Surprised, Bee-Lung raised herself on her arms, arching away from Gopal's sticky chest. "Enjoy yourself—for once!" The man's angry hiss belied his languorous expression. Or did it? A wicked slant to the brows above his dark eyes made the command a joke, the amorousness a trick to fool the watching qadi. Perhaps this youth knew what he was about?

Sighing, she rocked back, rearranged herself, and drew Gopal to sit upright between her naked knees. As she'd often dreamed of doing she swept the tip of her tongue along his hairline, tasting the wholesome tang of his sweat. Then gasped when he responded by flicking his tongue along the underside of her jaw. The servants went, extinguishing lamps as they left so that only one candle burned to light their performance. A furtive, yearning smell slunk between them. This smell she recognized: their audience was pleased.

Throughout their staged coupling the qadi's stifled enjoyment unfurled around them, dispersing itself within the flowering bouquet of their own bliss. Then, into the cloud rising from the aftermath of their exertions came a more intense version of that less familiar odor of the qadi's. And another odor which was familiar, and unwelcome: an oil-bathed, recently sharpened knife blade.

Pretending lassitude, Bee-Lung kept her eyes slitted open and rolled her face toward the rustle of the qadi's satin. Through one eye she observed him nearing the dais, his steps unfaltering in the shadowy chamber. On his hands he balanced a silver tray, source of the knife smell and the smell she couldn't quite place . . . and which, puzzlingly, reminded her of Miss Bailey . . . to the slightest extent. . . .

Gopal slept. His chest rose and fell beneath Bee-Lung's cheek with charming regularity. The qadi's arrival did nothing to disturb his rest. Often men slumbered this deeply following sex.

Not she. "You would like to see more?" she asked. No longer feigning unconsciousness she sat upright. "Give us but a moment—"

The qadi leapt straight into the air. "What? No!" He peered at her inquisitively. An uninoculated man should have been unable to make out Bee-Lung's expression. "I wanted to show you—to share with you this . . . cure—preventive, rather. In case your travels expose you to the 'flu."

The Russian organism! Could she obtain a sample for examination? May Fourth had taught her a technique intended to isolate it, as they'd taught several agents they sent into the field. Would the technique work? Or would some new vagary in the organism's growth or administration render it invulnerable to her tactics? Fear and curiosity warred within Bee-Lung's brain.

Of course curiosity won.

Zanzibar City and Aboard Xu Mu

Tink would rather have visited Rosalie at home, but her business address was the one he found. He waited to go in till midday, trusting that "La Bijouterie" would remain open despite the hour's heat, but that business then would be slack.

The iron lattice door slammed shut behind him and he stepped into the shop's cool dimness. For the moment he was alone. Banks of wooden drawers loomed slowly into view as his eyes adjusted to the lower light—not dangerously low, but in marked contrast to the burning clarity of the heat-reflecting white pavement outside.

A clatter announced the disturbance of the beaded curtain behind the shop's glass counter. A young woman fragrant with a mélange of herbal essences—lime peel and clove buds most prominent—parted its strings and came through. "Peace be upon you. May I serve you in any way? Do you seek a particular treasure? Precious stones? Cut coins?"

"Something more valuable," Tink replied. "The company of your mistress."

The woman's cheek dimpled with a repressed smile. "My mistress is not my mistress." She held up a hand to halt his confused protests. "I take your meaning—you're looking for the shop's owner, Miss Albin, n'est-ce pas?" She glanced back over one shoulder. "Rosalie? A man to talk with you."

He had only a moment to prepare himself. Then she was there. The resemblance to her dead sister, his first love, was more striking than at their last meeting. Three seasons ago, that had been, almost four. He had proposed to Rosalie at that last meeting—to no more effect than his subsequent proposal to Kwangmi.

He detected no embarrassment in her. No strong feelings of any sort. "Mr. Ho." She held out a hand for him to shake, white-style, and he took it, but also bowed. "You're not buying anything."

"Actually, I am. A betrothal gift." That got a reaction. "But also, of course, I wished to renew our acquaintance for the sake of days gone by. And I have questions—"

"You're marrying someone? Who?"

"Try not to seem so surprised!"

"I apologize. But is this a local woman—or man? I may be able to suggest the best purchase."

"It's not. Let me see everything you judge beautiful."

Rosalie showed him antique pendants on heavy chains of gold, decorative combs carved from white and violet corals, a brooch set with flowers trapped in amber, and an utterly impractical crystal diadem. At last he settled on a set of bracelets incorporating boar tusks. That seemed apt, given Kwangmi's birth sign, and they wouldn't impede her as she went about her business. She could easily wear them while steering *Xu Mu* or exploring and recruiting at future landing sites.

"I'll box and wrap these for you," the other woman offered. Amrita was her name, he had learned. She held aside half the curtain's strands. "Will you wait in here?"

Rosalie had a cozy office in the space indicated. Spikes jutting from its stone walls held lengths of pearls, rods of jade, and graduated bands of metal—gold, silver, brass, copper, tin, and lead, going by their looks and scents. Nails driven into the one wooden wall held net bags of more pungent bounties: teeth and bones, shells, feathers. Removing a stack of cedar blocks from a low stool, Rosalie sat. "Please take my usual seat," she said, indicating a wheeled and cushioned chair.

He rotated it to face her. "You seem well."

"I am." A mild annoyance tinged her breath. "As you might have learned without coming to see me in person. What do you want to know, then?"

"Have you been collecting intelligence? Spying?"

"I have." The annoyance changed to curiosity. "How'd you know?"

He hadn't till now. "For Everfair?"

"At times."

Was every answer going to be limited to two syllables? "Do you have a personal stake in Everfair's politics—particularly in the succession?"

"No."

One syllable. "What work have you done in connection with—"

"Let me stop you. I work when I'm interested, when I care. Mademoiselle asked me to ensure that the sheikhas here prevented British interests from exploiting the oil fields near Pemba, reserving them for Everfair. Princess Mwadi asked me to further the growth of the island's oil palm farms along much the same lines. I was able to do both. But I don't make a habit of that sort of thing."

She cocked her curly-haired head. "Have I answered all your questions now? Are you ready for mine?"

"What?"

"You thought this business went just one way?" Leaning forward, Rosalie hunched up her shoulders as if huddling with Tink over a secret. "Tell me more about your fiancée. How is she most like Lily?"

"She isn't!" Tink tried to control his outpouring of indignation, then realized Rosalie wouldn't be able to smell it. "She's Korean!" So, like Lily, not Chinese. And conventionally ugly. Two similarities he couldn't help. "Her parents are still married—she joined the May Fourth Movement with both their blessings!" Though since then his love had become estranged from her father.

"The May Fourth Movement? The Russians' enemies?"

"We're going to save the world! Them, too!" Silence. Then the rattle of crisp paper shaken out and folded came in from the shop: the sound of his gift being wrapped.

"I apologize. We've only heard about the Russians from the Italians," Rosalie said, as if that explained everything. Maybe it did; the two governments were allies. Was there more? Bee-Lung could fill him in with additional details. For now the answer to just one question mattered.

"So you're not in direct contact with the Russians. Are they recruiting you—directly or by proxy?" What if that was how the Italians were involved?

"No. Why?"

"Because we want you to work for us instead." Giving an edited version of the Spirit Medicine's effects and benefits—empathic links, sharpened senses—Tink spoke as if Zanzibar's contribution to the revolution was an accomplished fact. He had learned over his time as a node that this was the most effective way to lead: simply go where you wanted others to follow.

Midway through his description of the vividness with which he now perceived people's emotions, Tink sensed Amrita hovering just beyond the bead curtain. Her fascination was marbled with jealousy—of course! The two women were lovers? Or perhaps the relationship was more uneven than that: *My mistress is not my mistress.*

"Come," Tink instructed Amrita. "Listen."

Between strands of twinkling color he saw her shake her head. "Someone must take care of any customers we get. I'll stay out here." But she heard him to his finish. And as he tried to pin down the time of the appointment at which Rosalie would receive her inoculation, she tied the beads aside.

"We close for supper. Why not bring us both up then? Together. Or after—for drinks? Dagga?"

Rosalie's odor became more distinct. More self-assured. "You'd go too? You—*want* me to do this?"

"It's a good, direct way for us to share our feelings with one another."

"Yes! And whomever else you form your core with." A small stirring of anxiety twisted the shop's air. He tried for a reassuring tone. "So you need to select your core's members very, very carefully."

The door to the street opened and a man oozing prosperity entered. His goal was the purchase of tasteful gifts for two recently arrived European women, one the other's paid companion. He commanded both women's attention—first Amrita's and then Rosalie's as well. Tink left after making a promise to send an oil-burner to drive them the short distance to where *Xu Mu* was moored.

Several epics—hours of time, as whites counted it—remained till he'd be needed aboard. Who else could he get to help further the May Fourth cause? He reviewed the names of his contacts in this hemisphere. According to Tink's most recent knowledge Yoka, the longest standing of these contacts and Tink's partner since they were both children, served in his nation's priesthood—deep inside Everfair. The Tam brothers, the most likely candidates, remained in Everfair too, as did everyone else Tink could think of. Well, per-haps he would have to summon them to the capital when he had arrived and settled in.

He had paused unthinkingly at the basin of a public fountain, an edifice of spouting jets, wet stone, and rippling pools. So beau-tifully useful: women with clay jars scooped up its bounty to carry home for cooking, cleaning, slaking their thirst, watering their gardens. . . . The droplets saturating the surroundings with their freshness reminded him of the cascades of Kisangani. Would Kwangmi appreciate the cascades' joyous rushing? Would she im-itate their plunging abandon and leap headlong into the marriage he was asking her for?

Likely not. Vigilance and careful reflection were two of Kwangmi's most endearing traits. Some other goad was needed. Something that would speed up the time she took for consideration.

Twining through the fountain's mist came soft eddies of Rosa-lie's odor. Though the shop they emanated out of lay three corners away, he would recognize that scent anywhere. He allowed it to mingle with his memories of Lily, to infuse them and to be infused.

And that was the answer. He would convince his love that in Rosalie she had a rival.

Walking first to the hotel to bathe and pack, Tink took a wind-ing route to the Old Fort to ensure that his arrival was simultane-ous with Rosalie's. And Amrita's, too, of course—but her low-key jealousy of him would probably help rather than hinder Tink's plan.

Kwangmi had already ascended to *Xu Mu* ahead of them—he caught thinning traces of her, vanishing upward. Still, from the bridge pod where she was stationed, she would easily be able to smell his party. He ushered his two guests into the lift cage woven in imitation of Everfair's earliest basket-sided models, and was shutting the gate when his sister arrived. She also was accompanied: by Gopal and another, a stranger. This stranger was male, well-fed, well-pleasured—though he hadn't been pleasured by Bee-Lung or Gopal, judging from the low level of cross-scenting. Very little was detectable; they must have barely touched. A tassel buttoned to the neck of his white robe was the source of the man's main perfume.

Outside the lift car, the operator rang a bell and released its brake. Soon they had risen above the noisy evening throng. "You are Ho Lin-Huang, the inventor?" asked the stranger.

"I am."

"Your sister has told me of your prowess. And of your movement's growth. I'd like to join it."

Perturbed, Tink wafted a questioning air toward Bee-Lung. Something about this man pricked awake the hairs on the back of his neck. What was it?

"The Qadi Ahmed ibn Amir has cleared our permits for filming," said his sister. "And also he expresses interest in supporting our true mission—justice being his aim in all things." The breath with which she spoke bore reassurance, encouragement, a pledge of explanations—later. But there was something else. Something akin to a quality of the judge's, something troubling and elusive . . . something that dissipated into nothingness as they rose.

All of Zanzibar's passenger facilities hearkened back to Everfair's past: a covered wooden platform jutted out in a circle from the top of the lift shaft, and lightweight, ladder-like walkways could be manually extended to the hatches of moored aircanoes' gondolas.

Crossing these was often tricky because of the wide openings between their "rungs." As he escorted Amrita and Rosalie aboard *Xu Mu*, Tink managed to mark Lily's sister with a convincing swathe of simulated desire-filled sweat.

Customarily, when the entire crew assembled they did so either in the hold—if it was on the empty side—or in the two general quarters compartments, with the curtains between them pulled aside to allow the back-and-forth of smells and sounds. Bee-Lung paused in the corridor there, so Tink thought they were gathering all together in this spot, now, to confirm acceptance of their new kin. But then she went on again. He told himself this was no surprise. The infirmary was where she inoculated recruits, and evidently a lengthy consultation on the matter wasn't needed.

He had no objections to their destination. Here in the infirmary they were close to the companionway down to Kwangmi. She would receive a powerful dose of his manufactured desire for Rosalie.

Bee-Lung entered the small confines of the infirmary proper with only the qadi at her side. Gopal backed away into the crew crowding up behind them; that left Tink and Rosalie—and Amrita—standing on the tiny cabin's threshold.

His sister gestured for both women to come in. "Will you kin together with the qadi? Please?" she asked. Her invitation was a natural one from the standpoint of efficiency. But through the cloud of his own artificial longing Tink discerned no inclinations toward one another fermenting between the new recruits. At least . . . nothing at all emanated from Amrita, and there was only the mildest of intellectual interest on Rosalie's part. While on the part of the qadi . . . Wait. That . . . that was lust, yes, *lust*—though oddly accented, and muffled by the presence of—what?

From his low stool, the qadi smiled. "Perhaps you're hesitant to join together with me because I've been given the Russian Cure?"

"No, I—"

"STOP! NO!" Horrified, Tink grabbed Bee-Lung's hands and

thrust them up, out of her workbox. "We *can't!*" The Russian organism? Here? *That* was what he smelled!

"Brother! Brother! Be calm!" His sister tried reversing his grip, tried to grasp his wrists and stroke his hands, but he wouldn't let her. He wouldn't! It was a trap! Did she, too, harbor the Spirit Medicine's rival? Was that the source of that odd impression he'd gotten? And lost so quickly on the lift?

"Mr. Ho? What's the matter?" Amrita put a proprietary hand on Rosalie's shoulder, pushing her behind herself in the corridor. "Is there something wrong? We already knew about the qadi's previous inoculation and—"

Bee-Lung twisted free of Tink's hold. "The Russian organism won't hurt us—I have it too. I can control it!" She turned to the qadi. "Tell him!"

"But will he trust me? More than he trusts you?"

He would not. And now that he understood what he was dealing with, he wanted Kwangmi as his wife more than ever. He wanted custom, certainty.

"Listen! Tink! We know May Fourth is going to win—so let's prepare to organize the fruits of our victory! Let's study the specimens provided and draw conclusions as to how to handle the Russian organism's remnants when we've conquered Europe."

"I'll stay behind, on the ground, when you leave," added the qadi. "Out of your way—where I won't be able to interfere. Does that ease your mind?" Before Tink did more than open his mouth, the advent of the only one who really *could* ease his mind distracted him from his answer. Rising up the companionway, Kwangmi's emanations carried not the faintest wisp of jealousy—but they were thick with satisfaction, and as her glossy black eyes appeared they turned only briefly to meet his. Then they came to rest on those of Lily's sister. The satisfaction deepened, spilling fast from Kwangmi's pores.

"What a good find!" she pronounced. "We need more kin like

you, free of the stupid-making passions of animals." Finishing her climb, she wrinkled her forehead in unbecoming consternation. "Big Sister! Why do you hesitate? Make their mixture! Give them their night together here—give them as much time as you can! By dawn we must be on our way."

So *Xu Mu* would depart? So soon? Who had decided that? And when? Tink's confusion met Bee-Lung's comfortable acceptance of the situation. She had known! He glared at her accusingly. She shook her head and sighed a rueful sigh. Looking away, she selected a glass jar from her workbasket.

"There's a new message from Miss Bailey," Bee-Lung explained. "She won't be joining up with us until we reach Everfair." A flurry of scents traveled between his sister and Gopal, an exchange too quick for Tink to decipher. "Miss Sevaria will do all the filming there now."

CHAPTER EIGHT

May 1921
Kisangani, Everfair

You brought him!" Queen Mwadi grinned and opened her arms. Raffles jumped to her across the fruit-laden table.

"But of course! Didn't I promise?" Mam'selle Toutournier seated herself, moving still with the ease of a schoolgirl, though nearly an elder. The queen reminded herself to show Mam'selle the same respect as ever, despite her own recent ascension to the throne. She said nothing about Mam'selle's presumption but sat herself also. Her watchful attendants would act in accordance with their ruler's behavior.

"How was your flight?" Mwadi asked. "Not too cold, I hope."

"Child! I'm not so delicate as all that—remember, I've traveled by aircanoe since before your birth! I've ridden bicycles on roads and off of them—steam and oil-burning—and I've piloted waterfire climbers up the falls and the rapids—for miles! Surely you don't think a tame little trip on *Okondo* would cause me any problems? Unless you believe Nenzima an inferior captain?"

"No—"

"To tell you truly, you should be more concerned for your pet."

Mwadi frowned and attempted to straighten her arms to hold Raffles where she could see him. He grunted and wound his fingers in her palm-leaf crown. "No! Stop that!" she scolded him. The crown was braided to her head. "Hafiza—peel a banana and hand it here." With the banana as bait she was able to free herself from the monkey's too-close embrace.

"He seems unhurt." The banana vanished between Raffles's thin lips. "His appetite hasn't suffered."

"Really? I would have expected him to eat immediately on entering the room—did he not leap *past* the food to greet you? He's anxious not to risk a separation again, in my opinion."

Mwadi peered at the monkey more intently. His coat as luxurious as ever, Raffles was gazing longingly at a dish of tangerines cut open and arranged like flowers. But he remained in her arms. She relaxed her hold, which had been loose to begin with, and Raffles melted against her as if he were a dollop of warm grease. "You may be right."

"I often am."

"Bo-La!" Rima's voice sounded too clear to be coming from where Mwadi had left her, the bedroom all the way across the palace's courtyard. She must be standing right below the audience chamber's window. "You still holdin court? Ready to quit for the day?"

Mam'selle's face betrayed nothing.

"It's barely afternoon!"

"Ain't your brother due to be takin over about now? I want you to come with me an see how I fixed up that stage for filmin over at the Cultural Circus Buildin. An then I show you my new home!"

Mwadi looked questioningly at Mam'selle, whose expression remained bland. Well, it would do no good to expect otherwise. Mwadi knew that from all the roles she'd played—tutor, actress, spy—Mam'selle had learned to guard her face.

"What advice do you need from me?" Mwadi asked Rima. "I have no experience in setting stages or decorating homes. Whereas Mam'selle Toutournier—"

"Why not wait till evening?" This overfamiliarity was appalling! To dare to interrupt her queen! Mwadi glared, but Mam'selle continued speaking. "The drums say Madame Sevaria will arrive on *Xu Mu*. It's her film, after all."

"Her film. My country." She deliberately turned her back on Mam'selle and went to stand on the balcony outside the window, which was where she wanted to be.

"I ain't no good at waitin! Listen, Bo-La, you gonna keep me down here shoutin up these flimsy excuses for us to be together? Or you feel like duckin out? Come on!" Pleading now, Rima raised her strong arms and held them as if she expected the queen to leap into them off the balcony.

Mwadi looked back over her shoulder. Hafiza and the servants hired by Queen Josina had stayed inside. Mam'selle stood poised on the room's threshold, one swinging shutter in her hand. Only Mwadi had come this far. She wanted to go farther: her thighs strained against the balcony's pink stucco parapet. Irresistible, the dizzying lure of Rima—a woman sweet with the blossoming of a wilderness they tended together every night.

Yes. She wanted to say yes to anything Rima asked, go with her anywhere she wanted to go, and display her happiness to the palace—the city—the *world*. She wanted to be with Rima, to be *seen* with her. Where was Ilunga? Why couldn't he get out of bed promptly and take his turn upon the throne, when he'd cheated to sit there? He must come soon—

A stirring at the chamber's door calmed Mwadi's heart. At last she would be free. It was Rima, not Ilunga, but so what? Her duties for the day were done. "I'll order a carriage. Meet us by the side gate."

"What you mean 'meet *us*'? You ain't bringin nobody else, is you?"

Her duties for the day were done—except for those she owed her monkey. "Only Raffles."

"You oughta leave that thing here!"

"He's fresh off *Okondo*. I'd like him to become accustomed to me again—"

"You like to spoil it, that's what. Well come on then." Whirling away, Rima disappeared down the path to the courtyard's exit.

Experimentally, Mwadi loosened her hold on Raffles, hoping he would be tempted away by the courtyard garden's foliage. Instead he threw his long, fur-cloaked arms around Queen Mwadi's neck, wrapping her in a desperate warmth. One thumbless hand caressed her cheeks.

Sighing, she went inside, taking him with her.

Kisangani, Everfair

Gliding upward between the slick bellies of his two new favorites, King Ilunga withdrew his penis from the hot oven of one woman's vaginal canal and rotated to plunge it into the other's even hotter mouth. Her grunts grew muffled. But combined with the first's whimpers of disappointment they were still loud enough to drown out most additional noises.

"Get out of bed."

Most noises. Not his mother's voice.

His erection wilted. He kept it in place so that the woman's head covered him. He pretended not to know the hour's lateness. "It's morning?"

"No. It's afternoon. Your sister has left the throne vacant. Your subjects are waiting for you."

The pointy-breasted woman he'd been fucking was up now and holding open a kilt. He managed to put it on without drawing attention to his flaccidity. As the women toweled dry his torso he and Queen Josina went over the petitions to be expected. Nothing exciting; the plan was to nibble away at Everfair's protections for a season or more, thus lulling both the British and Atlantropan parties into believing they'd won.

"Also," his mother reminded him, "I have decided to furnish the doctor with a much nicer hand than he's expecting."

"Can't we just give him a standard replacement?"

"The Italians told him he had botched the job, and that they needed to redo it, maybe remove half his arm before they gave him a permanent prosthetic. I'd like to offer him a more attractive option."

They left Ilunga's rooms and descended to the courtyard,

following the paved paths winding through the garden and around Queen Josina's pavilion. A light rain pattered quietly against the dome of his bowler, forming drops that suspended themselves from its brim.

"You intend to join me in the audience chamber?" Ilunga asked.

"Your sister won't be happy that I continue missing her turns." Taking the stairs at a rate that showed her at least as fit as her son, Queen Josina—no one had yet summoned the courage to divest her of her title as they had done with Mwenda's other wives—arrived at the audience chamber's entrance ahead of him. Over the past few markets he had been glad of her counsel in navigating the feuding Europeans' tricky political waters, in pitting country against country. And he was even gladder that she deferred to him now in public, though he suspected her ambitions were high as ever. No matter. She waited for him to enter the chamber first, her face patient.

King Ilunga stooped to assume the throne. Devil had wished him to exchange it for one modeled on the Tudor throne of Britain, or that of some other European royal family. But Mwadi preferred this low, backless stool of silver-brass-and-gold-studded ebony, and his mother sided with her. Ilunga had kept silent on the matter, believing that to argue about it would waste time.

Apart from Gasser and most of the rest of Ilunga's personal retinue—his new favorites had stayed behind to prepare themselves and the bedroom for the next bout of sex—the audience chamber was empty. And so it continued for a long stretch. He had actually fallen into a semi-doze before the arrival of his first supplicant. And of course Dr. Kleinwald sought Queen Josina's help, actually, rather than Ilunga's own. The king struggled to appear interested in what they were saying. Something about the doctor's decision to self-amputate. Where was the pleasure in hearing about that?

"It wasn't painful," the white man explained. "Only frightening—and only that because I didn't understand what was happening."

"What were the symptoms, then?"

"My fingernails thickened and turned dark, then flaked away. There was discoloration of the blood vessels in the area around the wound—at first I suspected septicaemia, but I experienced no chills and had no feeling of feverishness."

"What color were the veins?"

"Green."

"Did it spread?"

"Initially. My entire arm seemed affected. But after I operated the color disappeared."

"For good?"

"Look!" Kleinwald untied and rolled back his unfashionably long sleeve. This revealed a gleaming band affixed between the base of his palm and the prosthetic's leather cuff. He pointed to the skin above the cuff that he had also exposed. "See? Nothing wrong."

Queen Josina held out one elegantly oiled hand. "Let me examine you more closely." She took the white man by his clumsy metal hand and drew him nearer. With a long nail she traced a snaking line up his pale forearm, and shook her head slowly, gravely.

Now King Ilunga was intrigued. He leaned forward, though from the vantage of the throne he saw nothing further. "What?" he asked, his voice high with impatience. "What is the problem?"

His mother dropped the white man's arm and frowned. "The color has not vanished," she explained. "All it has done is change."

Kisangani, Everfair

The stage of the Grand Ideal Cultural Circus was crowded with lumber and pungent pots of paint, glue, and varnish. Queen Mwadi admired the skill with which Rima skirted its colorful chaos, dancing easily between busy set-builders wielding saws, tacks, hammers, clamps, measuring tapes—

"Bo-La! What you think?" Swirling to a stop in front of her, Rima flashed a swath of gaudy silver fabric back and forth, up and down. "Costume for my character?"

Mwadi pinched the cloth between her fingers. It felt smooth and cool and heavy, like flowing water. "Who are you playing, again?"

"May Weather Syn-D the name. Livin in the year 2021. I give The Sleeper—that's Sevaria—her tour when she wake up from her coma. Ima be the future!"

Mwadi smiled. "Yes. Wear it." She looked around for Raffles. Her last sight of him had been just inside the theater auditorium's entrance, jumping for its balcony. "Do you need to stop for a fitting? I'll wait." She took a paper bag of sugared raisins from the bundle of picnic supplies she had smuggled out of the palace, right under the servants' noses.

"Won't be more'n a moment." Rima bustled away with a plump European, and Mwadi descended from the relatively well-lighted stage to the auditorium's floor. Before her, rows of brown velvet-covered seats slumped away into obscurity. A little illumination was provided by holes pierced in a few glamps burning along the auditorium's walls, but the majority of the lighting fixtures mounted there were dark.

"Raffles?" The monkey knew his name, knew her voice. She shook the bag of raisins. She should never have let him go. A collar or a leash would have given her some means of control. Mwadi regretted rejecting them.

There! Above her head, a sudden, impossible breeze blew by. And then a low wooden clatter came off the balcony—a pair of chair legs knocking together. Provoking creature! "Come here! If you missed me so much, why run away?"

There was a staircase in the Circus lobby. Mwadi aimed for the weak daylight seeping beneath the auditorium's double doors. But no sooner had she reached them and pushed them open than Rima reappeared on the stage at Mwadi's back. "Bo-La! Hey!"

With long strides Rima bridged the distance between them. "You ready? Ain't leavin without me, is you?"

"No—merely going up to the balcony to retrieve my monkey."

"What for? I done tole you it only be in the way while we havin our fun." She twined one sleek arm around Mwadi's waist. "Never-mind no monkey; let's go."

They crossed the lobby side by side. One last try. "Raffles!" Queen Mwadi shouted up from the foot of the stairs. "Raffles! Come!" The sole answer was silence.

Must she choose? Gratification or responsibility: Were these entirely separate paths for her from here on?

Outside, visible through the Circus's ostentatious new glass entrance, their conveyance waited. And there on the cart's roof, much to Mwadi's relief, sat Raffles, poking his thumbless paws into a bag she didn't recognize. Maybe if she went closer—

"See? Your monkey know how to look after itself." Rima pulled the cart door open for Mwadi; Raffles dropped onto the seat across from her as she settled herself, still clutching the still-mysterious bag. Rima spoke to the bikist, then climbed into the cart to sit beside her.

Down the steep ramp to the street they rolled. "So where are we headed now?" Mwadi asked.

"I found me a half-finished house near the airfield. Some hard-ass European businessman was expectin to live there—show you the one room where he thought he was gonna be scrubbin his back."

"A washroom?"

"You hafta see it."

Raffles pulled a shongun blade from the bag he was examining and held it to his mouth. "No!" Mwadi snatched the blade away. Its edge was sharp but poison-free. She relaxed just a little. "What have you got there?" She tried taking the purse away too, but the monkey wouldn't release it. "Let me look!"

"Bo-la? You need help?"

"In a moment." Mwadi relinquished the bag's drawstring and dug out the raisins again. She held them where Raffles could reach them. "Trade?" Still clutching the bag in one paw the monkey stretched out his other for the treats.

"When he takes—"

Like lightning the monkey's paw flashed forward and back—but Rima moved quickly too. "Got it!" She flourished the strange bag toward the cart's low ceiling. Raffles screamed and lunged at her.

Mwadi flung herself between monkey and dancer. The cart banged to a halt. They all crashed together and fell into the narrow space between benches. She managed to hug Raffles in a hampering embrace. Their bikist cracked open the cart's door. "Is everyone all right? I heard shouts—"

"Shut it! Drive on!" Raffles wriggled in Mwadi's arms but the door closed again before he could escape. The cart started rolling. Rima half-climbed, half-slid onto the forward-facing bench and gently pulled on Mwadi's arm to bring her up to sit beside her. Huddling in the cart's farthest corner, Raffles scooped clumps of raisins into his mouth and chewed them rapidly while eyeing the two women with what appeared to be suspicion.

Mwadi checked to make sure her crown had stayed on straight, then pulled the purse open. She found it hard to distinguish its contents in the cart interior's low, varying light. "Scoot away."

"Why?" Rima asked. But she obeyed, giving Mwadi room enough to dump the open bag between them. Curved steel glittered on the leather upholstery—five more shongun blades, which she understood. Most magazines took six—but why were they loose? And in a woman's reticule, from the looks of the other items: a jar of lip coloring, a lace-edged handkerchief, a tiny, square-looking glass protected by a sheath of black-and-violet brocade, a crumpled piece of paper with a torn edge, as if it were a page ripped from a book—

"Sumpn else in here." Rima was squeezing the ostensibly empty bag. "I feel it. Hard an small, caught up inna corner . . . Here!"

The object was a pearl-and-diamond ring, its setting mimicking a snowflake. A thread from the bag's lining was wound around its central stone. It seemed familiar ... where had she seen this ring before? She worked it onto her middle finger. A little tight.

"Okay. That's it. What the note say?"

"What note?"

Rima picked up the slip of paper. "This'n." She smoothed it out against her thigh. "Hunh."

"Yes?"

"You right. It ain't no note; itsa map."

Mwadi leaned over to peer at the page; it *was* a map, and as she'd thought, it had been part of a book at one point—an expensive one? No. She'd been supposing the plundered book's value based on the map's colors—but looking closer she saw that these had been added by hand, after its removal. The shapes shown were as familiar as the ring's, and similarly impossible to place. The words written over and next to them were neither English nor French—"Do you speak German?"

"Some. Learnt a little when I was tourin Venezuela—that an Spanish." The cart jolted; she nodded and kept nodding. "Good eye—'berg' mean mountain in Deutsch—what we call German. 'See' mean lake. This here is Everfair, Angola, Cameroon. . . ." Rima's words trailed into silence. "A bit down here at the bottom be talkin bout 'unavoidable casualties.' You know what those is? Sentence got cut off."

The cart put on a burst of speed. Mwadi steadied herself with a hand on Rima's white-clad knee—and a reverse image of what she was looking at painted itself across her mind's canvas: a white woman's hand splayed against dark fabric—purple satin—Mrs. Chawleigh's dress! Mrs. Chawleigh's ring!

Mwadi addressed Raffles as if he could answer her. "Where did you get it? Where did you find this reticule?" The monkey regarded her silently, solemn as an old priest.

Rima laughed. "What you think? He gonna tell you how he stole some poor refugee—"

"Don't pretend you're a slow-wit! Look at that lace, those jewels—this is no refugee's bag! It belongs to Clara Chawleigh, who is *not* supposed to be here. She's a spy! She and her husband—"

"Yeah. I know all about it. Ease up, awright?"

"You know? You knew and you didn't tell your *queen*?"

"Course I did. Queen Josina an Lisette got it all under control."

She should have expected Mam'selle to be part of any secret Rima kept from her. And her mother! Furious, Mwadi banged on the cart's ceiling to stop it. "Turn around!" she shouted to the bikist. "Back to the palace." The cart started up again but maintained the same direction. Had he not heard her correctly? She cocked her fist to hammer again for a halt.

"Bo-la? What's wrong? We almost there—ain't goin back now, is we?"

"Ilunga and Clara Chawleigh are lovers! We have to get to my brother and intercept any communication between them, now we know she's here in Kisangani."

"Now wait a minute! Ain't I tole you your mama got everthing covered? Ain't she always? An you know how I been plannin on you comin over my new place? Only a hopscotch from there to the airfield—you kin warn off King Ilunga tonight when he come out to welcome *Xu Mu*."

The cart's forward seat was higher now than its back; they were riding up the ramp of a roundabout. The splash of their wheels was replaced by rumbling echoes bouncing off the cobbles paving this major intersection of city street and country road. Mwadi pulled the window shade aside: the curving wall of the roundabout flashed into view, a blur of grey stonework. She gripped the barkcloth shade's edge nearly hard enough to tear it. "So Ilunga will go to the airfield tonight? How is it you're privy to the king's itinerary?"

"Got my ways. I kin be persuasive when I wanna be."

Yes she could. As the bikist's turn onto the road leading farther and farther from the palace demonstrated. As the implacably gentle hand Mwadi permitted to cover her own further showed. Strong as spider silk, that hand drew Queen Mwadi's gradually unclenching fingers to Rima's soft-lipped kiss.

She fought love's weakening effect. "You wouldn't dare!"

"Dare what?"

"To kidnap me."

"Kidnap you? I ain't doin any such a thing!"

"No? Then tell the bikist to stop. Tell him to turn around and take me home. *Let me go!*" A surge of fear and anger lowered and tightened her voice. Raffles looked up suspiciously from his raisins.

"Why you wanna run away? Ain't I always been real nice to you?"

"Yes. But why—why can't we just—" Frustrated, Mwadi tore back her hand and made a fist a third time. She only meant to beat it against the roof, but her monkey growled and bared its teeth and crouched to attack.

"Hey! Awright—it was spozed to be a surprise to you." Rima pouted and hung her head as if with shame. "You an your pet makin me wreck it." Her head rose high and proud again. "But okay! You gonna love it anyway. My new place got a full bath—like in a bath-house! Turkish style!"

"Oh!" Mwadi had adored the elegance of Cairo's hundreds of hammams. Though they'd been open to anyone— "Yours is private?"

"Now you unnerstan why I hadda take you there?" The cart slowed, made a sharp turn, stopped completely. "Take you here, I mean to say. At least look roun before you decide to head back."

"All right." Gathering up Raffles, Mwadi stepped out of the cart onto a modern, wheeled, metal mounting ladder and descended to a drive of broken shells. Barrows, tarps, and mounds of river stones still littered the grounds, but the house at their center radiated poise and finish. Beneath the green roof of its verandah, a pair of white-painted shutters were propped on either side of its opening door. Breaking free of her hold, Raffles vanished between them and into the house's relative gloom.

Mwadi followed him in and quickly reassured herself: he'd merely sought for and found a retired perch where he could find peace and quiet to digest what he'd gorged on. He often did so. She sighed, letting go of her anxiety and vexation, letting herself embrace the house's cool shadows, the soft echo of its welcoming emptiness, the freshness of its mud and mortar, its polish and promise—and at the end of that corridor, there, softly, she heard water dripping into a pool. She walked toward the sound. It would have to be a wide pool—and judging from the faint breeze blowing over it to her, so warm it verged on scalding hot—no, it would be cool—no, freezing cold!

All three temperatures awaited her. She stopped in the middle of the shallow archway leading from the house proper to a conservatory reminiscent of the home she and Ilunga had shared in Al Maadi. Except that this glass dome sheltered not tender plants and graveled paths, but a trio of tile-lined bathing pools.

Rima came to momentary rest beside her. "You like?"

Queen Mwadi nodded earnestly. "Yes—let's try it! I'll stay!" Together they continued past the closest pool to where scaffolding encircled one of two carved columns. Rima explained how each column would be topped by a showerhead, and pointed out the pipes installed along the ridge and rafters to feed them.

"But for right now this make a good rack for us to hang our clothes on. Attendants an them come later." Grinning, she shoved down her trousers and kicked off her sandals. A shrug and she was free of her loose, twilight-colored tunic.

Mwadi had too much on: sandals with knee-high laces; the long skirt of state; the tight-sleeved, frontless bodice popularized by Josina—and worst of all, the grass crown braided to her head. Light compared to European versions, her crown had never before troubled Queen Mwadi, but now she struggled to release herself from the tyranny of its frailty.

"Want me to help, Bo-La?" Rima's naked back bent over a table to their right. She straightened and turned with a shining blade held point up before shining breasts. "I kin get you outta—"

Mwadi's hands rose to cup themselves protectively around the crown's annoyingly intricate coils. "No! It's sacred! Royal regalia—you can't cut it into pieces—I wouldn't let you!"

"Who say I gonna? Bo-La, you too quick to jump! I was only meanin to cut your *hair*." Rima flourished the flashing blade again and Mwadi saw now that it was a pair of shears. "We can be like we twins!" Tilting up her chin, she mimed a vain self-caress to the bas relief sculpture of her coiffure. "Whatcha think?"

"I think . . ." Queen Josina would be shocked! What could be better? What could more thoroughly prove to her that her daughter Mwadi was a woman fully grown? "I think yes!"

Rima bit one dark red lip and closed her eyes. She opened them and shook her head no, as if getting her way displeased her. "This a big deal for you? Lemme make it bigger."

Rima gestured toward a bench on the room's other side. "I kin start on your hair while I try an explain."

"Is this more about your work for Russia?"

"Yeah! Ain't you smart! But this not about what we was discussin before, who my job made me hafta spy on. It's sorta like, well, it's somethin you gotta have done when they hire you."

Russia's government had noticed their neighbor China's relative immunity to the Maltese Influenza decimating Europe, and had connected it to its spread of the Spirit Medicine. But to avoid infecting themselves with socialism they had developed their own version. It was this, the Russian "cure," with which Rima had been inoculated two seasons past. The explanation lasted so long that by its end Mwadi's hair had been clipped down to a fine fuzz. Her crown, now too large to wear comfortably, rested on the bench beside Rima's sleek-muscled haunches. For a moment more she herself rested between Rima's marvelous thighs, on the unglazed tiles at her feet. Then she stood, brushing stray clippings from her lap and shoulders.

"Go on an leave that—when we get out my people be back and clean it up. Got to give you your final trimmin anyway, once you figured out what kinda design." Rima stood too.

"So how about joinin me this other way? Just a tiny little slit; you hardly gonna notice it. Won't hurt you, I promise! And afterwards we could be a lot closer to one another—that's what they tellin me."

Closer together than Rima and Mam'selle ever were.

"We be all in each other's emotions, accordin to my information. Yeah! Plus, I really ain't felt none a them bad effects you hear about, neither. No longin to be alone, no achy head, no sleepin all the day and half the night." Leaning nearer—as if there was anyone else in the room to overhear her whisper—Rima added, "Tween you an me, them things prolly only a problem for white people."

Leaning back again, she held up the shears, open now. "You ready? I have the fruitin bodies grown in that pot over there, right next to the warm pool. You ready now, or you need a while to ponder the question?"

Too long had she been leery of Rima. Too long had she looked at her askance, seen her as a possible danger—attractive but of dubious intent.

Once more her beloved knocked at the gates of her understanding, asking for Mwadi to arise and let her in. Nothing should separate them! Her heart was awake! She cast aside her doubt and what shreds of jealousy she could find. She offered Rima her right wrist, upturned. "Do it."

Kisangani, Everfair

King Ilunga regretted his insistence as the oilburner smoked and reeked and choked and screeched its way out of town. Why should he care how loyal he looked, with Devil leagues away, exploring Lake Edward? Beside him Queen Josina kept her face smooth, but surely the noise bothered her too? Surely the oilburner's jittery progress upset his mother as much as it upset his stomach?

"Sorry!" He had to shout his apology twice. The ride given by this machine was much worse than the one Devil had lured him into taking to the docks.

And longer. By the time they reached the airfield, Ilunga was nearly sober. From the field's far side a low, red-gold sunbeam pierced the clouds, a pointed reminder that the cocktail hour had begun. With a glance at his mother—even within the obscuring shadows of the oilburner's interior he must look sharp not to be caught out—he slipped a discreet, pigskin-covered flask out of his sporran. Up, up—only inches now from his thirsty lips—

"You will share your drink with me, my son?" His mother's hand covered his own.

"Of course. I'll just make sure it's safe." A small, closely super-vised swallow calmed his nerves, but not as much as he had wished to calm them. And then the gin's comfort was whisked away.

"Pah!" Queen Josina's plump mouth puckered, flattened, screwed down at the corners. "Not my favorite of the European liquors—where did you get it?"

"Gift from Mr. Chawleigh." Bestowed—with a knowing wink—as Ilunga left their ferry after spending a wonderfully sweet night in the arms of the white man's wife. And now—soon—he would be entertained by her again.

The bikist brought them to a stop. They had reached the air-field's mooring tower. Showy lamps powered by steam-charged waterfire batteries flickered to life near its top as he emerged from the cart. Above, thin clouds parted and regrouped around glamp-like stars. There was no sign yet of *Xu Mu*.

"Why are we so anxious to meet these particular passengers?" Ilunga asked his mother. "They're not part of our conspiracy." He paused. "Are they?" As he'd come to realize upon being sent to Cairo, Queen Josina was at the center of more than one intrigue.

"Rima's employer is of interest."

"The filmmaker?"

"Sevaria, yes. Sevaria binti Musa—which means newly built daughter of Musa. She is a Muslim and comes most recently from the island of Ceylon, though originating in Malaysia. She supports British oil interests."

He wondered how his mother knew all this. Which of Queen Josina's many intelligencers had provided her with such thorough background information? Most likely she'd used more than one.

On a portico jutting off to the right, the disengaged lift engine grumbled quietly to itself. They entered the tower and passed the bottom of the spiral staircase leading to the passenger platform. At first Ilunga was grateful not to be forced to climb it, as he expected to exert himself more enjoyably later that night. Once they had entered the lift cage and begun their slow ascent, though, he sighed in impatience. It would have been better to move rather than stand still, better to be doing *something*.

They arrived at last at the docking level. When not showing off to schoolmates and glossing over Everfair's weaknesses he had to admit to himself how shabby and cramped this place seemed compared to the palace and other public spaces. Mr. Beamond, the white in charge of the airfield, had never asked for improvements. As a result there was not even a stool to sit upon; Ilunga had to resort to perching on the lift cage's wooden parapet—and then his mother sent that back down and there was only the platform's too-high railing for support. And Gasser's arm.

Time crawled like a caterpillar. Why did his mother require his presence for whatever scheme she had in mind? Sometimes she explained, but the tilt of her eyelids told him she was once again judging him to actually be as stupid as she'd taught him to act. He was pondering a ruse within his habitual ruse, a way to escape her keen supervision and go off to finish emptying his flask, when finally the growing drone of an aircanoe's engine announced *Xu Mu*'s approach.

Ilunga leaned away from the support of his servant. A woman he hadn't noticed below—short and slight, but with an ample bosom—emerged from the staircase, bowed, and went to stand at the mooring controls. Her novelty was attractive; when he was finished with Clara he would have to acquire her services. And her name. Tonight? Perhaps. Or perhaps tomorrow.

The gangplank was got in position and passengers began to descend to it out of a square hatch in the bottom of the hovering aircanoe's gondola. First came a familiar-seeming man of about his father's age. Ho Lin-Huang, also known as Tink, that would be—he who had left the country rather than submit to the old king's rule. Ilunga glared at him, meaning to show by his displeasure that he himself would never tolerate such waywardness. But the Macao man's eyes avoided his and fastened instead on Queen Josina's.

"Mr. Ho." His mother extended both hands in greeting, as though to a family member.

"Most highly esteemed queen." Tink stepped forward to take the offered hands and bring them to his heart. "We're grateful to be able to slake our thirst for wisdom again at the well of your beautiful mind."

The queen laughed. "How long have you rehearsed that pretty speech? You don't sound much like the Tink of my memories." She gestured to a somewhat older woman still standing on the gangplank behind him, baggy trousers and vest detracting from her femininity. "Is this your sister?"

"Yes! How odd you never met! Ho Bee-Lung—"

A black-and-white blur sped toward the gangplank. "Raffles! Come here!" Queen Mwadi's voice rose unexpectedly from the lift shaft. "Raffles!" The blur stopped at the gangplank's near end. Yes, this was Devil's former pet.

The lift engine got suddenly louder, and the chains and cables dangling in the shaft began to move. Someone was riding up. Likely his sister—but no, her scolding came now from the stairway.

"Raffles! Hear me? Come! At once!" Sandal slaps punctuated her breathless shouts—why such a fuss over a stupid animal?

She appeared. Shocked, Ilunga gazed at his sister's nearly bald head. Where was her crown? Where were her plaits?

"Raffles, be good! Come—don't be scared of my new hairstyle. Come!" Mwadi bent and moved forward, both arms out. As she neared him he saw how designs cut in low relief curled and twisted like snakes through Mwadi's short-cropped hair.

"Look! Here—" Queen Mwadi held out a brown lump. "—I have a delicious date!" The monkey sidled away as if wary of her, then dashed to snatch up the offering. Mwadi caught and held him by one long arm. "Hah!" she cried.

Squealing with fright, the monkey lunged toward the gang-plank, but Tink stood steady at its foot, blocking the way. For a moment Mwadi's grip held. Then the creature wrenched its arm free and darted toward the lift shaft—but here came the lift's cage, with Miss Rima Bailey riding inside.

"All this commotion! Ain't you got better control a your pet?" The actress leapt over the gate in the cage's parapet before it stopped. Raffles shied back. "Want I should chase him for you to grab a hold?"

Ilunga realized his sister's haircut was a more elaborate version of Miss Bailey's. That explained it. Mwadi idolized the actress—as she demonstrated anew by disregarding Miss Bailey's impertinence: the actress had failed to properly greet either him or his mother.

Mwadi too ignored them. "Yes, please! And maybe with every-one else's help—"

Queen Josina assumed a mask of amusement and interrupted her. "Mr. Ho, please forgive my daughter. Mwadi, no—our guests need rest! They're just arriving! Don't pay your monkey any mind. He'll return to you on his own."

She drew Mwadi to stand by her on one side, Ilunga on her other. "As you've likely learned, with Mwenda's abdication my children have become Everfair's king and queen—joint rulers. We'll accept your formal obeisance tomorrow morning."

Her face once again smoothed itself of expression, as her eyes focused beyond those she addressed. "And who is this?"

Tink and Madam Ho turned simultaneously, swinging apart like double doors. Between them Ilunga glimpsed a voluptuous yet lithe woman clad in some light, gold-tinted fabric. As she approached it billowed with the breeze of her passage, dancing like flames.

"We present our passenger and business partner, Sevaria binti Musa, filmmaker and star." Ilunga vaguely registered that these words came from Madam Ho's mouth, which was odd, because—

He couldn't think why it was odd. He couldn't think why. He couldn't think. The flame woman was approaching. Nearer. Nearer. Her eyes flashed and sparkled; her red lips shone invitingly; her palms were laced with burning swirls that reached across the intervening air to lick against his skin and caught! The sweetest fire blazed up in him, a fuse of hot delight set off by the flame woman's markings.

He smiled. She didn't, but no smile was necessary to light her already-bright visage. She said something soft, something quiet, words falling like ashes from her white teeth, her flickering tongue; she tilted her head and raised her coal-black eyebrows as if awaiting an answer. She had asked him a question?

From his left he heard his mother laugh. More words—Queen Josina's. He made an effort and heard them: "I'm sure he will—his sister, too." Pressure on his shoulder forced him to face away from the flame woman. "You'll grant Miss Musa's wish, Ilunga?"

"Of course!" He managed to make this remark without choking on his own spit.

"And you too, Queen Mwadi?"

"Oh, yes! Rima's been waiting!"

Waiting for what? For this fire? Jealous, he frowned over his shoulder, but Miss Bailey appeared unperturbed. She hooked her thumbs on the sash of her trousers and strode forward. "I got us a perfect 'Hall of Memories' set," she announced. "Come an see it." She peered past the small gathering. "You say you brung Gopal? Where he at? I cain't—"

"We're mainly staying aboard *Xu Mu*."

"He'll sleep with the rest of his . . . friends."

First Tink, then Madam Ho spoke. No reason to be confused by the swiftness with which one answer followed the other. No reason to be irritated by his confusion—after all, it was apparently invisible to the only one who mattered. The flame-being was paying no attention to his discomfort, was no longer even looking at him, but at the tall actress swaggering toward their group.

Hurrying to interpose himself between her and Miss Bailey, Ilunga leaned forward and asked the beauteous Miss Musa the first thing that came into his mind: "Who is this 'Gopal'?" If they were a rival the king would have them gaoled.

"He a beginner." Miss Bailey slung her long arms carelessly around his sister's neck like a shawl. "We spozed to be actin together in Miss Musa's movie. She say he exactly what she needed."

No flush of embarrassment reddened the flame woman's cheek, though she was pale enough to show color. So very likely this Gopal was not her lover.

Nor would he ever be.

They descended to the ground. As they arranged themselves in the ample seating provided by three carts—his mother had drummed for a second to supplement the one they'd arrived in, and then Miss Bailey and Mwadi had come in the third—he took care to keep Miss Sevaria by his side. This meant suffering his mother's concealed pinches in silence. He knew she wanted to drive him off and have the flame woman's company to herself. He didn't care.

Only two carts pulled up at the palace entrance, as Ilunga observed on mounting the steps from the street. Out of the other cart climbed Tink and Madam Ho, assisted by little Gasser. There was no need for the apologies Queen Josina descended again to offer them. They hadn't exactly been abandoned—he'd entrusted their care to a good, reliable servant.

And so his sister's cart was missing. What of it? Mwadi and her Rima were sure to be all right. Besides, as the whites said, nothing gambled, nothing gained. He had played his mother and won. He tucked his winning's arm more tightly into his own, felt it throb with warmth and life.

"Here we are. Should I escort you straight to your room? Or would you like to see the grounds and gardens first? Or to be shown about the palace?" The encouragement and practice she'd given him during the ride from the airfield helped him talk to her as if she were just any woman.

"I want my own bed, I think." And to hear her voice answering him as if any woman used it to say anything. "Who will undress me?"

"I will." He felt the words spring from his mouth like plants sprouting up from seeds, pulled into the world by the sun.

"That will be perfect—thank you!" Her glowing regard fired his heart with courage. He was going to make her his wife!

Queen Josina started upward, their other guests following her. "Mother!" he called. "Miss Sevaria has the Pink Suite, yes?"

"Yes, my dear. Will you take her there? Bee-Lung is asking to see my surgery."

Ilunga grinned. His mother no longer fought his choice. Let her arrange all else as she would.

The glamp-lit corridors of the palace shimmered as he and the flame woman passed through them. The door to the Pink Suite stood slightly ajar, spilling a slim fan of rosiness onto the polished wooden floorboards. He pushed it wider. He released his flame woman's arm to usher her in. Her inner brilliance blended with the blushing radiance of the high brazier as she circled the room, taking in her accommodations.

"Are you satisfied?" he asked. "If not—"

"Where do we sleep?"

His heart sang. We, she had said: confirmation of their coming

consummation. "The bed is in your other room—past these curtains." He parted the folds of her silken hangings to reveal the
darkness of the Pink Suite's inner chamber.

"Oh!" Her tread light as smoke, Miss Sevaria came to stand at
his side. "And where shall you bestow my clothing once you remove it?"

He showed her. The tall chest that served as the suite's wardrobe
sat in the shadow of a dim dividing screen. Each layer of swathing
fabric he removed—veil, scarves, vest, smock, skirts, stockings—
increased the thrilling nearness of her furnace heart. When all
was bared he sank to his knees in triumph. There! The luminous
outline of her thighs and hips, the skim of her waist, the swell of
her breasts—perfection!

He surged to his feet, urging her before him, laid her swiftly on
the bed, lifted his kilt, and threw himself upon her. Possession!
Thrusting once, twice, thrice, he groaned and climaxed.

Too soon! No woman would be satisfied with such a brief engagement. But if—if he could rouse himself again— He kissed her
shining hair, a lustrous ear, her peerless brow, the translucent
lids of her dazzling eyes. She stirred a little beneath him—and he
within her! Yes! He was restored!

More measured now, his movements began slowly, barely rocking the mattress. Soon, though, he was grinding himself against
her with utter abandon, so lost in their conflagration he would
have missed Gasser's entrance—if not for the boy's shouts.

"No! Mr. Chawleigh—sir! I beseech you! You are in the wrong—"

"What is the meaning of this! You leave my wife dangling, waiting for your promised assignation— It is an insult! You insult an
accredited Beauty, you desert her for a mere—"

Ilunga rolled free of Miss Musa's flickering allure. Chawleigh
loomed against the false dawn of the curtained doorway. A sinis-
ter length distorted the silhouette of one hand—a knife? A gun?

CHAPTER NINE

"Commodious, and well laid-out," Bee-Lung pronounced the royal clinic. "Your planning is exemplary."

"Thank you. But of course much was already in place—the hotel's laundry and kitchens were both located here, and they used the same rooms for storage as we do."

"What do you store?" Bee-Lung asked the expected question automatically, but only half heard Queen Josina's expected answer. She could categorize most of the supplies she smelled: an abundance of bleached cotton, of alcohol, of water liberated of its stony impurities by distillation, and also traces of other necessities such as honey, sharpened steel, and salt. Those scents she didn't recognize must belong to unfamiliar names the queen recited as they walked the long room's circumference. Plants, mostly, and most likely local. Yes—there were whiffs, there, of two she'd learned to recognize during her earlier stay: pennyworth and periwinkle.

"And through here?" she asked, stopping at a doorway filled with a wooden door. Unusual in this climate, even in this building.

"A patient under observation."

"What for?" The door was tightly fitted. Yet between its joined boards threaded a male's aroma. A white. Not enough perspiration in it to warn of a fever.

"An infection that I don't think has run its course. Do you care to examine him yourself?"

Bee-Lung nodded, and Queen Josina's attendant opened the room. On a small bed built into its far wall stretched a sleeping man, thin and reeking of bad dreams. Black curls twisted on his pillow as he rocked his head from side to side, but his eyes stayed shut.

"Why doesn't he wake?"

"Drugs. His own. He says he needs them." The queen shrugged. "Won't it be easier for you this way?"

She went in. What was the matter? The closer she came to the man, the stranger she felt. Was it because of his race? No—she'd seen plenty of white men before, here and at home in Macao, and in Tourane and other stops along their route.

One forearm ended in a stub, with a reddened ring of scar tissue right above it.

She stood by the bed, looking down. Behind pale, twitching lids the man's pupils spun and danced. Something was missing— what? She shut her own eyes, to focus.

The air at Bee-Lung's back stirred as Queen Josina entered, and with the addition of her scent the feeling of wrongness faded and shifted a bit. Another's scent would have been better, though—

"His name is Alan Kleinwald. He's a doctor, but not of human wellness and disease," the queen said. "He studies how the entire world folds—I think that's what he'd say. How big is little and little is big. How we're all related."

Gopal's! Gopal's scent belonged here. Because the first time she'd encountered one particular ingredient of this room's blended odors had been in his company. In Zanzibar, in the qadi's apartments, in the body of the man himself . . . It was the odor of the Russian organism, the Europeans' equivalent of and rival to May Fourth's Spirit Medicine.

She opened her eyes and turned to meet Queen Josina's gaze. "Yes. He's still infected. And infectious. But I may have the cure."

Kisangani, Everfair

Tink paced the confines of the rooms to which he and his sister had been assigned. At least the windows were large, and plentiful.

But he had checked, and there was no sighting *Xu Mu* from any of them. He restrained himself from trying fruitlessly again.

He missed Kwangmi. He'd finally figured out what to say to her on the way here, and now they were apart again. For how long?

He missed Mwenda, who had failed to greet them on their arrival at the palace. Tink had known of his plan to abdicate—but where had the former king gone afterward? "Into the bush," Queen Josina replied to Tink's queries, as she directed him to follow the servant who'd come with them from the airfield. He parted from her as slowly as possible, but received very little elaboration: Mwenda would go where divination led him, and would include in his retinue General Wilson—another man Tink had looked forward to seeing again.

He missed Lily. Here, in her homeland, he admitted that silently to himself. His love for Kwangmi did nothing to lessen his sense of loss. Nor did reawakened awareness of Lily's death blunt his feelings for Kwangmi—in fact, it heightened their urgency. Death lurked everywhere, could manifest in any moment. When would he be able to impress upon his new love how crucial it was that they marry?

Questions without answers. Too many. And no relief to be found in wishing himself back aboard the aircanoe, with Kwangmi. Bee-Lung had insisted he descend into Kisangani tonight, for reasons mysterious to him but evidently not to her. She had exuded confidence as she invited him to join her, and he'd accepted with no reservations, expecting to engage in a final exchange of confidences with Mwenda—perhaps to refurbish his hand, or design a new one. He'd brought his sketchpad and toolbag for that purpose, retrieved from luggage lashed to *Xu Mu*'s old deck months ago.

How had his sister found them for him so quickly?

Tink shook his head. Pointless to wonder. So many better avenues of exploration lay before him—literally. Rather than lament what he couldn't see outside the rooms' windows, he should concentrate on what he could: a crossroads. The confluence of three of the capital's sunken boulevards made a six-armed star, the golden reflections of surrounding glamps on their shallow waters wavering and running together, going and coming along ways he too might take.

The scrape of metal on stone made him turn toward the door to the corridor. Its curtain parted to admit the sturdy-looking boy servant known as Gasser who bowed, then beckoned in another, scrawnier-looking boy dragging an iron basket behind him.

A basket filled with brass plates and rods, toothed gears, rings, pins, rivets— "Where did you find these materials?" Tink asked.

Through the arch came a woman's lilting voice: "Queen Josina sends her compliments, and asks your help." A woman clothed in a tunic and short trousers like himself or Bee-Lung entered. "A new refugee seeks a replacement for his lost hand." She smiled, bowing. "You are the best builder."

"That's no answer." A scarf sewn with green and yellow beads covered the back of the woman's head, visible as she bowed again. She straightened. The hair thus exposed, dark and lustrous, reminded him of Rosalie's friend's hair. That of their new recruit, Amrita. "What shall I call you?"

"I'm Hafiza, King Ilunga's woman. And these are Gloire and—"

"I don't care who they are, Hafiza. Tell me what I asked you."

The woman's round eyes widened. Shouldn't she be used to such brusqueness? But perhaps not from a stranger. Was he emanating too much hostility? He composed himself and tried again. "Is what you've brought me the gift of the queen?"

Relief flushed the air. "Yes. And I don't know—" Light embarrassment tinged Hafiza's emissions. "—I can't say precisely where this set of supplies comes from, but Her Prominence thought you'd like having them."

"Yes. I do. Gasser, Gloire—it's Gloire, isn't it? Leave that there, by the long table. Then go." He unpacked the basket, organizing its contents as he laid them out: rods and plates in descending order of size, gears by size within groupings based on the shapes of their teeth—

A flutter of green and yellow caught the corner of his eye and he looked up from his task. Hafiza and her scarf remained. Of course. He hadn't sent her away.

Perhaps she'd make a good recruit. "Is there any more you can say about this?" He waved one arm over the glittering arrangement of artifacts.

The woman gave a hopeful smile and secreted a matching flow of optimism. "Not specifically, but . . . the king's mother has said to him that she kept a collection of many of the things left behind by departing Europeans—and by you—in the case that they might someday prove useful."

"Ah! I did find several of these pins familiar, and a few of the finishing bosses, too." He picked up a faceted semi-round he remembered as one of the final products of his partnership with Yoka.

"Shall I assist you to prepare for bed?"

Tink frowned in puzzlement and eyed the curtain separating off the bedchamber. Why would he need help? Had he missed something about the arrangement or construction of the chamber's furniture? For months he'd slept in hammocks; under his first, cursory inspection the beds had looked easy to manage in comparison. "I'm fine."

Amusement tinged with curiosity drifted off the woman. "Yes, you are." Could that faint aroma be desire? If so, so much the easier to bring her under the Spirit Medicine's sway. He would consult his sister about doing so tonight.

Kisangani, Everfair

Bee-Lung walked into their palace suite and located her workbasket by its distinctive cachet. "There." She pointed and the attendant, called Sifa, nodded and picked it up from the closest of the room's two desks.

Her brother stood beside a long table covered in glittering machine pieces. When he'd lived in Everfair before, he had spent most of his days and many of his nights figuring out the best ways to make such things work together. Better than his current obsession. "Please leave that for the moment and come with me. I want to show you something I think will interest you."

Sifa conducted them back to the clinic, though this wasn't strictly necessary; because of the Spirit Medicine they could never again be lost. One of many benefits it gave inoculants.

The primitive prosthetic provided by the prison hung on a hook beside Alan Kleinwald's room. Her brother took it down at the queen's invitation, the creases on his brow shrinking and smoothing out as he became absorbed in examining it. Good.

Quietly separating Queen Josina from her attendants, Bee-Lung closed the door to the sleeping patient's room securely behind them. Then, whispering, she enumerated the advantages of swamping the fungal agent responsible for Dr. Kleinwald's lingering Russian enmeshment with a fresh inoculation using May Fourth's Spirit Medicine.

"Our organism is superior. The sensory enhancements it conveys are many times more powerful—and since we'll be with this man as he adjusts, we can integrate him into a good core and kin him with those sure to be loyal to your cause. Those you trust." She paused. "They'll be in deep, honest, and totally reliable communication with him. They'll keep him from making white errors."

Queen Josina nodded her shapely head. She whispered, too. "I've seen enough of that. Though a close connection can help. And persistence. Eventually, my sister Lisette's wife—"

A rustle of sheets drowned out the sentence's end. Bee-Lung shifted her attention to the bed. Alan Kleinwald's eyes remained shut, but he smelled awake. Why should he pretend? How did she seem to him? She adjusted her output to a more soothing

blend of fragrances, adding a maternal air to the general friendliness and eagerness to help. In her previous encounter with this
organism its sophistication had been unremarkable, so maybe
that was all she needed to do.

The man kept his eyes shut but sat upright on the bed, swinging
his bare feet to the stony floor. He coughed, covering his mouth
with the crook of his complete arm. Then he opened his eyes and
laughed.

"Queen Josina! Who is this with you? Have you given up? Are
you putting me under someone else's care?" He rocked forward,
ready to stand.

"Stay where you are." Bee-Lung tried to make her command
sound like a suggestion. "It will aid my examination," she added.
Not entirely falsely. Though most of what she needed to know
she'd learned while he lay unconscious.

"This is Madam Ho Bee-Lung," said the queen. "She's just arrived this evening with her brother—" She frowned and pivoted to
face the shut door, apparently noticing for the first time that she
was alone with Bee-Lung and her patient. "—her brother, Mr. Ho
Lin-Huang, once a trusted advisor to my husband. I've described
your case to her and heard her proposed treatment. I think it's
sound."

"Do you." The white man hunched over and began rubbing his
stump.

"My brother Tink's working on a better-designed hand."

"Two brothers?"

"One brother. Two names."

Queen Josina pulled the door open. "Sifa? Mr. Ho?"

Tink entered, followed by the attendant. The room was too
small for such a crowd; the attendant Sifa backed up to occupy the
doorway.

Tink's customary scent these days was a mix of devotion, determination, and self-denial, with a touch of mild, almost wistful
curiosity; right now he reeked strongly of inquisitiveness. "How

well does this thing fit you?" he asked the man on the bed, holding up the artificial hand.

"None too well. But it will do till I get a better." Quitting his massaging, Alan Kleinwald reached out for the prosthetic.

Her brother let their patient take it and sank to the bed beside him. "Before you put it on, allow me to make some measurements." He produced from a vest pocket a fine metal chain, a protractor, a stick of chalk, and a dark wooden shingle, and began fussing about with them, asking the patient questions about how he needed to use his hand, scribbling the answers and sighing.

The white man flinched once or twice—Bee-Lung couldn't tell whether this was from pain or a sense of violation. Fascinated by the mystery, she stared; he caught her at it and stared back.

"Is this your treatment?" he asked her.

"That comes next."

Tink withdrew, mouthing silent words, frowning and combing back his hair as he walked from the room without having acknowledged the presence of the queen. Bee-Lung sat down in his place and apologized.

"Please excuse my brother's manners. He becomes blind to everything else when solving problems."

"I remember, and I choose not to take offense at what is obviously his nature—for he has yet to acknowledge even my husband as his monarch and superior. Sifa, follow Mr. Ho and help him." Queen Josina shut the door behind her attendant. They were alone again. Bee-Lung opened her workbasket and began laying out her tools and materials on the bed's end.

Alan Kleinwald leaned forward to peer past her at them. "You've seen these sorts of things before?" she asked him.

"No."

So his inoculation with the Russian organism had been done in some clandestine way—certainly via a much different vector than any used for May Fourth's. Her self-inoculation with the qadi's specimen, for instance, had involved a blade, a cut, blood, a dressing. How could such a method be used surreptitiously?

She waved at the stoppered vials holding her selection of Spirit Medicine threads. "Do any of these speak to you?"

"What? What are they—ghosts in jars? I don't believe in nonsense like that."

"You don't have to believe in something for it to work!" At Bee-Lung's reprimand, Queen Josina's eyes flashed and a puff of surprise leapt from her skin. "These are forms similar to a compound you've already received, a botanical recipe rendering you more perceptive of others' emotional states and more receptive of connections to them." Those were the basics, all he really needed to know.

"You say I've already received it."

"Yes—rather, something like it, but weaker: what you've received comes of a different line. Perhaps even a different species." Bee-Lung wasn't clear on that yet. "I believe its influence can be overcome; to begin with, what the Russians gave you was never as powerful as what we use, and its remnants in your body are now quite faint. Plus we can easily keep you under observation here since you're not in a prison from which you need to escape. We'll be able to sniff out any buds of trouble before they flower.

"And we'll have even more of an advantage if we work with a formula for which you have an affinity. So—"

"Not in a prison?" Alan Kleinwald looked about the cramped, windowless room. "It's true I came here of my own accord. But what if I should decide to leave?"

"You must just let us know, then," said Queen Josina. "One of my women will go with you to make sure you're safe."

"A guard." The white man stood. He paced to the door but left it shut, turning back to pace the eight steps that brought him to the wall opposite. "All right." He returned to his former seat on the bed. "Is this how I pay you for my custom hand?"

"No!" Bee-Lung didn't want this to become a business trans-action. If Alan Kleinwald paid Bee-Lung for a hand Tink made at Queen Josina's behest, then what would she herself owe the queen?

"Yes." Queen Josina's pluming pride sheltered a stew of other scents. Satisfaction, Bee-Lung recognized, and acquisitiveness too—a curious combination. "Participate in Madam Ho's treat-ment program and you'll provide us both with the knowledge we need to defeat our enemies."

"Our" enemies? According to May Fourth, the ones to defeat were the world's imperialists. Didn't that include this country's rulers? And didn't its former king's favorite wife emit frequent whiffs of scheming to rule those rulers? So how could Bee-Lung have enemies in common with Queen Josina?

"I want this one." With his flesh hand, the white man fished out a flask buried beneath the ones Bee-Lung had offered.

"No," she said again. More gently she added, "That's still an ex-periment. It's not ready." He had selected the strain intended for Sevaria's match. Which would be the new king, Ilunga, if she had anything to say in the matter.

"Why not? It's the— It feels right!" Before Bee-Lung could stop him he put the flask to his mouth and twisted out the rag sealing its neck. Then he held it to his eyes. "Can't see much." As he tried to upend it she grabbed his wrist and snatched the bottle back.

"It's not yours!"

"I say it is." Queen Josina stood and opened her palm, lifted it like one presenting something to the sky. "This will be the variety administered. Prepare it. Show me how I too can perform this rite. Do you have everything you need?"

She should lie. Why not? Who would discover her falsehood?

But she must succeed, so that May Fourth's Spirit Medicine could vanquish the Russian rival. By studying the Russian organ-ism's effects on herself and Gopal in the inoculation she'd kept limited, Bee-Lung had come to hope that this victory was possible. She needed to demonstrate it now. "We can't do it here."

"Why?"

"Are you hoping to learn this technique? Then we'll need witnesses, and a record keeper of some sort."

"Shall I call Sifa back?"

"If you value her skill as an observer, yes, let's have her help. Only there ought to be others, too, to ensure impartiality, objectivity. And if we're to implant a story at the same time to reinforce the inoculation process— Really we need a larger space."

Throughout their move to the throne room and the gathering of additional attendants, Bee-Lung sought the opportunity to substitute another strain of Spirit Medicine for the one she had hoped to reserve for use on King Ilunga. Impossible. Occasionally Queen Josina's eyes left her, but never for long enough.

So instead, Bee-Lung got the queen to summon the king, her preferred subject. He arrived accompanied by Sevaria, passion streaming off the pair of them in a most gratifying manner. The star's glamor, switched on at Bee-Lung's behest, ostensibly to save the film from any further governmental interference, had done its job.

It ought now to have been a simple matter to inoculate King Ilunga with both versions of the Spirit Medicine right then—except that his seat of state stood next to his mother's, and that was where he installed himself. Sevaria, who graciously accepted the suggestion that she act as storyteller, stationed herself by his side. She also took charge of the pot of cocoa brought at Bee-Lung's direction, stirring into it the rough ground threads Bee-Lung gave her, the growth of one of May Fourth's standard forms of Spirit Medicine.

Then Sevaria settled into her performance, like a glamp's flame steadying. "Once," she began, "there was a lonely hunter. As a boy he had learned his father's trade, and spent many glad hours with him. But an illness swept the father away and deposited him—and many more besides him—at death's feet. So instead of growing up surrounded by love and family, the hunter lived alone, surrounded only by dogs."

Bee-Lung sat on a new-woven mat on the room's polished stone floor, chopping and mixing the ingredients for the inoculation of Sevaria's special Spirit Medicine coremate. Alan Kleinwald reclined on a longer mat rolled out to her right. Queen Josina's half-lowered lids belied her tight attention to the scene playing out before her.

Bee-Lung's hand hovered over the jar containing the threads she had intended to use. "What's that?" the queen asked, smelling suddenly of suspicion.

"A variety we're skipping." She made her hand continue to another container, similar enough in style and color she could be forgiven for mistaking the first for it. "Here's what we want. Charred platypus fur." It was nothing so arcane—merely hairs singed off a cat skin. But why should she reveal everything, all her secrets? What power did this woman think she had over her, that she sought so blatantly to direct events? With her husband stepping down . . .

"And the purpose?"

Bee-Lung thought quickly. "The intelligence of the Spirit Medicine will take the structural skeletons of our adjuvants as models and reproduce them within our patient." That sounded plausible.

"Very well. And they have drunk the preparatory brew—the basic compound? You gave it to them as the storytelling commenced, yes? So it's time to administer this special variety."

Bee-Lung was cornered. No more stalling—if she added further ingredients, the Spirit Medicine's action could potentially be smothered in a mishmash of low-grade corollary effects.

Desperate for an alternative course, she fixed her awareness on Sevaria's story. She needed a clue, a prod to her thoughts.

The filmmaker seemed to have reached a climax. "He saw the Queen of Forest! The prey he stalked lay at her feet. 'All my men wear red!' she proclaimed. Dipping her hand in the buffalo's blood, she anointed his brow. 'Swear your fealty to me!' The hunter heard and obeyed."

With an unmistakable effusion of sureness Sevaria held out her hand to Bee-Lung. *Now,* she mouthed. She wanted the Spirit Medicine! She intended to apply it—to the patient! Despite the sexual intimacies she'd initiated with King Ilunga, despite the shortness of her acquaintance with Alan Kleinwald, Sevaria had chosen the latter as her proxy brother.

Warm waves of love washed from Sevaria's glands, surging toward this white man. Bee-Lung was powerless to redirect them.

Was it possible that a connection as deep as the one she still meant to create between star and king could exist alongside another such? Alongside the bond about to be formed before her eyes? Reluctantly, Bee-Lung gave Sevaria the dish of powder on which she'd wasted as much time as she could. And the bamboo through which it was snorted. No more in control than Queen Josina, she watched and heard and *felt* the doctor ingest the specially prepared Spirit Medicine and succumb to its enlarging spell.

Zeroing in on him via her own olfactory enhancements, she recognized the Russian organism crawling through Alan Kleinwald's blood. Most likely it was mimicking the texture and tint of vessel walls; so it had wanted to behave inside her own circulatory system, though she kept it trapped in a custom cyst and filtered away its futile efforts at escape.

It did have a low cunning.

But compared to May Fourth's Spirit Medicine—despite being so long established in the white man—the Russian organism was as cold and sluggish as a bear waking out of a winter-long sleep, slow as a nest of half-frozen termites. On entering Kleinwald, the Spirit Medicine swept the Russian organism's nest away, licking up individual agents like a pangolin's sticky tongue. Brighter and clearer by the moment, the pulse of Alan Kleinwald's heart pushed nearer and nearer to Sevaria's, touching, matching, their fingers kissing, palm to palm, brow to brow, breath to breath, brain to—

"Fascinating!" Queen Josina's comment broke Bee-Lung's concentration—because she was too close! How had the queen come to stand here, right above the kinning pair?

"Yes. It's a success." A wilder success than Bee-Lung was going to admit.

"You can tell so soon?" The queen's odors aligned with her words: happiness, inquisitiveness, mild caution, a hint of something like . . . vindication, perhaps. But from her son, still seated, wafted a sour-ish jealousy mixed with acrid fear.

So soon, or sooner. You could sense the kinning sometimes before it actually occurred. "You'll be able to tell yourself, once you allow me to give you—"

"Not yet! We'll wait a while. I'll dispense a few doses first, be-fore accepting inoculation for myself." With judiciously impassive eyes the queen gazed down upon the twining embrace of story-teller and patient. "Are the subjects always so amorous?"

"No." When Tink and Bee-Lung had shared their joint inocula-tion with the special strain now in use, they'd felt glory, a mingling light that ebbed and crested a million times—but not the sexual throb emanating from the pair on the mat.

Had she done something differently in preparing this batch? Maybe one of her delaying tactics had affected the outcome, or she'd added a placebo that was not a placebo. As casually as she could, she retrieved the Spirit Medicine's dish—still holding an unused remnant of the powder—from its spot on the floor.

Kisangani, Everfair

Tink looked up from his worktable. Where was the woman he'd been given for help—Sifa? Yes, Sifa. When he'd sent her out with precise instructions as to what was needed, the suite's windows had shown unalloyed darkness; now they admitted moonlight to mingle with the flickering of this room's glamp and the low, steady glow of his sponge. How much time had passed? Too much. If she'd been unable to obtain the titanium wire for which he'd asked—a possibility all too likely—she should have gone to Queen Josina with his request. Or to King Ilunga; Tink wasn't sure yet how the royal hierarchy constructed itself.

Either would do. He stuffed the sponge in a pocket of his brown canvas trousers. The corridor was empty. The stairway up to the throne room was empty too—but not long ago angry, fearful men had shoved and beaten a white down those stairs. Why? Who? No one he'd ever met. Likely the matter had nothing to do with Tink, then.

But curiosity caused him to follow the scent trail a little ways, investigating. The white was male, too, and weirdly calm given the blows the odor of his clotting blood indicated that he was receiving. His captors smelled much more upset.

The stairs ended in mud and murk. If the Spirit Medicine hadn't enabled Tink to sense the guard standing to his left, he would have been startled when he spoke. "Where do you think you're going?" the man asked in Kee-Swaheelee.

Tink pretended to be lost. "I seek Their Royal Prominences." He answered in English, the tongue he and his sister had used exclusively since their arrival. Though of course he understood many more tongues—and was known to do so by some. But with this man his charade worked.

"Wait!" the guard instructed him after being subjected to a bit more faked ignorance. "I get one who talk you better." By now, however, Tink had had enough of this area's cellar-like lightlessness. Time to leave before he lost touch with his individual identity and became completely subsumed by the Spirit Medicine. Also, he worried that one of the other men's aromas could belong to an old acquaintance who would reveal Tink's fluency.

So as soon as the guard he'd been fooling left, Tink went back up the stairs. He kept climbing past his suite's storey and found the throne room complex right at the top. Inside was everyone he needed: Sifa, King Ilunga, Queen Josina. His sister too. He entered.

His client and the film star stood in the room's center, limbs

twining around each other like the knotwork of a decorative border. But this wasn't what Bee-Lung had intended, surely! Surely she
had meant to partner Sevaria with the king? Yet his sister sat calmly
upon a mat, smiling and emitting an only slightly puzzled satisfaction. It was Ilunga who broadcast pain and bewilderment. It was
Ilunga who turned to Tink as if seeking in his presence relief from
an intolerable loneliness—the very loneliness Tink himself prized
as a sign of independence from the Spirit Medicine's supremacy,
while at the same time hoping to exorcise it through marriage to
Kwangmi.

Tink bowed. He arranged his rising to coincide with Queen
Josina's rising interest in him. He expected her to ask him why
he'd left his worktable. Instead, her wide, beautiful mouth opened
to address Bee-Lung: "You and your brother are linked by the
same means as these two?"

"Yes."

"But you don't try to have sex. Have you never? Is this kind of
behavior in such a circumstance new?"

"Of course we two siblings don't want to have sex with each
other! We're not white! We're civilized people!" There was a brief
pause, during which his sister must have remembered that many
of Queen Josina's ancestors were of the Portuguese tribe. "And unlike European chiefs we have no need to control our dynasty so
strictly."

Apparently mollified by the voicing of this afterthought, the
queen turned her gaze to Tink. "Have you come to reclaim your
assistant?" she asked.

"May I?"

"No. Sifa is my particular attendant, and I want her myself to help
me retire. As she has witnessed an inoculation I also intend to question her on the process—tonight, while her impressions are fresh.

"Perhaps another is as well qualified." Without perceptible
physical movement her focus shifted to the king. "My son. You
will offer him Hafiza."

From anguish King Ilunga's emissions changed to sullen self-protectiveness. "Yes, Mother."

So that was who was in charge.

The king gestured and the woman who had earlier brought Tink his supplies emerged out of the cluster of servants standing along the room's far wall. "Go with Mr. Ho." She bowed and came to his side. He bowed again. She went to the door behind him, waiting to leave through it, but he stayed put.

The queen noticed. "Is there something else?"

Several somethings. Sifa's incomplete errand, for one. Also, his sister, whom he wished to consult, was ignoring his aromatic invitation to join him in his departure; she seemed rapt by the spectacle of Sevaria's and Dr. Kleinwald's embrace. Indeed it was a spectacle worth looking at, as the pair wound about each other in ways that defied gravity and made him wonder how they remained erect.

Nor did it look at all likely that he'd be able to consult now with the doctor about a practical method of getting his hand's manipulative powers to work on a sufficiently small scale, as he had suddenly realized he needed to do.

He picked the least important of these loose threads to pull. "I requested wire of a specific sort, made from a new metal: titanium. Sifa was to find it for me. Did she?"

"Mr. Ho?" Hafiza stepped nearer. He turned to face her. "I have instructions on where we may be able to acquire what you want. At the airfield there's apparently a depot of materials destined for Manono—"

King Ilunga interrupted. "But what do you need with such an arcane item?"

Why did the king care? He didn't—his odor remained sunk in primitive concern for his own individual survival. No genuine interest in what Tink was talking about. But Queen Josina—her aroma based itself on interest in everything. Tink addressed himself to her.

"I think that titanium's strength and ductility will match well with its resistance to corrosion and the relative ease with which our bodies accept its presence, to render it the perfect companion for my new prosthetic's external field generators."

Confusion thickened King Ilunga's aura. "Quite. But hadn't you best bring Doctor Kleinwald with you to test if this conductivity is enough for your, er, purposes?"

"What? Titanium's a very, very poor conductor!"

"But you just said—strength and conductivity—"

"No! I said ductility! That's a completely different—"

"Little Brother!" Bee-Lung emitted an un-Rat-like gust of harshness toward him—of anger, even. "Why do you presume to correct the king? Take the doctor with you, as he directs."

She stood and approached the entangled lovers. "Alan! Sevaria!"

Inexplicably, they parted. The filmmaker reclined upon the floor, gathering together her gauzy clothing. Dr. Kleinwald rose from his knees and smiled. "You have progress to show me?" He unrolled and smoothed his sleeves, pulled his trousers up and tied them in place.

Well, then. Tink truly had wanted to talk with him about the prosthetic. He left, the doctor and the servant following behind.

But outside Tink's suite Dr. Kleinwald frowned and stopped. "What's going on?" he asked. Tink wondered who he was asking—not Tink, for the doctor's gaze focused down the empty passageway, in the direction they'd come from. But no one was visible there.

Barely, though, someone was sensible, scentable. Someone climbing down the stairs that were around the corner. Mingling with the familiar updrafted odors of the captive in the palace's underground, and the familiar downdrafted odors of the throne room's occupants, came a new fragrance: a woman's, a white's, a seeker after growth and change. She was uninoculated as yet. As she came into view Tink registered the fact that Dr. Kleinwald still yearned past her. So he was being attracted by someone or something else.

The white woman reached them. "Sir?" She addressed the doctor,

ignoring Tink and Hafiza. "Might you be able to order a drummer to call a cart for me and my husband?" Heedless of her plump
hand on his false arm, Dr. Kleinwald shuffled hesitantly off toward
the corridor's corner. "Sir?"

"Please, Doctor, allow me to assist you." Tink set out after him.

"Wait!" The fear billowing from the woman's skin was all out
of proportion to the calm of her voice and expression. "You speak
English? Won't you arrange the cart yourself?"

Why not? It was the polite thing to do. Politeness frequently
led to recruitment. The doctor had vanished from sight, but Tink
could easily find him again. "Certainly I can do that for you. Your
name? And when would you prefer to leave? How quickly can your
husband join—"

"Mrs. Hubert Chawleigh." Dimples graced the white woman's
cheeks as she made a rueful grimace. "I'd like to leave as soon as
possible. I had an appointment with King Ilunga that went rather
poorly—in fact, he appears to have forgotten it entirely! So I've
nothing to do here. And my husband has got caught up in a small
disagreement, but I'm positive he'll be free momentarily."

So far every word the woman had said was true. Still . . . what
drove her to dissemble the emotions behind the words? And so
skillfully! Intrigued by the dissonance, Tink took Mrs. Chawleigh's
hand and bowed over it. "I believe Hafiza knows where best to find
the palace drummer at this hour."

"There's always one on duty! Wait inside and I'll go now." As
Hafiza hurried off, Tink opened the suite's door and ushered in his
guest. She went immediately to the unshuttered window overlook-
ing the intersection.

"I suppose it will take quite some time to get here, the cart."

Tink didn't know. "Mr. Chawleigh has plans to meet you at a
particular location?"

"Yes. No." She whirled to face him. "It's all such a muddle!
I'm meant to seduce the prince—the king—and win him to our
cause and— But why do I tell you any of this? I don't usually talk

so openly about Hubert's and my doings, and you're—" The white woman faltered. "Who are you?"

A node. A Dragon. "Ho Lin-Huang. A friend." In just moments he'd made great inroads, without needing to mention May Fourth or the spores. The charming gap between Mrs. Chawleigh's emotional state and her stance in the world made her wonderfully susceptible to the Spirit Medicine's allurements.

"I'm not—I'm not familiar with you, or any other Chinese. We've never met before—at least not formally."

"A friend in times to come. A future friend." Bee-Lung could see to that—perhaps at the same time she inoculated this servant woman, Hafiza. Would she want to create a whole new core?

The passage door slammed open. It was a white man—the same one whose weirdly calm odor had earlier haunted the stairwell. He slammed the door shut behind him and ran toward Tink and Mrs. Chawleigh. His calm air had intensified, hardened somehow. "Clara! We've got to leave now!"

"Hubert! But I'm still trying to get a cart for—"

"Who's this?" Mr. Chawleigh rounded on Tink. "What's your business?"

"I'm a friend," Tink repeated. "I'm assisting your wife in your escape."

Mrs. Chawleigh clung to her husband's shoulders, restraining him from taking hold of Tink's. "His name is Mr. Ho, dear, and—"

Loud anger spilled along the passageway—noise and smell. "No time!" Going far beyond polite behavior, Tink shoved wide the window and pushed the white man to the side. He stuck out his head. Sentries guarded the building's front, but they were focused on the street. "Jump! I'll provide a distraction."

"Right. You first, Clara."

"But Hubert! Where are we to find a cart?" Mr. Chawleigh bundled his protesting wife out of the window ahead of him. Tink dashed to the worktable and began sliding it toward the door to block it off—too slow. The door opened and several guards from the prison below streamed in.

Change of tactics. "Here! Help me!" Tink employed his most commanding voice and odors. "Push this out into the passage! He went that way—we'll tip the table over for a shield—he's got a shongun!"

No one asked how Tink had seen that. Together they lifted the table through the doorway, tilting it to fit and dumping all his carefully sorted tools and materials to the floor. Too bad. He would have to have Hafiza's assistance putting things back to rights.

Cries from farther off floated nearer. More minds to sway. More guards—and other people, not so geared up to fight—and one was his sister! He stood. Here she came around the corner, holding her workbasket in both hands, hair tidy, sweat proclaiming her allegiance. With her came Hafiza—whom he had sent entirely elsewhere! And the missing doctor. And Queen Josina.

The guards prostrated themselves. The queen spoke: "You let him get away."

A lean-muscled woman lifted her head. "Prominence, we didn't think—"

"No. You did not." The queen waved the guards up and away, shooing them past the table, toward the palace's entrance. "Go. Find again the man who dared threaten my son. This time, destroy him."

Later, in their shared suite, as he and Bee-Lung prepared for sleep, they recited to one another the events occurring during their times apart. The idea of recruiting the servant woman found great favor with his sister. Bee-Lung was already well-pleased that she had inoculated King Ilunga with her special Spirit Medicine despite Queen Josina's interference. And as she explained, the attenuation of the Russian organism's presence in the doctor's blood made it highly probable that the king's vector would be the more successful of the two.

To Tink's surprise Bee-Lung made no fuss over his encounter with the Chawleighs. Nor did she regret the missed chance to recruit them. "Let them escape. It's better than having to worry whether their inoculation would interfere in the king's and Sevaria's kinning. Already we have enough to concern ourselves with, and if the Chawleighs feel themselves in your debt, so much the better."

"I understand," Tink claimed aloud. This, too, was what it meant to be a leader: to plunge backward into the future, gazing blindly upon huge swathes of the past. To ignore his ignorance. To trust in boldness.

At first there'd been confusion as to how the furniture should be arranged. But their beds were now moved close enough that they could comfortably hold hands lying down—all night, if necessary.

INTERLUDE X

SIDE EFFECTS OF THE RUSSIAN CURE

On his diplomatic visit there from the former British colony of Zanzibar, Qadi Ahmed ibn Amir complained to the Italians that their prison camp on Nocra was far too hot. Shaded though he stayed in his assigned quarters—a shelter more hut than villa—the qadi missed the cooling zephyrs of his home. Rank sweat beaded the face of the prisoners serving him, drying to swamp in its sharp stink the softer effusions of the Russian Cure with which they'd been so humanely treated.

As he maintained afterward, it was due to the somnolent power of the day's heat, and not to any wish to evade his hosts' attention, that the qadi began making his solo excursions during the evening hours. And it was due to his preference not to impose on the signores that he failed to inform them of this, and to make these excursions accompanied solely by members of his own household.

The first time the qadi came upon the Prisoners' Grove, he mistook the men planted there for trees. Though he'd heard about the Russian Cure's unfortunate side effects, he'd never seen them, since very few of Zanzibar's citizens had yet received the Cure. There had appeared to be no pressing need. Besides, from everything he had been told, those affected spaced themselves too widely to be a match for what he saw.

In the faint moonlight, the victims' trunks mimicked the slim straightness of young date palms, and their hairy heads looked like saplings' crowns. Their limbs trembled, the qadi thought, with the night's breeze. Except that there was no breeze, and the limbs' motions became increasingly eccentric as he watched them, and the . . . bark was too smooth to be anything but skin. . . .

The second time the qadi entered the Prisoners' Grove he did so quite deliberately. He had heard, through discreet questioning, suggestions that the strains of the Cure with which inmates had been inoculated were experimental, meant to reduce the acreage wasted by victims of the strain currently in wide use. As he strolled along the grove's perimeter, this struck the qadi as plausible: though the number of the affected was high, they had arranged themselves so densely that their outstretched arms almost touched at the fingertips. So thickly, in fact, did they cover the ground, that the qadi missed the prisoner approaching him until they stood face-to-face.

The man was pale: an Arab or European. He spoke, and revealed himself the latter.

"Pardon, effendi, my attire—" The prisoner was clad in dirty rags, like his fellows. "—and my presumption. My name, sir, is Kleinwald. Dr. Alan Kleinwald. I ask your favor and support in my escape from this island."

The qadi showed no fear. Nor did he feel any, for his bodyguard was right behind him, and the prisoner smelled weak. "Why should I help you? I'm only here to assure the Italians that we'll keep up the extradition agreements they made with our British ex-governors." In exchange for certain considerations from the Italians, such as the inoculation with which the qadi had recently been provided.

"You should help me as proof of God's mercy!" The prisoner raised his right arm. The qadi's guard tensed, but the hand was empty. "They have given me their evil 'Cure.' A scratch, a scrap of its culture applied as I slept, and it has infested my blood—I feel it! Running wild within me!"

"But surely that's for your own good. If you're a doctor as you say, you know—"

"Not that kind of doctor!"

"But the Russian Cure is benign!" So the qadi had been told, and so he'd taught himself to believe. "Don't you want to live free of the 'flu?"

"Yes! I want to live a life free of all foreign bodies. You must take me with you. Smuggle me out. Bring me to the care of someone civilized, somewhere in Egypt or your own country—"

"I can't." The qadi gestured his guard forward. "You're blocking my way. Get out of it. Go back to your cell, or suffer the consequences."

The man shrank visibly, shriveling into a flaccid puppet of himself. "You can. But you won't. Why?"

If the qadi had taken Alan Kleinwald under his protection, this would have been a different story. There would have been no amputation, no throuple, no mergings.

The reason, though, that Qadi Ahmed ibn Amir refused Kleinwald's request was not because of any of this. The reason was its inconvenience: he had no wish to anger his hosts by openly adding their prisoner to his household, and no way to keep such an addition secret.

And so the qadi left the island as alone as he would ever be.

CHAPTER TEN

May 1921
Kisangani, Everfair

"Why do I—feel—so—*good*?" Mwadi stretched her thighs wider to better encompass the world of pleasure between them.

"Cause I wants you to. Cause I—"

"Don't stop! Don't talk!"

"You started it; you ast me! I was only splainin how we—"

"Rima!" Grabbing her lover's velveted head Mwadi thrust it back down again. "No telling—show me!"

All the morning's cool brightness, all her life's joy spun itself tight, entered inside her, opened wide to whirl outward, inward, outward, inward, out out out!

In the calm that followed the tempest of orgasm, Mwadi caught her breath and urged Rima up to rest against her shoulders. "Your turn?" she inquired.

"Don't gotta be like that, Bo-La, all tit for tat." Playfully the actress cupped and squeezed one royal breast. "Besides, them people that gave it to me was sayin their Russian Cure make us who got it feel the same as each other, an maybe that part's right? Yeah, gonna need to study it up—but later! Ain't you got your audience time comin pretty soon now? Let's get to the palace—maybe your mama be joinin you!"

When they arrived, however, the throne room was empty. "It still early," Rima declared.

Mwadi nodded. The stool of state's polished curves braced her coolly as she sat. "She may yet come."

A servant announced the first supplicant: another servant.

"Hafiza!" Mwadi tried to imagine what the woman could want. "Isn't it my brother you wish to petition?"

"I'll go to him too—but you were also my employer."

Mwadi gestured for her former maid to rise. "And so?"

"I wish to enlist in *Xu Mu*'s crew."

Rima scowled. "They ask you?"

The maid addressed her answer to Mwadi. "Yes, Queen."

Better if Hafiza hadn't answered at all. Better still if Rima hadn't interrupted the audience with a question. But since she had . . . best to end it.

"Have them make their request of me directly."

As the woman retired from the room, Raffles came in out of the courtyard, clattering open the balcony window's shutters. Mwadi held apart her arms, ready to embrace him in welcome. The stubborn animal stayed where he was, hooting sadly and bobbing his white-fringed head.

"He still scared a your haircut."

"Why?" She lowered her arms and nodded to Lembe, the servant at the door. "Bring us a fruit platter."

"Ain't you gonna need her to announce your next subject? Whynchu send me?"

"But I can announce myself. C'est moi, Mademoiselle Lisette Toutournier." Framed by the audience chamber's arched entrance she stood faultlessly erect: composed, lithe, elegant. Teacher. Co-conspirator. Rival.

Kisangani, Everfair

Fires slept. Fires lay down in beds of charcoal. King Ilunga was grateful that late into the night the burning had slowed so that come dawn he, its fuel, remained. Rolling to one side, he marveled at the smoldering beauty of the being who lay between him and his suite's curtain-hung doorway. Sevaria was her name. Sevaria binti

Musa. She would be his bride. His queen. His first and favorite. As Mwenda had always held his mother Josina in the highest esteem, so would Ilunga always hold Sevaria above all others—mere women.

A sigh, a swallow rippling her throat, a flutter of iridescent eyelashes foretold her waking. And then her eyes opened and he was once more aflame.

"Darling?" One hand, warm and fragrant, rose and lighted on his right cheek.

"Yes, my dear."

"What are your duties this morning? Are you able to accompany me to *Xu Mu* to arrange—"

"Anywhere. Anytime. Why ask? You know our story must take precedence over all other concerns."

The bed's other occupant stirred, then sat up. His new brother, Dr. Alan Kleinwald, who was a far better amplifier of sensations than Scranforth. Who had wooed and wounded him so gently in the night's darkness, the blood barely noticeable, the apology profuse. Who now asked, "And exactly what story is it we're telling?"

Ilunga smiled, confused. "What story exactly? *Ours.*" He handed the doctor his arm. "How we've met, recognized each other, fallen in love, and pledged to rescue the planet from the grip of capitalist hierarchicalism."

"Of course."

Kisangani, Everfair

Sometimes, when Mam'selle entered a conversation, its participants became more rational. Sometimes, though, they appeared to be more in thrall to their emotions. Queen Mwadi had observed this second effect in herself too often; she strove now for the first.

No prostration; no obeisance of any sort. As before, Mwadi ignored this probably unintended slight. "Be seated. Take my mother's chair." Queen Josina was most likely not going to grace her daughter's audience session. Again.

Rima stayed where she was, halfway between the throne's dais and the balcony by which the monkey had entered. Both she and Raffles were uncharacteristically still.

"So to this point, we've succeeded, yes?" Mam'selle sank skillfully into the chair, chin held high. "You're officially allowed to share the country's rule. And now?"

The servant was absent. Rima was in on most of Mwadi's plot. For the moment they could talk with relative freedom. "And now we find out what my mother thinks, and why she tolerates— encourages even!—Deveril Scranforth in his exploits. And also if she is truly going to destroy those spying Chawleighs!"

"Hunh!" Rima flung herself across the room and landed as if by accident on the dais's top step—at Mam'selle's sandaled feet. "Why you think she ain't? She give the order, right? An she offerin a reward, yeah?"

Mam'selle crooked a finger at Raffles. Provokingly, he came straight across the room to crouch before her like a courtier. "How are things with you, my friend?" Mam'selle asked with mock solicitousness.

"You like that monkey bettern me?"

"I'm fond of you equally." A wink! At Mwadi herself! Mam'selle sought to disarm Mwadi's jealousy by paying Raffles such close attention—but then she came down from Queen Josina's chair to squat beside Raffles, and that put her round haunches only a palm length from Rima's grasp.

Mwadi must not succumb to her feelings of mistrust. "I have physical evidence of these whites' evil intentions: maps, clandestine communications. Will you bring them to Queen Josina for me, Mam'selle?"

Mam'selle stood, with only the slightest hitch in her rising. "What good will that do? Be assured she knows all about the

Chawleighs' intentions, and has taken them into account in whatever schemes she's laid. She forgets nothing and foresees all."

"They're making a fool of my brother!"

"Ain't that hard. Sometimes your monkey smarter."

That wasn't true. Ilunga's appetites got the best of him with dismaying frequency, but Mwadi had seen intelligence shining from his forehead and heard it ringing in his silences and even, occasionally, in his words. Stubbornness was his fault, not stupidity—look how he had tricked her and left her behind in Kalima.

"Whatever my dear sister Josina has in mind, she's taken King Ilunga's character into account. She knows her son well enough to wield him with the ease of practice. She takes everything into account."

"Even things she ain't expectin? Like how her son been drug into some kinda three-way marriage with that doctor and my film boss?"

"What? How do you mean?" Mwadi leaned forward on the throne. A marriage? Why had she not heard of this before? Why hadn't she been invited to the wedding?

"But Rima, how does it happen that you know of this ménage?" asked Mam'selle. "I only learned of it myself because—well, because I made it my business."

"Ain't I said Sevaria my boss? Foun out through her." Rima splayed her hands over her face and shook her head. "Shootin schedule blown to hell; we gone have to reconfigure it so she can have her sumpn like a honeymoon."

"My brother married your film star? The woman who landed just last night?"

"Yeah. I guess. Sorta. Wasn't a actual ceremony but y'all's mama appeared fine with them gettin together."

So perhaps only a betrothal or a less formal connection. Still troubling, but not such a diplomatic blunder. "You say a doctor is involved also?"

"Doctor Kleinwald. You know him, yeah?"

"We met at Lady Fwendi's school. A European. A refugee."

"I see?" Mam'selle squinted. "And he is—"

"What I hear, he and Ilunga is both grooms to the one same bride."

"And to one another?"

Mwadi scoffed. "Ha! I doubt it! My brother has never been interested in other men."

"Prominence." Sifa spoke from the throne room's doorway.

Mwadi glared at the interruption. "You have the fruit?"

"No, Prominence, but Lembe will fetch it soon."

"What, then?" Was she never to be rid of these interfering servants, these outsiders and ignorant bystanders to the realm's political battles?

"I was present last evening. I observed and took notes on the kinning, as it was called, between King Ilunga and the foreigners. I come to reveal to you how this event figures in your mother's designs."

Mwadi felt her heart speed its beat. "You have been Queen Josina's woman for many long and loyal years. So why should you do any such thing?"

"Upon her instructions."

"Truly?"

"In exchange for certain pledges, yes, I am to explain her intent."

That sounded more like her mother's methods than merely giving knowledge away. "What pledges?"

"I may enter, Prominence?" Mwadi nodded and Sifa came forward to throw herself to the floor before the dais. "The message from Queen Josina is sent, she says, with love. The pledges she asks are to be made by you for the sake, she says, of our country's prosperity."

"You may ascend to your knees." Far up enough for a servant to be permitted. "Ought these others be allowed to hear more?"

Sifa settled her skirt panels in a smooth circle. "That's your choice."

Rima? Yes. Of course. Mam'selle? Mwadi had to, *had* to stick with her decision. She had to show confidence in the lessons taught at Lady Fwendi's school, and in their teacher. "Please proceed."

"Your mother of course wishes you to continue as a co-ruler. But in order to make available to you and King Mwenda—"

"*Former* King Mwenda," Mwadi corrected her.

"With humbleness, Prominence, I say that Queen Josina still calls him our king. His abdication is a ruse—in secret, he works to defeat the land's foes, in concert with his favorite wife. And in order to share with him access to the special powers bestowed by Madame Ho's Spirit Medicine, your mother asks you to journey to join up with him and his party on his pilgrimage."

"What powers?" The Russian organism had proved a disappointment in that regard. Her increased sense of intimacy with Rima could be put down to their increased time together. In all likelihood the Spirit Medicine's gifts would be just as strengthless.

"Is gaining such powers part of the bargain?" Mam'selle asked. What concern was that of hers?

"It will be. Forming a core with a member of your father's retinue should grant you the ability to spot his deceivers unerringly, and to learn of his well-being from afar. His choice of who you will 'kin' with is General Thomas Jefferson Wilson. You would prefer someone else? We can work that out along with the other details: who else will kin with you in this rewarding but risky venture, and who accompanies—"

"Bo-La! It gotta be you an me—we be more like we inside each other than ever, even with— Lemme come too!"

Sifa's skirt rippled as if she were trying to stand. "Miss Bailey, I believe my mistress has other uses for you."

"Now ask me do I care!"

What gratifying loyalty. Her beloved was so unlike Mwadi's mother.

As always, Queen Josina had her own agenda. She revealed

more of it that afternoon, in the garden's pavilion. More, but in Mwadi's judgment, less than the whole.

The pavilion's openness prevented the unseen approach of eavesdroppers. Its elaborately carved pillars supported its sheltering thatch, but they were too thin to hide spies. This was the perfect spot to meet.

For once, Ilunga had shown up for his shift on time; as usual, Queen Josina arrived with him. Then, as they'd been told she would do, she invited Mam'selle to promenade with her around the palace's courtyard. Mwadi was able to refresh herself in her room with a dampened washcloth before coming here to meet them, all according to her mother's plan. On entering the pavilion she had begun and won negotiations for Rima's inclusion in the proposed core. The price: accepting General Thomas Jefferson Wilson as her father's proxy rather than insisting on someone closer to her own age. Her co-wives' competing offspring, as Josina pointed out, were potentially problematic. Mwadi had no desire to form so close a connection with the General as with Rima—but he was old, and perhaps it would only be for a short time. Not for always. He must die sometime.

For now she lay on the pavilion's largest, lowest platform, striving to copy the careless attitude of her beloved, who sprawled beside her, occupying more than her fair share of pillows. Mwadi grudged her not one thumb's-width of stuffed satin.

With practiced sureness, her beloved rubbed scented oil into Mwadi's short, razor-sculpted hair. "You must teach Hafiza how to do this before you leave," Queen Josina declared.

"Why? We've agreed Rima's coming—"

"Separately. You'll leave separately and tryst later, afterward, on the way. We can't let your behavior here cause any suspicions." She occupied the second, higher platform, half-reclining on its couch. Her long-lashed eyes focused on Mwadi, closed, and opened apparently on Rima—for this was who she next addressed. "Your film has a shooting schedule, yes? So Lembe tells me. We won't need to interrupt it; you can still fly off to meet my daughter and my husband in plenty of time."

Even her tiniest victory was to be limited! Mwadi's control cracked and gave way. "'My husband'? You mean the king—the *real* king! The *real* one—who never meant for me to replace him."

The slightest of frowns furrowed Queen Josina's brow.

"Child!" Mam'selle stood from her perch on the second platform's edge and took two hurried steps in their direction—then stopped and stooped to accept Raffles's gift of a dripping, golden crescent of melon, whole and unbitten. She straightened, holding it to one side. "If your father pretends to forfeit the crown there is good reason—just as with the choice of General Wilson to kin with you. Isn't there? Shall I elucidate?"

Naturally, Mam'selle knew the intricacies of her "sister's" thoughts. Queen Josina, it transpired, was courting two distinct British factions: the traditionalists, who dreamt of restoring their empire's former glory by re-establishing its hold over its former colonies; and another faction whose members, in pursuit of new lands to conquer, had thrown in their lot with the Atlantropa project. Each group assumed the other was getting tricked. Both were right.

Still Mwadi smoldered at the injustice done her. "But he told everyone that Ilunga and I succeeded him!" she protested. "*Everyone!*"

"A necessary ploy. This way he'll attract less attention as he travels to the Americas—and eventually the claim will be true." Mam'selle's hand brought the melon slice to her mouth. She nibbled and swallowed.

"Lisette! Don't tell me you eatin that after this—animal done touched it!"

"For what reason should I not?" With a last bite Mam'selle licked her fingertips and returned to where she'd been sitting. She leaned toward the monkey and gravely presented him with her rind. "Raffles is probably as cleanly as the palace cook."

"You an your animals!"

They quarreled like old lovers. Which they were. "Control your-selves!"

"Of course." Mam'selle nodded emphatically and shrugged off her air of mischief. "We'll map out your itinerary for you based on Queen Josina's discussions with King Mwenda—we'll ask her to share his most recent messages."

"They a code?"

"Need you ask?"

Mwadi interrupted the exchange before it got too warm. "I'll begin as he did, by consulting the oracle at the atolo grove. That way no one will question the similarity of our paths."

The worship that King Mwenda had cobbled together from var-ious nations' beliefs continued to flourish even after his ostensible abdication. In his last act prior to leaving, her father had invited the ancestors' blessings by spreading a miniature feast before the house he'd established for them under the atolo. Three evenings af-ter the conversation in the garden pavilion, Mwadi stood in those same precincts and surveyed her own offerings: fresh fruit, creamy muamba nsusu soup, the inevitable kwanga sticks, and both rough lotoko and smooth ovingundu, served in tiny cups hollowed out of dogs' teeth.

A day from now she would leave. Queen Josina had offered her the services of Lembe, and more permanently, Sifa; already most of Mwadi's belongings were packed into trunks, baskets, and suitcases—clothes and cosmetics enough to keep her comfortable for markets and markets to come. Many of those markets to be spent without her beloved. Once more.

At least Mwadi got to reassert her claim on the woman Hafiza. Since the serving woman's inoculation with the Spirit Medicine, that nonsense about joining *Xu Mu*'s crew had passed. To make certain there was no mistake in the matter she had begun taking Hafiza everywhere, and Raffles quickly came to accept her presence as foregone, clinging to her scarfed head and shoulders like a baby.

Despite this new burden, Hafiza continued to perform her duties with becoming alacrity. Mwadi directed her to move the liquors to the right side of the painted mat where the ancestors' meal waited, and it was as soon said as done. Radiance shimmered inside the ivory cups. This was easily explained as a reflection of the glamps shining from the windows of the house of the ancestors.

The house of the ancestors had windows, but no doorway. Diviner Yoka sat with his back propped against the wall between its doorposts. His legs stuck out to either side of the offering mat, a stemmed glass of water tucked tight against the crotch of his trousers. Between the water and the mat, the hollow wooden belly of Yoka's sacred slit gong held bilongo: ordinary objects imbued with the extraordinary ability to communicate between realms. They had looked dull and unremarkable as they were dropped in the instrument's oblong hole, yet these black pebbles, strips of red bark, and twisted stubs of soft white clay were said to bridge worlds. Kneeling, Mwadi leaned forward to breathe softly, in and out, over the feast and divining tools.

Yoka smiled and covered the gong's opening with his scarred hands. "What is your question?" he asked, formally, and she told him what everyone had heard by now, that she journeyed from her home to find her father. "For this endeavor I ask my ancestors' guidance," she finished.

Not entirely a lie. Yes, she was going where her mother directed. Queen Josina had laid out Mwadi's course clearly. But the ancestors' guidance as to the manner of Mwadi's going could make a difference in what she encountered while on her mission, and in how she succeeded, and how and when she returned. The ancestors were well able to influence such inflections of the voice with which life sang.

For long, long minutes, though, they spoke only silence.

Mwadi stilled the urge rising within to reach across the mat and take up the slit gong herself. She would play the music of rebellion! Of conflict! Of change and excitement!

The music of Rima. That was what she wanted to hear.

At last the diviner untied the ceremonial mallet he wore about his neck and began striking the gong's twin tongues. Softly, softly, a call to ancestral spirits pulsed into the falling night. Between Yoka's surging and subsiding beats, Mwadi listened to the quiet sounds surrounding them: the rush of the evening breeze through leafy branches, the faint murmur of town traffic, the muttering of a wayward streamlet, its ephemeral course determined by the slant of tree roots and the careful paths on which querents approached the shrine.

The small splash and scampering steps of an otter shrew emerging from the water and coming toward them.

The animal entered the glamplight's glow. Its manner was bold. It put both forepaws on the rim of the soup bowl and dipped its narrow muzzle to feed. It examined the plate of sliced strawberries, and despite its carnivorous reputation ate several of these as well. An entire kwanga stick, too.

Then it turned to the gong. From the instrument's hollow sound chamber the otter shrew brought something forth, its long jaws obscuring the object's identity. It carried whatever the thing was to the glass and deposited it to be revealed as a black pebble slashed across its middle with a milkily translucent sky blue. Back to the gong's belly. Another black pebble, this one speckled with flecks of a fiery green. Another trip. The stub of chalk, which released sparkling, jewel-like air bubbles into the water. The white pebble. The scarlet-interiored bark.

Yoka's mallet had slowed to a stop as soon as the otter shrew appeared, then been withdrawn to rest alongside the diviner's leg. Now he took it up again to drum a flurry of notes, loud and furiously fast. Stubbornly the animal ventured back to the slit gong and darted once more into its belly and out again, dodging the mallet's blows. A last deposit was made into the water: a shining, gold-gleaming pearl. The otter shrew stood on its hindquarters, threw back its head, warbled a high trill ending in an even higher hiss, then fell to all fours again and vanished into the grove's shadows.

Kisangani, Everfair

Only room for one ass on the throne. Ilunga tried his best the first day of their kinning to make space for his flame and his new brother beside him. They all laughed together in the wake of the resulting tumble, but after that he put his mind to really solving their problem. However, between his bouts of quiet contemplation of the scab forming on the cut Dr. Kleinwald had given him, and their loud and vigorous physical engagements he made little progress.

His mother's seat would hold at least half the overflow. She always occupied it, though. On the third day he gazed thoughtfully upon her warm breasts, shields for her cool heart. Then he raised his eyes to her scheme-rich head and met her own gaze.

"Yes, son?"

It was his brother, the doctor, who spoke in response. "Will you be with us the entire day?"

She continued looking at Ilunga. "You need me."

"Why?" This question came from the mouth of the brilliant Sevaria.

"To keep watch. To intercede should the gods decide our present course is too dangerous."

"What danger could there possibly be?"

This time Queen Josina switched her regard to the speaker's face: Sevaria's again. "I deemed May Fourth's 'medicine' preferable to the whites' 'cure' when deliberating between inevitable infections. The Russian organism is blunter in possession of its hosts, yet seems to accord them fewer abilities. And the risk of causing pain during its administration is high."

She swiveled to address Dr. Kleinwald. "You are quiescent. Bee-Lung assures me that this is true, and I believe she believes so herself."

Was it actually the doctor his mother addressed? "What do you mean?" he asked her. "What makes the 'Russian organism' 'blunt'?"

A pitying look suffused Queen Josina's eyes and also her—smell? Yes, his mother's smell, which since his inoculation had become more noticeable, along with the scents of everyone else. "My son, I wish I had told you more before you left for university. Mwenda understood the extent to which we must maintain our distrust of Whiteness—not of whites themselves, of course, and so we did nothing to prevent your friendships with individuals. But—"

Again she turned to Sevaria, luminous vertex of all angles. "But the philosophy espoused by your Chinese sponsors as an alternative to Russia's looked so attractive! And as we waited and longed for you we learned more and more of the crippling sustained by the Russian organism's agents, which made the path splitting off in your direction an even better choice."

And back to Dr. Kleinwald. "And then, in such quick succession, came *your* arrival, Doctor, followed by Bee-Lung's. Her proposed course of treatment seemed easier to implement than execution—"

"What!" Ilunga found it impossible to believe, but: "You meant to *kill* him?"

Kleinwald smiled. *Smiled!* "I think you'll find that re-inoculation was not only easier to implement but a far, far more rewarding course."

Ilunga felt the sudden urge to touch his brother. He crooked a finger; the doctor inclined his head and stepped closer. Then remained there—within reach, but without making contact. Curse staying seated on this stupid stool! Casting dignity to the floor he got up and embraced Kleinwald with both arms, tightly, as he had ever wanted to embrace old Devil.

Triumph showered through the throne room's faintly eddying air. From behind Kleinwald's shoulder he heard his mother sigh and groan. From behind his own shoulder he—tasted—his light's approaching breath. Like vanilla, cloves, cinnamon—delicious! A warm and fragrant cloud surrounded him as she came to rest beside him and also opened her arms. They cradled his brother between them.

Words moved within Ilunga's throat and emerged from his mouth: "What is it you're scared of? Or ought I to ask 'who'? Who is it frightens you, mighty queen?" The question must mean something. To someone.

To his mother: she answered it. "I don't fear change. Or to be more exact, I don't fear change that comes gradually and with benefit to my people. The British have broken themselves into two factions: those who would restore their regime's old supremacy using the land's current contours, and those who wish to expand that land in alliance with other Europeans, by means of the Atlantropa project.

"It is the latter who would do the most damage. It is over the latter faction and their representatives that I would win."

"The Chawleighs." Kleinwald's voice. "They're uninoculated. So far."

"Would you like them to become part of me?" Said in Sevaria's sweet and fiery tones, sounding like the taste of peppers in honey.

"In exchange for what sort of favor?"

"Access to your daughter." Kleinwald again. "Queen Mwadi."

"Already granted. But only to your Chinese elements."

Ilunga frowned. He found himself asking a question. "But what if she wanted . . . *more*?"

"You are too unpredictable. For now, one child of mine is enough for the sum of you."

"Very well." Ilunga realized he had no idea *what* was "very well." He'd said it, though, so it must be true. "Let's think of something else to trade in."

"What makes you think I want to business with you?"

"Your son thinks you do. He has shared—" Confused, Ilunga stopped. Why was he talking of himself as if of someone not in the room?

Kleinwald shifted within their embrace, then broke from it to assume the throne. Alone. He seemed to continue the thread of Ilunga's speech. "He has shared a great deal of what you're planning."

"Has he? Then it's a good thing I haven't told him everything. Get up. That seat's not yours."

"And yet it is." With his new brass arm and his old flesh one, the doctor pulled Ilunga and Sevaria toward him. Ilunga lowered himself onto one of the doctor's knees as Sevaria alit on the other. Why hadn't he come up with this solution earlier? He laughed. It was so simple!

In through the audience chamber's doorway wafted the scent of someone known, a sister of some sort—though also a stranger. A moment later she appeared: Madam Ho Bee-Lung, the Macao healer. Her brother had provided Ilunga's brother with his latest and most satisfactory arm.

The healer bowed gracefully to his mother. But not to King Ilunga. He strove to feel annoyed. Instead, again, he laughed. "Why don't you come join us?" he asked, indicating the space on the dais directly before them. "You have all the same organisms inside you as we have. Why oppose your destiny?"

Queen Josina leaned forward sharply in her chair. "Madam Ho? You received the Russian spores also?"

"Yes. But only to a limited extent, one completely within my control." The healer woman drew nearer, peering at him out of the sides of her eyes as if he were a shy animal. "I admit to allowing too many variables for this kinning to work as a really informative experiment." She paced one direction, then the other, her sandals plopping back and forth along the floor's tiles like felt-covered mallets. Formerly their sound would have obscured her muttered words.

No longer: "This was only the second inoculation using my specially grown strain of Spirit Medicine. I ought to have simply duplicated the conditions of the first." She was scolding herself. Even with her back to him he heard her distinctly. Did she know?

"Instead, I connected non-siblings. Plus, I extended my special Spirit Medicine's ability to form its connection to produce more than two coremates. Add to that the presence, however weak, of a previous inoculation by another species. Three changes in protocol. Too many to track. I shouldn't have done what I did. I shouldn't have wanted to." She stopped to stare directly at him. Boldly. Insolently. She went on, no longer swallowing her speech. "But I did. Because I did as you wished. Didn't I?"

Sevaria replied, though not to answer the question. Not precisely. "You're going to be unable to rid yourself of my influence. Get over that idea."

Another's odor intruded. Its owner sauntered in past the servant who announced her. Miss Rima Bailey, his sister Mwadi's paramour. "Come on," she said to his darling fire. "We got the Circus stage till nine tonight. Wanna take advantage a how much work we been puttin into blockin, costumes, an makeup—you ready, aintcha?"

Sevaria nodded and stood. "We are. I am."

Ilunga found himself on his feet too. His brother rose also. Together they descended the dais.

"Wait!" Queen Josina sounded genuinely alarmed. "Where are you going? The day's just half over—you must stay to hear your petitioners. And this evening we're going to have visitors—the Italians!"

The doctor would do almost anything to avoid them. So, therefore, would Ilunga.

"You have no authority over me," he told his mother. Hadn't she figured that out by now? Demonstrating what he meant, he and his kin walked out of the room.

In the passageway, they waited for Miss Bailey to catch up. When she did, she rushed on to the stairway and waved for them to follow. "Hurry! We need to leave fore she stop us. Need to do our filmin now! I ain't about to stay here in Kisangani one more day than I hafta!"

A cart parked near the palace's entrance accommodated them. He and his coremates shared the forward-facing bench with only a little crowding, and Miss Bailey lounged upon the other between bouts of poking her head out of the vehicle's window to urge the bikist on faster. They arrived at the Grand Ideal Cultural Circus in what Ilunga deemed good time, but the instant they stopped Miss Bailey, who had begun mumbling complaints to herself about the bikist's slowness, grabbed Sevaria's hennaed hands and hustled her out of sight with whirlwind speed.

Bemused, Ilunga walked into the building in the train of the two women's aromas, his brother at his side. Down the sloping aisle to the area in front of the stage their mingled scents floated. Without giving the obstacle a great deal of thought, he navigated around a spidery-looking machine occupying the bottom of the aisle. Now the women's aromas came from the stage, from behind the intervening scenery. The four stair steps leading from floor to stage were blocked, though, by a man who was like Madam Ho—a newfound relative!

"No access till we're done filming for the day. No unfortunate interference with our story." The man ran a hand over his sleek hair, combing it back. "Unless you're late additions since we've landed—crew? Players?"

"I am King Ilunga! You should know me!"

A plume of contrition—pain, sorrow, and shame combined—burst off the man's skin. "Prominence! My deep apology! I'm only inoculated a little while myself, and still learning who we all are. Welcome!"

"Your name?" his brother asked.

"Gopal Singh. No—I'm Umar now—Umar Sharif."

"Lebanese?"

"What gave you that idea?"

"That's your new name's origin." Antanios Sharif had been a fellow student in Alexandria.

Umar's negating head shake became stillness, his frown alertness. "I must ask you to take your seats. We're about to begin shooting."

"You have guns!" Ilunga looked around, seeing nothing he hadn't already smelled. "Where?"

"Not guns—we 'shoot' with cameras. Here—" He put gently ushering hands on their shoulders. "Sit anywhere in the first row. I must take my place. You'll be able to see everything."

Ilunga supposed he would believe that. Umar breathed out sincerity with his words. Sincerity and a plea for patience.

Ensconced in brown velvet, his brother beside him, Ilunga perused the stage. It was lined with mirrors ranging from tiny spangles dangling in glittering chains to man-sized rectangles. Between the arms of the semicircle that the largest mirrors formed sat a long, low sofa draped in a silver tapestry, and decorated with golden pillows.

A serving woman came down the stage's steps. She, too, belonged in relation to Ilunga. She approached, but only bowed her head and continued past him to the equipment he'd been ignoring. It consisted, he saw now, of two separate pieces: a metal tripod that was topped by a wooden box featuring a protruding black tube about four fingers thick. From a cloth sack belted to her waist the servant pulled a third thing: a gleaming, double-barreled contraption like a tyre pump. She set it down and reached for the box's far side—but immediately Ilunga lost all interest in her, for Sevaria reappeared. She took the stage as if it had always been hers; Ilunga believed it must be glad of the taking. Anyone would be. Anything.

Sevaria lay down upon the silver-covered sofa, her expression blank, her eyes closed. Unmoving, yet vital as an unflickering flame. Like a candle that burns in a crystal chandelier, she shared her radiance via myriad reflections. And then a white blaze of switched-on waterfire lamps added to her glory. The box on the tripod began to whir and hiss under the servant's ministrations. Sevaria's lashes fluttered apart, and her sparkling eyes flashed back and forth as she lifted herself up on arms so softly curved they could have been sculpted of beeswax.

Suddenly, there was Rima Bailey. Ilunga didn't want to waste attention on her, but her movements forced it out of him. Her silver dress should have blended into the background of mirrors and tapestry and disappeared, but instead it whirled and danced around her like wind made visible. She circled the sofa to stand, rooted yet swaying, behind the end of it where Sevaria's head lay. Looking toward the empty auditorium she said, "You ready for today's tour?"

"Oh! More baby factories? More electronic gardens?" Sevaria looked in the same direction.

"Naw, we gonna be in town. I ast Doctor Shin to come take us round the hospital here. Then we go to the school and get a meal. Then we see the library an come on back here for the party."

Sevaria's glance upward was followed by more questions, again seemingly addressed to the nonexistent audience: "The party is to-night? So soon?"

"Yeah! People eager to meetcha—you the famous Sleeper." With a lean of her bare brown shoulder and a tilt of her silver-helmed head, Miss Bailey acted out hearing something. "Lissen! That the doorbells ringin—he come right on time!"

Umar entered, clad in a shimmering white gown, long sleeves bunched up and banded above the elbow with matching bracelets of amethyst, turquoise, and silver. "Sister! I greet you in the name of our victorious ancestors!"

Miss Bailey and the actor embraced. "An here she is—the ancestors' gift!" Pivoting to face Sevaria, she towed Umar around too. "Our Sleeper woman call herself—"

"STOP! We're filming! You can't come in while—"

The shouting was behind them. Ilunga turned in his seat to see who it was, since the air flowing to him from the entrance smelled confused. More relatives he'd never met: three women were trying unsuccessfully to keep out his mother's attendants and—yes, as they gave way to her she appeared—Queen Josina.

Leaving others to sort through the trouble, his mother swept down the aisle toward Ilunga as calmly as if she approached him along a palace passageway. Serene of face, swift of step, she quickly passed the suddenly silent camera, and the bowing servant who had ceased to operate it. A brief nod to the occupants of the stage, and then she was staring down at him as if he were the last morsel of fish on her plate and she was considering whether to grant the cook her approval by eating him.

"My son, if we leave for the airfield now there will be no unseemly delay in greeting our guests. Or if you prefer, you can wait a little and go to your quarters to bathe and change, and there will still be time to meet the Italians as you proposed, over drinks—for cocktails, as you said—before dinner."

Two choices. Both would give Queen Josina what she wanted.

So what did he, *Ilunga,* want?

He wanted to be big and strong, like his father. He wanted to protect his country against the Italian interlopers poised to extend Italy's borders via Atlantropa. His mother's plan was fine for that. No reason not to just go along with it—for now.

But also he wanted to protect his newfound kin—and in particular to protect his brother, Dr. Kleinwald, who had suffered imprisonment and maiming under the Italians.

Accomplishing both of his goals simultaneously would require division. Separation from those he sought to protect.

Reflecting his mother's hard smile back up to her, Ilunga announced his intention to remain at the Circus a little longer.

"Good. I'll wait for you in the cart and we'll travel home together. Don't be long." Seeming to notice Kleinwald for the first time, she bunched her eyebrows together as if puzzled. "I think that perhaps tonight you'd better not join us."

"Naturally not. I've arranged a berth aboard *Xu Mu*. Count on me to keep clear till your visitors depart."

Queen Josina left the way she'd come, with a minimum of fuss till she reached the doors to the lobby. There she appeared to listen patiently to the mixed grievances of the doors' guards and her attendants.

Beside him, Ilunga felt his brother stretch a comforting hand toward the back of his neck. Warm and moist—flesh, not brass.

"I don't want to go," the king confessed. "We'll be apart."

"Go," urged the doctor. "Then find the means to tell me all you observe. It's the only way I can know it."

"But this will be so strange! I—I'll miss you!"

"No. You won't miss me. Sevaria will be there. Besides, on a certain level we'll always be together. From now on. Forever more."

INTERLUDE Y

JOSINA'S INITIATION

If something's a secret, it can't be told. If it is told, it was never a secret.

The scene described in this interlude is not what happened, but it's near enough. It's what can be told. It's what you need to know.

At the age of twenty-five years (or fifty seasons), two seasons (or one year) prior to her marriage to King Mwenda, Princess Josina traveled from her home in the Angolan city of Luanda to Ile Ife, Nigeria, for initiation as a priest of the Yoruba deity Oshun. Already she was privy to the mysteries of Kianda, her country's mother of waters. Already she knew the secret ways of Mamba Muntu, Congolese crocodile divinity.

This was in 1890, long before aircanoe routes connected the continent's widely distributed population centers. The princess made most of her journey by sea, and finished by sailing up the Opa River.

The temple complex there was well developed and suitably maintained. Its separate shrines for Olokun, Olodumare, and various other members of the Yoruba pantheon displayed at their doorways human-sized sculptures of the relevant orisha (the Yoruba term for these deities), carved from the region's sacred clay. As young Josina's sponsors conducted her past these brightly painted figures, she strained to contain her nervousness. She told herself she must surely be worthy of the honor of her invitation here. Not only had her studies and service brought her to the attention of the Yoruba nation's spiritual teacher when he visited Luanda, but Josina's father Ha-

*mad, King of the Niassa, blessed and supported her mission to forge
this important connection.*

*They halted before the statue of a woman clothed in the colors of
the sun, and glittering with ornaments of gold and brass and glass.
Around this larger statue's bare feet gamboled smaller statues of
smiling children. The doorway beside them vibrated with darkness
and mystery.*

*"Close your eyes," Princess Josina's chief sponsor warned her. A
swathe of light fabric fell over her head, and firm hands guided her
through the dark door.*

*Inside, the scents of spices and sweet perfumes penetrated her
head's loose covering, and the chiming of many bells rose to fill
her ears. She opened her eyes, but no illumination entered them other
than a soft glow seeming to emanate from a spot midway between the
shrine's smooth floor and invisible roof.*

*The hands guiding Josina turned her around and urged her back-
ward to sit on a throne. The bells subsided. Now came sounds of
grinding, stirring, and chopping, and a trickling pour of liquid into
a metal cup. For a very long while—over a hymn—she waited silently for what would happen next. Whispers around her told Josina nothing, though she had more than a smattering of the Yoruba
language; she caught only stray syllables and unfamiliar words—
perhaps they were names?*

*Just as she was about to speak, the cloth obscuring her sight was
whisked away. Her chief sponsor stepped back with the cloth in her
hands, shook it out, folded it, and exchanged it for a shallow bowl
with a knife balanced across its rim.*

*Josina knew better than to be afraid. Out of the dimness—the
little light there was came from a tiny, flickering oil lamp on a low,
object-covered table—stepped another sponsor bearing a pair of
scissors. Snip snip! Josina's braids came free beneath the scissors'
blades. Rinsed frequently in the bowl's water, the knife shaved away
the remaining stubble of her hair.*

Then the knife cut her. The chief sponsor stood behind her now, with a third priest stationed in front of the princess and holding there the metal cup in which were the materials to be inserted into Josina's head. Swiftly the knife's edge etched the appropriate design on her bared scalp. Immediately, Josina's pain transmuted itself into a beacon of radiance, a shining signal showing her readiness to receive joy. And so she did: cool and satisfying, the mud-like mixture sank into the slits in her skin, into her blood, into her sparkling essence. She tingled with delight.

Now the length of fabric was unfolded and used again, this time to blot away excess mixture. Now the old and ragged garments she'd worn to this initiation rite were torn off of her, torn apart, and bundled up for disposal, as the new gown she had provided, never before worn, was slipped over her blazing head.

Now, clad so cleanly, the fresh initiate was brought to lie facedown before the oil-lit altar. A timeless moment she rested thus, listening to the quiet music of the incorporated materials' first promptings. Now she was helped to her knees and sang her prayer of gratitude to the animals, plants, and minerals who had contributed to her initiation.

Who were they? Items representing these contributors had been placed upon the altar. There rested a round of chalk from the dried course of an ancient river; there, a cluster of tiny seed pearls gathered in half the shell of a peahen's egg; there, what initially appeared to be the yellow flower of a grass called Xyris, but which proved on closer examination to be the fungus that mimicked the flower, Fusarium xyrophilum.

The organism's spongy ruffles emitted the flower's signature light waves and chemicals. Rather than a flower, though, it was a reason. Fusarium was the reason why, decades later, as one of Everfair's queens, Josina knew much more about May Fourth's Spirit Medicine than anybody had told her. Fusarium contributed mightily to Bee-Lung's special, modified version of the original inoculant, thus providing the queen with a visceral knowledge of the Spirit Medicine otherwise available only to those who received it.

In addition, the traces of Fusarium still seated upon her head were what allowed Queen Josina to envision and traverse the many worlds rising out of each decision her long life generously offered.

CHAPTER ELEVEN

June 1921
Kisangani, Everfair

All Hafiza's core kin had once been servants, just as she had: Trana and Jadida had been employees of Sevaria binti Musa since their respective girlhoods. Gopal had worked for Sevaria, too, though neither as closely nor as long as the women. Kafia had been stolen from her home and forced to act as a slave under the Italians, only escaping to Dacca after her "owners" left Somalia for Anatolia.

So Hafiza's core knew very well how to overcome Queen Mwadi's restrictions on their intercourse: self-effacement and silence usually did the trick. Once Aunty Ho made her secret way into the royal quarters to properly administer the Spirit Medicine's spores to Hafiza, there was no trouble with following most of the usual bonding protocols. The core slept together quite comfortably on the royal bedroom's balcony's cool floor, while Raffles, quickly become Hafiza's constant companion, lay atop its wall. The queen, unfamiliar with the names and faces of all the palace staff, never suspected them of belonging on *Xu Mu*.

Even when her duties parted her from her kin, Hafiza felt her core's presence. The diviner's music sang of them in her ears, his mallet beating harmonies that hung in the air like their scents, their pulsing hearts. And then the otter shrew's insistence on choosing that last object—was it not more than a metaphor? A sign? Her pet name, a joking reference to the lustrous whiteness she lacked, was "Luliwat"—and was she not in truth her core's pearl?

Oracles spoke to whoever listened; the creature's shrill parting cry could be meant for her as much as for her mistress. Hearing the diviner's interpretation confirmed this:

"More and more and more. You seek to rule. Your father, gone before—"

Hafiza's parents were pilgrims. Every spring they traveled from Cairo to some holy site. By this time her father should be safe within the walls of the city of Harar.

"—seeks to submit himself. Both these goals will be obtained. And more and more and more."

"How shall I go?" asked Queen Mwadi.

"How goes the hunter? Softly. With ears turned toward the game." The diviner hunched forward, dropping his head into cupped palms. "Listening . . . listening . . ." Eyes shut, hands shaking, he dipped the tips of his fingers into the goblet and flicked them upward, spraying liquid into the damp evening air. Dipping again, he turned his aim inward. Bright beads of water gemmed his face. "Listening for hints as to where to find that which sustains the prey: its drink. Its nourishment." He licked his lips briefly with a red tongue. "Hearing the cries and movements of that which feeds what the hunter would be fed upon. Learning its habits. Finding its favorite retreats."

"Who can teach such lessons to me?"

"Him you seek."

Queen Mwadi's response was an angry silence that lengthened beyond seemliness. When she spoke she sounded much calmer than she smelled. "You'd leave me with a paradox? You'd say I must find my father to learn how I'll find him?"

The diviner answered with a long, nasal drone: a snore. More snores followed it. Two apologetic young apprentices emerged from the shadows of the ancestor hut's walls with a mat, pillows, and covering, and as they eased him onto this makeshift bed Queen Mwadi stood and left. Her face was smooth, empty of expression, and her words continued polite—but she reeked of dissatisfaction.

Back in the palace, Hafiza tended to her mistress's bedtime preparations as best she could with so many toiletries packed for the next day's journey, then waited eagerly for dismissal. Instead, when Queen Mwadi got up from her vanity she ordered Hafiza to come with her out of the room. In obedient silence, Hafiza walked along the dim passageway behind her mistress, Raffles riding on her back.

Lembe greeted them at the entrance to Queen Josina's suite and accompanied them to her bed. With senses sharpened by the Spirit Medicine, Hafiza understood more of the interchange between mother and daughter than could formerly have been expected.

"You must trust me."

"I do." But Queen Mwadi lied. Though she firmly intended to obey Queen Josina, she exuded a light sweat redolent of doubt.

"As I've said, your father will be sailing to Brazil from Accra. In order to throw off any nosy meddlers he'll fly to Accra's port from Bangui or Bangassou, after a good, long immersion in the atmosphere of his spirit father's sacred grounds. There's an ancient forest reservation located between those two towns, and that is where you'll meet him.

"Sifa has been thoroughly instructed. She will go with you and administer your inoculations. They'll be pure—no Russian taint—"

A sharp surge of guilt and fear plumed off of Queen Mwadi. Why? Hafiza wished she could perceive more than emotions. None of the words either mother or daughter spoke gave any hint of what had caused her to be so upset.

Gradually, weak-scented composure returned to the room's air, and after a little while, a period during which no one's feelings altered, Queen Mwadi returned to her rooms. Aunty Ho had come and gone in their absence, leaving behind gifts for Hafiza and Gopal, and a slowly dispersing trail of mild optimism.

Kisangani, Everfair

Gopal disentangled himself from his coremates in the dawn's hazy light. So much to do! This was the last day in which he'd be able to film his scenes as Dr. U Shin—while at the same time he must assume a complicated additional role as part of the Italian entourage. He pulled his trousers free from the others' in the stack just inside the doorway to the bedroom proper. Past the low pyramid of neatly folded clothing, and partially hidden by it, sat his new Spirit Medicine workbasket, his present from Bee-Lung. He had to take that with him, of course. Queen Mwadi's apartments would be safe from disturbance by the Italians, but if he left the basket here today it was liable to be mistaken for Hafiza's and loaded onto the wrong aircanoe. After all, the baskets were practically identical, outwardly.

He stood on the balcony's threshold to dress. In the depths of the room behind him he sensed Hafiza slumbering lightly, near to waking. Soon the night's dreams would be lost in the tang of hunger, the fog of thirst. Morning matters. He inhaled their incipience, grateful as ever to be granted such a rich and rewarding life. Such absorption in the world's existence. Such bliss—such a compound of mundane joys.

That was the important lesson the Spirit Medicine had taught him: the beauty of the everyday. That was what he had here—also, though, there was something else—an unexpected depth to the scents surrounding him . . . more than the doubling that would be due to the presence of Hafiza's gift . . . a tripling effect he couldn't quite account for. . . .

All at once, he was uneasy. He turned to walk toward his newest coremate where she curled beside her mistress. Was it the monkey that threw him off? No. He'd smelled it as usual on waking, barely noticing that he did so. The creature had become Hafiza's responsibility and her constant companion. . . . Odd, though, that it perched so patiently on the bed's footboard, barely stirring at his approach. What was it waiting for? If it was awake, why hadn't it gone out? What could have proven a more powerful attraction than the courtyard garden's fresh, edible leaves? Even as Gopal asked himself these questions he realized the answer to the earlier one:

the reason why the scents of the precious spores, the threads, and the adjuvants of clay and fruit and flowers were so pungent—

Radiating irrepressible dread he turned again, and looked directly at his basket. Its top was askew—and the top of Hafiza's, set just past it, was fully open! The ingredients of May Fourth's Spirit Medicine—the monkey must have molested them! No!

He calmed his glands. The situation should be salvageable. Stooping swiftly, he slammed shut his coremate's basket's lid and secured that of his own—later they could sort out their contents, assess the damage, compile a list of items to replace. Bee-Lung would know what to do and how to do it.

But the odors of their precious supplies stayed strong—stronger than they should have been. They came not only out of the baskets at his feet.

They came from the bed as well.

Pivoting, Gopal resumed his advance on Hafiza and the softly snoring queen. His coremate's eyes fluttered open.

"Don't move," he whispered. If she did, she'd disturb Queen Mwadi—and the aureole of filched materials spreading out from where their heads lay, side by side. He bent to examine the display more closely, sniffing and narrowing his eyes. Yes, all the physical components useful for inoculation were here: shards of chocolate; living spores; fragile, lavender-tinted threads; sweet, slow-dried butterfly pea blossoms; pomegranate seeds; rich crumbs of mineral-stuffed earths, meticulously arranged in smooth arcs and glimmering rays.

Had the monkey done this? Entirely on its own? An animal? Gopal wanted not to believe such a thing possible. Surely this was a sign—but a sign of what?

He held out his hands for Hafiza's. She understood and gave them to him and he lifted her free of the art without spoiling it. Together they stood over it in mute admiration.

The queen woke despite their silence. One startled glance at them and she sprang up and away—then stopped. "You're— Who are you? How do I know—" The careful pattern was destroyed. "Hafiza?"

"Surely you remember Umar—Mr. Sharif? The actor? He means you no harm—"

"You can't know that!"

"But she can!" He wished he was able to pacify others as Bee-Lung did, but he could only regulate his own emotions. He steadied them, then realized with relief that somehow this was helping to ground Queen Mwadi's, too. Almost as if she were kinned with him . . . but that was impossible. There must be some other connection.

"I—I believe you! Why? Why should I?" A cascade of withered flowers slithered down the valley the queen's fist dented in the bed. She sagged backward, stiff arms supporting her quiet incredulity. A puff of spores swirled upward on the air she displaced.

Hafiza smiled. "Because strange though it may seem, we tell the truth."

Kisangani, Everfair

Bee-Lung wanted the visiting Italian embassy ignorant of her connection to Gopal. Or Umar, as they knew him. So despite his nearness—he sat just a double arm-span away, by the pavilion's entrance—Bee-Lung avoided looking in his direction. The only concession she made to her longing was to finger his sash, secretly, inside the front pocket of her silk trousers.

Never had she felt so deeply for one man. Not for her dead husband, not for her father—only her relationship to Tink came anywhere near this in intensity. The powerful link enabled by the special strain of Spirit Medicine she and Tink shared, added to the joint memories of their upbringing, made for a very strong tie—yet one still weak in comparison.

No. Sexual attraction. That was all this was. All. Gopal's scent slipped like a tongue between the aromas of roasted guinea fowl and freshly scored mango slices, and brushed delicately against her nostrils, causing them to flare wide. He smelled so full! Even in the midst of so much richness—the servers' trays were laden heavily with foods prepared in honor of the Italians' upcoming departure—his organs played a low, distracting song of seduction, an undertone, and his veins pulsed with the steady beat of his desire . . . for her.

That was the miracle. He knew her—he'd *had* her—and he continued to want her.

Now she wrenched her attention back to King Ilunga. Only the film star sat between her and him, and so far Sevaria had said nothing. She merely smiled when Bee-Lung inquired, politely and professionally, as to her good health. Of course Bee-Lung received and understood the star's reply without the cumbersome exchange of words: Sevaria and the doctor—who was absent physically, but present spiritually—were both extremely well. Sevaria's breath was even, her silence restful and easy.

Ilunga, however, had chatted loudly throughout the evening, aiming his remarks sometimes at Bee-Lung and other times at the slope-shouldered, mustachioed Italian ambassador on his left. Signore Quattrocchi's scent matched his appearance: affable, observant, and intellectually smitten with some idea—probably with the Atlantropa project, because of its promise to expand the acreage of his Sicilian homeland.

"What you're saying, then, is that your interest in this Doctor Kleinwald is no longer urgent?" The king sounded less concerned than he smelled.

"Exactly. Since you prove so pliable in the matter of pardoning the Chawleighs, we agree to leave it to them to handle his return to our care."

From Queen Josina, lounging prettily upon a leather-stretched chair frame, wafted a trickle of satisfaction. Bee-Lung believed Josina was attempting to train herself to emit less informative scents, but without inoculation that attempt could never be more than partially successful. Her scent of satisfaction meant she had never intended her exile of the European spies to be permanent.

"So delightful that we were able to come to terms of mutual benefit! My intended abhors violence!" Ilunga looked at Sevaria with an expression of adoration that pierced Bee-Lung's liver with jealousy. If only she could allow herself to look that way at Gopal!

Instead, she must part with him early tomorrow morning, publicly. The Italians would be watching. They must not know. They must leave Kisangani aboard *Omukama* without the slightest suspicion that a *Xu Mu* crewmember flew with them—and any hint of intimacy between Bee-Lung and Gopal could spoil his pose of innocence.

She would not endanger him with her eyes.

At last, at last, small bowls of lemon-infused water were brought round, each accompanied by a plate of cattail fluff. Bee-Lung rinsed and dried her hands. It was the feast's formal end. Once Queen Josina and King Ilunga stood and left, she did also. The searing aroma of Gopal's desire grew more insistent as she passed him, then faded under the lightly falling rain. Her usual priorities regained their importance.

Of course she was going to ignore his seductiveness. There'd be plenty of opportunities for sex—good sex—once the Spirit Medicine spores were more thoroughly distributed.

But the wasted hours between the dinner and his departure sorely tried Bee-Lung's optimism. She pretended to sleep, instead fretting uselessly at Tink's side till at last the fragrance of morning penetrated their shuttered windows. Time to go.

Despite the hour's earliness, a good many of last evening's guests were queued up ahead of them for carts to the airfield. In fact, she and Tink were nearly the last to board. Only Mademoiselle Toutournier and Miss Bailey yet waited. And before Bee-Lung could object, her brother offered to share the ride with them. Why did those two need to go? Why should they force an inauspicious number of passengers into Bee-Lung's carriage? Fortunately, just as they rolled down the ramp to street level, Bee-Lung spotted Lembe, Queen Josina's serving woman, standing stranded and alone. "Turn back! Turn back!" she shouted out of her window to the bikist.

Thus they became five, thanks to the Italians' inability to pack economically. Lembe had originally been expected to ride in the cart carrying their luggage, alongside Gopal in his semblance as servant rather than film actor, but the cart had become too crowded to carry both.

When questioned, Miss Bailey offered as an excuse for her presence an urgent need to see to the maintenance of her aeroplane. Mademoiselle's answer was more difficult to obtain, and when gotten, more difficult to understand. Apparently she was there at Queen Josina's request. The reasons for that request weren't forthcoming.

The rain had continued through the night. It began to fall harder, and they raised their cart's windows against it. Beneath her perfume, Mademoiselle gave off an air of sadness and weariness at odds with her cheerful expression. Miss Bailey's restless odor beat against the cart's walls like a caged bird's wings. These two avoided each other's eyes and touch, but Bee-Lung could tell that doing so was far easier for the older one. Perhaps this was due to practice. Perhaps quelling your lust became automatic over time. Or perhaps the Russian organism that Bee-Lung suspected of tainting Miss Bailey's system contributed to her anxiety.

Bee-Lung's brother frothed with worry, a scum of concern that floated uneasily atop the roiling cauldron of his craving for Kwangmi. "Won't they know Gopal's the same man as Umar? They met him! Won't they—"

"You jokin? They think all us 'darkies' the same! Ain't gonna notice nothin!"

"Discovery's much more likely to occur if he's still with them when they reach Tunis," said the Frenchwoman. "Prolonged exposure increases the likelihood of committing an error. Retrieve him before Tunis, at a stop in Algiers—at Biskra, or Batna—or earlier even; anywhere within twenty-four hours of there."

"Why do you want to help us?" Bee-Lung asked Mademoiselle. Some information was difficult to fully scent. "You're not kinned with any of our cores."

"No. But Queen Josina is willing to trust her own judgment in this matter. She maintains that your May Fourth Movement's 'revolution' can be made to work to Everfair's advantage. I also."

For the moment there was nothing to do but believe what was being said. And to keep all senses tuned to perceive any possible betrayal.

On the bench opposite Bee-Lung, Tink sighed up a lungful of frustration. Why? He, at least, had a course of action ahead of him.

"You gonna hafta ack like you ain't goin nowhere when you board your craft," Miss Bailey reminded him. "Just stoppin by for clean clothes."

"Yes. He will. And Gopal will inoculate *Omukama*'s drummers before anyone else," Bee-Lung assured Miss Bailey. "That way, there'll be no incriminating gossip between ground and air—nothing for the Italians to intercept once *Xu Mu* is on their trail." Bee-Lung smiled a small smile at the memory of Gopal's deft hands under hers, the rising of his air of certainty. He had learned the order and contents of his new workbasket by touch, memorized inoculation protocols with a quickness that both excited and disappointed her: it was good, it was proof she'd picked the right person for this job—but she could wish his lessons had taken at least a little longer. So pleasant when duty and enjoyment combined. Only there had been Hafiza's lessons to give, too, and that meant they worked in such a hurry. Even Bee-Lung's review and replenishment of the basket's contents after the monkey's incursion had lasted just a few drenched instants.

The rain's patter ceased, and Lembe lowered the cart's windows. The openness of the airfield allowed the dawn's breeze greater access. Newly arrived *Omukama* flew from the tower's mast alone; *Xu Mu* and another aircanoe were moored to two separate masts on the field's far edge, with Miss Bailey's aeroplane parked between them.

They'd hardly come to a halt before Lembe jumped out to join Gopal in handling the Italians' luggage. The servant organized a relay line with him and the aircanoe's loaders. This gave Bee-Lung no chance to approach Gopal alone.

So she and Tink walked the short distance to the tower in Mademoiselle's train. Looking back, Bee-Lung saw Miss Bailey heading in the opposite direction, toward her plane. Quickly they caught up with Mademoiselle. Then they passed her, and entered the tower while she lingered on the portico housing the tower lift's steam engine. The engine rumbled steadily as they faced the empty lift shaft; Bee-Lung surmised the lift's cage was already risen out of sight. It must be carrying the Italians and royals to the docking platform, since no one but loaders remained on this level.

"Shall we take the stairs?" said Mademoiselle. She had caught them up.

Tink wanted to stay behind. Mounting the coiling steps at Mademoiselle's side, Bee-Lung explained to her that this was because he wanted a closer look at the mechanism connecting the lift to the engine.

"I see. I sympathize.... Does it ever become a little too much for you, knowing someone else's thoughts?"

"What? No—because I don't!" The steps changed from metal to wood, and the scuffing sound of her sandals softened. How could she make Mademoiselle understand? "The Spirit Medicine— It's as if— You're married, aren't you?"

"Yes." The scent of sadness increased.

"For long?"

"No. But I've known my wife practically my entire life."

Women here could wed other women, that was right. "Do you . . . anticipate what she's about to say sometimes?"

"Often!" A laugh, a diminishment of the sorrow. "And often I say it for her." A rue-filled grin showed on Mademoiselle's face as they passed below a bright sponge. "It's like that? Like you're . . . in love?"

"A bit. You'll figure out what it's like for yourself."

"I will?"

From ahead and above came the muddled voices of the others. Bee-Lung ceased climbing and put out a hand to hold Mademoiselle back, too. "Aren't you curious about the experience? Don't you want to try it?"

"Perhaps. If I do, Daisy will try it with me. But I'll not experiment along those lines until after Everfair's political alignment is resolved to my sister's satisfaction. I'll help her son and daughter do as she wishes to that end. And then there are other puzzles . . . Haven't you ever wondered what it is the Spirit Medicine wants of us?"

"May Fourth? It—that is, *we,* we seek to overcome—"

"No, not your movement, the organism itself. Everything alive desires something—desires it more deeply, perhaps, than most people realize. And more of everything is alive than most people believe." Putting aside Bee-Lung's hand, she resumed mounting the stairs. "I intend to find out exactly what your Spirit Medicine is up to before I and Daisy let it become part of us."

"How?" Treading hurriedly, she caught up with Mademoiselle on the landing at the stairs' summit. Again she put out her hand, but stopped short of making contact this time. It would have been unwelcome.

"I will ask it!" Nodding briskly, as if she had satisfied the troublesome question of a student, Mademoiselle breezed out onto the mooring tower's passenger platform.

As Bee-Lung had anticipated, the Italians were there. Signore Quattrocchi straightened from his bow to Queen Josina and turned in quite natural surprise toward them at their arrival. Hadn't their rising scents preceded them? Hadn't they been expected? Evidently not. His reaction was genuine. His colleagues' startlement as well. The Spirit Medicine's rival was that much weaker.

Or was the Italians' surprise due to the deceptiveness that May Fourth's trainers had led them to expect in the movement's enemies? During the ambassadors' farewell banquet, the mingling of the many diners' scents had distracted her— No. In all honesty, the source of her distraction had been Gopal.

From the lift's shaft rose Gopal's enticing aroma and the sound of straining cables. Soon he and the heavy load of luggage would be visible.

Absentmindedly, Bee-Lung accepted Signore Quattrocchi's jesting, gallant invitation to visit him in Messina. She knew he felt no real attraction to her. Not like the feelings of the man the signore knew as Umar—or, in his current guise, as Vinay, the humble and happy servant given to the ambassador by Queen Josina in proof of her friendliness.

The lift groaned mightily and settled into place. Gopal-Umar-Vinay slid apart the top and bottom of its latticework gate. The two with him proceeded to transfer its contents to *Omukama*'s hold via the gangway. But he himself approached her directly. Rashness! They mustn't be seen together! Bee-Lung pretended not to sense him hovering at her shoulder. *Go away!* she signaled frantically, fragrantly. In vain. At last she had to concede that by ignoring him she only prolonged the time during which their ruse could potentially be exposed. She faced his lowered head and took from his extended hands a folded piece of paper.

It was addressed to her in her brother's hand. She opened it. A single black phrase was inked onto the page as if the brush, a flame, had charred it there: *Farewell until we rejoin forces.*

Stricken with a dawning sense of loss, Bee-Lung clutched the note to her breast. It wasn't just Gopal, it was Tink! And Ma Chau— her whole core! *Xu Mu*'s whole crew! They were all leaving—soon! Now!

"What troubles you?" Quattrocchi again. Gopal had deserted her to perform his new duties. Which were much like those he had been performing when they met: shifting large, heavy objects from one location to another. His legs, his shoulders, the long muscles of his back . . . how could anyone fail to notice him? How could the Italians mistake him for anybody else?

"Lady?"

This was not the moment to wonder about such things. Nor to pity herself. Though left behind, bereft of her core, she was not alone. Not as long as she continued to recruit new kin. Thanks to the Spirit Medicine, she need never be alone again. "I shall miss you," she lied.

Kisangani, Everfair, and Aboard Xu Mu

Tink hurried across the murk-filled airfield. No one was watching. No need to pretend to stumble or lose his way. Miss Bailey was now far enough ahead of him that the relative nearness of their craft to each other shouldn't matter. She would not notice how efficiently he moved in the dark.

Yes. He heard her pull off the Cloud Star's tarpaulin and climb into its cockpit. He'd have to be careful, though—nothing to keep her from flying off once the day brightened enough for the uninoculated to see. Soon.

He reached *Xu Mu's* tethering lines. Within their quivering ellipse hung its empty loading basket, very near the ground. Of course. They expected him. Raising the bamboo pole he had kept hidden on the tower's portico, he hooked it into the netting that was slung from the basket's sides, and pulled the basket low enough for him to climb aboard it.

Crouched between the basket's creaking walls, he signaled his readiness to be hauled up to the aircanoe. As the field fell farther and farther below him, Tink yearned with larger and larger outpourings of his own scents for his coremates—for all of them, but not for all of them equally.

Raghu and Kwangmi were waiting for him in *Xu Mu's* hold. Yet only a little of their combined effusions hovered below its opening—soft breezes thinned them and carried the bulk of them away. His love's essence blended silkily with aerial messages from everywhere, from places both nearby and distant: the smells of the mineral-filled waters of the Lualaba River's rushing cataracts; of the green juices of leaves torn apart by elephants roaming the forests far downstream; of the dry spiciness drifting free when the grasses of the high plateaus rubbed together, stem against stem. Almost he could hear the grasses' whispering—but no, he had arrived, and that susurrus was the sweep of Kwangmi's sleeves unrolling—no, the swish of her hair released from its work-appropriate topknot. No. The brush of her lips on the back of his outstretched hand. Yes. Yes. Oh, yes.

Raghu opened and hung a glamp. It swung gently on its hook, damp and glowing. "Welcome home, Brother."

Tink only smiled. Words were less necessary than ever, now—sometimes they were nothing other than a way to shape breath. Yet with Kwangmi he had to use them to explain so much. *So* much!

Her touch continued. Leaving Raghu to stow the loading basket, they walked together to the cabin Tink had previously shared with Bee-Lung. In its dimness—even though the Spirit Medicine enhanced his vision, the low light here made him half-blind—Kwangmi's caress stilled a moment, then resumed. Then was divided, doubled, tripled, quadrupled: fingertips and tongue, lips and teeth and sniffing, sensitive nose.

He broke from her embrace. "I've got a new explanation to give you. A better speech outlining the point of my intentions—plainer, truer—"

"Not necessary." She recaptured him, held him in arms light yet persuasive. "I've decided to marry you—"

"What! You—"

"Yes, but I have one condition." Now she drew away, though still maintaining all but physical intimacy. "We must be linked together as you're linked with your sister Bee-Lung."

Tink's open mouth emitted no sounds. Traitor words—where

did they go when he actually needed them? When he actually had something important to say? His pores released mere feelings: surprise and confusion. And then, relief. He was to have what he wanted! But his relief was followed swiftly by doubt.

Kwangmi disliked that emotion. She seemed to take it as refusal. "Don't you think the two of us deserve that same special treatment?"

"Yes! I only hesitate because—" He fought off panic. "I want this too!" He did! "Yes—the closer we get to one another, the happier we'll be. My sister has plans, however. What you're asking won't fit in with them."

"Plans? What sort of plans? Who do they concern?"

"Everyone. The world." His hammock must be just behind him. He edged backward and felt its comfortable give against the twin columns of muscle guarding his spine. A sponge should be hanging directly overhead.

In brighter light all this would make the most excellent sense. "Find me a dipper of water and I'll reveal to you what she—and I—have in mind."

Ever prepared, Kwangmi presented him with a drinking flask. He wetted the sponge and his surroundings sprang to gleaming life. Empty, now, of both Bee-Lung's and Sevaria's belongings, it seemed to Tink that the cabin's new spaciousness had an air of possibility, a width of choice he hadn't known was missing. And, as always, with vision's full return came clarity.

A small, flat-topped chest of precious gems, a consignment from Rosalie, occupied the nearest corner. He gestured to it. "Be seated—please?"

Kwangmi shook her head. "We'll sit together, or not at all." She glanced at his hammock. "Or we could lie with one another?"

"Why so eager?" The question burst out of him. "You've never before believed what I wanted was for the best."

"You agree to share inoculation by the special strain with me? Today?"

"Agree? Yes, all right, I agree—but what does that matter? And as for sharing it right now, this morning, that's impossible. It's not here."

"No. You're wrong. It is." Dipping a hand into her trousers' front pocket, Kwangmi pulled out a packet of barkcloth. Before she finished unwrapping it, he tasted the peculiar flavor its contents imparted to the air. These were the spores of his sister's breeding project, accompanied by the adjuvants with which they were applied.

"How did you come by this?"

"I—"

"She got it from me. And I stole it." Framed by the doorway's parted curtains, Alan Kleinwald spoke as unconcernedly as if discussing some quirk in the performance of a theoretical machine. Not as if confessing a crime. He entered and took the seat Tink had offered Kwangmi.

"Tell me your sister's plans."

"Why? Why should I?"

"Because I've made it possible for you to fulfill your promise and wed your bride without seeking Bee-Lung's permission. Besides, I'll find out anyway, at some point."

"How?"

"The Russian organism," Kwangmi explained. "Don't you remember that Big Sister took it in?"

What an odd way to put that. "Yes. But—it can't communicate! Not in enough detail; not in words—"

"However, it will ensure that *she* does." Kleinwald smiled, and it was a humble-seeming smile. "Come. What harm will it do to apprise me of your strategies? Don't we have the same goals, ultimately? Aren't we brothers?"

As far as Tink could smell, this was true. He decided, once more, to put his faith in boldness. To lead by sharing some large fraction of the truth. Well, the majority of it.

"We're on a mission to spread May Fourth's Spirit Medicine—

obviously. Recruiting coremates, sowing spores, forming cores in country after country. What's important, though, is how we've chosen our path. We're following—" He hesitated. "We're tracing the routes of several undersea cables. At certain crucial junctures we embed Spirit Medicine threads that will eventually grow and join together. Then there will be a means to send clandestine messages! A worldwide network!"

A laugh-like huff of breath left Kleinwald's mouth. "That's your goal? You yourself have said these organisms lack the ability to use words."

"We won't need them!" Excited by his own idea—it had been Tink who thought this part up—he sprang across the cabin and grabbed Kleinwald's flesh and metal hands. "They'll send beats! Like drummers—rhythmic pulses—a code!"

Kleinwald gave his half-laugh again. "Possibly." He turned to grin—to outright grin!—over Tink's shoulder at Kwangmi. "Or possibly we've already secured other means by which to send such signals."

Once more Tink felt the brush of Kwangmi's stern yet soft lips, this time upon his neck. And then he heard her murmured invitation to return to where he'd stood previously, accompanied by the pull of her strong, pliant hands. Lying back, he accepted his hammock's cradling embrace as if it were the embrace of his beloved. Who leaned over him now, offering a straw through which to inhale a new dose of his sister's special blend—a dose whose effects he already felt.

Bee-Lung often swore that the best kinnings were impervious to the flow of time.

He had left out one small yet significant element: the fixing of nodes. The special strain amplified and supported them, and they, in turn, would amplify and support the dissemination of May Fourth's truth. But including that omission would have done nothing except delay Tink's assent, the assent he'd realized he was going to give. No further need for delay. Since Tink himself was a node already, it could not—*could not*—affect Bee-Lung's strategy if he partook of the special strain a second time, with another.

Left nostril. Right. Glittering granules swirled up inside the hollow grass. Sweetness ran down the back of his throat. A brilliance like the songs of stars blossomed behind his eyes. Beyond his skin, five of Kwangmi's attractively capable fingers curled to receive the hollow stem he offered her. Her calloused right palm continued to cup the wooden bowl containing the mixture's plentiful remainder. She, also, inhaled, and it was exactly as he'd dreamt: the bridge between them changed from air to wings to the backs of birds on which they crossed and met together together together together together

Freed within her, Tink reveled in the unmediated feel of Kwangmi's blood and chi. His spark crested wave after wave of pleasure. They could be so close! They could be one—without barriers! Without misunderstandings! Without secrets!

But there—something had passed him by: a gliding shadow of—of what? What slipped away in avoidance of this inner dance of celebration? What hid itself from his joy? "His" spark . . . "His" joy . . . A—a separateness existed here. Was such a thing even possible for them anymore? Following the cool trail of his doubt he found his rapture sinking, his awareness settling once again into the confines of habit—though not before he sensed the tingling lips of a wound beneath Kwangmi's sleeve. It felt like the scar of a fresh inoculation made in the Russian way, as his sister had described it. And the air Kwangmi exhaled—how had he not noticed before—tainted! Worse than Bee-Lung's had become in Zanzibar—much worse!

Gazing on Kleinwald with eyes bitterly awake he found his fears confirmed.

"Yes. She is mine. Mine. And now she is yours and you are hers and soon—"

"No." Tink willed movement into his limbs. None came.

"Yes. Soon you, too, will be ours. Mine."

Kwangmi rolled over him to lie behind him. Kleinwald climbed in and the hammock stretched to hold all three of them—though it was a snug fit, tight as pork meat in dough. Almost Tink thought he would emerge unscathed from the confrontation, since as Kleinwald approached, he had been carrying no cutting tools.

Except for the arm Tink had created.

Buttocks pressing hard into Kwangmi's belly, back flattening her breasts, Tink had nowhere to go, no way to escape. The white man's slender right shoulder blocked his view. The prosthetic strapped to it rose, paused, and sank from sight. "The nape of your neck seems the best location for our incision." Tink felt a stirring of the stray hairs fallen from the knot he wore in imitation of Gopal. Then, very quickly, a line of heat—fire! A gentle rubbing like cricket legs came from the retracting mechanism of Kleinwald's knife—the fine-edged scalpel Tink himself had installed between the hand's thumb and forefinger.

"Wait! Don't administer the organism just yet—this man has another cache of secrets!" Kwangmi defended him by defiling the sacred privacy of their bond. "He said it would hamper Bee-Lung's scheme if we two were linked together in the same way as he and his sister are linked. Nothing he has admitted so far touches on such matters. Nothing about starting new cores or sowing the original spores anywhere *Xu Mu* went would prohibit what we did."

"True." Kleinwald's large, brown eyes regarded Tink as if gazing into the well of the world's sorrows. "So tell us the rest now, or later on, when you've fully integrated. The process can be a little . . . confusing at first, and it's better to take care of complicated explanations ahead of time."

Bee-Lung hadn't mentioned effects of that sort. He clamped his lips together firmly. There would be no ill consequences in terms of node formation. He'd said enough. His beloved's rank betrayal stank like charred kwanga sticks.

"Very well. I'll continue with our next step, and you'll answer after you've become accustomed to your inclusion. That's fine. Do you think holding out a few hours is going to make a difference? Not in the end." With a quiet click Tink recognized from workbench trials as the opening of one of the arm's storage compartments, a more potent version of the invading aroma snaked out.

The Russian organism smelled like pancakes soaked in beer. Also like spoiled cream. Also like the inside of a boxing glove made from wet clay. Also—but further attempts to characterize its scent dissolved as the organism itself dissolved in the cut and entered the stream of Tink's blood.

He bathed in raw wealth. Capitulation was not, perhaps, defeat. Greatly expanded senses told their stories from behind him, before him, above, beside, below. . . . Time was passing; he felt it run over him, slick as tongues and twice as thrilling. *Xu Mu* floated. He floated, too: as, with, in, up. Off. Onward. Gradually he realized he could close some of the pathways through which information entered him: eyes. Hair follicles. Nerve endings. Refining his refinements, he chose mostly familiar configurations. Memory helped. Guided by this he became what he'd once been.

Basically.

By way of a round hole in the wooden wall next to him, he saw that the sun was touching the rim of his horizon. Was its position the same as before? Different? He recalled, though barely, seeing a similar configuration earlier. Before. Similar but not the very same. Such moments were known as morning.

He was seated on Rosalie's chest. He was named Ho Lin-Huang, but called something else.

Tink.

Tink stood up. The sun, beside him, rose also. The hole stayed still relative to their heights. But it, too, was moving—in a different direction. Feet lifting, landing, levering his legs, his hips—this ought to be easier. It ought to be simpler. One word described it: walking.

Tink walked. He walked out. Into the dark corridor. He knew

where he was. He kept walking forward. No, aft. Toward the hole, the hatch, the way down to *Xu Mu*'s bridge. Reaching it, he traded walking for climbing, an operation which could go either up or down. Both ways were customary, but only one applied to these surroundings. Only one led to Kwangmi.

CHAPTER TWELVE

June 1921
Kisangani, Everfair, to Bangassou, Congo

Rima scowled at the short, busty figure making its slow way toward her over the airfield. She jerked her head to summon the woman's help faster. Rima loved to fly, but she hated waiting to take off. She'd already started the propeller whirling by herself; if Kisangani didn't require these stupid brake blocks around her plane's wheels, she'd be gone by now.

The mooring tower's long morning shadow moved off of her face just as the ground woman ducked out of sight beneath her Cloud Star's nose. A quick backward rock told Rima she was free! She shifted into gear and taxied away.

At least one good thing Beamond and his collective had insisted on: the airfield covered a huge area. Lots of room to build up speed. Gunning her motor, Rima raced over the primitive runway toward the tree line. The surfacing was so bumpy she shook and fizzed like a soda pop. Darkness loomed: leaves and branches stretching to snatch her from the air—but she tricked them! Throttle up! Rise to the sky!

High winds cooled and soothed Rima's irritation. Below, green orchards and pastures wheeled around and fell behind her as she followed the Lindi River north. In an hour she had reached Bengamisa; cocoa groves lined both the river's banks, accompanying it on its eastward bend. She continued north by her instrument panel's gyro and compass, frowning until she spotted the first buoy. On course. Good. Three more marks to hit before landing: Buta, Likali, and Bondo. She and Bo-La would spend tonight together as planned, in Bangassou's best guesthouse.

The voyage remained uneventful. Rima sighted only one air-canoe, near the end of the day: *Lukeni,* she thought. Its flight path crossed hers as the sun rested an instant on the horizon, the flags that should have proclaimed its name too dark to read in the twilight above its barkcloth envelope. With one star awake she glided down toward the earth's welcoming lights. No official landing strip, of course—Bangassou was growing in importance, but for even the best, largest airfields, aeroplanes such as hers were an afterthought. Too small for hauling loads large enough for profit—crates of machine parts or baskets full of fruit or dried fish—craft like Rima's Cloud Star were viewed as nothing more than expensive toys.

And that was all they were: expensive toys. Harmless—except when played with by spies such as herself.

By the time Rima had arranged for hangar rental and scheduled her refueling and departure dates, the sky was totally dark. Queen Mwadi was expecting her—now. And to tell the truth she was expecting herself. In a hurry, she splashed through the muddy ruts of the street outside the airfield's office—no raised walkways like in Kisangani here—to the drummers' corner.

First she sent a message to Bo-La at Maison Blanche, confirming her arrival. Then she summoned a cart—which turned out to be a new-style waterfire autocar. It dropped her unceremoniously before the broad, open, raised square of the guesthouse's front porch, which faced the town's famous market. Drizzling moisture had dampened the evening's activity, but not totally extinguished it. Picking her way among vendors who were taking advantage of the shelter of the porch's roof, Rima entered a hallway paved with gleaming brown tiles.

"Is it?" The voice of her beloved came leaping down the stairway, bounding step to step like a young gazelle. "Is it you at last?"

"Bo-La?" Rima's own voice quivered, naked. She rushed up to where the queen rushed down. "Miss me?" They twined their arms together like plots, embraced like conspirators.

"So much has happened in so short a time! Come—my room— *our* room is just here." Leading her to and across the sort of landing typically found in whites' houses, Rima's darling dove drew her on to an open door, a waiting bed, and a night of joy. As she'd been led to believe, Mwadi's inoculation improved their intimacy: Rima *felt* when to ease up pressing her fingers so hard on her lover's slick clit—*before* Mwadi had to pull them away, *felt* how the rising charge of her passion spilled power over the dam of her climax into shared bolts of lightning striking both of them, again and again and again.

In the end, morning broke, calm and quiet. Stormless. Rima got up and went to the room's window, parting its shutters, widening the splinters of light they admitted. On cushions piled against the wall to the window's right, the servant women Hafiza and Sifa slept. Or at least pretended to. Rima and Mwadi had been rather loud at times. Serve that Hafiza hussy right, sneaking around and sleeping practically in Bo-La's same bed.

The tree below the window rustled with sudden fury. A black face framed in white fur poked up through the damp greenery and peered at her as if Rima was the cause of every problem history had ever invented. That must be Bo-La's pet, stuffing leaves into the worried slit of its mouth fast as it could grab them, chewing vigorously.

Brown arms reached past Rima and out into the vaporous morning air. Hafiza had risen to stand beside her. "Raffles?" she called. She was its caretaker. The animal seemed to shift to a higher perch but came no closer. It gave Rima a suspicious glance.

"Raffles?" Hafiza repeated. Rima stepped back. The monkey jumped.

Bangassou, Congo, to Chinko, Congo

He hears his name called. Raffles. He knows what a name is: it's the sound of how he smells and what he does. How he smells and what he does become different now and again, while his name stays always the same, but this, he understands, is the way one sound—one *word*—has so much power. It encompasses all these changes.

Other names are in use for other beings. Not all beings need names. Do all names need beings? He tries to digest this puzzle. It goes slowly. On top of it comes the presence of the one who steals from him his hero's feelings, the one whose name is Rima. And quickly also comes the presence of Hafiza, the one who helps him reach his hero.

Rima retreats and Raffles leaps into Hafiza's comforting hold. She shares part of her air, and her taste of joining, and she carries him to his hero. His hero has so many names. Or are they all parts of the same name? Mwadi. Queen. Queen Mwadi, yes. But Prominence? And what Rima calls her is Bo-La.

Raffles has no way of making any of these sounds with his mouth. The decoration of bark and fruit and threads and flowers around his hero's and Hafiza's heads is the best he can accomplish, but it only speaks by being seen. And only he and the others with the Spirit Medicine inside them ever see it anymore.

The decoration shows in memory as in creation that the land and its growth surround his hero and all who come in contact with her in beauty and relating. That something in the milk she sucked from her mother's teats triggers and has triggered and will trigger a life rippling out far past anyone's expectations.

His hero wakes. Hafiza shows her teeth. It's a smile, a sign of happiness. His hero blinks and opens her eyes and mouth wide, yawning, which he finds much more soothing.

"Raffles, are you well?" she asks him. "Have you eaten? Are you ready for the next part of our journey? You must take care—there may be packs of chimpanzees out to get you!"

He hops onto the bed and pats her cheek in reassurance. So many words he knows! Knowledge protects him. The hunting habits of chimpanzee tribes depend on his ignorance.

"You tryna bring your monkey along?"

"Why not?" Queen Mwadi strokes his crown and cape. "His wild brethren thrive there, as I hear."

"All the more reason. He escape, how you find him?"

"Escape" is a new word. Raffles checks with Hafiza for its meaning. Behind him, her odor increases in response to his query. Her touch floods his senses further: the swift scents of running, the joy of feeling the world's immensity. These clues, plus her whispers—so soft only he hears them—help Raffles understand what Rima is saying. It's wrong.

Escape flees toward goodness to get away from evil. He is not escaping evil. He is held in his hero's goodness and he's never leaving it—what would he leave it for? He only ever plays at apartness. Pretends it only as a game. Because what is there without her?

Without her there is nothing. Less than nothing.

With her there is the flinging and flurry of clothes put in bags and baskets, the sweat of servants loading her belongings into cars and onto boats, the strange tenderness of river weeds in his mouth and the tame roar of engines propelling them up the river called Bomu, then up the river called Chinko, against the water's flow, into the day's last light.

They come to rest on the broad river's bank. Away from the water's openness, the night's first shadows lie upon gold-blossoming shelters, tents erected and illuminated by Hafiza and those helping her. Both he and Rima crowd into the tent where his hero's rolled-up sleeping mat emits her perfume. But she is absent—should he await her sure return? She is coming back here, he knows, and nearby, in the care of Hafiza and another—the one named Sifa—is the means to unite him with her permanently, and all is well.

Raffles chooses a corner of the shelter near the mat and settles himself to ruminate over his food and reflect on questions of procedure. How to inform his queen he has partaken in the means of her kinning? And when? Before the ceremony? But afterward it will be much easier to tell that passage of their story without the words to which she is accustomed. Afterward, the story will be shared by all.

Rima won't leave the quiet alone. "You finished here?" she asks. "Cause I ain't needin no audience. Me an Bo-La be feelin each other good enough on our own. You kin leave. Go stay inna same tent as the servant people.

"An don't pretend you cain't unnerstan what I say. I been watchin."

Chinko, Congo

Next morning, Mwadi woke feeling wonderful after what had seemed like just a brief nap. Rima was awake too, her deep eyes wide open. A long, sparkling glance and Rima rolled away from her and rose on one elbow. "Where the piss pot?"

She called for Hafiza and the tent's front flap lifted promptly. Good. The serving woman hadn't gone too far off. But her face wrinkled with worry. "The piss pot, Prominence? Were we to pack it? I would have, but Sifa said you traveled too light for—"

"Never you mine! Get back to what you was doin." Her beloved leapt up naked from the mat they shared. "Go on with you!" Darting another glance over her shoulder, she dragged her trousers off of the high line running the length of the tent's peak. "Lay on down again, Bo-La; I be right back!"

That was no way to address a queen. Hesitating only a quarter of a verse to find her own clothing, Mwadi left too. Silver morning light, filtering up from the river below, failed to show where Rima'd gotten. Only Sifa, and Gasser and Gloire and another boy whose name she'd never known, were about, assisting Hafiza to portion out the gifts they'd been instructed to offer King Mwenda. Pretending concern, Mwadi busied herself making sure it was all there: the freshly updated maps, the jars of liquor and oil and soup, baskets of dried fish, tiny nets filled with pieces of chocolate, and a special box of photographs from the filming of *The Sleeper*

Wakes. Rima reappeared and insisted on taking charge of the photographs herself.

Leaving behind a mechanic and her apprentice to watch over the boats, Queen Mwadi and her followers took the trail they had promised to take—and soon their promised guide met them to conduct them on. Inward and upward they climbed—sometimes on paths so high that she glimpsed the waters of the Chinko shining through gaps in the green forest below. Raffles rode Hafiza's shoulders and seemed content with eating what he could reach from that familiar perch.

The rain fell very lightly—hardly at all. Nonetheless, Rima hunched protectively over the photographs. When their guide called a halt for rest she fussed over them, evidently to her satisfaction, for when they set off again her lovely shoulders lay flat once more, and her long neck stretched erect and supple as a heron's. She bore the box of photographs now like a nest rather than an egg: something precious but strong.

A second halt. According to their guide they were nearly there. The rain had stopped, as it usually did midday. More remarkably, thin rays of sunshine trickled between the forest's leafy branches. Mwadi put Hafiza in charge of readying their gifts, never mind that Sifa was senior. This should show she still trusted her, despite that stupid petition to join *Xu Mu*.

The column continued with Queen Mwadi at its head. The way lay plain before them, though the guide stayed near, coming next after her. He bore the largest of the jars. The rest of her train carried the rest of her presents; only Mwadi's own arms were empty. No offerings. No weapons.

Tree roots formed a series of terraces in the path like broad stairs. Two trumpeters stood at their summit, and as she mounted the final step they played a familiar fanfare: her father's theme. Or rather, it had formerly been her father's theme. Now it was acknowledged as hers and Ilunga's also. She stopped to savor the sound of her birthright.

So where was the supposedly abdicated king? Below her the earth formed a shallow bowl—but not one of those visible within it had raised and then betrayed her. Only Mwenda's old advisers dotted the edges of the path's far end, with General Wilson's slim form standing in their midst, erect as ever, despite his great age. Should she blame him—or any of the others—for her father's deceit? Or should she believe that her parents acted only to protect her?

A breeze came from behind Mwadi, a soft swirl of air that settled down to become speech: Rima. "You ready? Gonna fight for the thing you want? Tell your daddy he cain't take you back offa your throne?"

She turned and touched her beloved's tight-clasped arms. "Yes! But what of my mother's warnings?"

"Igg em! That's my advice. So rulin Everfair puts you in danger causa all them foreign powers? Ain't nothin new there. She your mama; course she care what folks do to you." A close-lipped smirk and she continued. "I happen to know she also been lettin slip the secret a how your daddy still king anywhere spies might overhear it. Hedgin her bets. Proteckin you if they hedgin theirs.

"So come on."

On either side of Mwadi, the trumpeters posed with their instruments held chin high. Taking in a big, slow breath and letting it out as she pulled her hand free, Queen Mwadi started her descent. The fanfare repeated, gradually becoming faint with distance. Another music, the rush of water, greeted her as she reached the valley's floor. There it flowed: a stream turning that part of her path into round-topped rocks on which to balance. Then, past the place where the path crossed the stream, the two of them ran together, side by side.

On approaching the grotto, Mwadi saw it first as an immense mat thrown over the valley's far slope—a loose-woven covering of darkness with golden jewels somehow sewn to it . . . then she met her father's eyes, and space everted. Out went in. The bulging darkness became the hollow in which he sheltered; the jewels were fires flickering in its depths.

"Daughter." Mwenda beckoned her forward, eyes shining with welcome. When she stopped and tried to bow at the grotto's entrance he laughed and reached to pull her down beside him.

The beautiful russet hide on which they sat was covered in rippling white stripes. Mwadi stroked it with her fingertips as her followers brought Mwenda his gifts. Rough one way, silky smooth the other. The hide was the same thing in either direction, just differently felt. Much like her parents' love.

The procession was short, and finished quickly. Each servant knelt in turn, to then retreat back along the path and stand beside it, beyond her father's court. Mwadi saw that Rima stood among them, still holding the box of photos.

"Great Mwenda!" Her beloved's well-pitched words pierced the nearby waters' babbling easily. Mwadi stayed where she was. "We got one more thing for you—a new kinda story!"

"Come here. What's new about it?"

Walking toward them with careless grace, the actor balanced the box on her palms and forearms. "We call this *The Sleeper Wakes*. It's a movie—a film—a buncha pictures put together in order so—"

"I've seen films—many films. My first was in Alexandria, seasons and seasons ago. They're not new."

"You right! But this one here, it works a different way. Like you gotta share it." Nodding in the direction of Hafiza, she continued. "See, today y'all be treated with that Chinese thing, that 'Spirit Medicine' they callin it? Only Queen Josina, she think this story on toppa the Spirit Medicine can get whoever receive it on her same page, so to speak, believin and actin on the same plan."

"Ha. My wife's mind is a blazing watch fire in the night of my enemies' ignorance!" Mwenda turned back to her with a rare smile. "Truly, daughter, you can learn so much from her. She makes those who would use us for their own ends into the instruments of our redemption."

Mwadi nodded. But must she, too, be her mother's instrument?

The gifts of food her train had brought were carried off for distribution or storage; Mwadi didn't care which. Leaf platters holding nut pastes, dried grapes, and mounded slivers of smoked fish appeared before her, General Wilson, her father, and Rima, who sat at her side by her invitation. Raffles joined them as well, taking small tastes of her fare, though he'd been stuffing himself the whole journey. The box remained on Rima's lap. Shut.

"You and your brother will both carry May Fourth's Spirit Medicine in your bodies—though your mother hopes the Russian complication attending Ilunga's inoculation can be avoided." Mwenda patted Mwadi's suddenly twitching hand. "If all goes well, the powers and connections it affords us should save Everfair from Quattrocchi's flood. On this course Queen Josina and I agree completely—but one small matter has threatened for many markets to divide us. I insist on partaking of this Spirit Medicine personally, now, as well as giving it to the general. Now! I won't wait any longer to see how it affects others."

"But—" Mwadi felt objections she had no idea how to voice. Was this better than kinning with just General Wilson? Was she ready for such intimacy with her father? Could she trust him so much? And so soon in the wake of what was perhaps his betrayal of her? And then there were the vague hints Rima had dropped concerning sexual behavior between core members . . . "But that's not the plan!"

Rima backed her up. "You really wanna put Queen Josina's jaw tight like that?"

King Mwenda grew taller without moving. "Josina's jaw is her own. She must look to its condition herself. I am my country's leader. I go where I'm needed and do what must be done. And that is what this is."

He gestured to the general. "Go say we're ready." With the aid of a carved stick picked up from the ground before him, the lean old man rose and went out of the grotto's opening.

King Mwenda's attention returned to Mwadi. "Do I lie? Are

you sincere in your doubts?" With both hands he indicated the remains of their meal. "Already we've taken the first step; the dust of the common Spirit Medicine's threads was mixed into our food on my orders, in preparation for our inoculation with the special strain. Will you have us delay what comes next?"

Had they gone too far already? Her father was as buffalo-headed as Ilunga! "Until we know for sure—"

"—we gonna follow what you tell us to do."

Mwadi's anger at Rima's interruption flared—and vanished as her beloved's blunt nails dug deep into her skin. Rima's hand on her calf was safe out of her father's sight and due to their Russian connection her . . . air was probably safe from his sensing. Both touch and aroma wanted to reassure her of . . . something. Meeting her beloved's wide-opened eyes, she still had no exact idea what that something was—but she swallowed back her objections anyway. "Yes," she said. "Let us proceed."

"Good."

General Wilson returned and resumed his place. Mwadi inquired politely after his wives and children. As he answered, Sifa came with chocolate. Arranged next to the steeping pot at her tray's center were short pieces of hollow bamboo and four shallow metal bowls filled with purple-grey powder. Bowing low, she retreated to the grotto's opening to wait with Hafiza and the other servants.

Though the general contested with her politely for the honor, brave Rima went first. Fascinated, Mwadi watched her beloved insert one end of the bamboo into a flaring nostril and the other into her tiny pyramid of powder. Those black and brilliant eyes, that mouth like berry wine . . . They were going to be hers—and far more certainly than they'd ever been Mam'selle's. This was more powerfully linking them than the weak bond given by the Russian Cure.

General Wilson partook smoothly, without incident. Next was Mwadi's father. From close beside her, Rima radiated her confidence that his unexpected inclusion was going to work out for the best. How could King Mwenda deny his daughter the succession once they became so much more solidly connected? Mwadi's fears evaporated.

It was her turn. She touched one end of the bamboo to the mound of powder. She bent over the tray. She breathed the powder in—and a screeching grunt made her blow much of it right back out. Coughing and gagging and crying, she dropped her bamboo straw and wrestled off Raffles's white-furred arms.

"Bo-La!"

"Mwadi!" Through tears she saw her father's horrified face. "Are you good?"

"Yes. Yes!" But she choked on the rest of what she wanted to say. The monkey embraced her and filled her mouth with his hair and smell. She would suffocate!

Suddenly his weight vanished. Freedom! Mwadi opened her eyes. Beloved Rima floated before them, blurred though still unutterably, ineffably beautiful. . . .

"Girl! You ain't dyin on me! Water!"

A cup—the general held it to Mwadi's lips and she gulped down its contents, rinsing clean her tongue and throat.

"Are you good?" her father repeated.

She could speak again. "I'm okay. Quite well enough to proceed." She sat up—when had she toppled over onto her side? "What more is there to do?"

"You jokin? We ain't doin nothin! No way you puttin yourself in no further danger over this—an that's flat!" So much for Rima scoffing at caution.

"Restrain that animal," King Mwenda ordered. "Get it out of here. That's the problem! Then we can go on."

But Raffles was already gone. Reluctantly, Rima allowed Mwadi to consume the rest of her share of the inoculant powder. She inhaled the few streaks that were left in the bottom of her father's bowl, too.

And then, finally, as shadows unfurled from the grotto's cool depths to dance outward, dimming the air, Rima opened the box of photos. Within lay a wrapping of heavy, rubber-blessed cotton, a barrier against the damp. Her deft fingers undid the wrapping to reveal the precious, hard-won treasure within: representations of their important story. Lifting the first of these, Rima held it by its corners and showed it round. Simultaneously there came a commentary:

"Here we begin: a panoramic view of the city of the future. See our shining towers, our rational gardens and plentiful park-lands? How well-planned our thoroughfares—like the thoughts of giants—like the melody of time—"

Who spoke? The voice was Hafiza's, but these were not a ser-vant's words.

"Next comes The Sleeper's awakening. We're inside the Palace of History, now, in the room dedicated to Dr. Shin's scientific labors."

A second photograph appeared. Mirror upon mirror reflected row upon row of white-shrouded cots. The draped outlines resting on the cots looked like corpses. On the closest and most central cot the covering lay pulled back to show the face of its occupant: the film star Sevaria. Her brother's lover. Who lifted her long-lashed eyelids. Whose dazzling eyes burned away the photo's whiteness, turning silver to gold. Queen Mwadi blinked. The colors contin-ued to well up and spread. The woman in the photograph pursed her lips, then parted them.

"From here, we'll proceed to The Sleeper's breakfast—" The picture talked! With Hafiza's tongue! Mwadi looked away. The darkness surrounding her shifted, slid aside, replaced by another picture: a table laid with gleaming crystal, steam spiraling up from the cups, and delicious odors permeating the atmosphere.

"So begins The Sleeper's education in the time to come, the time of plenty. While drinking and eating her fill, she meets May Weather Syn-D, who takes her on several guided tours." A mon-tage of moving photographs depicted scenes in which Mwadi's beloved, dressed as May, led Sevaria onto trains, into unguarded vaults piled high with gems, and to various other happy spots.

"Then what are the roles we're supposed to play? If these photographs represent our story—" Mwadi noticed how closely her father regarded her, as if her example showed him the way to handle their new awareness. But was this attitude something she saw? In the ever-increasing dusk of this chamber? Or did she feel it also? Or smell it—

"—then how do we tell it?" He looked directly into Mwadi's eyes. But she waited for Rima to answer him.

"We gotta make our story come true. We gotta do what The Sleeper remember she done by the movie's end." Like the speckled darkness of the nightjar Mwadi had once ridden right across Mombasa, the luster of her beloved's hair caught every fleeting ray of light. Sculptured curves of raven black, rich brown, and dove grey surged around her beauty.

The scrape of a thin blade emerging out of a wooden scabbard sounded in the grotto's gloom. "You wanna watch better how it goes? Lemme introduce you one more medicine: mine. Then you be like Mwadi an me."

"I don't remember this as an idea of Josina's."

"It ain't. But it's a good one. Cain't you tell?" It was good—yes! Mouth-watering enthusiasm wafted all around them.

"So." Her father's right hand shone suddenly bright. He had kindled his glamp. In the glory of its illumination he extended his all-flesh left hand. "Give me your gift."

A quick flash. Mwadi winced with the pain of King Mwenda's scored skin. He, of course, gave no visible sign of being hurt. And soon came the soft lick of the Russian Cure's cloth, cleansing and binding his wound.

"Now your turn, General."

Then, rapt, the four of them absorbed the remaining photos' import, watching one scene glide into the next. The future they were to build thrummed with deep wonders: cageless zoos, teacherless schools. Crops without diseases. Clinics dedicated not simply to maintaining health but to amplifying it: to sharpening patients' senses, improving their abilities, increasing their fertility, extending their lives.

The work necessary to make these things happen was the labor of love. In a trance, The Sleeper viewed herself taking journeys around the globe to share her understandings with friends and strangers. Mwadi and her core kin went with her. Upon waking all celebrated their evident success.

The display was done. The story had been viewed. Rima rewrapped the stack of photographs in their length of blessed cotton and returned them to their box. General Wilson crouched to receive it, squatting in the hole they dug for him in the soft, dry ground. Together the remaining three filled it in, leaving uncovered his shoulders and his gleaming head.

Even as she scooped the loosened soil into place, part of Mwadi worried that water would get inside the box and spoil its contents. A kind of double consciousness split her mind. The doubt, concern, and anxiety peeled away like dead skin: limp and translucent. Through it she perceived a different feeling: gladness. Gladness! Their story was alive! It would sprout! It would grow!

Hafiza stood, shedding Raffles from her rounded back. "And now you'll spend your first night together as a core." She left them.

Kisangani, Everfair

"More hot water!" King Ilunga commanded. The bath would cool unacceptably unless replenished in a timely fashion. "Now! Go get it!" He waved the serving woman away. Once he would have seduced her, but these days all his desire was for his brother and his bride-to-be.

Milky with lavender-scented soap, the merely warm water

slopped against his skin as he polished his darkness with a sponge. Of his two coremates, only Sevaria remained in the palace physically. Which was enough. Dr. Kleinwald's love came to him quite clearly over *Xu Mu*'s drums. Ilunga had only to climb to the palace's roof each evening to feel it throbbing in his blood—fainter and fainter with the increasing distance, yet still distinct.

The room's curtains swung apart, but no one came through them. After an irritated pause, he called out to hurry the servant in. Nothing happened. Also, an aroma different than the one he expected began seeping past the soap's overwhelming perfume: Madam Ho's.

Ilunga swiveled his head. There she stood, old and sturdy and wise, a bucket balanced on one vest-hung shoulder. "Greetings, mighty king. I bring you what you've asked for—and also what you need."

"You may approach."

"I will." As if there'd been no question to the contrary, Madam Ho strode firmly forward and poured her bucket's contents into his brass and wooden bathtub. Splash! Invigorating heat soaked into him, and with it the realization that his own aroma carried his self-doubt to the nostrils of one who could easily recognize it. A small shift in the elder woman's emanations told him she had marked the moment of his realization.

"And since you'll never ask me for it, I offer you this advice unsolicited: reserve the particular mix of the three inoculations you've received for those you trust absolutely—those with whom you would breed children."

Ilunga drew himself up to sit taller in the tub, mustering as much dignity as he could find it in himself to feel. "What's your basis for saying so?"

"Your mother, Queen Josina, has secret plans."

"I'm aware."

"Are you?" Slinging the empty bucket back toward the door, Madam Ho took Ilunga's sponge from his surprised hands. Before he could prevent her she had dipped it in his bathwater and raised it to his face. "Can you see with your eyes shut?" Cleansing streams coursed down his cheeks like tears.

He pushed her away. "I don't need to! I can catch a scent, trace someone by smell and know where they've come from, who they came with—"

"Yes. We can all do that and more. But what we perceive are emotions, not thoughts. Your mother's mind is complex, while her heart is simple."

"She'd never let me be harmed. Never. She loves me!"

Madam Ho held up a huge towel, soft and white. "Assuredly. Here, let me dry you off before a draft comes."

Swathed in close-clipped cotton, Ilunga stepped free of the tub's vapors and immediately identified the smoke of his sweet fire approaching. Still a long ways off, though.

"So what does Queen Josina tell you? That she's grooming you and your friend Scranforth to establish the least harmful configuration of this country's rule she thinks possible? That in the worst case, your most powerful enemies will believe themselves your closest allies and will count on you to oversee Everfair's drowning?"

Nearer. Nearer! Ilunga hurried to rub away the last of the bath's lingering moisture. "I suppose. Something like that. Why?"

"Don't you understand that she treats the Spirit Medicine as if it's a necessary evil? An accommodation your country must make to forces beyond her control? Whereas in fact there are, as you're growing aware, many advantages available to those of us who are inoculated. Advantages which not only profit us as individuals but mean we're poised to save the world from plunging into all-out war—again. The Spirit Medicine is a force for good!"

So Ilunga had been coming to convince himself. "You believe I can correct my mother's oversight. How?"

"By allowing me to form in you a deeper, broader connection with our—"

A soft breeze borne in past the window blinds interrupted the focus of his attention: a nymph's breath, warm with Sevaria's wonderful aroma. And then she poured her fragrance up the stairway, along his corridor, under the curtains. And then she was wholly there!

The creases radiating from Madam Ho's eyes smoothed out and relaxed, and her smell shrank back a bit. "Let me show you some of what I mean." She bowed toward Ilunga, but beckoned Sevaria to her side, away from him. Irked, he willed his fumes to flow more strongly, more seductively. This had no apparent effect.

"You see? You lack influence—your very coremate resists your call." Looping several strands of Sevaria's soot-black hair around her fingers, Madam Ho pulled them back and arranged them behind his intended's ears.

"Now. If you follow my advice and become a node—"

"Aunty!" His bride's voice leapt in, its brightness breaking apart Madam Ho's softer tone, which he suddenly realized had been sinking lower and lower. "I know what you want to happen. Why must you explain it to the king? Why try convincing him to do it?"

"Primarily because he's here. Your other coremate is sadly far away."

"But are you certain that you need your next node to be a man? Use me!"

"What? Of course he'll be a man! Just like Tink—"

"A woman—just like you! You're the real node!"

"No. It's Little Brother who has been sowing the spores in the telegraph cables, ever since we left Beijing. . . ." Ilunga sensed Madam Ho's certainty evaporating as it met Sevaria's passion.

"Who has inoculated us? Who has driven forward our quest for more potent strains? No one understands the stakes of our expansion better!" Now she turned on him her full regard: eyes, ears, pores, follicles—and his essence floated to join hers on a cloud of joy.

"Do you consent, dear one?" he asked himself, and answered silently. Yes. Alan Kleinwald also, from the reservoirs of him Sevaria held, communicated his agreement.

"The process involves no tools, no further materials, as you have partaken of the necessary special strain," Madam Ho explained. "I simply send the news of our selection home, and make sure it's distributed to all our cores."

"How long does that take?" This question felt like Alan was asking it.

"It depends. How easy and regular is contact between us? We'll use drummers where we can, but until we finish incorporating the telegraph cable system, many distances will require physical travel."

Without warning Madam Ho's usually even output shifted, becoming jagged, pinched—stuttering with clumsily suppressed pain. She crumpled to the floor. Ilunga stared. Sevaria bent at the waist and swayed over her, brushing the air above her with outspread fingertips. "Aunty!"

The breeze entering between the room's door curtains stopped. His mother stood in its way. Behind her he smelled Mademoiselle Toutournier. "What's the matter?" Mademoiselle asked.

Queen Josina swept in, her skirt and bodice fluttering. "Madam Ho seems to have fainted." She fixed him with a measuring glare. "Did you do this? Give her a shock of some kind?"

"Of course not!" Ilunga had to back up to make space for his mother, Mademoiselle, and a pair of attendants. The hard line of the bathtub's rim impressed itself into his buttocks.

Mademoiselle had joined Sevaria in hovering over Madam Ho. "Her eyes are open," she announced. "They respond to movement. Oh, tears! She's crying!"

Pain continued to rise from Madam Ho's huddled form. Pain and longing.

"Aunty!" Sevaria spoke in the fashion he knew as her own. "Why do you miss your coremates? Why do you miss anyone? You have the means. Stop denying yourself their presence."

A long shudder interrupted Madam Ho's breath. Then she sat up. "Dare I reach out to them? *Can* I?" she asked.

"Reach out to who?" Queen Josina demanded. "Your brother? Some spy for the Italians?"

"What? The ambassadors are innocent!" Every effusion Ilunga received from them had been sincere.

His mother laughed. "Are you completely sure of that? It must be as certain as the ground we grow on. And their servants, too?"

Ilunga couldn't recall whether he had met them all.

"A puzzle!" Madam Ho's hand took Sevaria's; together they lifted her to her feet. "I see it clearly: for fear of this you sent Gopal with them as Vinay, and not as himself—or as Umar. He will uncover the truth. And when the truth is determined, you'll share it?"

"Why won't you question him on that point directly? There's no call to be scared of getting ready to reach out to him—you're both inoculated with every element necessary, though you belong to different cores." Again Ilunga detected the patterns of Kleinwald's mind in the words said.

"But how is this possible?" asked Mademoiselle.

"Spooky action at a distance," Ilunga explained. "We're still learning what's possible. The three of us—" He began to understand what he meant as he said it. "—not only are we three people, Ilunga, Sevaria, and Alan, yes, but also we are yet another trio: your two kinds of Spirit Medicine plus remnants of the Russian organism. Combining these elements makes something new."

Was that all? Only three? Or was there a shadow, a fog, a fourth? He paused, doubting, and Sevaria continued. "Sometimes we can . . . fill one another up. At night, dreaming, we come together. Try it, Aunty!"

Another pulse of desolation. In its aftermath, quiet, calmness. Emptiness. Ilunga remembered feeling lonely like that. Now, though, too many people were in here.

"Where are my clothes? Where's Gloire?"

"He went with your sister," Mademoiselle answered, not looking away from Madam Ho's trembling attempt to stand unaided.

Mwadi had taken Gasser from him also. And before that, Hafiza. Must she appropriate *all* his servants?

"How do you do it?" his mother asked him. "Is it constant? Can Doctor Kleinwald initiate the connection, or must he wait for one or both of you to contact him first, since he's so distant?"

"The effect is somewhat intermittent," Ilunga's brother explained via Sevaria. "At times we're extremely close—effectively inside one another, as now. But then there are other periods during which we exist practically in our original isolation."

Sevaria went into the next room to find him a clean shirt and kilt, and Ilunga took over talking. "However, we can rely on our entanglement to be there always, though not always to the same intensity."

Queen Josina nodded, seeming unperturbed by the transfer of the thread of discourse from mouth to mouth. "So I can communicate with the inoculated Italians through Madam Ho?"

"We should try that. It may work."

Dressed at last, Ilunga sighed happily as he followed his bride-to-be to their throne room. Behind him came his mother, and then Mademoiselle, one arm draped over the sinewy shoulders of Madam Ho. Then one of his mother's favorite servants, Lembe. A young European-looking man stood aside from the doorway as Ilunga approached it. "Prominence!" he called. The king ignored him, but Mademoiselle urged the white man to wait for an audience. He filed in alongside some other petitioners.

Only two asses today. The stool of state held them both, though cozily.

His mother took her accustomed seat and indicated the spots on the dais where Mademoiselle and Madam Ho should stand. The petitioners and guards arranged themselves against the chamber's far wall.

"What do we need to do to form this link?" asked Queen Josina.

"First," said Ilunga, speaking for his absent mate, "we need to obtain Madam Ho's full cooperation. There's a—a barrier you've erected. We can't get past it unless you let us through."

A tang of cunning crept from the elder's pores. "And why would I do that?"

"Why wouldn't you?" his mother asked. "To help me. To reach your lover."

"You— How can you know about that!"

A smooth, self-satisfied air surrounded Queen Josina. "Well? It's true, isn't it? Will Gopal think you're real or a dream when you come to him?"

"He may not want to believe there's a difference."

Next to Ilunga, Sevaria smiled. "Then lie down, that you may teach him."

"Here? Now? What about your petitioners?"

"They can wait," Queen Josina declared. "Since we're all present, and we have a way of finding out how the inoculation's going, we'll do so as quickly as we can! Yes?" She looked at him—at them.

"Yes," he said. Sevaria rose from the throne and gently guided Madam Ho to rest comfortably upon the dais tiles before him. Mademoiselle sat by Madam Ho's head and cradled it in her lap.

"Inhale deeply," he instructed Madam Ho, and then he entered her nostrils via his and Sevaria's shed particles.

Warmth. Darkness. While at the same time conscious of the room's occupants and its atmosphere of shifting shade and solemn sweat, Ilunga felt himself travel deeper, deeper into the pulsing channels of this new relative's life. It was easy to tell his two surroundings apart. Different senses for different experiences.

At first he voyaged effortlessly, as if swimming without arms, or sailing without a boat. But then he stopped.

He had reached the barrier.

It was tight—a basket of will. Vein-like tissues bulged out as if containing an infection, swollen with the effort of holding the Russian organism within. As Ilunga observed it, the barrier before him relaxed, thinned and stretched, became permeable. Out between its interstices curled the scent, the force and sway, of the organism the Russians urged on all Europe.

On its own, this entity would want its hosts to clump together. It would clumsily direct them to assemble, and get them to champion the birth of their own nation, Atlantropa—unless, of course, it caused the strange syndrome making each seek to be planted in a plowed field. This was a disorder, a malfunction of its reproductive urge.

But combine a healthy Russian organism with the existing forms of Spirit Medicine and a new, more powerful creature was generated: the creature that enabled Ilunga's joyous commingling over any distance with his brother and his bride-to-be.

So soon as he sensed the release of Madam Ho's barrier, Ilunga withdrew his main focus from her inner workings. With the aid of the doctor's lingering presence she should now be able to discover how to contact Gopal—even supposing he, also, had isolated the Russian growth away from the rest of himself.

With one arm, Ilunga beckoned the European-looking petitioner forward. This was a big, muscular youth whose round grey eyes and sand-colored hair made Ilunga feel oddly awkward. He studied the effect as the man explained what he was seeking. The foreigner's features reminded Ilunga vaguely of someone. . . . He interrupted the rushed and stilted speech: "What's your name?"

"Gregor Strasser, Prominence. You remark something familiar in my face, don't you? I wouldn't presume on such a slight connection, but I believe you have a previous acquaintance with my sister, Frau Schreiber. As I was saying, my family, and in fact all Germany, understand how much we will owe to Everfair for your support in ridding Namibia of this British conspiracy."

CHAPTER THIRTEEN

June and July 1921
Chinko, Congo

Paddling barefoot with Sifa among the streamlet's reeds, Hafiza was content. The inoculation was a success—and what did it matter that the physical steps with which it was accomplished were the work of one uninoculated? She had narrated it. The specified story had been planted, literally and otherwise, and this latest core's members had spent the night rehearsing their fresh relationship—a framework established in an attempt, she understood, to overcome the Spirit Medicine's latent tendencies toward sexual love with a differing propensity, one favoring the sort of love tying Bee-Lung to her brother. Judging by the laughter rolling toward her out of the grotto's entrance, that trial was bearing happy fruit.

The trill of a spiderhunter's song subsided. The morning was quieting to noon's stillness. Time to verify that the new core's formation fully supported the weight of its members' needs and discoveries. Beckoning Sifa to come with her and stepping carefully to avoid stirring too much muck, she left the shallow waters for their low, soft banks. Here, clay jars stacked in the shade of overhanging trees kept the encampment's beer cool. Each took a jar and balanced it on her hips. Fermented liquids supported the Spirit Medicine the best.

As they approached the root-sheltered entrance to the grotto, Hafiza was a little surprised to see someone emerge from it. Long legs, long arms whirling—it was Miss Rima Bailey. "Hey!" Miss Bailey hailed her, waving her over. "You all bringin somethin for us? We started plannin how to spread ourself all over the world. That is some challengin work. We grateful for whatever you got."

Queen Mwadi and King Mwenda appeared and stood alongside Miss Bailey, so she and Sifa offered them their swallows of the beer first.

"Yes!" King Mwenda stretched his throat appreciatively, chin to the pale, blue-grey sky. "This feeds us! Daughters, you both must drain it down!" He handed the half-drunk jar to Rima without looking at her. "What's next?"

Hafiza had her instructions; they'd have to do in the absence of the envelopment of her kin. Sifa's physical nearness only teased at true intimacy. Hafiza sent her away with the empties and stayed to carry out her assignment.

"Now that you're feeling your core's closeness you'll want to maintain it," she explained. "Yet your core's story will remain rooted here, while your voyage, King Mwenda, must still be undertaken. But eventually, once May Fourth's Spirit Medicine is brought everywhere, you four will communicate freely via May Fourth's inoculation of telegraph cables."

"Okay, sure. An I guess me an Bo-La be stickin together pretty tight right from the beginnin. Ima fly us to Lake Edward. We gotta see what that white man Devil up to over there."

They were going to spy on Mr. Scranforth? No—that wasn't what her core wanted them to do. Nor Aunty Ho. Nor Queen Josina. Whence came this initiative? Puzzled, Hafiza opened her nostrils wider. There must be a clue in the air as to why the core wanted to take this unforeseen direction. Was there already a node? Whose scent prevailed in its new-formed blend?

It was Raffles's scent. The monkey's. How could that be? The core had chased him off before absorbing their story. Furthermore, he was of an entirely different species! Surely humans had the greater influence on the core under the sway of an organism adapted to their systems. The troubling scent came from vines framing the grotto's opening—and there the monkey clung, swinging by one arm, gesticulating with the other to show he meant to jump. Even as Hafiza held out her arms to receive him, she questioned Raffles's presence there.

But then, heavy and sweet, the monkey's joy spilled into her own emotions and drowned her doubts with simple optimism. Of course Queen Mwadi and Miss Bailey would journey to intercept Scranforth's interference. That way they'd be handy when Queen Josina needed help managing whatever predicament King Ilunga's core got into. As for sowing spores at either end of the transatlantic cable, King Mwenda and Raffles would be able to handle that task by themselves.

"My brave monkey! Exploring a new world!" Petting the crease between the double tufts of his crown with one hand, on the spot where she knew it gave him the most pleasure, Hafiza briefly clasped Raffles tightly to her breast.

Then King Mwenda claimed him, and the monkey draped himself over the king's head and shoulders like a living hood. The king's solemn face melted into smiling serenity. "Yes," he whispered. "We go. Together, preparing the way."

Sudan, Aboard Omukama

Gopal had been too alone for too long. The inoculations he'd accomplished didn't help that much. *Omukama* used four drummers; forming them into an exclusive core made sense, though that left him on its outside.

Now, in the aircanoe's dark, cramped galley, he considered the cook. A spy. A woman. Bharatese, like himself, though of a "higher" caste. The Italians called her Brenda—close to what she called herself, Brinda. Mixed with the smoke of the tiny iron stove box, her smell conveyed impatience, weariness—and a grudging attraction to him. This last he had managed to engineer into a conversion to the cause.

May Fourth insisted that Spirit Medicine inoculants must give at least token agreement to what was done. He had to urge her on to action. Eyes shut, Gopal imagined the two of them together, skin to skin, groin to groin. "Vinay," said the cook, her voice sharp. "Come here." No need to move his feet; he simply leaned forward and lifted his arms to embrace her. And finally, after his words and emanations convinced her that inoculation would increase their enjoyment, he was able to administer the spores that he had guided her to choose, the same crop he'd first shared with his core.

Then came the entanglement. Perhaps inoculation improved the sexual aspect for Brinda. For him? Bareness. Thinness. In the arms of only one coremate, Gopal's solitude ebbed only a little lower. He missed Trana, missed Jadida, Kafia, Hafiza, even his lover taken from outside their core, Bee-Lung.

Crouched in the storage cubby between the galley and crew's quarters, he told Brinda the core's story, but knew there'd be some variation in his solitary telling. Some separation from the truth. Despite this, she assented to assisting him in his mission.

The best spot, the likeliest opportunity for recruitment—and really for the entire process—was *Omukama*'s viewing lounge. Retrofitting had placed this on the aircanoe's highest level, to the fore of its baggage compartment. The two-deck climb up from the passenger cabins kept away most casual visitors, but Signore Quattrocchi spent much of his time there, Gopal had noticed, drinking fermented grape juice. The signore's entourage usually kept him company. This afternoon was no exception.

With his workbasket strapped to his head and leading his brand-new coremate, Gopal mounted the companionway to the cold, windy baggage compartment. Freezing air and faint stripes of wan light made their way between the hull's intentionally loose-fitting boards. Difficulty breathing in the thin atmosphere here was probably another reason passengers preferred their cabins when *Omukama* flew this high. But on the other side of the rubber-blessed gaskets of the door Gopal opened, warmth and comfort reigned.

To the room's customary furnishings—a quartet of wicker tables, a row of wicker stools—the four members of the Italian party had added a pillow-lined hammock hung between window frames. Here the signore reclined. His three attendants—also diplomats, according to Bee-Lung—sat on the stools, twisting to face Gopal as he entered. Naturally.

He bowed and sensed the cook, behind him, bow also.

"Vinay? Did I summon you?" Quattrocchi stared pointedly from beneath his bushy brows.

"Not exactly, Esteemed. But as we set out you asked me to remind you when we reached our journey's halfway point. And we're nearly there!"

"I see. Gravina! Ercolano, Gentileschi! Come have your glasses filled—a toast! We'll be in Europe in a matter of days. Here, yes, that one will do all right. Pour the wine!"

Gopal drew the leaf-wrapped bottle Quattrocchi had indicated out of his basket and removed its cork. Then he acted hesitation. "Esteemed, may I suggest an additional way to celebrate? One more in step with the latest customs of our land?"

Chubby, boyish Gravina snorted. "The land we're leaving? What do we care if we're a bit off from its beat? The main thing is—"

"The main thing is that we may at any point return. *Any* of us. We'll observe the customs you bring to our attention when we can, Vinay." Signore Quattrocchi turned from his junior aide to Gopal, nodding encouragement. "Go on. Explain."

Leaving the bottle to Brinda, Gopal pulled the necessary tools from his workbasket: slim bamboo straws, a chopping knife, a brass bowl, jars of the adjuvants Bee-Lung recommended. The precious spores, the same strain as his own. He began telling the inoculants their story. A new story, because they were forming a new core:

"Once there was a people who wandered. Slowly, over long years, they made their way from home to home. On the road they traveled they came across many surprises. They saw immense towers whose tops pierced the clouds. They waded through rivers flowing with pearls, fed on snakes' eggs and glittering cakes of ice. But they belonged nowhere. And despite all these wonders their journey took its toll in exhaustion, illness, and death.

"So, weary of the endless road, their tribe split apart. One faction decided that they would end their search to focus instead on building a country to call their own. They would fill it with the best of all they'd seen and remembered, and settle down to rest.

"The other faction recognized the uselessness of their quest but felt the remedy for that issue lay in getting help. They developed the method I employ with you here and now: a ritual designed to invoke the aid of plant and animal spirits." Naming each ingredient as he introduced it, Gopal cut, ground, and blended them the way he'd been taught. And then, as he'd been taught, he offered to partake of the mixture right along with the inoculants, allaying, as he could smell, their suspicious fears.

Kisangani, Everfair, and Aboard Xu Mu

Lying flat on the throne room floor as if overtaken by a fit, Bee-Lung shut out annoyance, shame, all the emotional fumes threatening her focus. Only the doctor's instructions conveyed via Miss Sevaria mattered. First Dr. Kleinwald used the film star's voice to urge calmness and then, when he—it—they—judged Bee-Lung ready for more specific guidance, the film star began to whisper:

"Remember his scent? He has never ceased to emit its particles. They have never ceased to age and change on their release. Feel them kiss you, floated on tender winds, mellowing and dispersing with space and time. Now grade them, and sort out their classes into a path ranging from least to most pungent. Follow that path and you'll find him."

Out of her desire she built a bridge through the air. Her will walked it. Automatically, she continued muffling the distractions emerging as obstacles, such as birdsong and the skyborne allurements of strange new plant species. So far . . . so far . . . Soon, despite her efforts to ignore them, she couldn't help noticing how the land's exudations became drier and drier. Stones and sand predominated: desert. Rain vanished; its blurring effect had irritated Bee-Lung for most of her trip, but now she missed it.

And now she reached her destination: the rich clustering of Gopal's odors. Now what?

Disconcertingly, Sevaria's commentary started up again in her ears. "You're close, yes. Go closer."

But where *was* she? How could she be in two places at once? The fragrances she had tracked began to fade; the ribbon beneath her—feet?—began to break apart—

"No! Don't give up!"

Wrapping itself in and out of *Omukama*'s busy aromas, Gopal's thread thrummed stronger than ever. She could hear it, sniff it, twirl it around her—tongue? Around herself! Plunging forward, Bee-Lung smothered her longing in his salty sweetness, gulping, swallowing, beside him, within him, surrounding and surrounded.

But to no effect. His thread refused to bind with her. It acted as if she simply weren't there. Rearing back in fear and confusion, Bee-Lung felt a tug pulling her farther off, farther away. What was it? She surrendered to find out. And there, that! It was nearby, a beckoning nexus that sensed her and accepted her presence as real.

It took her in. She had clear boundaries now. Two sets. The cool tiles of the dais pressed against her back and shoulders, and the strings of a hammock pressed there also. She lay still and rocked. She listened to Dr. Kleinwald's questions twice: in Sevaria's voice and in his own.

"Have you made full contact? Are you integrated?"

"Yes," she replied. Her words were doubled, too. She said them as herself and as Tink.

"Yes? But just with your brother? Well, that was the danger of trying now, with *Xu Mu* in *Omukama*'s vicinity." A whiff of consternation—worry, self-blame, and uncertainty—bloomed out of the doctor's skin. Sevaria emitted a tiny replication of it—for whose benefit? Most likely on reflex.

Bee-Lung opened Tink's eyes, leaving her own shut. The hammock hung in the cabin they had shared. "Why try it, then?" they asked.

"It should have worked! I was formed from the commingling of the Spirit Medicine and the Russian organism."

"*You* were formed? Meaning who? Doctor Kleinwald?"

"Meaning me, I, the one who is all three of us." A quick flirt of the doctor's eyes. "Or should I count you and say all four of us? Five? Six?

"Ha! The waft of your fear! No, I'm joking you. It's only three. I appear limited to my original kin: Alan Kleinwald, Sevaria binti Musa, King Ilunga. Therefore I believe that you are limited also. Mr. and Madam Ho, of course. And Kwangmi. But not, it seems, Umar—or Gopal, or whatever we're calling him."

Bee-Lung had heard that some lichens were in actuality a blend of algae and fungus. Perhaps the entity addressing her was similarly amalgamated?

As a dense and powerful wave of interconnected odors billowed into the cabin, she let Tink's head turn toward the curtained door. She allowed his arms to rise to embrace his wife, Kwangmi.

She clasped Kwangmi to their chest. Kwangmi clasped them back, and then . . . then, Bee-Lung became confused.

"Well?" The voice in Bee-Lung's ears was Queen Josina's. "Have you found out how the Italians responded? Is Gopal successful? Is he ready to be recalled?"

The voice in Tink's ears was both Bee-Lung's and Kwangmi's. "A slight problem has cropped up," it said. "I'm entangled with my brother, aboard *Xu Mu*."

"Not unexpected," said Dr. Kleinwald and King Ilunga. All bodies heard their simultaneous declaration. "At least, not *completely* unexpected," the doctor and the king continued. "Though we've focused so far on establishing their equivalency, we must now zero in on any detectable differences between our inoculants, however small."

Supine upon the dais, Bee-Lung tried her best to filter away Tink's distracting surroundings. She must grow used to missing him. The alternative would be to grow used to missing herself. With a harsh effort she raised up the dormant body—*her* body! She rose up on her elbows and forced her eyes open. Mademoiselle's lap had deserted her, and the European petitioner who had entered behind them knelt in the place where Mademoiselle had sat—though he wasn't holding Bee-Lung's head, but facing the king's throne, hands folded. Mademoiselle now hovered at Bee-Lung's feet.

Anger crashed over her—she would drown in rage! No! Whose anger was this? As it ebbed she tracked it to its source: Queen Josina. Quickly as the anger had risen it dissipated, leaving no trace on that smooth face. What had so enraged Queen Josina? What had Bee-Lung missed while busy being Tink?

"Will a thousand veterans of our civil war do?" King Ilunga asked. "Plus the hundred we've trained to be guards?"

"Yes! Any troops you can give us! And supplies? Anything at all—shonguns, bombs, jumpsheets—"

The queen's voice was flat, and chill as frost. "For how long will you want these things?"

"Till the invader leaves!" The white man didn't look away from the king.

"You, too, are an invader."

"But—that is to say—we're not—*they're* invading *us*! I mean—we're your allies!" At last the petitioner turned his head to address the queen. "The British are your enemies—so of course you're supporting us, not them. Aren't you?"

"Perhaps. But wouldn't it be best to wait before deciding, my son? To consult your sister on this matter?"

Sevaria, seated again by King Ilunga's side, shrugged. "I suppose we'll wait for her return—in two markets, right? Come back to us and we'll consult her then—and through her, my father, if the inoculation has gone as we expect."

The inoculation creating the royal core—the completion of May Fourth's plan for Everfair's advancement! Bee-Lung wished she could have traveled with Queen Mwadi's party and made sure of a good outcome. But then who would have kept watch over King Ilunga and his disturbing coremates?

King Ilunga's mother seemed unconcerned by Miss Sevaria pronouncing what were obviously her son's words. Or by anything else—for along with the anger Bee-Lung had found so overwhelming only minutes ago, all Queen Josina's emissions had dried up. Though Bee-Lung moved to stand close by her, brushing off Lembe's assistance in rising from the floor, she caught no scent of further emotions coming from her.

Lembe led the dissatisfied European away and gestured the next petitioner forward. With a graceful flourish, Mademoiselle plunged her hands into the melon-sized basket he presented and lifted them, full, to show their contents to the queen. Brass beads cascaded between her fingers. The gift came with a plea for protection—but not, this time, protection from greedy or dishonest neighbors, as was usual.

Also different was the petitioner's origin: he came from a long distance away, from very near the border with dead Leopold's possessions. His town was called Inongo, and he claimed to "humbly" represent its citizens. "It is said," he continued, "that our lands will be sacrificed in the production of a new country, along with many other farms and forests. All river valleys, all low acres of any sort west and south of here, are to lie underneath a deep lake."

"Who says this?" asked Queen Josina. "Diviners? Mothers of Wisdom?"

It was clear to Bee-Lung that the man was referring to Atlantropa. Obviously word of the plot had gotten out. Perhaps one of the Italians had talked too freely—but then why had this rumor surfaced so far from the palace?

A shiver coursed through Bee-Lung's bones. Not because she felt chilled; the room was sufficiently warm. Another shiver—and another! Was her body not her own? No, it wasn't; the Russian organism she'd kept isolated so long was loose in her blood. She had managed to ignore that fact all this time. It was no longer possible.

Now beset by one continuous quiver, Bee-Lung attempted to edge off of the dais unremarked and sneak away. No luck. King Ilunga snatched the corner of her tunic.

"Have you just figured it out?" he asked, cutting the petitioner off midsentence. "You're never going to be the same."

"The same as what?" Bee-Lung wanted to sound brave, but her voice shook too much. "As you?"

"As me? Perhaps not, though likely you'll turn out somewhat similar—but what I mean is that you've changed from who you once were. Irrevocably."

"Come sit down, Aunty," Sevaria ordered her. To Bee-Lung's surprise she did exactly that. The tremors radiating from her center outward slowed, but increased in strength. What did that mean? What was happening? What could she do?

"Continue," King Ilunga commanded the petitioner. "You say you seek our help preventing this massive flood?"

She let one arm surrender. It curled and kinked and waved about before her face, then over her head, then went arching downward—

"Madam Ho?" Mademoiselle Toutournier had interposed herself between Bee-Lung and the king's throne. With her filmy wrap unfurled like the wings of a flying insect, she bent to whisper a worried question. "I think I know how to handle this—will you trust me?"

Mademoiselle smelled good, crisp and clean as sliced loquat. Amid the background scents of the rest of the room—frustration, duplicity, fatigue—her aroma of solid yet daring practicality refreshed Bee-Lung with hope. Something could be done!

She nodded—and Mademoiselle nodded too, her blond head

matching the motion of Bee-Lung's black head. Straightening, Mademoiselle took hold of Bee-Lung's right hand—the one she still fought to control—and pulled her back to her feet. Then Mademoiselle clasped her winged arms around Bee-Lung and whirled her off the dais, down to the audience chamber's floor. The soles of their sandals struck its tiles in time to the shuddering pulse beating through Bee-Lung's veins. And steadied it. And grounded it. And gradually slowed it down.

Mademoiselle smiled. "Is this not a better method of handling your problem? You *see*—and now you must *listen*." Low in Mademoiselle's throat a humming started—a song. The same crest and trough throbbed in this music as had shivered along her body. An answering trill bubbled up in Bee-Lung's chest and spilled between her parting lips: not in unison with Mademoiselle's melody, but in harmony and counterpoint. The incident reminded her greatly of that dance a dozen markets ago on the roof of their hotel in Zanzibar. Except that had been the interplay of coremates, while this . . . What *was* this? Call it what you wanted, it was happening between an uninoculated woman and some agency carried by Bee-Lung.

Like a spring issuing water into a wild ravine, Bee-Lung's mouth poured forth music. Like a wound up toy unwinding, her body moved of its own accord: her arms and legs turned round, leapt up, pointed high, bent out. And soon she was addressed by her own words, though still singing.

"Your friend is good. Your dance partner? She knows you won't beat me."

Mademoiselle's grey eyes narrowed. Her song acquired a burden of sense. "I'm right here," she crooned. "Talk *to* me, not about me—say things directly to *me*, whatever you have to say!"

For a moment, Bee-Lung only warbled wordlessly, a big, dancing bird. Then, again, the notes she sang came out mixed with speech. "You find me new and learning of my power," the entity inside her said. "So much that I don't know! What am I for? Why is there me and you? What can I want? What can I do?"

Complicated claps rose from a small group of petitioners stand-ing near the impromptu dance floor. Their cadence fit! "You're asking me the questions I wish to ask you." Mademoiselle turned away, seeking to catch someone else's attention. "I don't know the answers. But I believe that together with the other of your kind we ought to be able to find them all out."

"The other? Of my kind?"

King Ilunga and Miss Sevaria rose up out of his throne and de-scended the dais. They began to sing as well—a third harmony, above Bee-Lung's, to simpler and more intermittent beats: "I am like you, made up of more than two; I also want to know what we can do and how we'll grow."

"We celebrate ourself! We feel! We breathe and hear and taste! We're real! We understand all this and more. So maybe that's what we're for? To meet and share? To be aware?" So she sang. What did she mean? Bee-Lung struggled, but the music ruled her, outside and in. The only effect she accomplished was to bring her careen-ing path nearer the exit. Door guards spun into view. Could she run past and escape them? But she would carry her usurper with her wherever she went.

Meanwhile, an opera's worth of vocalizing continued gushing from her mouth and from the mouths of Miss Sevaria and the king. The sense of the libretto seemed to have shifted. Now the song's burden was that these entities—hers and King Ilunga's—should try to increase their presence by inducing their inoculants to spread their spores more widely, and without any regard to forming nodes or evenly distributing cores. Their only object, they opined, should be to broaden the fields of their experience.

Algeria and Sudan Aboard Xu Mu *and Kisangani, Everfair*

Tink had the hang of it now. *Xu Mu*'s familiar comforts helped. And Kwangmi's new and deeper interpenetration of his senses overcame his initial fright at what still sometimes seemed a new world.

Still, yes. Yet the changes the Russian Cure had wrought in him could be called improvements.

Waking from the light trance he experienced instead of sleep now, Tink found himself on the bridge, seated between two coremates. Chen Min-Jun remained focused on the far-off glitter of what he knew to be *Omukama*'s propellers. Raghu, though, noticed Tink's return to consciousness and brought him a cup of honeyed water.

"Thank you, Brother," he remembered to say. "This is good." Raghu nodded and said nothing, but a question smoked and fizzled beneath his silence. How to get it out where Tink could hear and quiet it, with an answer or some other strategy?

Worry flavored the unasked question. What did Raghu have to worry about? Tink sipped his cup and took a guess. "Finding water's not going to be a problem on this flight. We'll use the same oases as *Omukama*. After all, we're following the same route."

"But won't they have drained them dry ahead of us?"

It wouldn't do to laugh at the idea. "Gopal can make sure they leave us plenty." Imagining even such unlikely contingencies marked Raghu as a potential future node—if and when Tink left this one to form another core.

As soon as Tink had formed this thought, his larger awareness flagged it as calling for deeper examination. What were nodes? How did they figure in the execution of Bee-Lung's plan?

Kwangmi was calling him. He got to his feet and met her at the ladder's top. They entered the forward cabin. His hammock was empty. They let it remain so and embraced each other upright.

He ceased to strictly define himself, stopped giving himself exact boundaries, and let his understanding flow. Nodes, he knew, acted like magnets in electric motors, pulsing and driving the revolutions that gave dynamos their power. Decisions came out of nodes after a careful sampling of possible choices had been presented by the members of many cores, with the greatest weight given to the node's immediate coremates. Actions were instigated by nodes based on information gleaned, again, from several cores.

These points slithered together in a blending that dissolved the last trace of seams running along the edges of Tink's and Kwang-mi's melded minds.

What of the plan, then? Sister's scheme required nodes to be evenly distributed across the globe, not clustered tightly around one group, in one particular spot. If Bee-Lung's special, sibling-strength strain was employed too frequently, if the protocols she insisted on weren't followed, more nodes than needed could develop, and in futile proximity to one another.

And how did this strain produce these nodes?

All of a sudden, a jerking down and aftward pulled them to the cabin's deck and jammed them against its rear bulkhead. Their arms wrapped protectively around their bodies. Bee-Lung's peculiar mix of faith and worry percolated up to just below their surface. Was she back with them again? Yes—or rather, they were back with her.

Their Bee-Lung mouth was open, singing. Their Bee-Lung arms enfolded another's body, a body uninoculated, redolent only of fruit and the juices of flowers: Mademoiselle's. They danced with her. Their body bent and swayed to its pulsing blood and pounding truth, and Mademoiselle mirrored them, step for step. Their two ears filled with sound: the breath of their audience, which sighed to the same pattern being beaten by its hands and feet.

And now, approaching them like a lover, came the timid, trusting tread of an organism wedded together in a structure like to their own, though its bodies here numbered just two. Through the Bee-Lung eyes they saw the bodies of King Ilunga and Miss Sevaria, who carried invisibly within their sweet-scented clasp a third, present non-physically, much like much of themselves: Dr. Kleinwald.

For long moments their orientation toward Mademoiselle

faded. At first she reflected their faltering movements. Then they stopped moving completely. So did she.

"Uncanny." That was the king speaking. But it was Sevaria's small hands that, loosed from Ilunga's larger grasp, reached for Bee-Lung's. "We never thought we'd meet another one such as we've become."

"Explain yourself, my son." Queen Josina! Seated on her throne—of course she was. With effort they detected her smell—as faint as if it came from the other side of the palace. No wonder the queen's command had surprised them—though Bee-Lung had known of her presence all along. A quick glance explained a possible mechanism of suppression: the queen's skin shone with grease. It moistened her lips and glistened at the edges of her hair exposed by her crown.

"Here's another entity such as us, Mother."

What of the queen's breath? Inhaling slowly, they just barely detected it, filtered thin by—as Ilunga's knowledge noted and Kwangmi's confirmed—the charcoal of burnt oil palms.

"One such as you? Madam Ho and her brother are part of this entity, I gather; who else? Madam Ho's lover?"

Interestingly, as Queen Josina spoke, her exhalations increased only slightly in pungency. Was the charcoal inside her mouth? That would have muffled sound as well as scent.

"Not her lover. His. Kwangmi. Who is aboard their aircanoe."

"What good does that do? I want better surveillance of the Italians—I need a source of intelligence closer to them than *Xu Mu*."

"I'm sorry. It isn't possible." Sevaria's words sounded only a little sorry, but the regret King Ilunga emitted was sharp.

"Why not?"

The queen's son didn't answer, instead releasing such fear and shame the emotions threatened to overwhelm them. Hurriedly, they had Bee-Lung explain the problem as the doctor had explained it to Kwangmi: "Though Gopal has received all three inoculations needed, he must undo his quarantine of the third before we can formulate one of ourselves within him."

"Three inoculations?" Queen Josina narrowed her eyes and flared her nostrils. Nothing comprehensible came out of them. "Why so many? How many sorts of this organism exist?"

Bee-Lung's learning made up the entirety of their response. "May Fourth sent us on this mission with several varieties of Spirit Medicine, believing they'd appeal to potential kin of many bodily phases. Also, they encouraged our development of the special strain."

"The one you used on my child?" What sense hid behind these words?

Bee-Lung's indignation at the words' shallowest meaning brought her to their fore again. "First I used the special strain upon myself!"

Mademoiselle intervened. "Why portion out blame for what's done and over? Tell us something helpful, as you did while dancing. Tell us what we've asked. Do you know how many kinds of Spirit Medicine there are? And have others been tasked with spreading them?"

"What do you mean by 'kinds'?" Kwangmi's argumentativeness flavored that question. "There are many varieties of Spirit Medicine, as we have been saying, that are yet of a single ancestor. They count as one. Then there's our innovation, which uses a trick to fold this ancestor's genetic structure back upon itself and double its powers. That's two. Number three is the Russian rival, the—"

An odor of evil impinged on their Bee-Lung nose. They quit speaking. Their Bee-Lung head turned toward the room's entrance, where the odor's source stood. Chawleigh.

Aboard *Xu Mu*, Dr. Kleinwald had claimed to Tink that Chawleigh was an assassin. Certainly he reeked now of death. Perhaps this was the power of suggestion—or perhaps he always had. Advancing toward the throne, Chawleigh carried himself as if proud of his humility, bowing his neck but holding the rest of his spine tightly erect. He laced his hands together behind his back, though he smelled more as if he kept them at the ready near some hidden weapon than as if he were restraining them.

Chawleigh straightened from his brief bow. "Your Dignities, my thanks for allowing my return." Via Bee-Lung's senses they perceived that King Ilunga winced at this seemingly simple statement; from his broad smile, no one uninoculated would have guessed it.

Nor would the king's gracious reply have tipped anyone off: "You're most welcome here, and anywhere else in Everfair. Your charming wife also."

As Queen Josina nodded in approval, they realized that their awareness of the audience chamber was growing more and more restricted. First to desert them was sight: blurring and blackness crumbled off the scene's periphery till only the dais was visible. Then sound: the constant, quiet murmur of the court's breath died, followed by the footsteps of Mademoiselle's departure from Bee-Lung's side. But soon she could be seen again, coming into view as she approached the dais. Her lips moved in silent interrogation of the newcomer. Her glands released skepticism and self-assurance.

With her as its center, their shrinking circle of vision irised shut. Next the feel of the floor under Bee-Lung's feet, of her clothing, of her sweat-damped hair, faded and were gone. Then, quickly, the most important category of impressions: scents. All of them became faint as memories save Queen Josina's; her scents vanished.

Utterly.

They were no sooner bereft of sensation than rescued from its absence. The comforting familiarity of the odor of sunbaked wood coalesced, background for Kwangmi's body's pragmatic and deeply lusty effusions. Tink's body, too, was present, emitting odors of confusion, happiness, and, as touch registered again, satisfaction. While they sorted out the knotted threads of these effects, sight, too, returned. With it came the power of distinguishing movement, as together they entered *Xu Mu*'s bridge pod to sit, bodies close, almost touching, and blended together inside. But they were

missing their vital third: Bee-Lung. Apparently she'd stayed behind in Kisangani, stuck in her own body.

Behind them, reflected in the glass showing them the darkening sky, Raghu stood at the pod's bank of control levers. Above
them, leather shoe soles scuffed on ladder rungs, descending. They
looked up. It was Dr. Kleinwald, Alan, trailing a fragrant cloud of
achievement.

He spoke as he approached, clarifying the source of his gratified
air. "Your infiltrator is almost finished! We should prepare to pick
him up tomorrow evening."

"Already?" asked Raghu. "Do the drums say where?"

"Ghardaia. On the Wadi Mazab."

"Is there a field? A mooring tower?"

"No."

"Why not?"

"It's a bad site. Too windy."

A complex aroma drifted toward them: fear overlain with determination. Raghu had piloted *Xu Mu* before, but the only arrivals
he'd previously overseen were to fully modernized facilities. "Then
how will Gopal disembark from *Omukama*?"

Kleinwald shrugged. "Ask him when we arrive. The town's tall-
est edifice is their temple—perhaps you can tie us up there."

The Kwangmi of them thought that might be a bad idea. "Unless it's the custom, we'd be guilty of blasphemy."

"Then we'd better wait and see." He shrugged once more.
"Come. Time to sleep."

The need to lie unconscious for hours was less pressing than
ever. But they followed the doctor up to their core's cabin and
climbed together into a hammock slung next to the one he took.

Easy in the dark to reflect to themself in detail on events. To
themself and themself alone. Their ideas were formed and communicated without words, without the slightest sound. Kleinwald,
the Chen twins . . . anybody who was inoculated could monitor

their feelings, really—but that was all. No one could hear them wonder why Tink's maneuver to recover passengers from the roof of the Christian temple in Tourane had been all right, while this endeavor was not. No one could eavesdrop on their internal dialogue, or their resulting realization: the difference was twofold. The Tourane situation had been an emergency, and it was of such brief duration that no rituals were interrupted.

Here was yet another way in which Kwangmi's trap had helped him. Helped them: no one would detect anything except their emotion, their contentment at reaching harmony on the subject. They shared this harmony gladly with the rest of the resting crew.

Dawn came early at these altitudes. When sunlight crimsoned the cabin's rafters, their shift quit its hammocks for duty. They relieved Raghu from his stint in the bridge pod and assigned parts of their awareness to the routine tasks of flight. Chen Jie-Jun went with them, though they explained to her that serving as backup was redundant, since they numbered two already, if you counted bodies as separate entities. After a long massage session she left to inspect sun damage, she said, to *Xu Mu*'s envelope.

Brightness.

All that day, waves of sand unrolled beneath them. The air-canoe's swift shadow billowed and dwindled, its outlines changing with the rise and fall of the dry sea over which they sailed. Only age rose up out of the lower airs: it was the dust of ancient eras, the life-burying layers of time's passage, that marked their crossing from south to north. Nothing stirred. Nothing else smelled.

Until evening, when the wind shifted momentarily: veering away from *Xu Mu*'s stern, it came briefly out of the east, bringing them a hint of moisture—was there to be rain? They spotted a low bank of clouds, but lying to their south, in the wrong direction. And of the wrong color: brown rather than grey.

The prevailing winds reasserted themselves. The southern clouds came closer.

Raghu rejoined them, now in the role of navigator, accompanied by Ma Chau, scheduled to work *Xu Mu*'s levers, and Aito, Ma Chau's trainee. They were free, then, to visit the familiar bow cabin where they'd been born, and for this reason become a favorite place.

Using Kwangmi's eyes they continued searching for signs of the aircanoe's destination, as they had done below. Finally, just as they were about to send Tink to investigate the unease filtering up and forward from the bridge, they caught their first glimpse of Ghardaia's red-and-white dwellings. Like the doll-sized houses of particularly well-organized imps, they covered the sides of the slopes ahead in regular rows and columns. As *Xu Mu* approached their appearance grew steadily, revealing the thoughtful orientation of doors and windows in arrangements that left none blocked from the sun.

But suddenly all the houses were covered in gloom. Twilight? So early? No. The air assaulted them with anguish. Raghu and Ma Chau were terrified, and the reason why blew up from behind to loom over them, darkening half the sky: an immense sandstorm.

They returned to the hatch leading to the bridge pod; the companionway down from the hatch was already crowded with crewmembers pulled there by the same emotions. Dr. Kleinwald peered at them from its foot. "We're going to try to beat the storm. Ma Chau is speeding us up."

Behind them, Jadida objected to that plan aloud. "We have to stop. What about Gopal?"

More practical-minded, her coremate protested, too. "Where will we go?" asked Trana. "Where is it safe?"

They heard Raghu's shouted explanation, scented his desperate confidence over the rising general stink of lostness. "We'll fly east-northeast, make for the port of Gabes and the sea, where the storm will die."

"No!"

"But—"

Both Gopal's coremates started and stopped talking at the same time.

"We'll come back for him," Ma Chau promised. That smelled true.

But Jadida was unsatisfied. "When? What if he's in trouble? What if— Will we be in time?" Without looking at Trana, Jadida reached to touch her forearm. "You have an idea, Sister. Say it."

"*Xu Mu* can drop us here. We'll use jumpsheets. We'll find Gopal and get him home ourselves." Smoothing a wing of tiny braids back over one ear, she leaned into Jadida's touch. "Yes?"

Love flooded the space around them. "Yes. If we may."

The love turned to something else. The Tink in them recognized it as deference. Deference to him, the crew's node. They gave his permission. "You may."

"Kafia too?"

They sought for her and found her in Bee-Lung's former dispensary, using a bowl of drinking water to wash her undertunic.

"Her too." That core had split enough times. No more separations. "I'll bring her to the hold. Be ready."

CHAPTER FOURTEEN

July 1921
Bangassou, Congo, to Isiro, Congo

Rima adored everything about her Cloud Star: the thrum of its engine, the shine of its steel fore-fuselage, the gleam of its rubber-blessed silk rear. Its cockpit's openness, exposing her to the wind's rough kisses. The movement!

And now she shared these delights with Mwadi, seated just behind her—and also, though only faintly, with Mwadi's father, still making his way through the forest.

Far below them, Bangassou spun like a slow plate, its lights glistening like mounds of caviar raked into rows by a giant fork. Far above, stars and cirrus wheeled in a lazy dance of dull grey and twinkling black.

She took them south, toward Bondo and the Uele River. Perhaps they'd be able to requisition fuel there. Some must be kept for boats.

As they flew, though the air traveled mostly from front to back, at first Rima missed Mwadi's humming dread. The wind whipped by so fast that hardly any scent got to her—but their commingling had thrown up a chain of invisible sparks between them, a chain lying along the Cloud Star's skin. Over it came Mwadi's frightened realization that she and Rima contravened Queen Josina's wishes.

By now the sky was white with dawn. Rima assumed an attitude of laughing defiance for the bonds uniting them to share. It worked—sort of. The anxiety ebbed to about half its former strength. They landed, and Mwadi had to assume an arrogant air to demand that the field's committee break out their palm oil reserves, which helped to keep her worry bearably muted. But then her fears crested again as they taxied from depot to runway. Rima pulled the Cloud Star into takeoff position, stopped, and rose to stand and face her passenger.

"Bo-La. Ain't you think your mama woulda change her mind bout what we spozed to do if she knew the whole story?"

"Maybe. Maybe! But who's going to tell her?"

That was a point. "We gonna. Us. After we done scarin that spyin Devil back where he came."

"But what if I—what if we fail?"

Rima laughed. "Child! That what this about?"

Anger rolled off Mwadi's silky skin. "I'm not a child!"

"Course not!" She did her best to beat down her amusement and succeeded. She reached out to offer her lover the reassurance of touch and caught and held Mwadi's hand. But contact intensified emotional transmissions. Past that shallow surge of anger lay a deep spring of fear. It gushed up! It overflowed—it inundated her feelings! Rima had to fight it back—for both of them! She stroked Mwadi's tender palm and slowly, gently, brought it to her lips. Nuzzled it, licked it, cradled it against her cheek.

"We gonna do it. You know we gotta. I know we *can*. So we gonna. Now Ima siddown. Les go."

Their next stop was Bambesa. The sun had set an hour ago—one-and-a-half ballads as Everfairers counted time—but there was no need to stay the night. No need to sleep. They found the fuel depot unstaffed. They took what they required from it and took off again. No need to see where they were flying; Rima could smell and feel it. The soft splatters of moonlight escaping the overcast gave her plenty of illumination as she lowered her aeroplane's nose for their third landing. Isiro shone dully in the near distance; the runway stretched through its neighboring grasslands.

The airfield was deserted; no surprise, in the middle of the night. Rima climbed down from her seat and hoisted Mwadi to the ground. "I'm thirsty," Mwadi complained.

"I know. We outta luck; ain't no river." It seemed they needed water more since their inoculation, and food less. "Couple three more hours—okay, maybe eight or nine—anyway, soon as we reach Lake Edward, there be gallon on gallon waitin for us to drink." No water here. No more fuel in range of any of her senses. They had enough to get to Kyavinyonge—just barely.

"Can I fly us the rest of the way?"

"What? You crazy? You ain't never—" Rima closed her mouth. Was it really such a bad idea to let Mwadi pilot? Most likely their connection would provide all the control Rima needed.

"No, I've never even tried. I should start now. Now! How hard can it be?"

"Hardern you think." Rima shivered at a breeze coming off the high plains. "Tween the two of us, though—"

"Yes? Yes!" Queen Mwadi jumped up and down and waved her hands above her head in excitement. "Oh, Rima! I'll be brilliant! I'll show everyone! I'll fly so fast and so far— You won't be sorry! Wait and see!"

Bangassou, Congo, to Yaounday, Cameroon, Aboard Brigid

Raffles misses his hero Mwadi. But Hafiza is always with him, and a new companion, also constant, has many of Mwadi's same scents. Plus the companion's name, Mwenda, starts with the same impossible sounds as hers, sounds Raffles hears and knows and cannot make. Raffles stays with Hafiza, who stays with Mwenda, who is also called King. It is a little puzzling. But traveling far, Hafiza tells him, is how to make his hero nearer. The brightness in his blood agrees.

The river flows and they ride its waters to a town Raffles remembers. They pass through there on tossing waves. With difficulty, Raffles sleeps. He wakes as they slow and bump to a stop. It's another town. Hafiza carries him to a place of many aircanoes. Exciting! They climb the stairs to board one—the pole that their stairway rises around is smooth and barkless. They enter, and though there's now much less space overhead, he continues to occupy Hafiza's shoulders. Mwenda follows them. One name to call him is Prominence, which is exactly the same name as his hero's—so Raffles is even more right!

He goes to a corner of their cabin for resting. With eyes shut and ears open, it's a safe time and place to let the brightness expand again throughout him, grow wider and dizzier and wiser and more at home. This is safer than while they were floating on the river.

Through small gaps around the room's window enter traces of the river's dampness. Raffles wishes he could touch the water's body, swim up against its broad currents to his last sight of Mwadi. The sight of her leaving him behind! The sight of her getting out onto the river ahead of him, in a canoe with his rival, Rima. The moving water has taken her away—can communing with it bring her back to him? He breathes its droplets in, lets them soak into his throat and lungs.

This is stretching his ideas. This is good. The brightness—the medicine for loneliness—does more than heal. It helps him spread his understanding. Like in a dream, his sense travels along the river's slippery banks. Connections forming at the speed of feelings lead him back up it—stronger and stronger! Now on wet land—no, *under* it—he can run along threads thickening, clumping, sprouting more paths, more ways to reach more spots . . . but he goes straight, no branching.

Here it is: the heart of their knowing. The limbs of the member guarding it, slippery with protective secretions, curl around the wooden box in which live their planted hopes. And from this secure site unfurl all their ambitions, all their webs. Which one takes him to who he wants to be with?

With something not his mouth, Raffles tastes each path. The best one, the one truest to his hero's scent . . . disappears. It is faint, then gone. Vanishing in the air.

But how? Air exists; it is not nothing. Withdrawing, returning to his corner, Raffles is aware that part of his journey happens through air. The steps between particles of brightness trapped in water drops and clinging to pieces of dust are longer steps to make in the air, yet he makes them.

The cabin rocks and rises. And now it's moving in one direction. Gradually the air thins and loses the last of the river's moisture. Raffles is unable to keep himself from uttering an anxious sound. Hafiza hears him and comes away from the window.

"Brave Raffles! We're embarking now on a new stage of your journey to the New World. I can accompany you and soothe your disquiet—but I can only come along a little ways. Only as far as our stop at Yaounday."

They are flying on an aircanoe. This is a familiar thing. But this flying is on an aircanoe having another name: *Brigid*. With tricks taught by the brightness Raffles compares *this now* to *that then*, and notes how besides the name there are other differences. The walls of the rooms of *Brigid*'s gondola—the part in which humans generally keep themselves—are better at allowing the outside in. They do it through the tiny chinks between layers of cured vine juice coating the woven plants of which the walls are made. Whereas *Okondo*'s walls are tighter. Also he has less space to jump within these walls—but then Hafiza shows him how to open the hatch for climbing the net around *Brigid*'s envelope and he can be free! He can glide! He can flip end over end as he leaps from one mesh square to another.

Again they go lower. The air warms and thickens. Prominence Mwenda joins Raffles in the open air, emerging from below onto the gondola's roof. They are close now in understanding, which is good: the effect of sharing the same brightness.

"We're coming to our mooring. Here is Yaounday." Prominence uses so many words. Like Hafiza, like all human people. Yet even before these words are said, Raffles sees and smells the city: home buildings, food markets, walking ways, and the smoking fires of human engines.

He hears their sounds. He jumps and lands to squat beside his Mwenda.

More words: "Time to bid Hafiza farewell. She must return to Queen Josina with my report." Mwenda's metal hand raises the hatch open; his meat hand clasps Raffles's own. "With my report, and with as much sense as she can give of what you would have her say."

Isiro, Congo, to Lake Edward, Everfair

Mwadi knew she was born to fly this machine. She knew it in the highest recesses of her head. Had she not ridden birds for years in unwitting preparation? She gripped the round-topped stick protruding up between her knees in a tight caress. Beneath her bared feet, two slick pedals vibrated with power.

"Higher!" Rima's shout trailed back to Mwadi from the passenger seat. It whipped away as quickly as her fragrance. But Mwadi felt their shared desire for freedom! For exploring! For the wild and strange, foreign and faraway—for the sky! She raised the Cloud Star's nose and exulted as the forest's canopy fell farther below.

"Now we gotta peel our eyes for a town called Gao, so we see where to turn south."

Was there going to be a sign? A flag? Suddenly anxious, Mwadi scanned the vast, green velvet landscape for something obvious. "How will we know it?" she asked. Against the headwinds her words weren't going to be heard. But the subtle bridge laid along the aeroplane's wooden trim and cotton-fiber fabric could carry the sense of her question to her beloved, and bring back the burden of her reply.

Of course! There would be a flag, but first an airfield, visible from this great height as a broad swathe of earth cleared of trees. And yes, appearing ahead she spotted just such a configuration. Grinning, Mwadi swung the aeroplane sharply right. The move's suddenness jammed her hip against the side of the cockpit. A loud creaking groaned out along the wings.

"Hey! Don't do nothin crazy, Bo-La!"

Crazy? What a worthless word! Mwadi would do what she wanted—and it would be glorious—not "crazy"! She thrust the control stick left, then quickly right, then left and right again, again. There! They veered back and forth like swallows catching grasshoppers.

"Bo-La!" A fluttering squeal tore across Rima's fearful cry. It peaked and flattened, turned into a low, soft drone. "You wanna crash us? Stop foolin!"

Straightening out their course, Mwadi felt a definite drag slow the rudder's response. But the aeroplane stayed up, and Rima stopped complaining, her mood fading from alarmed to mildly annoyed, so everything must be fine.

And everything *was* fine—for most of the rest of the day.

They were so close to landing. They'd been in the air about four epics, or six European hours, when Mwadi noticed that the leaves of the treetops had become much more distinct, despite the creeping growth of the afternoon's shadows, despite the grey mists tangling together over the forest. And then a tentacle of mist wrapped around the Cloud Star. She shook off the image of being seized by a hungry monster. The mist had no force, no means of pulling them down . . . but its touch meant they were too far down already!

"Rima!" Mwadi's fear burst from her like spit from a trapped weasel. No response. "Rima!"

The aeroplane's engine sputtered, died, coughed, caught again. "Rima! Rima!" Desperately she hauled and stomped at the controls, fighting to bring them higher. What was wrong with her beloved? Why was there no answer? Tears of frustration fogged Mwadi's goggles. The aeroplane responded clumsily to her struggles, staggering up from the rumpled carpet of the forest canopy as if drunk.

Trying to keep them level, she found herself leaning heavily to her right—starboard. Their left wing hardly supported them—they

could tip over! Flip! If Rima was unconscious she'd fall out! Mwadi
had to wake her, but shouting hadn't worked—she'd have to use—
what? That thing they'd shared, yes, that feeling, that fungus—

Its presence had withdrawn while she concentrated on the
aeroplane's instruments and controls. Now she needed it back. So
should she cut herself again? Cover her eyes to duplicate the grotto's
darkness?

A sudden burst of speed sent the aeroplane zooming into the
blue above. Nothing but heaven ahead of her—and the engine
died again. And stayed dead. Shoving harder on the useless pedals, hugging the control stick to her belly, Mwadi heard her own
sobs, the wind's thin whistling—and a low humming she *knew*
but could not name.

In the relative silence of the emptiness around them, that humming grew clearer, louder, became words dropping sweet as honey,
kind as milk—from the lips of her beloved—awake! Alive! And
singing—singing the same way Mwadi herself sang when entreat-
ing passage from the souls of birds. It asked the currents of the
atmosphere for safe passage. Rising higher, higher, Rima's melody
peaked like amazement and fell like fate.

So did their aeroplane. Its nose tilted, pointed downward to the
distant earth. Sent them diving to the ground.

Now the wind screamed! But Mwadi joined her voice with
Rima's to chant over it in ferocious counterpoint, to plead for a
miracle. She flung her body side-to-side to balance their descent
and sang! Sang! Clinging to the seat and stick as she hoped Rima
clung to whatever she could reach—

Despite all Mwadi's efforts they started spinning. Slowly, then
faster. The green below wheeled wildly around them and dizzy
blackness rushed in from all sides. Singing frantically, Mwadi
abandoned the pedals and put her feet on the cockpit's wooden
instrument panel, bracing for the inevitable crash. Who would tell
her story? At least she died a queen. But alas for her beloved, who
should never, ever have an ending.

She tucked her head between her knees and pulled them close and tight. And still she heard Rima's music—and it sounded even louder now. It was coming up through the wood, through Mwadi's leg bones—lower notes than the air carried—how did Rima make them? Faintly, Mwadi continued to breathe out her higher harmonies. The notes seemed to wind their way beneath and between the chiming weights of her beloved's melody, to draw her along their reverberating scents like flowering vines.

With eyes shut, Mwadi saw the forest's treetops rush to embrace them. Shaggy green crowns bursting with life were whirling, pirouetting, dancing to their tune. So beautifully! Terror fled her skin, flushed away by the shouting wind of their descent. New feelings plunged out of her: the joy of having mounted to such heights! The thrill of knowing how far was too far—and going there! Golden in her throat, new refrains poured forth—the last she'd ever give the air. Let them be strong! Brilliant! Let them call every other singer to join in with them! Every other song!

And then two things: a mass of twittering birds erupted from the canopy of leaves. Mwadi felt and heard their flight. More varied than a flock, they smelled of turtledoves, of swifts and buntings, dark indigos, gaudy weavers—too many species to count! In a swirling cloud they filled the world with the clamor of their crying and swept apart its air with the beating of their wings.

At the same time, Mwadi's hands released their cradling hold on her shins and grasped the control stick. Why? They pushed it forward, away, while her right foot crushed the rudder pedal to the cockpit floor. The spinning stopped.

Now her arms tugged the stick in to nestle against her crotch. And gradually—would there be enough time?—their course leveled out so that they glided scarcely a soldier's height above the canopy. For the moment there was no immediate danger.

Why had she done what she did?

Because I knew you could, sang her beloved Rima.

Because their connection ran that sure and that deep. Because together they were better than anyone or anything who came against them. Because Mwadi gave Rima her whole self: head and heart and hands. Because she was her beloved's—just as her beloved was hers.

But pure though it was, this shining moment would never last. Already the distance down to the treetops had halved itself. Now no more than the height of a sturdy child stood between the Cloud Star and the leaves fanning out from treacherous branches. . . . Already they had slowed so much that the swarm of birds surrounding them was passing. Dull feathers and dazzling ones outflew them in a confusion of sounds: caws, warbles, chirps, screeches, fluting hoots and fluid trills—and choking sighs? Gasps and muttering groans? Which of these many breeds made *those* sorts of sounds?

None. The sounds came from the aeroplane's engine, which was trying to start again.

Rima understood how that could happen: the wind was pushing the propeller, which made the rotors turn and pistons leap—irregularly, but somehow that helped, and for one long verse they really flew. Gently, she and Rima urged themselves higher, higher, and a little bit higher.

Now all traveled at the same rate, birds and Cloud Star. Thick breezes buoyed their feathers and fuselage. Using the front-flyers' eyes—so surprisingly easy it must prove all shared the Spirit Medicine—Mwadi spotted a twinkling on the horizon. It grew rapidly from sparkles small as tasty insect wings to a glittering smudge of blue and grey. Lake Edward! Their destination! They would make it!

Like a swimmer drowning, the noise of the aeroplane's engine disappeared a third time. Mwadi waited in an agony of impatience for it to resurface. Instead, they began to lag behind their companions again, to drift lower and lower, sinking through layer on layer of birds. And then she was reminded by Rima's song that the airfield where they expected to land was on the lake's far side, in the realm of the Ugandahs. Miles farther off. Still over the Earth's curve.

Too far. Though Lake Edward was coming much nearer: her fastest selves saw the shining crests of its waves. Surely its beach would be wide enough to accommodate them?

The Cloud Star was last of the flyers now, and Mwadi's original body and her beloved's trailed close behind the others. Oddly, the sense of sinking seemed to have lessened quite a lot. As they cleared the edge of the final cliff—barely—Mwadi could almost believe the aeroplane was being lifted up. By what? She didn't know. Rima thought it was due to an atmospheric effect she called an "updraft." Or maybe they suffered an illusion? Maybe the ground had dropped so suddenly so far beneath them it only felt as if they'd risen?

An illusion? An updraft? Perhaps the aeroplane was being dragged higher by the wake of the birds flying before it? Yes, perhaps—but whatever had caused it, the feeling vanished as Mwadi scanned their surroundings for a good landing site.

There shimmered the white gravel of the beach. Mwadi tried steering to starboard to get the aeroplane into a better position. The control stick refused to move right. She began to shove harder—but Rima warned her to stop before she broke it.

Up from the pebbles and weeds and mud and sand came a wave of new birds: red-necked grebes, black-beaked flamingos, fast-spiraling snipes, and white terns unhurried even in their surprise at Mwadi's advent. They mixed with the rest of the flock of flocks, expanding and continuing the Cloud Star's escort as the aeroplane started to cross the lake's waters. And clearly, definitely, the birds' wings *were* helping—though that help was only a very little.

By now they were as near to those waters as they'd been to the treetops. Now nearer. Now skipping, skimming, fresh fish for the snatching crowding the troughs between the peaks slapping them, slamming them, skidding them to a stop. Sinking them.

Mwadi split in pieces: part of her in the sky with the rapidly dis-

persing birds; part in the water with the rapidly gathering schools
of fish; and part still in the aeroplane, in both the body of her birth
and the body of her longing, in Rima's sleek limbs and supple waist
and elegantly drooping head.

What to do? Should she leave? Ride the last of the birds heading
shoreward and abandon her flesh, her claim to queendom? And
abandon her beloved too? No.

Catch for us the fishes, the little fishes ... Quickly she brought
their gold and silver backs to bump beneath the Cloud Star's ruined undercarriage. Buoyed by their thousands, the aeroplane
sailed triumphantly for land.

When hosting her in Bookerville, Mrs. Albin had called the
Song of Solomon an allegory, saying its verses meant something
other than what they said. But Mwadi admired them for exactly
what they were: the poetry of love.

Her fish followed her birds, surging under the lake's surface the
way dreams move inside sleep, bearing Mwadi and her beloved
in a basket woven of wood and cloth and flashing metal. Happy
splashes bathed their air as one body after another leapt toward
the sun and fell rejoicing to rejoin the water. Ahead, the bright
eyes of her waders and wing-feeders spied weather-bleached boats
resting high on the beach. They saw for her how women and men
lifted and carried these boats down to the lapping waves to launch
them. Mwadi and Rima were going to be rescued!

Everything and everyone she ruled was working together to
provide Queen Mwadi with the best of all possible reigns. Her
mother would come to accept this someday soon.

So would everyone else: May Fourth, the Russians ... both factions of the English. She'd begin winning support now by making
good on her original goal of finding her brother's British friend,
Deveril Scranforth, and enticing him back to Kisangani. That
would show the effectiveness of her powers.

Kisangani, Everfair, and Ghardaia, Algeria, Aboard **Xu Mu**

Almost entirely his original, single self, King Ilunga stepped cautiously onto the palace roof. Queen Josina and his wife Sevaria walked a ways ahead of him, arm-in-arm through the misting rain. Like moist smoke, the rain blew across his line of sight, obscuring their figures—and everything beyond them. His sense of smell was hindered by the rain, too, but Ilunga knew that the assassin Chawleigh waited in the pavilion on the roof's far side. His mother had arranged this meeting, and had seen to it that their party arrived last.

When he and Sevaria appeared in the audience chamber, promptly enough, the queen had sent his sweetness off with Lembe to be re-bathed, re-clothed, and re-perfumed. While these pleasures were soothing them his mother had gently—gently for *her*—hinted that the entanglement the two of them were part of ought to be suppressed as a secret. Then she urged that Ilunga delay his approach to the meeting's site until after she went there with his wife, so that the two of them would arrive separately. "No need to hurry," she had told him, as she left him fretting on the throne over his unaccustomed aloneness.

He had probably not paused there long enough to satisfy her. As usual these days, though, a protective layer of fat stopped the release of Queen Josina's scents and made her mood difficult to gauge.

The mist cleared for a moment, and Ilunga saw that his mother had stopped midway to the pavilion on the roof's far end, detaining his wife by her side. Was there some problem ahead? No—judging by the queen's words, all was well. "Come and meet your new sister," she crooned, soft-breathed. "Come and see her tintings and taste her nectar, my children." That invitation would have been addressed to the royal beehives. Or rather, to their inhabitants.

Like the mysteriously absent Mwadi, his Sevaria pleased the insects. Unlike his primary self, whom the bees disliked. Humming tunefully, they circled Sevaria's head, some landing to crawl delicately along her soot-black brows and down the bridge of her nose. Her laughter hissed out between closed lips; their feet tickled her! Ilunga laughed too, and continued toward her.

But a cloud of bees burst from the ring of hives at whose center she stood. They zoomed toward him—a threat! He froze. Must he pass this present danger in order to deal with the next one? Couldn't his wife quiet the bees with some emission?

"There you are!" Hubert Chawleigh's lying placidness coated his voice like soap. As ever, under his show of calm he was tense and wary. No doubt this dissonance between inner and outer song was what had disturbed Ilunga on their first encounter. Zeroing in on where the voice came from, Ilunga saw the European glance up, his pale face contrasting with the shadows cast by the pavilion's eaves. "Trust you're ready to give me your decision?"

Sevaria's scent had prevailed. Yes. The angry swarm slowed and swerved away from him. Sevaria opened her silk-draped arms to embrace it, and within a wink it had covered her in a coat of living velvet. Ilunga walked past easily, nodding to his frowning mother.

"We have consulted." He had no qualms about uttering the falsehood. Give one, get one. Dish it out and eat it. "Your plan to speed the flooding project meets with my sister's favor."

"Good! Then let's set the first part of it in motion!" Gesturing to a spot beside him on the pavilion's cushioned floor, Chawleigh invited King Ilunga to sit—invited Ilunga to sit in his own pavilion! On the roof of his own palace!

Queen Josina joined them. Her small smile spoke epics about the lack of attention Chawleigh bestowed on her as she sat behind him. What she expected she could employ to meet her ends. Ilunga had a somewhat hazy idea of what those ends were; they involved ruling the world, partially by means of some reign of his own.

Sevaria shed her robe of bees and came to kneel at Ilunga's feet. She took his feet into her lap; his mother had counseled him that the European would see this as subservience rather than as his wife using him to channel her power. So it was: Chawleigh ignored both women and addressed Ilunga. "When shall we start digging? And where?"

"How soon can you bring in the necessary laborers?" the king asked in response.

A puzzled pause, then swiftly stifled annoyance. "But isn't Everfair going to provide its own workers for the Atlantropa project? At least the part done here?"

"How? How should we pay them?"

"Yes. Well . . . Can't you print special currency? Or issue bonds of some sort to be redeemed later?"

"'Redeemed later'? No one's interested in promises of money in the future! No! As for currency, I'm going to strike coins. We have plenty of precious metals to mine, and people want solid, immediate returns for their sweat. Everfair is still a young country, with much to build." Or so his mother said.

He checked again for what he could detect of her emotions. Released by the day's heat, which thinned the protective fat she wore there was . . . something besides her usual resolute political intentions: a sunken weariness, a tired bitterness . . . Something distasteful. He sought refuge from it in his wife's energetic ambrosia. Her fingers licked at his ankles and the arches and soles of his feet like the warming tongues of a flame. So delicious!

"You'll at least order your warriors onto the job—won't you?"

"Given that we've sent the greater part of our soldiers to fight in Namibia, no, we won't. We can't. There are none to spare."

"But you may simply draft more into service! Press them!"

His mother uttered her sour pungency aloud. "We are not making slaves. That's not our business. Nor is it yours."

Sevaria's honeyed fire burnt away the barriers between them. The hot delight spread by her touch soaked deep into him, borne by his blood direct to his heart and beating up, out, everywhere!

"I beg pardon. I have no wish to offend you, or anyone in the royal house."

Through a honeyed haze, Ilunga was aware that though the words of the apology were offered to his mother, Chawleigh's attention stayed focused on him—as Sevaria was even now observing. His mother had correctly gauged Mwadi's uselessness in such interactions.

"We say it's better that the Italians draw on their own resources."

Now, at last, the European's focus turned to the queen. "You think so?"

"I know so."

"You know." For a moment, Chawleigh's smug disbelief swamped Ilunga's and Sevaria's fresh-springing confluence. "What resources are these you speak of?"

"The Italians' prisoners; those they keep on the island of Nocra."

A shock coursed up Ilunga's spine. Like a bolt of lightning the name of Kleinwald's old jail leapt into the sky—and brought the doctor awake! Brought him down! With them! In sudden fury, they jumped to stand on Chawleigh's either side like two guards.

"Nocra! Do you deny its existence?" they asked the startled European. "You can't! You've been there yourself—hunting me! Trying to kill me!"

"Dignity, no!"

Chawleigh could see only Ilunga. "I meant my brother," they amended. They used the king's mouth.

"Your brother? A half brother? I know of your sister Mwadi—"

"Doctor Alan Kleinwald." Was "brother" still the right term for that connection? It was a more intimate one than what he had dared to call the earlier, more primitive connection with Devil. It would do for now, since the ceremony of their marriage was yet to be performed. "He escaped."

"I—I am sorry! I didn't know. . . . But yes, the Italian authorities can send you a few of the criminals they've locked up—"

"They can send the island's entire population! The ambassadors have our demands and will deliver them." This was what Queen

Josina had directed them to say, and saying it accorded with their own desires. Their work was done. Now to relax.

Stepping down from the pavilion, they clasped hands and retired gracefully to the bees' garden. No venomous stings would trouble them now, enveloped together as they were in their Sevaria's compelling fragrance. Indeed, one group of insects seemed to indicate where they should lie, hovering invitingly over a platform planted with a bed of rare and precious clover.

They reclined there carefully, ignoring Chawleigh's puffs of outrage and his vain attempts to call them back. Let the queen handle him. Shifting the center of their sensorium to the doctor's input was much easier done lying down.

Eyes shut. Ears nestled in foliage and fabric, the shallow cups of those organs filling with the whispering beats of their blood. Skin on skin, nostril to nostril, they sent their awareness out and up, north and high, to where *Xu Mu* flew over a mirror of salt. And inside the aircanoe, to where their Kleinwald's new hand smoothed the dry folds of a silken jumpsheet. Fingers measuring its black pleats, they contemplated taking hold of its corners and leaping out of the hatch before them. But then they'd be left behind, just as isolated as the core they sought. More so.

They went instead to disturb Raghu at the aircanoe's controls. Descending the short ladder to the bridge pod, they were met by a surge of goodwill. "Brother," Raghu said aloud. "We are heeding your advice; we pause soon."

This was puzzling. "I gave you advice?"

"Didn't you?" Raghu left the wall of levers and came toward them. He had finished setting up the halt. Already the relatively milder smell of the dampened engines drifted between the wall's half-opened louvress. "Perhaps it was Tink."

Chen Min-Jun left the forward lookout to meet them. "No."

"No, my sister?"

"I think the thought came from inside your very head."

Raghu laughed. "Then why wouldn't I recognize my own idea?"

"Because of the way you got it. By listening to . . . no, grasping upon the trails of others' scents. That's what you did, and then you blended your findings together for your conclusion. So of course it felt—smelt—like the answer was someone else's." She ran her stubby fingers through Raghu's hair and smiled. "Check how I'm right."

"Yes! Ah!"

Xu Mu had completely stopped its forward movement. They returned to the hold, where an anxious Ma Chau and her core kin hung over the smaller of its hatches, now open. The air rising from the hatch bore the faint chill of the desert dawn. It also bore, more emphatically, traces of the four crewmembers who'd been lately absent: Trana, Jadida, Kafia—already excited to be so near to seeing her lover—and a weak but triumphant Gopal. And someone else: a stranger. A mystery.

The aircanoe bled height. Nudging aside the others, they leaned over the coaming and saw the brown-shadowed ground coming steadily closer.

In wordless harmony, the watching core deployed the passenger basket. When it was full they all raised it together; the aid of Kleinwald's superior mechanical strength was very welcome.

The core that had done the retrieving lapped the core of returnees in warmth and joy. The celebration of the arrival would soon spread. Even before climbing out of the basket, Kafia offered Ma Chau a drink from her water jug, which she said had been filled at a cave spring sacred to smooth childbirth. From Ma Chau's hands it passed among them all.

But Ma Chau wasn't pregnant. In her air was no sign of gravidity. In no one's air . . . Another mystery—could it be connected with the first, the presence of one unknown?

In a way it was.

Gopal helped the stranger to alight. Her nostrils flared wide. "We're all inoculated with the same Spirit Medicine here?" she asked with her mouth.

"More or less," their Kleinwald replied. "Within the larger group there are smaller . . . entities."

"To which do I belong?"

"To mine," said Gopal. Trana, Jadida, and Kafia said it with him.

"But what of Hafiza? How will she receive this new coremate of yours?" Sevaria asked via their Kleinwald. "Is your story in danger of splitting?"

Gopal didn't like that. "Isn't yours? You three have been apart even longer—and you aren't even properly a core."

That wasn't a problem for them. They could be together whenever they wanted. Wherever they wanted.

Ordinary cores, though, those who weren't group beings, had trouble connecting over distances. Her physical absence put Bee-Lung in danger of alienation from Samara, Aito, Kang, and even her old friend Ma. Something must be done about this. Something permanent, and something immediate—though these would not necessarily be the same somethings.

Tink was close by and could be called upon; with him would come a chance to remind Bee-Lung of what she risked, and also to access her expertise. At their Kleinwald's urging they invited Tink's presence; with Kwangmi's guidance he would come soon.

Reassured, they started speaking, their goal to give Gopal the impression that the time in which they waited for Tink was being spent constructively. "We think—" Abruptly they stopped talking: Raghu was at first closer than Tink, and then he was right there. And he was different. Fuller, heavier, suddenly smelling surer of himself. And redolent also of Bee-Lung's special Spirit Medicine.

A new node. The birth for which Kafia's water prepared the crew.

They began again. "We think your rescue expedition will become another story. One Hafiza won't share. Raghu? Am I right?"

"I believe you are." Raghu nodded and released a tide of solemn anticipation. "And the best way to show what this means is to put it into practice. Let's retire to a place better suited for listening."

"The forward cabin—the one that Tink and Bee-Lung took over?" they suggested. The one where Raghu had sought and found the materials to support his new role. When they met their equal coming toward them on the way, they waved to signal to both its bodies to turn around and go back there.

But only eight bodies fit into the cabin. Raghu stood on the room's threshold, holding aside the door curtain so that their Kleinwald's eyes could look in over Raghu's shoulder. Brinda and Gopal lay in the cabin's hammocks, with Trana, Jadida, and Kafia spacing themselves evenly between them. Tink and Kwangmi sat on each other's laps on top of Rosalie's chest; the combined airs of those two were pungent enough to penetrate far into the passage where Ilunga, and Sevaria's Kleinwald, waited with the kin of other cores.

Though Gopal lay quietly for the moment, his scent was one of protest. Raghu emitted soothing odors, and from behind his back they did their best to support him with their own. He talked, too, probably out of habit. "Which of you begins your new story?" he asked.

Trana was oldest. "We fell like feathers, light and pretty, blown softly to the ground by the last mild wind before the approaching storm. At first, like feathers, we knew nothing of where we were— empty sand and shadows kept us apart. Then, just as we found ourselves together again, the first fury struck: blasts of sand like the blows of a giant fist. Where was there shelter? Where would we find Gopal?"

"The brown air blinded us," continued Jadida. "When we had been able to see the city, it lay spread out below our landing spot. We headed for the place where we remembered it to be. Green palms bent toward us, bowing their shaggy heads so low they touched the sides of the hills down which we ran." She pretended to plunge down a steep slope, her knees raised high. "The scents surrounding us were strange and muddled and thin. They whipped by so fast! They tore apart!"

Kafia took her turn in the telling. "Still, we could smell that our brother Gopal was near. Closer and closer to him we came. Buildings rose to block the terrible howling winds, and within their cover we found stronger proof of his whereabouts. Crawling along in the dirt, we raised and inhaled small particles of his pungency and tracked them to the source from which they flowed: a mouth of earth. We entered its hush."

Now Gopal should have spoken. But his silence lengthened, and the story's gap widened and stretched and deepened, till in the quiet the loud rub of cloth on cloth told how Tink rose and came to lean over him. "My love," Tink said, revealing the presence of his sister's heart within his words. "Do you want our bodies to be together again? Then finish what you've started, that you may return to Kisangani."

Gopal groaned and raised his head. "Yes. The cave. The spring bubbling up from its floor. We waited there and then they came to our rescue. And then we went together with them into the dying storm's death and traveled here."

A bare summary. Brinda's ending flourish could match the style of this part of the story or of the rest. Not both.

And Gopal had referred to his coremates not as us but as them. Different. Others.

The addition of a sixth member to the core had cast him out.

Despite the impending awkwardness, Raghu smiled and nodded. "And?"

Trana and Jadida took Brinda's hands in their own. Going to the hammock's top, Kafia touched her forehead to Brinda's and cupped her new coremate's lean cheeks. One of them said, "Sister?"

"And now we are welcomed home. We're with ourselves at last. Home. Here."

Raghu passed the soft weight of the door curtains to Kleinwald and nudged his way to Gopal's side. A whiff of bravery lifted off of him to mingle with the cloud of concern he'd left behind. He addressed Tink. "Bee-Lung? Has this happened before?"

Kwangmi answered. "No. It's not unexpected, though. May Fourth prepared me to understand that some cores could perhaps form themselves out of parts of others instead of germinating on their own."

From Kleinwald's vantage, Tink appeared to be stroking Gopal's face, gently, repeatedly. "Given the circumstances, we'd better bring him down to Kisangani as quickly as possible," said Tink's voice. "The sooner he's back with Hafiza, the better."

"And with you." Imposing Kleinwald's scent over the scene, they dared their equal to face and deny their truth. "You want him back with your Bee-Lung."

"And that's where you will take him." So said Raghu, the newborn node.

INTERLUDE Z

THE STRANGULATION

Hubert Chawleigh did exactly what he was supposed to do, exactly as he was supposed to do it. He accomplished his goal. But also he failed utterly in its accomplishment.

He was observed entering the palace during the darkest, moistest verses of the night's song. Inside, his scent curled up from the guarded foot of the staircase climbing to King Ilunga's chambers. The guards were easily distracted by waking dreams of the glorious recognition they would earn by their eternal bravery someday soon, very soon. . . .

Chawleigh put down their lack of interference to his skillful exercise of stealth. He mounted the stairs to the guarded landing and silently approached the guarded doorway. The curtains he swept apart swished softly, a sound the women on either side of them seemed to ignore. Likewise those disposed before the entrance to the occupied inner room. Chawleigh passed between them unmolested.

Ilunga was awake. His open eyes shone through the gloom and caught his assassin by surprise. In three steps Chawleigh crossed the room and snatched the king by the throat. "Wait!" croaked Ilunga, but that was the last word to come from his lips. Grunts, gasps, and choking gurgles don't count.

When the final breath had left the king's body, Chawleigh assumed he was dead. An understandable mistake. Especially as the assassin had to leave the scene of his crime in haste: Chawleigh's keen ears heard the noise of someone's approach. Being uninoculated, he couldn't tell who that someone was—perhaps a tardily responsive guard? But he judged correctly that this didn't matter.

Only one way led back out to the corridor—blocked by whomever was coming in—but the balcony window beckoned with a light breeze even Chawleigh understood. Just a quick dash and a jump one short storey down, and he was safely surrounded by the whispering leaves of garden plants. After a startled moment, the chorus of nocturnal insects resumed. The chirring masked whatever sounds the newcomer made, and darkness masked him from Chawleigh's sight: all he could see was a vague black silhouette against the charcoal grey of the balcony window's curtains.

Light flared behind the silhouette, sharpening it. Out over the background buzz and hum came cries of horror—his deed had been discovered! Time for him to flee! But—

"Wait! Stop! I'm still alive!"

The voice was Dr. Kleinwald's. Yes, and it was Kleinwald who stood revealed there now on the balcony. The words, though—

"We'll go and tell my mother." The words were King Ilunga's.

Others, the guards, came in, gasping and muttering curses that would have been plain to Chawleigh had he been inoculated. Only the woman who joined Kleinwald on the balcony was clearly audible to him.

"Prom—Prominence? Is that you?"

"Of course it is."

"You are not dead? But lying on your bed is your— You have been strangled!"

"Fortunately not. Come, let us take this matter to the one with the best understanding of the European evils we face. I'm sure Queen Josina will be interested in your report." More was said, but Kleinwald and the woman—probably a guard—left the balcony, and Chawleigh no longer heard them.

After a moment more the room's light was extinguished. The assassin paused to be certain he wouldn't be seen, then started toward the arched passageway giving access to the street. Then froze. Glamps and sponges glided into the palace's courtyard and spaced

*themselves apart to form a long, bright line—a moving line. Search-
ers had been deployed. There was no safe escape route. None.*

*Chawleigh was an experienced killer. He knew he had only one
option: to stay put. Not to stay exactly where he was, though, for the
line of searchers stretching unbroken from one side of the garden
courtyard to the other was progressing steadily toward him. Quickly,
while shadows yet disguised his actions, he swarmed up the palace
wall and regained the balcony.*

*Epics passed. The searchers, with their glamps and sponges,
passed beneath him. They doubled back, advanced again, and
again retreated. In the interval between the first and second waves,
Chawleigh ascertained that the king's bedroom was empty and went
to hide inside of it.*

*Empty of life and full of death. Blindly, the assassin attempted
to retreat to the corner farthest from the balcony window. The bed
had been moved to the room's center. He stumbled and fell upon it,
landing on King Ilunga's corpse. Which lay motionless and uncom-
plaining. Growing cool in the night air.*

*It seemed to Chawleigh that the king was indisputably dead, de-
spite Kleinwald's argument against that fact. If proof was required,
here it was. If necessary, such proof could be brought elsewhere.*

*Chawleigh sat up slowly, showing no sign of fear or disgust. He
pulled a large knife from the sheath strapped beneath his shirt, a knife
he kept well honed. He tested its blade against the pad of one finger.*

*By touch he located a length of cloth upon the bed, a sheet or blan-
ket, and wrapped it around both of the corpse's wrists to contain any
excess blood and keep himself from getting soiled. Twice he raised
his knife and twice brought it down, collecting his sadly mistaken
trophies. Without a beating heart to pump them out, there were no
great red gouts spurting high and wild. Only sluggish trickles damp-
ening the severed pieces of cloth. It was an easy enough task.*

*But when did this happen? It's helpful to remember that time is a
not-always-convenient lie.*

CHAPTER FIFTEEN

August 1921
Kisangani, Everfair

Desire gratified, Bee-Lung released her warmth and comfort to wash along the air channels linking her with Kwangmi and Tink. How fortunate that she was able to offer such fleshly splendors to them—the delightfulness of connecting with other organisms, other cores . . . someday soon, they hoped, with other multiply-bodied intelligences like themself.

One person potentially responsible for creating such a being lay beside her: dear Gopal. Languidly, she turned her head to enjoy watching him as he rose from their bed and donned his shirt and trousers. Beyond him the palace windows admitted the faint, dull grey light of evening. It coated him in quicksilver; his bare arms gleamed like loyalty and shadowed his torso with deep belonging. Such fullness in his every movement! Not a moment of such ripeness should be wasted. Why was he leaving? He should return. Immediately. Quickly she emitted an inviting perfume.

His amusement teased her nostrils and he laughed. "Oh no! You won't get me to stay just because you want to feel me sleeping. I'm going to meet Hafiza's father."

Sleeping? Yes, that was how Gopal dreamed. And dreams were how the Russian organism imperfectly contained inside him communicated with them. At some point, Gopal must become aware of this.

For now, Bee-Lung let him leave uninformed. A while she lay still, following the winding trail of his scent down the palace's broad front steps to the raised walkway before it, then along the sunken boulevard the walkway bordered, to the intersection where a crossing swing carried him beyond her powers of distinction. After that, only brief whiffs of him surfaced through the swirl of others' odors.

They knew which house he was headed to, anyway.

Now in full night's darkness, Bee-Lung slipped unnoticed past the soldiers guarding the passage to Queen Mwadi's chambers. Kwangmi and Tink were waiting; together they entered first the sitting room and then the crowded bedroom beyond it. There the other two group beings were patchily represented: all three of the first—King Ilunga, Dr. Kleinwald, and Sevaria—lay stretched on the wide, pillow-strewn mattress side-by-side. But of the bodies belonging to Queen Mwadi's and Rima Bailey's questionably sentient new core, only Mwadi's and Rima's were there.

Despite the danger of being overheard by her guards, Queen Mwadi spoke aloud. "Welcome! We greet you individually and as a whole."

"'We'? In what sense do you talk of 'we'?" That was Tink's voice, from Tink's mouth.

"Gonna needta change summa how we say things." Though this was unmistakably Miss Bailey's way of blurring words together, those words could not have come from between her lips, for these were engaged in kissing the tips of her sovereign's fingers. Who continued: "Raffles sayin we spozed to give ourself a name. We could call ourself Ranga-Danga-Whoopty-Doo far as most of us cares, like me—but for Raffles it a serious matter."

Frowning, Dr. Kleinwald levered himself upright and away from Miss Sevaria's fragrant arms. "Raffles is your monkey body?"

"Yeah. The power a names real fresh for him since he got into it right when he took him summa y'all's Spirit Medicine." Queen Mwadi frowned back. "You got a problem with that? With him? Cause if you do, you got a problem with us—"

"No, no, my sister!" King Ilunga still reclined silently on the bed, but his placating speech originated out of Kleinwald, who leaned forward now to pat the queen's shoulder tenderly. "We're too new to make rules; nothing to make, nothing to break."

"Names would help. I sometimes wonder who I mean myself when I say 'you' to you." Miss Sevaria rolled toward them to the bed's edge and propped her head on a hennaed fist. "I know who *I am* and I know who *we are,* but is there the same sort of relationship between your minds and bodies as there is between ours? And the same sort of all-overness too? What do we call such a quality? How do we discuss it?"

"We gotta use words?" Rima's mouth was free now to ask her questions. "Why we don't sing an dance? Or why we don't put our ideas straight in each other's brains? That's how me an Bo-La do family."

"'Family' is the designation you give your aggregation?" Tink's penchant for precision felt odd on Bee-Lung's tongue, but she indulged it lovingly; hadn't he given her access to the courage to return Gopal's voluptuous touch to her skin?

"Well we ain't talkin bout no kinda 'mates,'" Rima replied. "Bo-La don't wanna make no sex with King Mwenda cause he her daddy, and ain't *none* of us gettin it with no monkey. No old man neither, even if he wasn't half-buried in the ground."

"General Wilson's not 'old'!" Now King Ilunga raised his body up. "Just nicely ripened."

"Uh-hunh." Neither Queen Mwadi nor her consort smelled convinced.

"He's like wine—"

"Listen. We can argue later. Right now, we have problems to solve, decisions to negotiate." Bee-Lung did her best to breathe patience out with her words. "We have complicated maneuverings around pre-inoculated people's politics to plan. Let's get to work."

"Agreed. If we wish to start with names, I'm Sevaria, no matter who is hosting me. Call out to my spirit."

"You're certain that you're always separate enough to be that one person?" That was Bee-Lung's body's brother, Tink, in her body's brother's body.

"Yes."

"So what we gone do in a case where there's more'n two?"

"More than two in one? Three? Four?" Ilunga asked. She thought it was Ilunga.

"Yeah."

They could arrange themself in almost endless ways. "It's worth asking." She consulted her Bee-Lung knowledge base, aided by the ease of Tink's ability to calculate. "Naming each possible configuration could result in too many names to keep track of, and the problem will only become worse as others like us are born."

"Then let us simply name our wholenesses, and keep the rest of how we call one another the same."

"Name em what?"

The mouth that asked that question answered it. "We should take our stories' titles to be our families'. I am Queen Mwadi of the family group *The Sleeper Wakes*."

"That makes sense! So then I am Sevaria binti Musa of the family *Wear Red*." The star turned. "You are Bee-Lung?"

"I am. Our name is—" She hesitated. Kwangmi and Tink belonged to one core and she to another. Their stories were different. Yet all belonged to the same sentience, the same "family" . . . So what story *did* they share, then? Had they given it a name? "—is *The Mission*."

Atlantic Ocean, Aboard Brigid

How far back is his hero? Raffles dangles two-pawed from the net around *Brigid*'s envelope and gauges the thinness of the thread of Queen Mwadi's scent. It stutters on the wind, each faint burst a seed in the dwindling stream of seeds spit from the mouth of the lands they leave behind. Though the going's hard, he knows this is the route he must travel. Away. Over the sea. To and through newness.

As the blue waves below surge and smooth out and surge again, the brightness he attends to in his hero's absence leads him forward and downward, downward and inward. Forsaking his aftmost vantage point for a spot under the envelope's midsection, Raffles drops from there onto *Brigid*'s gondola, and enters the place he shares with Prominence Mwenda. He understands that this space is for sharing something besides sleep: dreams. And he also understands that dreams are a way of contacting his hero, a way his new kin can help him find her.

Accordingly, despite the daylight still filtering between the bamboo slats covering the window hole, Raffles jumps to join Prominence where he lies in the cabin's cushioned hammock. He curls against the human's hairless pelt, its savor so reminiscent of that of the other Prominence—and yet so different.

Their heartbeats match, cresting and ebbing like the sea's waves. A feeling of lightness comes over him, the same feeling he has when leaping tree to tree, a feeling of lifting himself out of himself, off of himself, skimming the sky's lowest reaches, breathing its closest airs and soaring free.

They are free.

Behind *Brigid,* their wake unfurls in a long vine of whispers, mists of thoughts of other places, other things, other *times,* other parts of *themself,* of the being known as *The Sleeper Wakes:* of Raffles's hero. And his rival. And his roots.

Before *Brigid,* the course to Brazil teases them on with whiffs of strange jungles and surprising rivers . . . and just emerging over the Earth's curve, mountains topped with water crystals—ice! Snow! This land has such promise, so many secrets to open wide. And so many kinds of people to persuade to aid them.

A fruit-like swelling approaches along their wake, an invisible bulge they sense speeding nearer by its . . . loudening sound? Its intensifying odor? By the sweetening of its colors, that's the best way to describe what's happening. Yes.

The bulge is her! Queen! A visit in their dream! Quickly, they create a welcoming environment, mimicking the grotto where they were born. Now it is as if they lounged there *again,* in their separate bodies. But switched: Prominence Mwenda locates in the likeness of the planted human whose name is General Wilson; Prominence Mwadi locates in Raffles, a delight! Raffles can take his pick: Rival? No. Hero? But then she will perhaps be disappointed by the simplicity of such a straightforward mirror trick. To show he's smarter than that he chooses instead to inhabit the counterpart of the other Prominence, the Mwenda one.

They talk using words. Raffles is happy he has a human mouth. "What is bad?" he asks. "What can you need with us?"

Prominence Mwadi hops the pretend-Raffles into the pretend-Rima's arms and makes his rival say, "We need us some answers." Is she still where she was? Yes, but also in other places—everywhere? All around?

"We gotta decide whether we enough or we oughta make more."

"More kin? More cores?" Either Raffles is asking this or Prominence Mwenda or both of them.

"More a what we is. What me an Bo-La calls families. Cores is fine, but they ain't capable a gettin together while they apart. Look how we doin."

The figure of the planted man begins to sway as if in a wind or to music. "We defy space. We play and dance and sing with ourselves and rule and challenge each other." Raffles feels the urge to sway, too—it comes tingling along his expanded senses, rushing in and out of him. He makes the image he occupies move to the same rhythm and they are all caught in its mesh, a spell of their own weaving, all in agreement that this is their answer, and *this,* and THIS.

The likenesses swirl and drain off as if the dream holding them pours them from a cup. They drip down his chin. As if they are juice. As if he swallows them.

Raffles wakes. Bent into a loose cage, Prominence Mwenda's arms and legs trap him in their hammock. Soft whuffing sounds issue evenly out of the human's nose. Raffles sneaks away between crooked knee and cocked elbow. On the room's threshold he pauses.

Where is the dream? Vanished. His hero is gone also. But he knows better how to proceed with her blessing now that they have stepped together to the pulsing of the brightness in their blood.

Kisangani, Everfair

Hafiza welcomed her coremate Gopal at the front entrance of the apartment her father shared with three other travelers—all, of course, absent at the moment. This shrunken core of just two must grow, but none of those three travelers were among their potential kin, for two of them had already been inoculated with the variety distributed at the sawan held on the island of Ceylon and had joined a core originating there, while the third categorically refused any "taint," as she called it, of the Spirit Medicine, the Russian Cure, or any other fungus.

Gopal smelled pleasantly of sex and rain. They greeted each other with small, reassuring touches to shoulder, cheek, hand—nothing that would surprise or alarm any neighbors peering out of their doorways into the passage. Closing the curtains that divided off the rooms her father had leased, Hafiza brought her coremate to meet him and their European guests.

She introduced them all, then left for the floor's kitchen to fetch cups of warm chocolate. On her return the Europeans, Herr and Frau Schreiber, had resumed their chairs to examine her gift to them: the Chawleighs' map showing the coastlines finally resulting from Atlantropan flooding.

"Where is Everfair?" the woman asked. "Under this . . . lake?"

"Most of it, yes," Hafiza's father said. He had seen the map earlier and agreed as to its accuracy based on his many journeys. "Some of the mountaintops remain as islands. Everfair's mines—"

"Queen Josina has shown me where to mark those on the copy we're making for her." Hafiza's unfeminine talent with brush and pen had not escaped the queen's notice. Little did. "The cost of losing access to our mines' metals and earths is going to be one of King Mwenda's strongest arguments for stopping the project."

"So what should we do with this copy?" asked the man, the Herr.

"Keep it safe." Mademoiselle also had a copy, which she'd taken home with her to Kalima. "Bring it to the attention of your backers."

The two whites exchanged a quick look, and the scent of trepidation leapt from their pores. "Our backers are no longer interested in our discoveries," said the Frau. Defiance edged her strange air of shame.

"But they sent you here!" Hafiza protested.

"They let us come here. That's somewhat different." Herr Schreiber smelled more of fear than shame. "We Anti-Atlantropans are divided on all but one point: Everfair's growing infiltration by May Fourth's Spirit Medicine is—"

"'Infiltration'?" Gopal leaned forward to interrupt him. "That sounds as if you're describing something bad."

"No! The Spirit Medicine is perfect! The perfect path to continued resistance!" The Herr leaned forward also, as did the Frau, his wife. "My English ought to be better after all my practice—I was about to say there's a way that this substance could unite us— you—the world—against our enemies." The two clasped hands. "Which is why—"

A burst of coughing cut the sentence off unfinished. Hafiza got a cup of water for Herr Schreiber from the table, but when she turned to give it to him he waved her off, though his panting breath reeked of smothered fear.

"Please, my honey," said Frau Schreiber, moving right to the edge of her seat. "Let me ask, as it's my idea."

"Very well."

Husband and wife both nodded, and the wife's aroma became self-consciously sweeter, like a sentient flower bent on attracting bees. "We want—we would be extremely honored to kin with you and form a core together. Our friend and mentor Princess

Mwadi—I mean queen, Queen Mwadi—has explained the various benefits of inoculation. But we don't think that she—that her core is the best one for us to—to enter."

Gopal smiled a huge smile. "Welcome home!" He opened his arms wide and closed them both in his embrace. "You and our host Bahir will complete us!"

Was that right? Bahir, her father, had agreed to join them? So if Hafiza's core was to be modeled on the core to which her former mistress belonged, which of them would be planted? And what kind of animal would they kin with?

Others also had questions. "Now?" asked the Herr.

"Do you require anything else?" asked her father. "How can I help?"

"Why not now? Let's do it; we're all here. But we need a story." No frown appeared, but Hafiza scented her coremate's hesitation. "One making sense to all of us despite our different backgrounds. It's most important."

"Many widely respected scholars of folklore and mythology conclude that there is only one truth underlying all the world's fictions—one tale told in numerous versions." The Herr's effusions turned timid as he made this assertion. "Can't we just agree that we mean the same thing when we choose our group narrative?"

Hafiza's father laughed. "Whose meaning will we agree on?" He swallowed a mouthful of chocolate and shook his head. "These 'scholars' are Europeans, aren't they?"

"Different meanings shouldn't matter. King Ilunga kinned successfully with people from quite other cultures," Hafiza pointed out.

"I brought my workbasket." Gopal bent to retrieve it from the floor. He opened it. "This is the strain Hafiza and I received originally. Does it call you?"

"Literally?"

"In any way, Frau Schreiber. Herr? Bahir?"

Her father nodded. "Yes. It's good. The rest are interesting, but this bottle is nearest to satisfying me."

"'Nearest?' So it's not exactly where it—what it ought to be? What you want?"

A scratching came from the flat's entry. From too low on the doorframe—was it done by a child's hand? Who was there? Hafiza strained but could smell no one until the straying air currents finally carried to her the odor of a cat—perhaps their animal! The door's curtain lifted at its bottom as a sleek grey-and-black head protruded into the room.

"Mmmrrrup?" Round green eyes examined her father's living arrangements and apparently found them acceptable. The cat's body followed its head. For a moment it posed before the curtain like a dancer awaiting accolades, then stalked straight over to Hafiza, ignoring the others present.

She recognized it now—its black stripes and crooking white-tipped tail. This was the former inhabitant of Lady Fwendi's washhouse. Extending a hand to stroke its sinuous spine, Hafiza stopped mid-reach. How had it got here from Kalemie? What did it know?

The cat arched its back against her still palm and pushed forward, initiating its own caress. Automatically she pressed downward as it slipped by, and again when it looped back for another pass. It leapt into her lap, forcing her to sit suddenly upright.

Though it purred and kneaded her thighs, the cat didn't seem to want to settle on them. Instead, it peered over the table's edge. One paw established itself there. Then a second—

"There you are! Provoking beast!" A woman—also somehow familiar to Hafiza—stood in the doorway, curtains pushed rudely to the sides. Even more rudely, she entered without invitation.

"My apologies! My cat's no respecter of privacy. I'm Professor Janota. And you are?"

Hafiza's coremate bowed. "Umar Sharif, actor. These are Mr. and Mrs. Schreiber, late of Germany—"

"You have my sympathies for any losses—"

"—and our host and hostess, Bahir Haji and his daughter Hafiza, who serves the queen."

"Ah!" A peculiarly satisfied odor emanated from Professor Janota—Miss Janota she'd been called when she taught for Lady Fwendi. "Then you can help me in my quest!"

"Your quest is for your cat?" Hafiza's father asked. "Take him!" While their attention was off it the cat had jumped to the center of the table.

"No, but I may as well collect her. Come here, Carmelita." Gathering her European-style skirts in one fist, the professor swept toward them. "Come!" With her arms open she attempted to pick the cat up. A hiss and a warning growl made her back away.

"Wait!" Hafiza leaned sideways in her chair to put a hand on Professor Janota's sleeveless forearm. This would increase their understanding. "Leave her where she is; I think she's choosing which kind of Spirit Medicine we should take."

"What? 'Choosing'? She can't choose—she's a cat! Just an animal!"

"Is she? You know of Lady Fwendi's history as one who has ridden in such animals' flesh?"

"Rumors! Superstition!"

The cat called Carmelita was examining Gopal's workbasket with intense concentration. Its long front legs probed deep into the basket's fragrant heart, and its graceful neck stretched to extend its nose in swift, exploring thrusts. The thrusts ended; Carmelita's muzzle remained buried in one place for several moments.

"Nonetheless, I believe this will be our best selection." Removing her hand from contact with the professor, she coaxed the cat's head away from the jar it found so fascinating and pulled it free. "Interesting!" she remarked, trying to sound as if surprised. "It's the same variety as we gave to the old king." And to the new queen, and her lover, and the monkey, the general . . . all the members of what Gopal called *The Sleeper Wakes*, the very core and family whose structure they were planning to replicate. Hafiza could easily have predicted this would be the strain picked.

Now Hafiza transferred its prize to Gopal's care, and the cat seemed to transfer its fascination to him as well. Professor Janota was able to remove it from the table—to Hafiza's father's evident relief—without growling, hissing, or any other protests on its part. It wriggled and twisted in her arms, but only so that it had a good view of Gopal as he chopped and blended its preferred spores into their Spirit Medicine. The professor made no move to leave, and Carmelita made no move to escape her hold.

Not until the preparations were complete. Then, as Hafiza's coremate pushed forward the wooden bowl containing the materials that would form their new connections, the cat broke loose and bounded across the tabletop, back into Hafiza's lap.

"Carmelita! Naughty puss!" The professor leaned over the table to make a failed try at recapturing the animal, then started around toward Hafiza's seat.

"Leave it alone!" Hafiza knew now she was no longer a servant: she was telling this woman she'd once waited on what to do. "This animal is not your property."

"Yes she is!"

"I say she's not. No one belongs to anybody."

"Carmelita is mine! I rescued her, fed her, brought her here—"

"Why?"

"You rescued this cat? From what?" Her father's focus strayed from her own. That would change.

"Why?" Hafiza repeated the question. "What made you bring it with you?"

"I—" Professor Janota stopped as though Hafiza's words formed a physical barrier. "I don't know. I—"

"You brought her where she wished to go. To us. She made you."

"Rubbish!"

"She will be our coremate," said Hafiza. "Obviously."

"You're not serious! You're going to—to give Carmelita some dangerous drug? Some people have hallucinations when they— You can't! I won't allow that—it's immoral!"

"How is it immoral?" The scent of calm cheerfulness overlay Gopal's ever-present, always-pungent determination as he spoke in Hafiza's support. "Was it a crime for us to inoculate ourselves against capitalist trickery?"

"I won't argue about that." In two quick steps the professor was beside Hafiza and reaching once more for "her" Carmelita. Who flattened its ears and swiped at Professor Janota with one paw. Its throat rumbled threateningly, and its eyes narrowed to green slits.

"The cat has made clear what she wants. I must ask you to leave."

"But—" A sudden wave of slyness arose in the professor's emanations. She cocked her head as if listening to an internal voice. "Then I will sell her to you."

"We're poor! We're Germans!"

"Why would you assume I meant to you personally, Herr Schreiber? You or your wife? No." Though she stood nearest the Europeans, Professor Janota still had her eyes fixed on Hafiza. "Not when it's most assuredly the queen's handmaiden who has won my cat's fickle heart . . ."

"I have little money of my own," Hafiza admitted. While traveling she had lived gratefully upon the gifts of others who were inoculated.

"There's another mistaken assumption—I don't want notes or coins. Your influence is far more valuable." She smiled and crooked an eyebrow. "You know. Put in a word with Queen Josina so that she supports my new teaching establishment—and Carmelita is yours."

A whirl of uncertainties circled through Hafiza's thoughts. The cat had come from Lady Fwendi's school, and so had Professor Janota. Why would either now be divorced from it?

But she promised what it was necessary to promise. Her father escorted the professor out of the door of the apartment. On his return they partook of their Spirit Medicine, mixed expeditiously into the gourd from which they poured their cocoa.

Gopal drank first and began their story. "Once there was a group of revolutionaries who understood that in order to succeed in their mission they would need special help. So they sought out the wisest doctor any of them knew. This doctor contrived a formula based on a plant lately found in his own garden—a lowly looking specimen which revealed itself possessed of many unique properties. Among these was the ability to instill in those who ingested it powerful sensitivities to the glandular secretions of others."

Hafiza took the gourd from him and swallowed down her portion. She knew what should come next: "The revolutionaries distributed the doctor's formula widely, aided in their endeavors by its unerring guidance. Deceit, fear, greed, anger—by the formula's powers, all these motives and many more were unmasked in their opponents. Knowledge of their enemies' inmost feelings gave them an enormous advantage.

"But those ranged against the revolutionaries concocted their own formula designed to do what they believed was done by the doctor's, and to bestow on *its* ingesters protection against an infectious plague raging across the globe. Now in this belief as to the formula's powers they were mistaken, as they were mistaken in a great many things. The connection between taking a dose of the formula and escaping a case of the disease was not one of a cause and its effect."

Softly kneading claws and a droning, humming weight settling onto Hafiza's thighs reminded her that the cat called Carmelita must have her part in these proceedings. Sans chocolate. She swept away a fingerful of the residue remaining in the bowl where Gopal had prepared the mixture and offered it to the inquiring muzzle. Carmelita licked it up.

Understandably, the cat said nothing to contribute to the story. Yet. Instead, Gopal spoke once more. "What the connection really meant was that the same groups who welcomed the formula's liberating properties had also been subjected to an earlier and less harmful strain of the plague. So now they were immune to it—but not for the reason their foes thought."

Now the cat stood on dainty yet steady feet and leapt once again onto the tabletop—this time only to trot over it to the Europeans sitting on its opposite side. It pawed tentatively at the space between them, thereby indicating it was the turn of one of the Schreibers to spin more of their story's thread.

The Herr received the gourd Hafiza passed him with great ceremony. He made a sort of seated bow in her direction and another toward Gopal. After tilting the container to dribble a little cocoa into his cup, he passed it on to his wife. He sipped and cleared his throat. Twice.

"Shall I go on with our composition? Very well. Ignorant of the error underlying their supposition, the revolutionaries' foes devised a mixture of their own intended to guard against the dreaded disease, a mixture which also seemed to check undesirable outlaw behaviors. Though the treatment came too late for many countries—" Herr Schreiber's voice caught, choked, then started up again, much shrunken. "—it was touted as a miracle drug. For a while its side effects were unknown, and when that was no longer true, knowledge of them was suppressed. Suppressed . . . suppressed . . ."

The Frau, having drunk her dose, patted her husband's shoulder and took over the tale's telling. "Those escaping that suppression found that their exposure to this so-called cure and its aftermaths made them eager to explore any alternatives. Thus many came to side with the revolutionaries and those who sheltered them. Thus was their alliance born. And thus, happily, it was nourished and grew, unhindered, to fulfill its destiny."

Though it was obvious from the repetition included in her last three lines that Frau Schreiber believed their story had come to its conclusion, and though the bowl between them had of course been emptied by her, the cat looked expectantly at Gopal. It knew there was something more. Its knowledge spiced the apartment's air with hope and joy. The moment stretched, filling with the soon-to-be-familiar smells of her freshly inoculated kin, enticing Hafiza into opening all her pores. Wider, deeper—there. Thudding below Gopal's heart, the secret rhythm, the pulsing of the Russian

Cure he carried, encysted, inside. With her eyes she asked. With his mouth he answered: "Yet the key to this destiny lay in understanding and encompassing its enemies. In hearing and retelling their stories."

With his hands they reopened his workbasket.

Kisangani, Everfair

Gopal's regret tinged his every emission. Even as he swam in the warmth of his new coremates' breaths, he longed for something other, something more. Revolutionary thought discouraged wallowing in the wastewater of wishes made in vain. Reach for the possible, he reminded himself, taking out Bee-Lung's latest addition to his inoculation kit: the special Spirit Medicine she herself had developed. The one he still expected to use to form a stronger connection between her and him someday soon.

But for now he would try to mimic the structure of the most recent core—the one that seemed to have given rise to a new mind.

"Again?" asked Herr Schreiber, as Gopal poured the contents of the white clay jar into the wooden bowl.

His wife shushed his lips with one finger. "Can't you tell? We're being treated royally!" She shut her eyes and smiled and sighed as if in ecstasy. "Isn't it obvious? Can't you *feel*? Our host, and our hostess, and Mr. Sharif—we are *all* so *excited!*"

Hafiza's memory helped Gopal select the proper adjuvants. There were more of these than the first mixture had called for, but in smaller amounts. Administration was quicker, since there was no further recitation to accompany it. None was needed. And yet . . .

And yet still something was missing—not more story. But something . . .

Pondering this perplexing, indefinable lack, Gopal set his hands moving through the steps of preparing their core's second inoculation. It would work—it was working already, for as Bee-Lung had observed to him, a well-fashioned kinning operated independent of time's accustomed flow. The deeper, surer connections it would establish already worked. The center of his consciousness drifted from coremate to coremate: first, naturally, to Hafiza, with whom he felt most familiar. Her viewpoint fed him to that of the one she was gazing on: the refugee woman, Frau Schreiber, whose narrow nostrils flared suddenly wide now that she began scenting the full range of her kin's outpourings. A look of surprise dawned on her pale face as she took in Herr Schreiber's no longer concealable attraction to Hafiza—had it never occurred to her that her husband could want sexual relations with someone else?

Next, Gopal inserted his consciousness into the white man. Thanks to this coremate's astonishment at the ease with which he sensed the chemical traces left by the apartment's absent occupants, Gopal appreciated that ability as if he'd never before experienced it. And entering Bahir the shared pleasure deepened, doubled, reflected back upon itself and tripled and quadrupled and—

Gopal realized that though their second dose had made it all the way around the table, he had yet to immerse his awareness in that of the cat. Prejudice on his part? Probably; animals ought to be either wild or domesticated, but cats were both. Or neither.

Gingerly, he brought his attention to bear on this final coremate, but met with resistance—no, met with himself! As if cast by a mirror that reflected odors rather than images, Gopal's savor flung itself up in his way. Would it be possible to sniff past his own smell to detect and incorporate the cat's? Stubbornly, he persisted in trying. There had to be a path in, a means of connecting with this member Hafiza seemed sure their core needed. Focusing on visuals he found yet another barrier in the guise of a match: his gaze was challenged by a pair of staring, slit-centered eyes like polished emeralds. For age-filled instants neither he nor the animal blinked or looked away. Impasse.

Swift pain wrapped his left wrist. Blood welled from four red stripes—the beast had scratched him! Furious, Gopal clenched his uninjured hand into a fist and cocked it back—then froze with an abrupt realization: the cat continued to sit where it had been sitting, continued to stare at him, unmoving. Unafraid.

Innocent of ill intent. Or so it smelled.

Then why hurt him?

The vibrations stirring Gopal's chest had started so slowly he'd ignored them at first. Now they sped up. What were they? Waves of rightness spilled upward from—the cyst! The Russian Cure—encased in the strongest, most secure cage he'd been able to fashion of his own flesh . . . Now it strummed against its gristly confines, playing him like a ghost would play a haunted harp. Its song's chorus was "Let me go free!"

Why shouldn't he? Bee-Lung had unleashed her own encapsulation of the organism many markets earlier.

Because European solutions created their own fresh sets of problems. And because, stubbornly, he clung to the fear that the Russian Cure, no friend to workers such as himself, would impose on him some insidious evil—some inescapable means of control.

But even back in his own body like this, he sensed how firmly Hafiza insisted that the cat was correct. Gopal needed to release the Russian organism into his veins and let it bleed out of his wounds. So he did.

It took a few lines. As the cyst's tissues finally separated, the thrumming warmth caused by the organism within suffused him from toes to topknot. An answering thrum emanated from the cat's throat as it licked the marks it had made on him, its tongue pleasantly rough. Then it snaked its head back to bite its own flank.

"Well enough," declared Hafiza. "That takes care of the third phase for the two of you, but to finish the inoculations of we four I must ask—"

"There's yet another step to our proceedings?" asked Herr Schreiber. "This is more involved than I had bargained for—it's too much work! Let us leave, my treasure."

"No!"

"But—"

"One small adjustment is all we need—isn't that so, miss?" Frau Schreiber's appeal to Hafiza was accompanied by a breath of imperfectly stifled jealousy. "Then we'll be able to truly join together. We will be as one!"

"We will be so at times, yes. When that's what we prefer." Drawing back the draped folds of her white scarf, Hafiza bared a well-muscled arm. "Come, you're not frightened of real intimacy, are you? For this final inoculation you must let our animal break your skin.

"I'll demonstrate." She leaned forward past her father and extended her hand to where the cat crouched, alert, tail curling like a furred avatar of one of Saraswati's arms. With a quick swipe of a paw, Carmelita gave Hafiza a wound identical to Gopal's. His coremate was brave; she barely flinched.

The cat licked her. "See? Smell? I'm fine. Now you do it, Baba." Bahir offered his hand and received the final stage of their inoculations. Herr and Frau followed suit—the man reluctantly, the woman screwing down her resentment of Hafiza, an emotion she deemed unworthy. Grudgingly, the edges of Frau Schreiber's scent blended with the scent of the woman she had judged to be her rival.

Then it was as if their two airs were notes of music, forming the base of a chord. Gopal and the rest of his kin built on that base. They made perfume together, a mighty swell of meaning all their own. Not anyone else's. Their name. In words: *The Blending.*

"To the roof," said somebody—Bahir? Hafiza? Gopal himself? No matter. In unison they left the apartment, walked along the passage to the floor's exit, and climbed up four flights of the stairs clinging to the building's wood-and-metal walls. The openness of the evening sky beneath which they ventured dispersed their cloud of feeling only a very little.

Most of the building's flat roof was occupied by growing beds.

Lush with moisture, cool with night, bushes and curling vines rustled around them as the new coremates walked their winding path. Chairs and couches circled the drummers' platform just beyond the roof's center.

As they approached it, a young woman Gopal recognized from the palace rose to greet them. Za, her name was. She belonged to a core that had been born within the last few markets; her trips supplying fresh eggs to the palace kitchens and clinic had ended soon after the core formed, and this must be why: integration into the drummers' guild. Evidently her new duties brought her here instead.

Others stood too, and gathered with them on the raised stage where the instruments were arranged. Though of several different cores, every one of them had been inoculated. Naturally. Spirit Medicine–enhanced senses were speedily proving the best key to forming clear connections between drummers' stations.

So touching hands, drenching the soft breezes chasing between their skins with messages of love, *The Blending* began their dance. An explanation was extended by each dip and pivot; a plea for support by each whirl and clap and waving hand and swaying hip and yes! Their steps were met and matched! Drumbeats followed their story's timing, the rhythms pounded by their hearts. Soon Gopal's particularness felt the grasp of calloused palms caressing him, carrying him, lifting him skyward like a prayer.

The rich odor of wet earth welled into him: first through his nostrils, then via the soles of his feet, his toes and heels and ankles, calves . . . the circle surrounding him receded, drew back, let him sink into the knee-high loam filling the clay pot in which they planted him. Into the soil, the universal medium of communication—

But he would be blind! No roots traveled between the denizens of this garden! No path existed for sending or receiving his signals—

Except the air. The thick air. Thick with vibrations. Thick with sounds.

The air would deliver their blessings to the country. To the continent. To the world.

With a thrill, Gopal accepted his part in *The Blending*'s structure. Like General Wilson, he would work as a transmitter. He would speak the language of the Spirit Medicine to all who had received it.

And like Queen Mwadi and King Mwenda, Hafiza and Bahir would widen their scope, the cat aiding in their core's outreach just as Raffles aided the outreach of the royal core, the group being that was their template. Their Herr and Frau would fill the need for lovers, these two comprising a role played originally by Queen Mwadi—again—and by her consort in sweetness, Miss Bailey.

This was the burden of the song they sang with no words, the music *The Blending* made with their bodies and their shared dream. Nourished by the fluids and minerals seeping in at his feet's wide-open pores, their Gopal's blood flowed happily, heedlessly, circulating quickly from scalp to groin to cool, dark feet— feet dancing without steps. Joy rushing without the necessity of movement as they spread their delight on waves of cadency, crests and troughs of truth and change and growth! And knowledge! So much to distribute, and such pleasure in the distribution, such enhancements to life provided by these Spirit Medicine–multiplied points of view. Those formerly frightened of integration realized their freedom within the Spirit Medicine's embrace. For not all saw the same.

But that variance was strength, was everything ever to be required. Little need now to pull and push and lift one lone mass of flesh.

Perhaps, though, it was a call for that shifting about that was at this moment approaching them? The soft-plushed resonance of the night sang with a familiar scent, one their Gopal had tasted quite recently: Bee-Lung! Coming closer . . . higher . . . closer . . .

She was here. *The Blending* sensed her seeking how to join their dance. They clasped her with Herr Schreiber's arms, and mounted the cat upon her head. Out of Carmelita's eyes they saw too much, a bobbing confusion on which they lowered the cat's lids. But with that adjustment all became beautiful, and energetically organized. Swirls of pungency underscored the nearness of their desire. Supremely tight currents tunneled among the crowding of their individualities, telling each and all how their stories supported so many different versions of themselves. So many realities. Steady and ripe and glorious was the feeling of their rhapsody—

Then came the news of King Ilunga's murder.

This was why *The Blending* needed Gopal to stay here. Because anything happening anywhere in the capital would come directly to their attention via the drums. Dispatching their Hafiza and Schreibers to the palace—those kin who could enter it most easily—*The Blending* conferred hastily with Bee-Lung as she walked with them there.

"It's probably Mr. Chawleigh who killed him; this Mr. Chawleigh and one of King Ilunga's coremates, Doctor Kleinwald, are enemies," she pronounced.

"But Mrs. Chawleigh and the king were lovers—so isn't that why her husband assassinated him?" Frau Schreiber still hadn't mastered the trick of accessing every corner of her kin's minds.

"You'd say jealousy was the motive? Yes, they *were* lovers. When Sevaria and the doctor kinned with King Ilunga, however, that earlier relationship withered on his heart's vine. Unlike the preserved fruit of his rapport with Devil, it has died a genuine death. Which— hmmm—perhaps there's a shred of a connection to that circumstance after all? For Tink has told me King Ilunga's loss of interest was taken by Mr. Chawleigh as an insult.

"If this matter has sorted itself out as I expect it has, we can ask the dead king himself who did the deed. Possibly he'll even know why it was done."

The palace's facade looked as calm as Bee-Lung felt to them, as if nothing terrible was amiss; only a few glamps more than normal glimmered beside the steps up from the water-filled street. Whiffs of panic blew from the doors as they opened, however, and the door guards' skins were sheened with it. Inside, the stone floor above their heads whispered with the hurried passage of bare and sandaled feet.

"Unless we're asked to enter it, we'll avoid Queen Josina's presence. For now." Casting about, Bee-Lung chose their direction. "The king's coremates are with my family, up this way. Come."

CHAPTER SIXTEEN

September 1921
Kisangani, Everfair

Queen Mwadi closed the curtains on her suite's sitting room and turned to face the sprawling bodies of her brother's keepers. "Success!" she announced. "And they're here. Bee-Lung is escorting two of the new being's coremates up to meet us now."

"Good." That was Sevaria's voice. But was she using it for herself? "Who are they, then?"

"My German friends."

"Them? Those poor refugees? They're not who we want." So that must be Ilunga speaking.

Kleinwald answered him. "Of course they're who we want! Displaced whites will flock to the cause." With his brass hand he tried to unhook Sevaria's earring from the bed covering in which it had become entangled. "If you'd rather approach the parties who were backing your claim to the throne, say so, but there's no call to limit ourselves. We can court both sides. Think big."

The others entered without scratching on the doorframe. Understandably. They couldn't help breathing in her expectation of them. Still, Queen Mwadi felt a part of herself upset at this presumption.

Releasing her individualistic dismay into the room's slowly circulating atmosphere, she hoped it would be quickly overcome. And it was! Bee-Lung's brisk effusions of pride and enthusiasm flushed away most of Mwadi's embarrassing feelings in a pair of lines, while the Schreibers' less intentional emissions—a blend of fear and curiosity—broke apart and scattered the rest. They reduced her vanity to an empty gasp.

"Your Prominences are well? Both of you?" Bee-Lung understood. "Was there any pain?"

"Yes, of course there was pain," Mwadi answered. "To some degree all the inoculated who were in the general area felt it, even those of us whose consciousness rises out of other bodies than those of the king's coremates."

"You felt the assassination? What happened?" asked Frau Schreiber.

"Why not ask me? I'm right here." Again her brother talked to them through Sevaria. "He choked me with his bare hands. He smelled like he rather enjoyed the effort."

"Mr. Chawleigh, was it? Do you know why he killed you?"

"Yes, I do." Sevaria tilted her face from Schreiber to Schreiber as she answered their questions. She frowned Ilunga's frown. "Can't we dispense with this ridiculous notion that I'm dead? Just because my original body stopped breathing."

"I don't believe our country is quite ready to accept rule by your coremates. One of them is white," Mwadi pointed out.

"Jewish." Now Dr. Kleinwald was speaking, from his own mouth. He still struggled to free his coremate's earring.

"How is that different?" Mwadi asked, bending closer. "Here. You've got to thread this spiral bit under the edge...."

The slightest scrape of thumbnail on wood was all the warning they got. Ten odorless guards rushed in. Two each seized Bee-Lung and both the Schreibers by their arms. The other four dragged Sevaria and the doctor from Mwadi's bed toward the door.

"Wait!" Ilunga's coremates protested in unison. "Where are you taking us?"

"Come," said one man. From his opened mouth came a reassuring stream of impatience mixed with sleepiness. Since Mwadi detected no excitement or dread in his breath, things must not be that bad.

"I am your queen! I order you to stop." She saw now the shining grease blocking the emissions of the guards' pores.

Another guard, a woman, sighed and bowed her head. "Prominence, we're only following the orders given to us by your mother." The sigh and the words bore the scent of the woman's resignation as her smothered sweat had not. "It's the wish of Queen Josina that we bring your guests and visitors to the atolo grove for the dawn deliberation."

"The deliberation?" Mwadi repeated stupidly.

"The deliberation to determine who has killed the king."

"No one!" That was the doctor's voice. "No one has killed me—but that bounder Chawleigh certainly tried to!"

"Come," repeated the man who'd first spoken. "We're not supposed to talk to anyone, just to do what we're told." Now his worry surfaced. And fresh-brewing confusion as to who was answering him, and why.

"Very good." Mwadi wanted to reassert her supremacy. "I will precede you."

As she swept past the guards and their docile captives, she let loose a blast of summoning alarm for Rima to discover when she arrived for their morning sex. Trailing her fingertips along the passage walls, Mwadi left behind more of the same scent plus quickly devised hints as to where they were headed.

But only two carts waited at the bottom of the palace steps. A rare oversight—these would have nothing like enough room for their entire party. And the morning was early, the sky barely grey, the street below empty. No bikists in sight. Additional guards were called to watch over the white couple till a second trip could be made.

Maybe Rima would arrive first and disrupt whatever scheme Mwadi's mother had in hand. Disruption was one of her beloved's best skills.

Kisangani, Everfair

Alan never forgot himself. A mind capable of comprehending that the world's basic building blocks were both particles and waves could handle multiplicity quite easily.

He rode in two carts: as Sevaria, seated opposite Queen Mwadi and between two guards; and as his primary, original incarnation, Dr. Kleinwald, seated between this body's two guards and opposite Bee-Lung and hers. Outside the carts' raised windows rain suddenly materialized, lashing down as if it would wash away the air. Despite this interference he maintained the two bodies' connections. The storm stopped as swiftly as it had begun; by the time they came to the grove's ramp it had cleared up completely.

Wear Red's Sevaria was their first to alight. With the guards' and King Ilunga's help, they found their way to the ceremonial plateau. A carpet of overlapping straw mats covered its center. Most of its circumference was marked by a circle of standing women and men, a circle crowned by an arc of courtiers their Ilunga recognized. Thrust forward, all entities took their places facing Queen Josina and her most immediate companions: Yoka, advisor, priest, and diviner; Mademoiselle Toutournier; Josina's two favored servant women, Sifa and Lembe; and an older man their Ilunga greeted as Alonzo, one of his parents' longtime counselors.

A slight disturbance rippled through that section of the circle as its constituents moved apart for Queen Mwadi to join them. A pair of drummers to the right beat a few fast measures; in the near silence following this outburst, their Sevaria's ears detected the pattern's distant repetition. It was the dissemination of their doings. Over that came Alonzo's proclamation of this deliberation's purpose: to find the king's cowardly killers. Then he called for Bee-Lung to step onto the mats.

"But first," Mademoiselle cautioned her, "remove your footwear."

Sandal-less, Bee-Lung came to kneel in a spot a bit off of the circle's defining midpoint. *Wear Red* resisted Alan's urge to correct her.

"Whomever you hold holy, you must swear by them, and by your ancestors," Yoka declared. "Do it now, and do it aloud. They will hear and guide us in our proceedings."

"Those whom I hold holy? All creation is equally sacred in my eyes—" Her face turned upward. "—stars and moon, rain and sun—" Now her head bowed downward. "—plants and animals and insects flying, crawling—"

"Then you betta swear by everybody. Alla them. Everthin you can think of." Queen Mwadi's lover Rima swirled in between two of the circle's members like a loud whisper, a badly kept secret. "Cause you got a big job to do convincin these people ain't no murder been committed."

"We have seen the corpse. We have the killer's confession." Alonzo's statements were accompanied by a scant air of doubt, leakage filtering through his body cream.

"Then why question me?" asked Bee-Lung.

Queen Josina laughed. Her protection was complete; they had no way of knowing whether the laugh was genuine. "Causes have causes. Perhaps your Spirit Medicine treatment contributed somehow to my son's death. Can you deny it did? Truthfully?"

"And if I lie? How will you know?"

With a smile as enigmatic as her laughter, Josina waved a hand at Yoka, who stood beside her. "We have a system."

Suspicious, they targeted the diviner using both bodies' senses. As with Alonzo, the unguents masking his emissions had been applied a little too skimpily. But only suave certainty emerged from his skin.

"No. Nothing I have done, nothing the Spirit Medicine did, was responsible in any way for King Ilunga's death. In fact—" Bee-Lung gave her own smile and waved with her own hand, her gesture and its underscoring aroma aimed in *Wear Red*'s direction. "—just the opposite. Your son lives, Queen Josina—inside his kin.

"This I attest to and affirm as fact, resting my sureness on the certain divinity of our shared world, and the certainty of the coming revolution."

Yoka bent forward. For a couple of lines the muted click of cowries came from beneath his hands. "Correct," he announced.

"She's telling the truth!" Mademoiselle Toutournier sounded and smelled astonished—apparently she hadn't opted for the odor-camouflaging ointment.

Queen Mwadi emitted offendedness. "You ought to have asked me first!"

"I thought you wished to rule alone. That could have influenced your answer. Couldn't it?"

Silence lapped around them. A reluctant nod and a whiff of shame made known Mwadi's agreement.

"So. So they—he—they must join Madam Ho upon the mat," Queen Josina decreed.

They found themself summoned forward by gently inviting aromas. Bee-Lung took and kissed two of their hands. "Are you all here?" she asked.

"Of course! Why not? Are you?"

"My son?" Queen Josina inched forward on her throne. "You live? Prove it to me."

"Ask your oracle whether I live or not—or don't you really believe what it says?"

Yoka nodded and lowered his eyes. "It is as we were instructed."

"Yes. Very well." Their Ilunga's mother crooked a commanding finger. "You will answer one question the ancestors want me to pose to you. The right answer will match the one they gave us.

"Come forward."

They went in both their bodies, though they could have heard her whisper where they stood. This way, though, the sensory pleasures of incorporation doubled and supported each other, like a note played in octaves. Pure as wind fluting through hollowed stones came the queen's words: "Who supports your claim to inherit Everfair against your sister's claim?"

So many possible truths: the Chawleighs. The Chawleighs' employer, King Edward. But based on their King Ilunga's longstanding knowledge of Josina's confidence in her ability to manipulate him, *Wear Red* understood which answer to choose: another.

"You."

Kisangani, Everfair

Rima twined her mind around Mwadi's. The pair of them fit together better than ever, and already, on the flight to Lake Edward, she'd begun to learn the hang of basically bypassing King Mwenda and the monkey. It had only gotten easier—maybe because those two were so far away, and getting farther. Rima could connect with Mwadi at any time, and neither of the others would have to be part of the picture—at any rate, not a big part.

The constant presence of General Wilson was a different song to sing. He was impossible to ignore. Often Rima felt him vibrating along her veins as the blend of Russian Cure and Spirit Medicines they'd taken opened every gate between her and Bo-La. In a way, the general's humming seemed to help them reach one another: via his buzz the same electric juice flowed in the sighs they blew into one another's mouths, and the same sugar sweetness lit her tongue and her lover's.

But this ceremony, these sacred grounds, were no place for such rapture. That much she gathered from the streams of scent many of those in attendance gave off. Enfolding her Bo-La now in greeting, Rima dared only to dart a chaste peck to her cheek. Even so, the closer contact made Rima wise to what it was that Mwadi considered their biggest problem: Queen Josina's lack of trust.

Ducking up out of their embrace, Rima spoke aloud her lover's challenge: "Mama, why won't you let me show you? I can be in charge of everything—all by myself!"

Queen Josina shook her head. "My plan is for you to go abroad like your father and demonstrate to America how useful distributed senses can be—how we benefit by sharing immediacy across oceans and mountain chains and deserts. How smoothly government can go. Your brother was meant to stay here with me. Now . . ."

"I can still stay!" From the middle of the mats the king's male coremate voiced Ilunga's objection to the idea of a change in Josina's plan. "I'll be even better—less distracted, less liable to fall into traps. Alan can warn me, and Sevaria, and—"

"Who gonna believe you who you say you is? Who gonna?" Bo-La's anger threatened to make both bodies' throats choke on Rima's words, but she kept going. "Unless your sister here to keep swearin it, an to do her part a the job, probably look to everybody else like it set up just the way your mama wants, with her still stayin on top. Without you."

"Then do you suggest that Queen Josina herself leave? That she desert Everfair?" asked Mademoiselle.

"Course not!"

"Or worse, that I should break us in pieces? Throw us into fighting a war against ourselves again?" Though no hint of her real feelings scented the air, Josina looked and sounded shocked and disapproving. "But thanks to the Mothers of Wisdom, who guide us, we know there is another, easier way."

"Easier? What way is this?" asked Sevaria.

"We'll convince our enemies they've done nothing wrong. The assassin and his wife will be happy to accept exile instead of death, naturally enough."

"Have you sentenced him yet? Let me do it! Then he'll be forced to admit I'm alive!" The woman must be speaking for her undead coremate.

"Good. Yes. But we'll need to do some further convincing, since

Mr. Hubert Chawleigh will be seen by many as caving to our assessment of the situation because of his cowardice." Josina pursed her lips and smacked them together lightly. "So I've chosen another target to persuade to our understanding of the situation, if we should agree on what it is. Another enemy."

Rima and Mwadi knew which enemy she meant: the oil-explorer they'd brought back from Lake Edward. Ilunga's erstwhile companion. But Deveril Scranforth's stubborn refusal of the Russian Cure kept his mind inaccessible. Would he accept the king's noncorporeal presence? Hard to tell; they had no influence there, and his reaction was entirely unpredictable. "You got a third backup?"

"The Italians we've inoculated will support us in this. They'll be likely to understand. And in the worst case, supposing that they're unable to persuade any other important Europeans that King Ilunga's still among the living, we'll have to pass my son's decisions off as yours." Briefly, Queen Josina closed her eyes, which made her state of mind even harder to decipher.

But within the mingling of their own minds, the minds of *The Sleeper Wakes*, all was singing crystal. They saw a way to get what they wanted: to have their commands treated as if they were Ilunga's. As irresistible.

All they needed to do was ingest him, and King Ilunga's decrees would be indistinguishable from their own. For they would in fact *be* their own. Rather than favoring one of King Mwenda's heirs over the other, the syncretized organism formed by the combination of Russian Cure and both Spirit Medicines would render that contest moot. Neither brother nor sister would win their battle for succession. And both.

Could they make this ingestion happen? Ilunga's two coremates were present, so here and now should be its happening's where and when. But how would they do it? Undoubtedly Bee-Lung knew the best means of merging cores. They could ask her.

Before Queen Josina and all those assembled.

In the bodies of Queen Mwadi and Rima, they stepped bravely

forward. The silence immediately surrounding them deepened. The gaps they'd left in the ring remained, and admitted large bursts of the messages also stealing quietly above the heads of the bystanders: rustling leaves, tapping twigs, low winds whistling over seamed barks and cracked reeds. The music of the grove played sweetly on their skin and in their ears . . . The future was about to happen. Who else could feel it coming? Who else were they entangled with? The swamp nightjar their Mwadi rode in Mombasa? The flocks of birds who had carried them to Lake Edward? The fish who bore them over its depths? Very likely the plants with underground tendrils encasing their General Wilson's legs. And the lives these plants communicated with, at second and third and fourth and fifth removes, perhaps . . . Eventually they would use whoever, whatever was necessary to make themself right. They could even bring in Madam Ho, and both her families, too: her coremates on *Xu Mu* and her Kwangmi, her Tink . . . Potentially, doing that would offer them access to all the cores she had caused to be seeded. All across the civilized world.

They cradled the airs of their present bodies' essences in two of their hands. "Here's what we've got to share," they said, using words, to be sure that they got everyone's attention.

A breath of caution plumed off of Madam Ho. "You don't worry you'll be drowned out?"

"No! We afraid a nothin!" Their Rima shouted this with their Mwadi's approval—but then they thought again and summoned their Mwenda, whose melody filled them with stern, bright love. And in harmony another presence manifested: their mascot, Raffles. The one who cared about names. And names, they understood then, were the key. Good names worked like stories: they told everything about those who had them.

As long as each member of their family had a name, they each had a story. As long as there was a story, there was a self. Expanding the family group past the Spirit Medicine's former limits would change an old group into a new group singing a new story, and most probably would create a new self. But the new self wouldn't erase the old selves that sang what made it. They kissed to celebrate the joy of their understanding.

Their Rima roused her mouth from the kiss to reassure Bee-Lung. "We only hafta keep thinkin separate names: who we is an who we gonna end up to be. We oughta be able to handle that."

"Are you sure? Are you ready to do something so complicated?"

"We ready to try."

Giving off great swells of encouragement, Madam Ho turned to face Queen Josina. "If you'll allow a moment before proceeding further, the core holding your son can encompass your daughter's core. Then he'll have that much more support for his pronouncements."

"Here? Right away?" Josina widened her large eyes. "Will Sifa again observe and remember for us how this process works?"

"If you like. If you're letting us go ahead with it."

"Yes—provided you're quick. You have the time it takes us to prepare the white man for judgment."

"You are gracious! How many verses till then?"

"Alonzo?"

"It will be no more than eleven, Prominence."

This would be long enough to attempt the merging, Madam Ho's confidence proclaimed. She guided them to sit in what they presumed to be a propitious arrangement.

Who was to be judged? There appeared to be only one uninoculated white man within sensing range: Deveril Scranforth. And his odor came from a cart far up Batwaboli Street, a cart very slowly approaching the grove's ramp. Worry salted their courage. Who else could Queen Josina mean? Not Herr Schreiber, who, according to Gopal's drums, he and Hafiza had just kinned with last night. Not the doctor, soon to be one of themself. No.

No. She must be referring to the judgment of another white man, one still unrecruited. Chawleigh? Probably. He'd been accused and assumed guilty of strangling King Ilunga, and would

now be awaiting conviction and sentencing. But where was he waiting at? No trace of him laced the air—or? Except for? What they
barely managed to perceive was something so faint . . . something
like Chawleigh's scent but compromised, confused . . .

"Attention! We begin!" Madam Ho clapped her hands and released an invigorating aroma.

"Will you need your workbasket fetched from the palace?"
asked Mademoiselle, her air that of an attentive hostess. "Should
we send a messenger?"

"I could easily ask Tink to bring it, but we have everything that
matters right here."

Kisangani, Everfair

Their Ilunga understood. What mattered was the story they sang.
Their Sevaria had provided different stories for their different
births: "Wear Red" for the first entity, kinning her with him and
with their doctor. Stills and an oral summary of the film *The Sleeper
Wakes* for the second entity, the one comprising Mwenda, Mwadi,
Rima, Raffles, and General Wilson. Would one narrative prevail
over the other?

No. Rather than clashing, their stories combined. The hero of
"Wear Red" became a forest dweller contributing some of the wild
ingredients used in the movie's Spirit Medicine mixture. The Deer
Woman stroked to sleep in her home century the character Sevaria
had played, and stroked her back awake one hundred years later.

From their mingling at the mats' center, *Wear Red* watched
their fiery darling dance their story's changes. When the time
came, they added their Ilunga's voice to their Kleinwald's recitation. And heard and yielded to new tunes, new branches of their
tale. New minds. New means of belonging together. New kin.

Already low, they let their awareness sink even lower—into the
roots channeling food and thoughts from flower to tree to spreading moss. And they floated, too: higher and higher, drowning

theirselves inside water droplets, drifting lighter than a fly's wings on the stillest of breezes.

They could be anywhere, everywhere. They stood up in all their bodies, but such limited movement was not enough. They had to run, to burst away from the watching ring of others—at least with the legs of their Rima and Mwadi. Escape! Freedom!

A guard was sent to follow the two lovers; they led him past the tree where Mwadi had released the royal shongo, past the hut where she'd received Yoka's prophecy, to the atolo grove's wildest recesses, and lost him among the morning's mists and shadows. Straying vines and springing mosses caressed their arms and ankles, wound around to trip them and cushion them as they fell.

They realized that they simultaneously lay on hidden green leaves and crouched on the deliberation's brown and grey mats. Using the redefinitions just acquired, the bodily boundaries of their Rima and Mwadi's lovemaking—bared nape and cupped breast and thick thigh—had shifted to include the sight and feel and smell and sound of dyed silk, and supple leather, and minutely articulated brass.

A ripple of horror passed through them. Was this incest? Even though one of the bodies implicated had ceased cohering? Could they learn how to keep these two members' sexual feelings separate from their Ilunga, as they had isolated them from their Mwenda? Or would it be necessary to tear theirself apart? And what then would happen to their nonincarnate king?

Stubborn Ilunga trusted in his individual actions to prevail over all else. Straining his particular self out of their enmeshment, he wrested their Alan's mouth to his usage with rude abruptness. "Mother," he made it say, "I'm here for now, but we'll need other arrangements in the long term. I can't—I *won't* continue to share my—*me-ness* with Mwadi."

They inhaled Mam'selle's shocked huffs of relief, savoring them all the more in lieu of any decipherable emotions coming off of

Queen Josina, whose even voice and placid expression left her words shallow: "For now, then. Our prisoner is ready."

Still they received only the vaguest hint of Chawleigh's smell. But now they heard a struggle approaching the plateau: rustling brush, and kicking feet, and panting curses that reeked of mountain juniper berries came closer and closer. The partial signatures of half-camouflaged guards' scents accompanied the nearing noise.

Rousing up from a forest-sheltered embrace, their Rima and Mwadi remounted the sloping path and retook the mats' center. There, with Sevaria's hands, Raffles groomed them, while King Ilunga kept speaking.

"Just make sure you realize that until we can reconfigure, I'm part of the most royal being ever. Whatever I say will matter three times as much as whatever you say, Mother, because I'm also King Mwenda and Queen Mwadi."

"In a way that's true. In spite of what you say, though, your best plan will be to let me guide you. I believe your father would agree?"

Their Mwadi's head nodded. Their Rima's, too. "He do."

The noisy swearing arrived at the mats' edge, accompanied by the faint yet recognizable aromas of juniper and Chawleigh, and the more definite presence of wet ropes—and another aroma, one almost heavy enough to blot out even that, though so all-pervasive that until this moment it had been paradoxically unnoticeable: fresh mud. And when Queen Josina's guards forced the prisoner onto the mat before them, they saw the reason for the scent's sudden density: the assassin's bonds and naked skin were thickly coated in clay.

"I find you guilty," said Queen Josina. They could know only what she said. "However, my son wishes to sentence you for the far lesser crime of accidental injury. This is provided you acknowledge that he's still living."

Chawleigh spat on the mat. His spittle formed a small black puddle to his left, redolent of dirt and alcohol and resignation.

"Are you trying to say I failed? But you know I didn't! I killed the king! I achieved my target! My wife has already gone to collect our fee."

"A fee you will die before receiving. Wouldn't you rather live? Behave rationally!" Mademoiselle admonished him.

Chawleigh's barking laughter changed into a spasm of coughs. He bent his head forward to bury his mouth in his chest a moment, recovered, and spat again. "Behave rationally? Here? In Africa—the world's armpit? This cesspool of superstition? This—"

"Silence!" Queen Josina *sounded* furious, though she looked no more than slightly annoyed. One of the two guards standing behind Chawleigh raised her baton suggestively, but Josina waved this punishment away. "Your outmoded opinions count for nothing. Your only usefulness lies in your ability to convince your chiefs you missed your chance to kill my son."

"And how am I going to do that?"

"Tell them you've seen me," they said. "Turn around and it's true."

The mud-covered European swung his face back and forth between them and Queen Josina. "You're serious! You think my bosses will credit some hallucination, some ghostly vision of mine, with being Everfair's rightful ruler? Still alive?"

"I'll prove who I am." They were talking out of their Mwadi's mouth. "Clara has a pink mark shaped like a flower's silhouette—on the underside of her right breast."

The white man scoffed at that. "Any spy could find out so much by asking the servants a few choice questions."

"She also has a strong preference for getting the soles of her feet caressed as her sexual climax begins."

"Perhaps she does. Again, that's a detail which could be discovered by any diligent operative." Past the masking odors of mud and vegetation, though, came a hint of chagrin. They kept going.

"She has a special word she whispers in her lovers' ears when urging them to—"

"She has your hands! At least one, and maybe both! I came back and cut them off before my capture, and sent them to her by separate runners so they'd not get lost."

"My . . . hands?" Their horror at what this butchery signified thickened the saliva in their Mwadi's throat and almost stopped her tongue. "You—cut them—"

"Give me your weapon." Queen Josina's rigid face and steady reach declared her deadly calm. Her eyes stared nowhere, at no one. The nearest guard genuflected and gave her his shongun. She took it and stood, glanced down, then shook her head. "No." She gave it back. "That would work best from a distance."

Carefully removing her sandals, Queen Josina stepped forward. Once. Twice. Four times. "Your club." Her eyes were now fixed on Chawleigh, but they could tell it was his guards she addressed.

"My bosses wanted physical evidence! They *made* me— Please— DON'T! PLEEEEE—"

Blood and piss broke through the clean smell of drying mud. They shut out the sound of the white man screaming. All sound. Most sight, too, but with their Rima's eyes they observed how Mam'selle threw hampering arms around Queen Josina's heaving shoulders and flailing arms, how she drew her away from the hunched, quivering back of the would-be assassin. How Mam'selle dared to scold Josina—or so it looked and smelled: she exposed her teeth and flared her nostrils, took big, angry breaths in and exhaled a fog of frustration.

Queen Josina's genuine reaction was of course opaque. But soon her usual coolness of demeanor returned, and she appeared to direct Chawleigh's guards to carry the white man's semiconscious body off the mat.

They waited four lines after that before opening their ears; the prisoner's moans and whimpering had faded, baffled by leaves and distance. Mam'selle's lecture was done, her lips set in a hopeful smile. "You agree with me?" she asked.

"Yes. You're right, my sister, as you often are," said Queen Josina. "He's not going to do us any good. Fortunately, however, we have access to another white man who possibly can help. My son's old friend, Scranforth. We'll use him."

Kisangani, Everfair

Bee-Lung located and followed her brother's scent, a fine strong thread. Tink was seated in the first of the two carts that had earlier carried them to the atolo grove, now returned to the palace. His yearning for his wife trailed up the steps he'd just come down, a plume of possessiveness and anxiety.

On the bench opposite Tink sat the Schreibers, who were connected to her dear Gopal. Could those two somehow bring him closer? Perhaps if her brother's hands touched the hands of Gopal's coremates, her dear would feel her love? Hands were important. She submerged her awareness fully in Tink's. Their eyes peered through the cart's shutters as Kwangmi appeared, with Deveril Scranforth walking beside her. It was just as Queen Josina's drummers had directed. Their guards, grease melting and washing away in the misting rain, gave off the dull odors of met expectations.

Scranforth and *The Mission*'s Kwangmi got into the second cart. The separation was sad. But though they longed Tink's longing for the joy of greeting Kwangmi's body physically—feeling the soft skin beneath her jaw, tasting with their tongue the fragrance blooming out of the creases behind her knees—at least here there was the refugees' delighted opening of pores and senses, and the gratifying enmeshment of the essences of their Bee-Lung and the Europeans' Gopal.

Which was best: Flesh or air? Neither. Both. With a shrug, they ceased the effort of making such an artificial distinction. It was most natural now to fall into the encompassing mode exemplified by the combination of Spirit Medicine and Russian Cure. To knit together extremes, and in their meeting find truth. As this most recently born entity had found its name: *The Blending*.

All the way to the grove *The Blending* touched them and sang. The stories of their songs caught up with the present and flowed onward from there like the shallow waters of the streets through which they traveled. Herr and Frau Schreiber relayed excerpts to Gopal and the drummers. Some of these they translated into speech—reiterating them thus unnecessarily, and probably out of habit. They would learn.

"And now that we have broken down the false barriers erected by the guardians of the status quo, we welcome the advent of our golden age! Abundant food and the easy ability to share it; abundant work and the right to profit from it; abundant knowledge and the promise of more to come!"

So it went. Repetitively. Slowly. But by the time the subtly decaying wooden walls of the city's shops and homes gave way to the glad growth of living trees, the refugees had ceased talking and wrapped pale arms around the body of *The Mission*'s Tink. The rest of *The Mission*'s short ride was spent awash in the mingled sensations and mirrored perceptions of their kin's multiple surroundings: the rooftop garden, the grove's hilltop, the interiors of both jouncing carts.

Kwangmi's bikist was an uninoculated solitary. Along with about half of Kisangani's citizens, he chose not to let existing Spirit Medicine–generated cores take him in, and he refused to start a core of his own. But he knew enough to follow the other bikist's lead and to pull up to the grove's ramp behind him so they could disembark.

At the ramp's top they paused. Scranforth, the last up, clung to Kwangmi's arm as if a tight enough grip would give him a grasp of what was going on. "You say Loongee's here? Revived him some-how, I gather—mystic arts and such . . . Never underestimate the power of blacks' magic!"

"It's science, not magic!" their Bee-Lung insisted.

The day's cloudy light was about to reach its peak. Their path to the plateau was plain. "What's the hurry?" the white man asked as

they mounted it. "Too hot to run! Impolite to keep the queen waiting, of course, but still, I'd rather not—" Breathlessness caused by
the path's steepness quieted further complaints.

They reached and entered the mat-centered circle. It took a
moment for Scranforth to recover. "Hi! Hello! Understand you
want to see me?" He bowed and removed his slouch hat, signs of
respect—though his sweat revealed that this was merely a matter
of form. No real humility emanated from him, and even his pretense was poorly aimed: Was it meant for Queen Josina? Or for
Queen Mwadi, who knelt beside their Bee-Lung's original body, a
good three soldier-lengths away from her mother?

"Remove your boots." Again Mam'selle was instructing someone on proper behavior.

"What? Really? Very well, if that's the custom. Never one to
willingly offend the natives." Stooping, he untied his boots and
pulled them off. "Here you go." He attempted to give the boots to
their Tink. "No starch. That's a joke."

"You may keep those," said Queen Josina.

"As long as they don't touch the mats," Mam'selle added when
Scranforth bent to set his burden down.

"Ah? Yes? Well, let's—er, shall we? Waste no more time." He
straightened, his arms awkwardly full. "I gather you want me to
vouch for Loongee? King Ilunga, that is. Shouldn't take me a moment to verify his identity—he and I go back a bit. And then I'll head
off home, reassure the backers, that sort of thing. Check that they're
still on board to take advantage of the oil license he's granting us."

Scranforth craned his neck in what smelled like true confusion.
"Are you taking me to him or is he coming here?"

"Neither." At the sound of Queen Mwadi's voice, the white
man's wavering attention swooped her way. "He's here already."

"Where?"

"In me. In us."

"His flame burns on." Sevaria smiled sweetly and held out a
hand. "Here. Touch me and you touch him."

"Er . . . You sure of that? You seem, ah, rather better looking than old Loongee. Much more exciting, too! Nothing like I remember—but far be it from dear little Devil to turn a gal down." He pinned the boots between hip and elbow and seized Sevaria's hand.

Or tried to. Quick as striking snakes the four arms of Rima and Queen Mwadi intervened. They parted the air in unison and shoved him away. "Unhand my wife!" they ordered with both mouths.

The entity was not of one mind! *The Mission* sensed the disturbance this caused, the ruffled scents its members emitted as Ilunga struggled to tug their Sevaria into line, to get her to accept the need for withdrawing her offer of physical contact.

"My apologies for my curtness—but this is serious, Scranners! Sevaria is the light of my life!" their Alan explained.

"Serious, is it? Well, I suppose another darky's more your type than a married white woman. Especially with that rotter Chawleigh for a husband. Say, do you think that's why he choked you to death?"

"He didn't! I'm alive!"

"Yes, yes, if you insist."

"You'd do well to insist on my son's continued existence yourself," said Queen Josina. "That's if you wish to retain the oil rights he granted you."

"Ha! An excellent point, Prominence."

"Then you'll serve as our witness?"

"Small matter of the—the hands? The little Oriental girl here was tellin me they got sent off as a guarantee the deed was done? I can swear till I'm blue, but in the face of concrete proof no one will believe a word I say."

Queen Josina laughed. "The hands are an abomination, a reminder of the evil days of Leopold. Any nation allowing them to be transported over their territory is going to be despised and hated, and even among the Europeans there'll be consequences. I don't fear the hands.

"Besides, they may be stolen before they arrive at their intended destination. The journey ahead of them is a long one, full of uncertainties."

Kisangani, Everfair, and Aboard Xu Mu

The drums informed Raghu that Bee-Lung was on her way to *Xu Mu*. Jie-Jun and Min-Jun lowered the cargo basket in anticipation of her arrival. But the essences rising from the cart that trundled onto the stretch of airfield beneath them were only those of the bikist and Raghu's missing coremates, Tink and Kwangmi. Certainly these presences were necessary, but without Bee-Lung's expertise, how was he to sever their ties to him for good? How could he even know that what he wanted to try with the Chens and the others was possible?

Conditional though it must be, Raghu exuded a welcome into the air of the bridge. The first to climb down the companionway and approach him was Kwangmi. The second down was Tink, who smelled faintly nervous.

Raghu stayed seated at the control levers. "Where's your sister?" he asked. "She's the one we're looking for."

"I'm here. In a way." Though Tink's apprehensive bouquet remained the same, his eyes, his expression, even the pattern of his breath, and when and how he swallowed, all shifted to Bee-Lung's. Was he talking for her, then? Tink had never performed that trick before. "Will this do?"

"Perhaps it will, yes. We'll see."

Raghu was determined to make the most of his own abilities. With a curl of scent he summoned the twins and *Xu Mu*'s yet-unkinned May Fourth recruits, Amrita and Rosalie. He continued talking. "I have a question an expert should be able to answer: How do we manage now, with two nodes in one core? Must either Tink or I degrade? Or is splitting the core a better option? And is it possible?"

"Ideally you'd first expand, then split naturally, as Gopal's core did."

"There were nodes in that one?"

"Not necessarily—none were identified. Regardless, the principle's the same."

"Of course it's the same—because nodes don't exist!" That was the voice of Kwangmi, high and skeptical. "They are strictly hierarchy in disguise: a flimsy excuse for our woefully retrograde behavior!"

More crew members crowded onto the companionway: Ma Chau. Her lover, Kafia. Amrita, and after her, Rosalie. At the sight of the last two, Tink's pulse stuttered perceptibly and the edges of his breath turned ragged. "What are they doing here? How'd they get here from Zanzibar?" he asked, obviously speaking this time for himself.

"We flew commercial routes. The cores we left behind are well-enough established, and the qadi sufficiently enmeshed in us that we feel safe coming."

Still an atmosphere of anxious curiosity spilled from Tink's skin. But Raghu had his own question to ask.

"Wait—you're saying there's no reason we shouldn't reconfigure ourself, but also no reason we need to?" He let his scent convey his blended relief and hurt pride.

"If you want to pretend you're the most important part of your core, and everybody else's as well, go ahead. You too, Tink. We'll argue about it later."

"But whose core will you belong to, my wife? Will you stay with me or go away with Raghu?"

Kwangmi smiled, and a surge of splendorous joy blew around the cabin. "I vowed to share my life with you—didn't you believe me? And didn't I say we would argue later?" She lifted her arms to encircle him. "We must be together in order to do that! But first let's find out if your sister has work for us."

Tink's head nodded Bee-Lung's yes. "I do—so long as all wish to proceed." All did. Each by each they went up to the aircanoe's infirmary.

Via atmospheric currents curling back to him along *Xu Mu's* sponge-illuminated corridors, Raghu felt the Chens enter the infirmary, followed by Tink's body functioning as his sister Bee-Lung. Behind them trailed Rosalie and Amrita, who stationed themselves in the doorway. Raghu settled in between them, ready to soak up their essences as these were shared: to start with, cloves and cardamom and other sweet spices, smothered longing, laughing regret.

Channeling Bee-Lung's expertise, Tink prepared his new coremates' doses. The precision Tink had practiced as an engineer and inventor made this physical part of the job quick.

The new story emerged out of the old one: a tighter version of their mission's launch and success, updated to include all that they had discovered since leaving China. Now Jie-Jun and Min-Jun led the new recruits to quarters as Raghu lingered behind to thank Tink for his ready acquiescence—but no, he had not acquiesced! Not attempted or allowed severance—not removed himself and his wife from the rest of the core—no!

Instead of billows of fresh strangeness to be pushed through, comforting familiarity surrounded Tink. "My friend!" Raghu couldn't keep his surprise from manifesting in his voice and odor.

"You don't mind that we've stayed connected?" his persistent coremate asked. "With the abilities stemming out of our tripartite inoculation, we have powerful gifts to offer."

The soft breath of Kwangmi's happiness alerted Raghu to her emergence from the bridge. "Allow us to demonstrate," she said— not in the manner of someone asking permission. "The best method would be for me to cut you and put the Russian Cure directly in your blood. But since you're too timid for that we'll just—"

He was tired of others' belittlement. "I'm not afraid! I'm simply careful!"

"As you should be. As befits a node—but we must take risks, too."

Lapped in Tink's supportive effusions, Raghu knew that that was right. But . . . "But there is also another way?" An easier one, he hoped.

"It's experimental; as long as we're in the same core, we ought to be able to broaden our contact to include all levels and forms of inoculation."

Kwangmi had gotten close enough to touch him. Her strong arms enfolded him and brought him to her work-scented suede vest. "An exchange of vital fluids can help, and of course blood's the most direct—but why should we waste time talking? Not when showing's more efficient. Here." Cradling the back of his skull she kissed him purposefully on his mouth. To invade and be invaded, he parted his lips—only to find that he was ingesting the taste of Tink's pleased sweat. And then there was more. He saw and smelled and tasted himself. He *felt* himself as both subject *and* object—as the new node standing dazed next to the infirmary's doorway, and as the warm coremate folded securely within their Kwangmi's embrace.

Then more again. The blossoming darkness of the living quarters filled Raghu's already overflowing senses, each unfurling petal a touch, a sound, an intensity rich in newly deepened connections between the Chens and Amrita, between the Chens and Rosalie, between Amrita and Rosalie, and on and on, permutation after permutation, till all thought of separateness vanished. All.

Even some of those who were at that moment outside our core were within reach of this potent understanding. We crossed the bridge linking Tink with his sister, plucking up the tips of the threads of the bridge's special Spirit Medicine and assigning these their proper places within this newly expanded realm of ourself.

That accomplished we sank away, down and out of *Xu Mu*, toward the earth. Toward Bee-Lung's busy body. Toward the throbbing drums and swaying hips and lightly stepping feet of the dancers on the deliberation's mats.

How many could we be at once? The tap and snap of fingers making music bore us from dancer to dancer like wakened spores on invisible winds. Ourself settled onto the cracks and crevices of every inoculant's being, shrouding them as if with fine, translucent silk. We moved in concert with our Rima's leaps and grinds and dips; draped ourself over the suppleness of Bee-Lung's shoulders; careened back and forth and back again from Schreiber to Schreiber, and then from king to king, dead to absent.

But though we tried we could not go from queen to queen.

Of course Queen Josina was still uninoculated. The question, though, was why?

Our Mwadi had never understood what held Josina back. Nor had our Mwenda. Even poor strangled Ilunga, who when incarnate had been lavished with her approval, brought us a very limited understanding of his mother's schemes. She wanted to put on a show to convince the weakening Europeans that Europe was in no danger of losing its grip on Africa. She sought to project his supposed foolishness as her own, her country's, her government's, as the foolishness of an entire race. So if this was indeed her goal, how could she refuse our help?

To find out what noninoculants believed, words worked best. Especially when smells and other more reliable indicators of the emotions were masked or smothered.

We chose Alan Kleinwald to do our speaking. Narrowing into his perspective, we slowed the wide-swinging arc of his waltz, then stopped before Queen Josina's throne. A deep bow and a precisely calibrated flourish of his new hand accompanied his grinning invitation: "My queen, won't you join us?"

"*Am* I your queen? *Yours?*"

She knew of whom she asked this. Gallantry provided our answer: "We swear you are! Our whole allegiance is yours if you'll only accept it. Come! Dance!"

To our satisfaction, she rose and wrapped her fingers around Kleinwald's flesh and metal wrists. So odd, to touch and yet feel no more than the other's pressure. "And when you give me your allegiance," Josina asked, "what do you expect to get in return?"

Too hard to explain that without authentic communication. We called ourself closer together. "At least to enjoy your full presence." Even with all nostrils flaring, even after Queen Josina had gone without replenishing her protection for seven ballads, hardly any information reached us from her muffled pores. And what sniffs we gleaned seemed strangely contradictory: Hope and resignation? Comic grimness? Weary excitement?

"Are you sure? You want nothing more?"

What was happening? The blankness covering Queen Josina was spreading out from her and rolling over everything. Sight remained, and the loudest of the surrounding sounds, and a greatly lessened sense of our individual bodies' placement. The broad, powerful flow of scents we'd so quickly grown accustomed to had dropped to a thin rivulet.

Our Kleinwald faltered. "How—what are I—why did you— dwindle us?" We sank to sprawl untidily on the overlapping mats.

Mam'selle's face swam into view. She bent to brush our Kleinwald's forehead with one professionally cool palm. Our Rima remembered Mam'selle's medical training. "Is that what you perceive?" she asked. "A dwindling down?"

Queen Josina—our mother, our wife—towered above us. "You haven't asked me for anything, but because I am wise and generous, I'll share my secret with you. Also because, if you spend enough effort examining your members' minds, you will discover you already know it."

"A secret? Tell us! Who among us has hidden it from ourself?" We lay on our Kleinwald's left side. We willed that side's elbow to prop up the torso. After a grudging moment it did so. A tight tunnel concentrated our vision on Josina's glistening face.

"You are the collective being formed by combining inoculants of three separate organisms. My secret concerns the source of one of these organisms: Madam Ho's special variant of May Fourth's Spirit Medicine."

We blinked in perplexity. "She is the source! Obviously!" We knew this. Our Bee-Lung provided memories of the variant's development.

From beyond our extremely constricted field of vision we heard Mam'selle's voice scoffing lightly, her breath ruffling the hairs on our Kleinwald's cheeks with her skepticism. "Did she pull these spores out of her fundament? No? What was *her* source? From where did she obtain the materials she experimented upon?"

She answered herself with detectable relish: "From Everfair."

Was this so? Forsaking outside input, we focused on determining our Bee-Lung's response. We let our Kleinwald's body relax and lie on its back again as we sought that long-familiar reach and stretch. That powerful combination of discipline and curiosity which, yes, had found in a sample collected on her first visit here the means to expand the original Spirit Medicine's actions.

Which discovery we would have revealed to ourself if that revelation had been requested. And if it had worked within any part of our story.

Via our Bee-Lung's eyes and ears we made out Queen Josina saying more. "The plant chosen is one with which I was previously inoculated—though that wasn't exactly the intent. But during the ceremony initiating me as a priest of Oshun, a bit of it was introduced under my skin. It remains there and reminds me of my ties to the sacred. Not to risk adulterating that connection, I have held myself aloof from you.

"This is my first reason for doing so. But there's a second, too." She turned her odorless body to nod briefly in the direction of her servants. "Lembe, recite to me the events of the evening when King Ilunga first kinned with his husband and wife."

"Prominence?"

"Quickly. In one verse."

"Madam Ho provided the materials for your son to claim two supplicants as his kin. She tried to withhold her most potent mixture, but you were watchful to prevent that. You made sharing the founding story you told them contingent on her compliance. Once the king's connection was established—"

"What? No—that's not what we remember!" we protested through our Bee-Lung. "Miss Sevaria told the story." For the moment we ignored Josina's implied accusation of an attempt at deception. "It was hers . . . a folktale from her childhood." Our Sevaria confirmed this. "Naturally that night was a little confusing—"

But Queen Josina held up a hand to halt us midsentence. "It's not the night which has confused you.

"Go sit, Lembe. That's enough."

We hadn't been the ones confused. Had we?

Josina continued her explanation. "I have found other discrepancies, most in reports given by those multiply inoculated. My daughter's impossible flight to Lake Edward, for example. My son's insistence on the Italians' innocence. I don't trust these versions of events. I don't trust *your* version of the past. Or of the present. Possibly not of the future, either." Her almost entirely scentless breath sighed out. "For I have experienced my own."

Our Bee-Lung's eyes were failing now, too. Just a small circular patch of skin remained visible, pale and smelling of Mam'selle's patient inquisitiveness. Then it was gone. Those eyes were blind.

"You must go back. Dissolve."

We sought our other bodies, vague dimples in the boundless matrix in which we . . . stood? Sat? Lay? We willed movement. Toward the suddenly loud singing of Rima Bailey—our Rima? No! Now we shredded farther apart! Hurrying to gather the last wisps of our tattered self, we caught the corner of a glimmer of light, the faintest touch of a breeze, the barest tang of dampened folds of flesh, the tickle of raindrops running beneath root tendrils and traveling out, out, out—

We went with the water, under the ground, along pathways our

General Wilson had pioneered. Divided and diluted—our consciousness simultaneously spreading and shrinking, suffusing us with a sourceless brightness that we realized was our own—we carried with us nothing except our stories. All true! The stories' threads came apart as we did, each imbued with knowledge of its place in the pattern. Every single incident, each twist, took flight and landed in territory eager to receive it. And so we were many and yet still, potentially, one.

"Yes."

Who spoke that word? How did we hear it? Who asked these questions about what was said and what we heard?

Our Bee-Lung assembled, became palpable and visible. "Visible to whom?" she asked. Audibly. Around her, shown by her shining, was the hilltop we remembered, strewn with the same mats, on which stood most of those who had stood upon them previously. All were back but Mam'selle. Mam'selle was absent. Gone. Other absences broke the circle of onlookers. Large gaps, dark and troublingly difficult to gauge, separated Lembe and Sifa from one another, and Queen Josina from—herself? Multiple Josinas occupied the ring that surrounded our Bee-Lung and yet one more Josina, who took Bee-Lung's hand and emitted freely—generously, even—an aroma of amused delight.

"You're good!" said the queen. "You won't have to learn much before our land can absorb and accept your channels."

Beyond the silent backs of Josina's seated selves, our Bee-Lung glimpsed shimmering movements, vague shapes swelling with low-humming songs and rippling with honey-like perfumes. She knew that if she could just get closer to them, their meanings would come clear.

She also knew that yielding to such urges led to falling into traps. "Where are we?" she asked for us.

"We dwell in possibility."

A riddle. Or poetry. She tried another vector. "Why are there so many of you?"

In unison all the queens replied, "More than you know." The closest queen elaborated on the statement. "You have observed that your kinnings take effect in advance of your inoculations? With the help of the herb embedded in my flesh I can become more present in more ways, on more paths through time." This Josina reached out to take our Mwadi's hand. "And I believe that with my instruction, you can, too."

We switched to Mwadi's senses. These also perceived several Josinas against an indeterminate background of colors and lights. "Will you, then?" we asked. "Will you teach us?"

We found we sat. We found we held our hands, and hers as well. We found we no longer needed to look to see what lay outside our circle.

"I have already begun."

COROLLARIES

1. Like stories, time wants to tell itself.
2. Life defines its own meaning.
3. The resolution of opposites can be reached without either side's defeat.
4. Spreading sentience incorporates and advances any and all native intelligences it encounters.
5. Continuation depends on the proper perspective.

Common Measurements of Time

These equivalencies compare the units Everfairers most commonly use to measure time to those more familiar to readers. Priests and scientists prefer different, more precise terms, especially when considering periods of shorter duration.

Season = six months

Market = four days

Epic = approximately ninety minutes

Ballad = approximately forty-five minutes

Hymn = ten to twenty minutes

Verse = two to four minutes

Line = ten to thirty seconds

Coinage

Queen Josina and the group sentience including her son chose to exploit the rich metallic deposits in the country's mountains and coined four monetary denominations. They are, in order of valuation (lowest to highest), drops, cacaos, shongos, and glamps. Drops are primarily composed of copper and marked on their face by a stylized water drop, with a map-derived representation of the course of the Congo River carved onto the reverse. Cacaos, struck from silver, show a whole and a cut cacao pod on their face, with a stylized representation of the cacao tree's branches on the reverse. Electrum-forged shongos have a throwing knife on their face and a tern on the reverse. Golden glamps feature Everfair's iconic pierced, globular lampshade on their face and a mechanical hand on the reverse. All denominations are marked with the date they were struck and the motto, in English, "Everfair my home."

A series of printed bills featuring engravings of early aircanoes was also produced.

APPENDIX C

Group Beings

Wear Red
Sevaria binti Musa, King Ilunga, Dr. Alan Kleinwald

The Mission
Ho Bee-Lung, Ho Lin-Huang/Tink, Kwangmi

The Sleeper Wakes
Queen Mwadi, Rima Bailey, Raffles, General Thomas Jefferson Wilson, King Mwenda

The Blending
Gopal Singh, Carmelita, Herr Paul Schreiber, Frau Hanna Schreiber, Hafiza, Bahir Haji

The Sleeper Wakes to Wear Red
Sevaria binti Musa, King Ilunga, Dr. Alan Kleinwald, Queen Mwadi, Rima Bailey, Raffles, General Thomas Jefferson Wilson, King Mwenda

ACKNOWLEDGMENTS

The only way I could have written this novel was by accepting the persistent kindnesses of many overlapping and deeply rooted communities. I'll try to name some of them now. First come my family, my ancestors, my deities, my friends, and my loves, who as always have, by supporting me, extended my reach.

Second, because I wrote most of *Kinning* during the early years of the COVID pandemic, a great deal of what went right with that process is due to the input and constancy of my online colleagues-in-creativity. This includes STEW members Betsy Aoki, Kristin King, Caerdwyn Torres, Jo Rixon, Jesse Stewart, and Patrick Hurley, as well as the motley gang who showed up for daily Zoom sessions: James Leonard, Paul Martz, L. Timmel Duchamp, Eileen Gunn, Brittany Selah Lee-Bey, Sara Ryan, Emily Jiang, Be Kaye, Cindy Ward, Alethea Kontis, Stina Leicht, K. Tempest Bradford, Tamara Sellman, Robert Mullen, Jason Andress, teri clark, Victoria Garcia, Richard Pearce-Moses, Mark Sturek, Monica Valentinelli, Leslie What, Valor Levinson, Manju Menon, moses moon, Tegan Moore, Claire Light, Meghan Hyland, and Siobhan Carroll. (They never showed up all at the same time, though. Thank goodness.)

Third, the biology behind *Kinning* derives from Suzanne Simard, author of *Finding the Mother Tree*, and Peter Wohlleben, author of *The Hidden Life of Trees*. There are those, of course, who question the existence of a fungal information superhighway; I choose not only to grant its existence but to extrapolate from it.

Fourth, Mary Anne Mohanraj put me in touch with a Sri Lankan native who consulted helpfully on the country's architecture, furnishings, food, and gardens.

Fifth, my wonderful editors Aislyn Fredsall and Lindsey Hall got me to promise you how my story would end with the way its beginning went.

So please join me in thanking them and all the others who made *Kinning* work the way it works. If you don't like this book, well, I wrote it. But if you do like it, remember I had help.